MESSENGER FROM GOD

MESSENGER FROM GOD

The Last Eulogy Series Book One

A Novel by

ANTHONY R. DIVERNIERO

Columbus, Ohio

This book is a work of fiction. The names, characters and events in this book are the products of the author's imagination or are used fictitiously. Any similarity to real persons living or dead is coincidental and not intended by the author.

Messenger from God

Published by Gatekeeper Press
2167 Stringtown Rd, Suite 109
Columbus, OH 43123-2989
www.GatekeeperPress.com

Author can be reached at tdproph20@gmail.com

Visit my website at www.anthonydbooks.com

Edited by Alice Peck
Copy edited/proof reader by Ruth Mullin
Cover design by Duane Stapp

ISBN (hardcover): 9781642374490
ISBN (paperback): 9781642374483
eISBN: 9781642374476

Printed in the United States of America

Dedication

To the memory of my younger brother Bobby

Robert D. DiVerniero
August 14, 1960–August 16, 2012
Gone from this world but never from our hearts

Acknowledgements

WITHOUT THE BRILLIANT direction of my editor, Alice Peck, this novel would never have been published. Thank you to a wonderful woman with the patience of a saint who allowed me to be creative and steered me on my wonderful and passionate journey of bringing these characters and their story to life.

To Duane Stapp, my cover designer, who continued to blow me away with his designs, thank you for your patience and insight.

To Ruth Mullen, my proofreader and copy editor, who scoured over one hundred thousand words, checking facts and correcting errors—thank you, thank you.

To my friend Chris Little, a big thank you, for reading the first manuscript and prompting me to continue the process of publishing.

To the Italian village of Ottati, where my grandfather was born and whose picture adorns the cover of this novel, I will forever hold the beauty, the stillness, and the character of you in my heart.

To the following people who read the book and gave me their honest opinion, thank you! Thank you!

Toni Jane Pallatto, Lisa Souza, Barbara Radigan, Mary Jean Luppi, David Carano, Peter Parisi, Dale Pearce, Cyndi Nadeu, Kasey and Courtney Kesses, Sherri Lynn Ramo, Mary Jo Pallotto, Marc and Karen Pallotto, Alicia Luciani, Beth DeRosa, Randi Peterson, Lynn Wakefield Testa, Lynn Ferrucci, Steve Kosinski, Mary Connor DeMaio, Maureen Stephens, and Noreen Augliera.

To B&N of North Haven, especially Lisa, Deni, Noelle, Wendy, Brian, and Jean-Marcel, thank you for allowing me to spend my mornings in the café drinking espresso macchiatos and eating cinnamon scones while I wrote *Messenger from God* and as I continue to write the sequel. Your friendly faces and kind words are greatly appreciated.

To Eli at Staples, thank you for all the help in printing the manuscripts.

To Mike, Kathy, Mathew, Olivia, Michaela, and my goddaughter Paige Leavitt, thank you for the excitement you showed and the happiness of your family in my life.

To my dear friend Frank Arciuolo, to whom, when we worked together many years ago, I would often say, "let's go write songs." Thank you for the wonderful comments even though I knew the book was not your cup of tea—you made my day. One day, my friend, we will retire to our passions—your music and my writing.

To my children Anthony and Dominique, thank you for your support, your love, and your courage. You are the loves of my life—ever entrenched in my heart.

To my family—my mother Lucille, my father Dominic, my sisters Rosalie and Lenore—thank you for your support, inspiration, and love. To my other children—Bryan, Ben, and Gabriella—thank you for being who you are.

They say that behind every great man there is a woman. I am far from a great man and she is definitely not behind me, for no woman should ever be behind a man: she stands beside me, she is a rock in adversity, she is a strength that inspires me, and a driving force that makes all that is bad good. Thank you, Lynn Panico, for being you—my Sydney without the issues.

Neither must you be perturbed when you hear of wars and insurrections. These things are bound to happen first but the end does not follow immediately. He said to them further: Nation will rise against nation and kingdom against kingdom. There will be great earthquakes, plagues, and famines in various places and in the sky fearful omens and great signs . . . On earth, nations will be in dismay, perplexed by the roaring sea and the waves.

—Luke 21:9-11, 25

In our journey through life, we meet many people.
We walk through the passages of time entangled in the forest of life.
In our journey, we meet both friend and foe.
To know one is a friend
Helps one overcome the foe.
We all end our journey in the same way,
Walking out of the forest of life and into the safe hands of God.

—Paolo DeLaurentis

Spring, 1963

FORTY-FIVE MINUTES HAD passed. His father held a cool, wet facecloth in his rugged hand and gently patted his son's face. Tears trickled from Tony's eyes as he watched his son approach death's door.

"What's his temperature?" Lynn tried not to panic, but her voice betrayed her.

Tony withdrew the thermometer from the boy's mouth and sat back on the toilet seat. He angled the thin glass pipette. His wife continued to try to keep the child cool.

"Shit. You have to call Uncle Doc," Tony said, his voice filled with trepidation.

"What's his temperature?" Lynn pleaded again.

"Do we have another thermometer?"

"No, just that one," Lynn's voice was frustrated. "What is it, Tony?"

"Almost one hundred and seven. The mercury is all the way at the top. He's burning up, Lynn."

Lynn ran to the kitchen and picked up the handset of the white princess phone. A religious calendar with an image of the resurrected Jesus hung on the blue-painted wall. She dialed her uncle's number. Dr. Joseph Esposito answered the frantic phone call from his sister's daughter. He listened patiently to the pleas of the crying mother.

"Relax, Lynn. I'm sure he'll be fine. I'll be right there. Try to keep Paolo cool and most of all, try to keep calm. I'll call the ambulance."

"Okay, the front door is open—we're in the bathroom. Can you call Uncle Anthony?" Her voice cracked, tears streaked down her face.

"Yes, I'll call him. But Paolo is not going to die." Uncle Anthony was the priest in the family. He was called whenever anyone was sick, so he could perform the Last Rites. It was always better to be safe than sorry.

Paolo had shown no signs of being ill; it was sudden and quick. The day before, he had been his feisty self, playing with his friends. It was the first hot day of the season. Soon the trees would blossom—nature's way of giving birth to new life.

The screened front door swung open, and in rushed Uncle Doc. He ran to the bathroom. What he witnessed would forever change him. Lynn sobbed. Uncle Doc mumbled a prayer that sounded like the Our Father.

Father Anthony came next. "Am I too late?" asked the priest.

Tony shook his head. An ambulance's siren echoed through the neighborhood as the four adults stood in the small beige bathroom in total silence, staring at the little boy in the tub.

Chapter 1

Forty years later, 2003

"MY TALK TODAY . . ." Paolo paused. He looked left, then right, and noticed the two Secret Service agents, trying to look anonymous. He continued, ". . . will forever change the way you think, provided you desire to accept what I say. Is there anyone here outside of the faculty who has heard me speak before?" Paolo was astounded when more than half of those gathered raised their hands. "Wow, I am humbled by your presence. In my previous talks, I spoke about the need to give back to society. The need for you," he spread out his hands to the assembly, "to accept responsibility for your fellow man and to give back to those who need your help. The option of what you choose to do rests deep within your consciousness. I say to all of you," Paolo paused once again, "look deep within yourselves, trust and rely on the goodness that resides within you."

Paolo stopped, feeling the eyes of his audience following his every move and gesture. He pointed, and in a voice powerful with intent, he said, "Within each of you is a love so divine in nature, a love that waits to escape your being. The love I speak about is a love meant to be embraced by all humanity. We as a people keep this divine secret dormant for our own personal use. Our own stupidity allows the greed of society to suppress this precious gift and stifle the love within us, a love we keep absent from the world in which we live. I say to you—I challenge you, the future leaders of our world—allow this hidden secret within you to escape. We are a misguided people—life is not about money, possessions, social climbing, being number one. No, my friends, life is about love and how we as a people, as a society, love one another. My mother used to say to me, 'Treat others the way you wish to be treated.' What a magnificent way to live your life. In all the speeches I have given until recently, the one essential ingredient I left out was love. You can do all I mentioned, but if you do it without love, you have done it for nothing. For without love, life does not exist."

Paolo continued to talk about love, the need to forgive, and the relationship between God and man. He gave examples of how to incorporate love in a capitalist society. "Love lies deep within all humankind waiting for its shining moment."

With heartbreaking vigor, Paolo described the destructive nature of humankind in the absence of love. He gave the attendees the quintessential choice—to accept love over greed, pride, and selfishness. His ending statement: "The unwillingness of man to give love and accept love will be the downfall of all mankind. You," his voice boomed like a Baptist minister as he made his point to his congregation, "who are going out into the world . . . can change the deplorable moral attitude of society with a simple act of unconditional love."

There was a moment of absolute silence in the Providence College auditorium. Then, in an explosion of applause and cheers, the audience rose to its feet.

Chapter 2

PAOLO'S BOYHOOD WAS anything but ordinary. Raised in a faith-filled Catholic family, he was the fourth child of Tony and Lynn DeLaurentis. Paolo was unexpected. Not believing in birth control, Lynn became pregnant at the age of thirty-seven. Ten years of making love without getting pregnant came to an end. The parents were shocked and their oldest child, Anthony, was embarrassed at the idea of his parents dancing naked between the sheets.

"I can't believe Mom is pregnant," the fifteen-year-old said to his younger brother, Bobby.

"What do you mean?" the thirteen-year-old inquired.

"You know, they still do it."

"Do it? Do what?"

"You know." Anthony's face grimaced.

"Oh, you mean they're still fucking," Bobby said as he tried to keep a straight face. He was schooled in the ways of the adult world—more so than Anthony.

"Oh my God, Bobby! Do you have to use that word? It's Mom and Dad." Anthony turned and walked away in disgust.

Bobby laughed.

* * *

Paolo learned early on that being the youngest had its benefits—not having to fend for himself, always being protected and coddled. His sister Veronica treated him as if he were her own child. By the time Paolo was ten years old, Anthony and Bobby shared an apartment and Veronica was in her second year of nursing school.

He grew up with an extraordinary intellect and an uncanny ability to retain knowledge. Early in his life, Paolo showed a capacity for deep thought. He often sat for hours by the backyard swimming pool in a lounge chair—the type with multi-colored strands made of woven plastic—and gazed at the twinkling stars of the night.

"What on earth are you looking at?" his father would ask.

"I'm thinking, Pop . . . just thinking about Italy. Someday I'm going there and I'll find out who I am."

As his dad walked away, Paolo would hear him say, "That child—what a doozie-pots." What a crazy kid.

* * *

On one warm spring night, his homework finished, the fifth-grader sat in the broken-strapped lawn chair. The stars blazed overhead, the smell of approaching summer filled the air. His mind flooded with pictures and scenes of a foreboding future, a picture soon to become a reality. Unnerved, he stood and walked toward the porch. His father sat inside at the table, reading the evening newspaper.

The screen door squeaked shut; a lightning bug glowed in the distance. Tony placed the paper down and looked at his son. "Paolo, are you okay?"

"Yeah."

Lynn walked through the open sliding glass door; she carried a coffee pot and two mugs. "Paolo, *yes*, not *yeah*. What are they teaching you in school?"

"Yes, Mom," the youngster replied.

She placed mugs labeled Mom and Dad on the red-and-green plaid tablecloth next to the sugar and milk and poured the hot brown liquid. "You do look a little pale. Come here, let me see if you have a temperature."

Paolo walked the few steps to his mother. Lynn leaned over, placed her cheek against his, then her hand against his forehead. "You're fine, no fever."

"Don't worry, Mom, no high fever like in third grade."

"God forbid, we don't need to go through that again," Tony said. The parents looked at each other.

Tears welled in Lynn's eyes, and she turned her head. "Yes, we don't need that excitement again." She walked back into the house.

Paolo slid one of the brown wooden chairs out from under the table and sat close to his father. "Dad?"

"Yes, son?" Tony took his mug, added two spoonfuls of sugar and some milk to his coffee, and asked, "What is it?"

The young boy fidgeted in his chair, struggling with his words. "Dad, I . . . I . . ." Paolo started to stutter.

His father put his hand on Paolo's forearm. "What is it, Paolo? Are you in trouble?"

Paolo shook his head. "Dad, I have weird dreams."

"Are they nightmares?"

"No."

"Well, what do you mean, Paolo?"

"I'm awake when I have them."

"Oh, I see." His father leaned forward. "You have daydreams. Nothing to worry about," he said as he rubbed Paolo's hair.

"But Dad, they seem so real, as if I'm there."

"They seem real because you have a vivid imagination. Now go get a deck of cards and we'll play a couple of hands of war."

Paolo sat frozen for a moment, not saying a word, his head hung down.

"Paolo, look at me."

He raised his head and looked into his father's eyes.

"Daydreams are perfectly normal. Now, go get the cards."

Paolo pushed the chair back and went into the house.

Chapter 3

PAOLO AWOKE THE next morning. Both beating his father at cards and their conversation eluded him. He lay in bed and pondered his dream. *She floated toward him, her eyes focused on his. Mesmerized, he could not move. She began to speak, but he heard no words. Tranquility engulfed them. Paolo knew he was dreaming; his heart began to race. She touched his face, her hand smooth; she looked in his eyes, her head tilted. Her hand dropped to his chest. He took her hand and placed it within him. She clutched his heart, withdrew her hand; she placed his heart onto hers. Their two hearts beating as one, she kissed him and disappeared.* "Wow, what a dream," he said to himself. Above him, taped to the ceiling, was a poster of Italy.

He jumped out of bed, grabbed his black marker, went over to his wall calendar, and crossed off the day. "Only twenty days left of school," he said to himself. He walked to the bathroom, brushed his teeth, and took a shower. With a towel wrapped around his thin body, he went back to his room. His mother had laid out his clothes—brown chinos, a light-blue button-down oxford shirt, and a pair of brown socks. He dressed and went downstairs to the kitchen.

On the counter sat a bowl of Cocoa Krispies and a brown paper bag. He opened the refrigerator, took out the half gallon of milk, and poured some of it over his cereal. He left the carton on the counter and ate his breakfast; he disliked it when his cereal became soggy.

"Paolo?"

"Yes, Mom?"

"Don't forget you have to clean up your room today after school," Lynn said as she climbed the stairs from the utility room to the kitchen. Dressed in a blue bathrobe, she walked over to the counter, took the carton of milk, and placed it back in the refrigerator.

"I won't, Mom."

"I packed your lunch—Genoa salami and provolone cheese."

"Did you pack any Yodels?"

"Yes, I did."

"Thanks, Ma."

She patted her son on the head, kissed him on the forehead, and went upstairs to get dressed. "Don't be late for the bus."

"I won't. Do I need a jacket today?"

"No, it's warm outside."

"Okay."

Paolo finished his breakfast, rinsed the cereal bowl, and placed it in the dishwasher. He wiped his mouth with his hands, grabbed the brown paper bag, jumped down the three steps to the foyer floor, and ran out of the house. He got to the end of the driveway, turned, and looked back to make sure he'd shut the front door. He glanced at his Timex and jogged to catch the school bus. He arrived at the corner at the same time as his friend, Bill Conti.

"Hey, Paolo."

"Hey, Bill." Bill was an inch taller than Paolo and a little chunky around the stomach. He sported a Beatles-style haircut. His dark brown eyes hid an inner intensity of reckless abandonment. Bill was always ready to take the dare before anyone else. He loved the adrenaline kick; his heart raced with the sensation of indestructibility.

Paolo, the conservative, always weighed his options; he often refused to take risks. Bill always stuck by Paolo's side and defended him vigorously. The two were best friends; both liked the New York Yankees, the New York Giants, and Wilt Chamberlain. And, of course, they liked pretty girls. The two partners in crime—nicknamed by Paolo's father—did everything together.

Intellectually Paolo held the edge, physically Bill; they defended each other and neither one would betray the other.

The two boys waited patiently at the bus stop. "Hey, we're going to the sandpits today, are you gonna come?" Bill said.

"Sure, I have to clean up my room first. Who's going?"

"Tony, Steve, Vinnie, and Mark."

"Neat."

The thirty-five-seat yellow bus screeched to a halt. The door swung open and gobbled the two boys as they climbed the short set of stairs. They walked down the aisle to their favorite spot at the back of the bus.

"Hello, Paolo."

"Hi, Lisa." He blushed.

"Hello, Paolo," Bill said in a high-pitched voice as he puckered his lips and formed a kiss.

"Shut up, jerk," Paolo said as he pushed his friend into the green padded seat.

The boys talked about the previous night's Yankees win as the bus pulled up to the entrance of the school.

"I'll see you at recess," Paolo said.

"See ya later."

They went their separate ways to their classrooms on the third floor.

Recess was every morning at ten-thirty. Today there was a kickball game between the fourth- and fifth-grade boys. The girls mingled about and sat on swings, chatting away. Lisa and her friends, Rosalie and Maryann, watched the boys.

The school bell rang, ending recess. The fifth-graders, victorious, gave a yell and patted each other on the back. The students filed in a single line toward their classrooms. Paolo trailed behind.

"Paolo, Paolo," Mrs. Sullivan shouted. "Are you coming with us?"

"What, what? Ah yeah, I mean yes, Mrs. Sullivan." Paolo trotted up to the line.

Mrs. Sullivan walked to the young student, "Paolo, are you alright?

You look a little pale. Are you warm?" She touched his forehead. "You don't have a fever, but maybe you should go to the nurse."

"No, Mrs. Sullivan, I'm okay, really I'm okay."

"Alright, let's get back to class."

As he walked back to the classroom, Paolo tried to erase the daydream. The distraught faces of the parents, the hands sticking up out of the dark sand like dead sticks in a garden, the dirt in the open and lifeless eyes of his friends.

On the ride home, Paolo sat quietly next to Bill and looked out the window. The bus made its stops. Lisa stood in the aisle and turned around, "See you tomorrow, Paolo."

"Bye, Lisa," he said, without moving his head.

"Paolo, I think she likes you," Bill said. "Paolo and Lisa sitting in a tree, K-I-S-S-I-N-G."

Paolo looked into Bill's eyes. It was the last time Bill ever made fun of his friend. "I'm only kidding."

"I know. Scared you, though, didn't I?" Paolo said. The two boys laughed.

As the bus approached their street corner, the boys stood and walked down the aisle. The clamshell doors opened, and they jumped the three steps to the sidewalk. As they were about to go their separate ways, Paolo said, "I don't think we should go to the pits today."

"Why not?"

"I don't know," Paolo paused, his head hung down. "I think something bad is going to happen."

"Something bad? You're crazy."

Paolo continued to look down at the sidewalk and said, "I don't think I'm going."

"You a girl or somethin'?"

"No," he replied curtly.

"Yes, you are, you're a sissy," Bill punched Paolo in the arm.

Paolo gazed at Bill, their eyes met. "Stop looking at me like that—it gives me the creeps."

Paolo continued to hold the gaze. “I’m not going,” Paolo’s voice was stern.

“Sissy.”

“Am not.”

Bill, angry, said, “Yes, you are, you’re afraid.” He walked away.

“Am not, you jerk. I’ll be there after I clean up my room,” Paolo yelled.

Chapter 4

PAOLO OPENED THE screen door to his house and announced, "Hi, Mom. I'm home."

"Hi, Paolo, how was school today?" Lynn walked out of the kitchen. She wore a violet flower-patterned apron.

"It was okay. What are you cooking?"

"Your favorite."

"Raviolis? Are they homemade?" His eyes brightened.

"Yes, of course."

"Jewel," he replied.

"Jewel? What does that mean?"

"Boy, you're getting old, Mom."

"Well, what does it mean, this word 'jewel'?"

"Neat, cool, nice."

"I see. Well, why don't you get your jewel fanny upstairs and clean your room and I will get you a snack."

"Jewel, Mom, jewel." Paolo ran upstairs. Lynn watched her son, shook her head, and walked back into the kitchen.

Twenty minutes later, Paolo flew down the stairs. "Paolo, your snack is ready." He stopped in the kitchen doorway. Lynn looked up from the stuffed pasta, her hands covered in flour.

"Paolo, what's wrong? You're so pale."

"I have to go, Mom. Bill is in trouble."

"What do you mean, Bill is in trouble? You stay right here." By the time Lynn reached for a towel and wiped the flour from her hands, Paolo was out the front door.

Tears filled his eyes as he raced his bike down the street. The playing cards attached to the forks of the wheel clacked against the spokes as he stood, pedaling ferociously toward the sandpits. As he approached the center of town, he heard the sirens. Dread overcame him, and then a wave of deep sadness. As he reached Elm and Broadway, an ambulance sped around the corner toward the dirt playground. Stunned, he turned around and went home.

The sandpits behind the high school were a common place for the boys to ride their bikes. They would race their two-wheeled vehicles in and around the mountains of dark sand as if they were professional car drivers. On occasion, the friends would leave their bikes and climb the slippery slopes to the tops of the hills.

The company that owned the eight-acre parcel surrounded the property with a six-foot-high wire fence. Signs stating "No Admittance" hung on the steel barrier. Over the years, the boys found ways to enter the prohibited area, and kept their playground a secret from their parents.

Paolo opened the screen door to his home. His mother stormed out of the kitchen, her voice angry. "Paolo DeLaurentis, Jesus, Mary and Joseph, where on earth did . . . ?" She suddenly became quiet. Paolo sat at the bottom of the stairs in the foyer, sobbing and gasping for breath. "Bill, Bill is dead." He fell into his mother's arms. Lynn cradled his head against her chest. He sobbed, "He's dead. Bill is dead."

"What happened?"

The screen door opened and Tony walked in. "What's going on?" The phone rang. Paolo pushed away from his mother and turned to his father, still sobbing. "Bill's dead."

"What?" Tony looked at his wife; she shrugged and ran off to answer the ringing nuisance.

Tony knelt near Paolo. "Tell me what happened."

"We were supposed to go to the sandpits. I had a daydream—I saw the sand and the dead bodies of my friends. I called Bill's name."

Lynn rushed back to the foyer. "That was Joyce, Bill's mother. There was an accident at the sandpits. She called to see if Paolo was alright."

"See Dad, they're, they're all dead," the small fifth-grader sobbed uncontrollably.

His mother knelt beside him, her voice soothing, "Paolo, Bill is alive, he didn't die. Bill is okay."

"He is?"

"Yes, he is fine, a little scratched up but fine."

"What about Tony and Steve?"

She looked at her husband. Tears welled in her eyes. "They took Tony and Steve to the hospital."

"Vinnie and Mark are dead?" Paolo asked through his tears.

"Yes. I'm sorry, honey, Vinnie and Mark went to heaven."

"Oh," the child cried. "Can I go see Bill?"

"Sure, I'll call his mother after dinner. Okay?"

"Okay, I think I wanna lie down." He turned around, "Mom, Dad?"

"Yes, Paolo?"

"Who am I?"

"You are Paolo DeLaurentis, our son."

"Thanks, Pops."

"Go lie down, I'll call you when supper is ready." Paolo walked up the stairs to his bedroom. Lying down, he fell asleep.

That night, Lynn and Tony tried to wake their youngest son for supper, but Paolo, oblivious, slept soundly. Later on that evening, they received a phone call from Bill's father. He wanted to say thank you to Paolo for saving his son's life. He went on to say if it weren't for Paolo's yell for Bill to move, his son would have died in the landslide. Lynn accepted the thank you. Tony didn't tell her that Paolo hadn't been there.

Chapter 5

"HEY."

"Hey. Wanna go outside?"

"Sure."

It was the first time the two boys had been alone together since the accident. Their parents watched as they trotted silently toward the brook by the two willow trees. The green grass was interspersed with bright yellow dandelions. Paolo and Bill approached the Mill River and sat on a large rock overlooking the slow-moving stream. The water rustled over twigs and stones. A dove cooed in the distance.

Bill's hands were still swollen and bruised from trying to dig out Vinnie and Mark after the landslide, the two buried under ten feet of sand.

"Why didn't you help us dig out Vin and Mark?" Bill waved his swollen hands in the air.

"I wasn't there."

"Yes, you were. You yelled at me to get out of the way! You saved my life, and Tony's and Steve's."

Paolo gazed intently into Bill's eyes. "I had a daydream after recess. I saw Vinnie and Mark's mom crying. I had a bad feeling about the sandpits. That's why I didn't want us to go. Then when I got home, I was cleaning my room, and I had another daydream. I saw the guard chasing you guys, and you were hiding behind the hill. Vinnie and Mark climbed up the hill, you were at the bottom with Tony and Steve. I saw the sand slide on top of Vinnie, and I yelled for you to get out of the way. Then I snapped out of it and ran downstairs and got on my bike. When I got to the corner, I saw the ambulance going to the pits. I turned around and went home. I thought you were dead."

"So it's true you weren't there. Dad said that when he got there, he didn't see you, so I thought you ran away." Bill's father, Jack, was a firefighter and had been the first person on the scene. "I guess I should've listened to you and not gone."

The two boys sat silently. They didn't hear their fathers approach.

"Well, you two partners in crime, what are you doing?"

"Just talking, Dad," Paolo looked at his father and smiled.

"You guys want some lunch?" asked Jack.

"Sure, Dad. How about McDonald's? Come on, Pard."

"Pard?"

"Yeah, partners. Thanks, Pard, for saving my life." The two boys jumped off the rock.

"McDonald's it is," Jack said, "and after we eat, we'll go see Tony and Steve."

"Jewel, Dad."

"Yeah, jewel, Mr. Conti." The two boys walked ahead of their fathers, Bill's arm around Paolo's shoulder, and Paolo's arm around Bill's.

Chapter 6

When Paolo was in eighth grade, his clairvoyance and empathic sense became stronger. Nearly five years had passed since the high fever. Lynn first began to question her youngest son's normalcy when the phone rang. "Mom, it's Aunt Lenore," Paolo would tell her before she could answer it. "Mom, Uncle Johnny is calling." Lynn tried to discuss it with Tony, but Tony already knew; he kept the secret to himself.

The straw that broke the camel's back was Monday, June 3, 1968. Paolo was eating his Cocoa Krispies and reading *The Journal Courier,* the local morning newspaper, before he went off to school.

"Anything interesting in the paper?"

"No, Mom, just the normal political stuff about Kennedy."

"Do you think Bobby Kennedy will be our next president?"

Paolo gazed off into the distance.

"Paolo, are you there?" Lynn waved her hands before his eyes.

"Yes, I'm here, Mom."

"So, do you think he will win?"

With no emotion, Paolo said, "Bobby Kennedy will be assassinated, and Nixon will be our next president."

"That's a terrible thing to say, Mr. DeLaurentis."

Paolo shrugged his shoulders and said, "Yeah. Sorry, Mom."

Two days later, Kennedy was assassinated. Lynn became frightened. Paolo was not like his brothers or his peers. Lynn needed to know there was nothing physically or psychologically wrong with him. She told her husband of the incident, and he agreed to have Paolo examined.

The following day Lynn called Uncle Doc, who referred her to a neurologist. Unbeknownst to them, the doctor they would see was involved with a government study on extrasensory perception.

"Mom, why do I have to see this Dr. Payne? I'm fine."

"Because your father and I want you to."

"Ugh, but Mom."

"No buts, you're going. And who is Dr. Payne? We are seeing Dr. Piccolo."

They arrived at the medical building and were ushered into a stark green room with white cabinets, a small sink, and a window that overlooked Howard Avenue. A blood pressure cuff hung on the wall and a round stool with wheels stood in the corner. Paolo jumped on the examination table, crunching the white paper beneath him.

"I really don't want to be here, Ma."

"Paolo, stop it."

The door opened. "Mrs. DeLaurentis?"

"Yes." She stood to meet the doctor.

"Please don't get up. My name is Dr. Payne." His voice sounded nasal.

Paolo looked at his mother and mouthed the words, "Told you so."

The five-foot-eight, broad-shouldered man wore a long white medical jacket over a white button-down Oxford shirt, black pants, and black shoes. His hair was thinning. A stethoscope hung around his neck.

"You must be Paolo?"

"Yes, I am." An uneasy feeling came over Paolo. "Are you a Russian?"

"Paolo, that is none of your business," Lynn jumped in.

"No, I'm not a Russian. I'm American." The doctor laughed.

Paolo stared at the young physician. Their eyes met, and Dr. Payne turned his head.

"Mrs. DeLaurentis, I see from Dr. Esposito's notes that you are concerned about your son's . . ."

"Mom thinks I'm a wacko because I know things."

"Paolo DeLaurentis!"

"Well, it's true, Mom."

"Paolo, why don't you tell me what you know?"

Lynn answered for him, "He told me when Bobby Kennedy was going to be assassinated, and he can also tell me who is calling on the phone before I answer it."

Dr. Payne's eyebrows rose. "Is that true, Paolo, or are you just a good guesser?"

"My mother doesn't lie."

"Paolo, answer Dr. Payne."

"Yes."

"Yes what?"

"Yes it's true, Dr. Payne." Paolo rolled his eyes.

There was a knock on the examining room door. Paolo said, "That's Dr. Piccolo."

"Come in."

"Excuse me, Dr. Payne, I didn't realize you were seeing my patient."

"I knew you were busy, Dr. Piccolo, I hope you don't mind."

"No, not at all, thanks for picking up the slack." Dr. Piccolo looked at Paolo, "You're in good hands, son." The door closed.

After Dr. Payne gave Paolo a thorough cognitive assessment, he turned his attention to Lynn. "Mrs. DeLaurentis, physically your son is fine." He flashed his perfectly white teeth and his eyes twinkled. "I would love to test Paolo further to explore his abilities."

Paolo shook his head.

Lynn ignored him. "What type of testing?"

"A simple psychological examination that will test his extrasensory perception. In other words, ESP."

"I will have to discuss this with my husband but I don't think it will be an issue. Will it, Paolo?" Lynn's voice was stern.

"No, Mom."

"Paolo, it won't be that bad, we'll make a game out of it. Plus you can have all the soda and ice cream you want."

"Really?" he said sarcastically.

"Absolutely."

The doctor stood and patted Paolo on the head. Paolo grimaced at his touch.

"If it's okay with you, Mrs. DeLaurentis?"

"Please call me Lynn."

"Okay, Lynn, I will have my secretary call you and arrange the testing for next Tuesday."

"That would be great. Thank you, Dr. Payne."

"Please call me Colin."

"Thank you, Colin."

* * *

As the mother and son entered the car, Lynn reached over and slapped Paolo in the back of the head.

"Ouch! Mom, why did you do that?"

"Because you were very rude to Dr. Payne."

"But Mom, the guy is a snake."

"Paolo, that is enough! You will go for testing and you will do what he says."

Paolo sat resigned, sulking. "Yes, Mom."

* * *

Paolo scored one hundred percent on the entire test. Throughout the three days of testing, he showed an incredible, if not fantastic, sense of prediction. Not only was Paolo clairvoyant and telepathic, he also had an innate ability to understand complex problems, Dr. Payne explained. Paolo's brain absorbed everything and in quick fashion. In layman's terms, his brain was like a computer.

In Payne's opinion, Paolo was a savant. The problem was that he had no other physical or mental incongruities associated with savants. He showed no signs of autism. He had no mental retardation and no brain injury other than an extremely high fever in third grade. According to his parents, the fever exceeded the thermometer's limits.

Dr. Payne found no record of Paolo being in the hospital. He used his government contacts to obtain a copy of the police report of the incident. Within a day of his request, a messenger dropped off the information. The report stated what the parents had said—the child had a high fever—with a vague description from an emergency medical technician.

Dr. Payne sat at his desk in his office on Howard Avenue. In the room cluttered with books, he read the report on Paolo DeLaurentis. There was a knock on the door.

"Come in."

An older, gray-haired woman entered. "Dr. Payne, Mr. and Mrs. DeLaurentis are here."

"Show them in, Estelle." His tone was curt and arrogant, that of a physician who placed himself above the multitudes who sought his help in healing their disease.

"Yes, Doctor," Estelle's response was equally curt—more like, "Yes, asshole."

The twenty-nine-year-old neurologist stood and tucked in his white button-down shirt. His hands brushed his pants, then smoothed his hair. He walked around his desk to meet Paolo's parents. The attractive couple held hands and smiled. Dr. Payne went over to Tony and shook his hand.

"Come on in."

"How are you, Colin?" Tony said.

"I couldn't be better. Please sit down." Payne pointed to the two chairs opposite his desk.

Lynn looked quizzically at Tony. "You two know each other?"

"Colin belongs to the country club. When you mentioned his name, I didn't put two and two together."

"That's because you never listen."

"Sorry, honey."

"Lynn, I'm not sticking up for your husband, but I only go to the club occasionally. I didn't know Paolo was his son." He pointed again to the chairs.

The husband and wife sat in the upholstered chairs. The sharp-nosed neurologist sat at his desk and leaned forward, hands folded on the black blotter, waiting for the question he so often heard.

"Well, Colin, is my son okay?" Tony asked.

"He is more than okay, he is truly remarkable. Paolo has a unique gift. I'm truly amazed. Paolo told me how you used his gift to bet on football games."

Lynn looked at her husband. "You did what?" Her face was red with anger.

Payne, embarrassed, said, "Sorry, I thought she . . ."

"I just did it a couple of times and besides . . ."

Lynn cut him off. "Nevermind, we'll talk about it when we get home. So is he okay, Colin?" Her anger subsided.

"To answer your question, yes, he is quite normal." The doctor continued, "Outside of his intellect and his paranormal ability, he is a well-rounded teenager, which in itself is astounding. You and your husband have a unique and exceptional child."

Lynn asked, "What do we do?"

"Nothing, allow him to be a teenager. Don't question him about the gifts." Payne turned his head toward Tony, "Or ask him to use his gifts."

Tony lowered his head.

"It's okay, honey." Lynn grabbed hold of her husband's hand.

Payne continued, "Paolo is extremely cognizant of his gift." He leaned forward, "Treat him as you treated your other children. Allow him to grow and have fun. He will find his way."

"Okay," Tony said, placing his hands on his lap. "We know you are busy." He pushed up from his chair. "Thanks for the help, Colin."

"Yes, thank you," Lynn said.

Colin stood, holding a medical file. He walked the two to the door. "Here," he handed the folder to Lynn. "This is Paolo's file. Destroy it. We don't want anyone to find out about him." With a puzzled look, Lynn took the file.

"Tony, maybe we can play some golf in the next week or so. My schedule is pretty light. I have to be in Washington for a couple of days. How about Saturday morning at ten?"

"Is that okay with you, honey?"

"Fine with me."

"Great. I'll meet you at the clubhouse."

"Sounds good, Colin."

Lynn grabbed her husband's hand. They walked to the elevator.

* * *

The history of governments using individuals with so-called paranormal abilities dates back to Biblical times. Stories of extrasensory perception reached the intelligence agencies of the United States as early as World War II. An allied spy network in Germany came across documents that showed Hitler relied on astrologers and seers to move his armies.

In the early 1950s, intelligence agencies throughout the world explored psychic research. The Cold War brewing, covert agents of the leading powers navigated the massive chessboard called Mother Earth, spying on one another to determine the war capabilities of their enemies. The three superpowers conducted tests on individuals with presumed paranormal abilities. It was a psychic arms battle, with the Russians and the Chinese well ahead of the United States.

A collective effort began among US intelligence agencies to find the ultimate secret weapon—not a destructive weapon, but rather a weapon with all the answers.

The government began to fund secret projects dealing with the paranormal. The CIA coordinated the extensive nationwide research and Dr. Colin Payne of Yale University, a well-known neurophysicist, became the government's lead researcher.

In the mid-1960s, one of these projects involved using extrasensory perception to try to infiltrate communist spy networks within the United States. At the time, the White House had no idea that a thirteen-year-old boy had the paranormal ability they so desperately sought.

Payne closed the door. He walked back to his desk, opened the drawer, and took out a copy of Paolo's file. The physician walked over to his wall safe and placed the file inside, next to the 8mm movie of Paolo's testing.

Dr. Payne concealed the information from the government. He classified Paolo as a remote viewer; he also believed the young boy had the ability to bi-locate but he had no actual proof.

By definition, a remote viewer has the ability to obtain accurate psychically derived data on persons, places, and events anywhere in the world. The ability to bi-locate is defined as the appearance of an individual in two places simultaneously. Bi-location was an ancient phenomenon, experienced by mystics, saints, monks, and holy people. Saint Anthony and Padre Pio had this uncanny ability, and so did Paolo DeLaurentis.

When the university discovered that Payne secretly worked for the government, they promptly terminated his employment. The doctor then joined the NSC. Payne kept Paolo's secret, hoping to manipulate the child for his own benefit. Over the years, Dr. Payne stayed in contact with the family.

Chapter 7

PAOLO AND BILL graduated at the top of their high school class, first and second respectively. Paolo was accepted into Yale University and Bill into the Naval Academy. The two would converse weekly via phone. Bill was Paolo's best friend through thick and thin. In high school and during his freshman year of college, Paolo's gift was dormant, other than his recurring dream of a woman who took his heart away.

Paolo's ability to enter into the psychic world as a remote viewer began when he was a sophomore at Yale. One Sunday while at his parents' house for dinner, a family tradition carried down from his great-grandparents, Paolo and his brothers flipped through a family photo album. They came across a picture of their cousin Carla and her friend Adriana.

"Madonna mia! Look at the boobs on her," Paolo's brother Bobby said. "Paolo, maybe Carla can fix you up with her."

Anthony said, "Look at that face! Dooze brut-ugly." He placed his thumb between the forefinger and middle finger and shook his hand while raising it toward his chin. His eyes said, "What, are you crazy?"

"Who cares if she's ugly? Look at that body," Bobby said as he held the picture.

"No, she's not my type," the nineteen-year-old said.

Their mother stood in the doorway of the family room, a yellow kitchen towel in her hand. "Boys, dinner's ready. I need one of you to get two extra chairs."

"I'll get the chairs," Bobby said.

The seventeen family members took their places. Anthony, the oldest, sat by his father. Paolo, the youngest and still unmarried, sat opposite his father at the other end of the table with the nieces and nephews. The men sat on one side while the women sat closest to the kitchen. The children were all close in age. Eleven-year-old twin boys belonged to Anthony and his wife Tina. A second set of eleven-year-old twin boys belonged to Veronica and her husband Evan, referred to by the family as "the American." Both couples each had a younger daughter, as well. Bobby and his wife Maria had two daughters, ages nine and six.

Tony and Lynn loved Sunday afternoons. Having the grandchildren around was life-giving. Lynn loved to cook for the family. Life was good. Life was safe.

After dinner, Paolo went back to the den. He sat on the couch, the photo album open to the page with the photograph of Carla and Adriana.

Bob was right, she has a great body.

The picture of Adriana ingrained in his mind, Paolo sat back and closed his eyes. *Adriana sat on a doorstep. She noticed Paolo across the street and waved at him. He waved back.* Suddenly he heard his niece.

"Look at Uncle Paolo. His eyes are open. I think he is dead."

Paolo said, "Boo." His niece jumped back and started to laugh, a nervous laugh.

"I'm not dead, you silly girl. I was sleeping."

"You sleep with your eyes open?" the nine-year-old asked.

"They were closed, silly."

"No, they were open, I swear, Uncle Paolo."

The phone rang. Lynn answered it. Paolo listened.

"Hello? Hi, Carla. How are you?...No, he's here. Of course I'm sure. Would you like to talk to him?...Really? And where is Adriana?...In Boston? And he waved to her? No, he's right here. Tell her it wasn't him. Say hi to your mom and dad. I have to go take out the apple crisp . . . Love you, too. Bye."

Lynn walked into the room. Paolo sat there and shook his head.

"Dr. Payne?"

"Yep, I'll call him in the morning."

"Okay." A mother's sense, in tune with her youngest son.

The next day Paolo called the doctor. Being coy, he told Payne what he saw, withholding the interaction between him and Adriana. He had begun to realize that sometimes it was best to keep some of the truth away from the doctor.

* * *

The following November, Paolo's junior year at Yale, he arrived at his apartment later than usual. He drove up in his forest-green 1970 Firebird, Neil Young's *Southern Man* playing on the 8-track tape player. His oldest brother, Anthony, waited on the stoop of his apartment. Paolo opened the car door and said, "Antnee, what are you doing here?" Then he noticed sadness in his brother's eyes. He walked over slowly. "What's going on?" His voice cracked, a lump in his throat.

"Dad died of a heart attack this afternoon. We've been trying to reach you."

"Damn, damn." Paolo turned away from his brother, walked the short path to his car. Anthony followed behind. The young scholar leaned against the vehicle. Tears streamed down his face. Arms folded, his head bent, he said, "Son of a bitch." Then with his left hand, he banged the side of the car. "Is Mom okay?"

"No, the doctor gave her a sedative to sleep."

"Shit, I can't believe this," Paolo's lower lip and chin wobbled.

The older brother reached out, pulled Paolo to himself. The two hugged, sobbing in each other's arms.

* * *

The next three days were a blur. The Italian custom was to wake the body for two days. Family and close friends attended the viewing the first day. The second day was open to the public. The third day was the toughest—the final goodbye, the funeral Mass and burial in the family plot. Paolo's mother and siblings asked him to give the eulogy.

The limousine pulled up behind the hearse on a dreary, rainy November morning. Paolo blankly gazed out the window. A small crowd surrounded the entrance to the church. The family sat quietly in the car waiting for the six cousins and Paolo's childhood friends Steve and Tony to remove the casket from the hearse.

"Are you okay, Mom?" Veronica asked.

"I wish this was over with." A tissue held to her eyes, Lynn said, "How I loved your father. At least he's at rest with Nonnie and Poppie, God rest their souls." She made the sign of the cross and began to weep.

Anthony wrapped his arms around her. "It'll be alright, Mom, it will be alright," he said. A lump rose in his throat and he held back a heavy sigh.

The driver opened the door. Cold air swept through the black limousine. Bobby got out first, helping his mother, followed by Veronica and Anthony. Tears in his eyes, Anthony looked back at Paolo and said, "Make us proud, little brother." The funeral director lined the family behind the coffin. Anthony and Bobby stood on either side of their mother. On either side of Veronica were Paolo and Bill, dressed in his naval uniform. The funeral participants gathered behind the family in the vestibule of the church. Lynn's uncle, Father Anthony, had died several years earlier, so Father Bob, a long-time friend of the family, walked down the aisle to meet the coffin. After Mass, he invited Paolo to come forward to give the eulogy.

"On behalf of my mother, my brothers Anthony and Bobby, and my sister Veronica, thank you so much for being here. Today we share in the celebration of a man we desperately loved. The words I speak come from my heart because my dad is now with me in my heart." Paolo tried to hold back his tears. His voice quivered as he continued.

"Dad's undying and steadfast love for our mom was an example for us all to emulate in our own lives.

"When I was sixteen, hormones raging, independence beckoning on my doorstep, dating, falling in love, Dad decided the time was right to have the talk. He told me this: when you fall in love, fall in love for the right reason. Not lust or desire, but love from the heart, from the soul. Seek out the woman of your dreams, the woman you would die for, sacrifice your life for. When you find her, tell her you love her. Tell her you need her in your life. Do what she asks of you and most of all, respect her. If you respect her, she will respect you.

"You see, my father was telling me more than just how to love a woman. He was telling me how to love life. He showed us by example how to love your neighbor. Most of all, he taught us the love of family.

"My father was a man of greatness because he had a loving wife . . . Mom, we love you. What we learn from my dad's life is love, unconditional love. May my life be blessed with the love he had in his heart. If he were standing here today, he would say to you, I love you. Dad always said I love you. Those spoken words are sometimes misinterpreted. When you heard those words from my dad, you knew they came from his heart.

"Thank you all so much for being here this morning to celebrate love . . . the love of my dad. On his behalf, my family and I, 'I love you.'"

* * *

The casket lowered, Paolo and Bill watched as sand was thrown into the grave.

"Come on, Pard, I'll drive you back home," Bill said.

"Thanks for coming, Pard, I really appreciate it, and so does Mom."

"I had to be here, he was like a father to me. After all, he gave us our nicknames."

"Yeah, that he did."

"I take it your ESP gave you no warning?"

"Nope, as I tried to tell Dr. Payne, it comes and goes."

"He still calls you?"

"Yep, he wants me to work with him after I graduate. I told him no. He wasn't happy. He said I owe him because he never told anybody about my gift. He said he would ruin me if I didn't help him."

"How would he do that?"

"He'd let it leak that I have paranormal gifts."

"And you still said no?"

Angry, Paolo said, "Yep, I'm going to use the gift for myself. I'll become wealthy enough that I won't have to worry about a shithead like him."

"Be careful, Pard, rumor is he has a lot of power. He was at the Academy recruiting last week. He wanted to talk to me. Then when you called and told me about your dad, I booked. I'm definitely going to avoid him now."

"Good idea, Pard, good idea."

They continued to walk to the car, weaving among the gravestones. Bill stopped at a concrete cross with the name Augliera at its base.

"Pard, I still don't understand how it works. The ESP shit. I mean, I know you saved my life and Steve's and Tony's that day at the pits. But . . . how does it work?"

"I don't know, Bill. I really have no clue. It just happens. And let me tell you, it's frustrating. I'll have a vision in my mind like I'm watching a movie, bizarre stuff like buildings crashing and airplanes exploding, and none of it happens. Yet I know it will. Something inside of me convinces me it's true. Sometimes I just know, like betting on the football games. I can look at a picture of someone and out of nowhere I feel like I am transported to where they are."

"Are you kidding?"

"No."

"So do you experiment with it?"

"No. I'm afraid to."

"Why?"

"Because I feel like I'm playing games with something I shouldn't be."

"I understand—like testing fate."

"Yeah, something like that."

"You know, Pard, what you are telling me is amazing. You should start to document what you see and keep it in a safe place. And most of all, Pard, take care of yourself. Use your gift for the good."

"You're right, Bill, use it for the good."

“Listen to me, Paolo, write the stuff down. You never know when you might need it.”

“Yeah, maybe I’ll do that. Oh, by the way, start investing in gold.”

“Why?”

“I don’t know. The thought just popped into my head.”

“You’re freakin’ weird.”

“Thank you.” The two friends walked back to Bill’s car, arms around each other’s shoulders.

Chapter 8

PAOLO GRADUATED FROM Yale University on Memorial Day. The campus was alive with parents and students milling about. A gentle breeze circled the quad on the warm spring day. Over twelve hundred matriculates waited patiently to receive the prestigious diploma. The ceremony lasted nearly two hours. Paolo waited his turn by daydreaming about his upcoming trip to Italy. Afterward, the family gathered at his cousin Franco's restaurant.

Drinking a glass of Chianti at the bar, Franco said, "So, my little cousin, you excited about your trip?"

"I can't wait. I hope I'll be able to track down our relatives—if there are any left."

"You're going to Amalfi, Messina, and Ottati."

"Yep, the place I really want to go to is Ottati."

"Our grandfather's birthplace?"

"Yes, with all the research I've done on our lineage, Ottati is the missing piece of the puzzle. I know absolutely nothing about Poppie's hometown. I plan on staying there the longest until I can uncover the details of our family history."

"How you gonna do that?"

"I'm going to start with the records located at the town hall. If I find no answers there, then I'll go to the church."

"The church?"

"Sure, the church has all the records—baptisms, death certificates. I should be able to find some answers."

"Paolo, why you so interested in all this family stuff? Our family is here now, what difference does it make?"

"I ask myself the same question. There is something inside of me telling me to go. I have no idea why, other than I know I've got to go. There are answers in Ottati for me, answers that will tell me who I am."

"'Who I am'? What the hell does that mean?"

"Let me explain it this way. When you gamble on the football games, you sometimes get a feeling that one particular team is going to beat another, right?"

"Yeah, but more times than not, those feelings are wrong."

"Well, this feeling I have," Paolo put his right hand over his heart, "is coming from in here. I have to go."

"Hey cuz, you gotta do what you gotta do. I'm jealous, someday I'll get there." Franco paused, then with a curious look, he said, "Paolo, can you do me a favor while you're there?"

"Sure, what is it?"

"Can you get me some recipes for the restaurant?"

"Absolutely."

"When you get back, make sure you stop in the restaurant."

The two cousins embraced each other. The party over, Paolo drove home.

* * *

Before Paolo departed for Italy, his mother made him promise he would visit the Vatican.

"Maybe you'll meet the Pope," she said as she fixed the collar of his shirt, followed by a pat on the shoulder and a kiss on the cheek.

"Okay, Mom, sure, no problem, the Pope and I can have dinner together," he said with a chuckle. The Pope was the farthest thought from his mind. Paolo was more interested in finding a classic Italian beauty, the likes of Sophia Loren.

She laughed and looked at him. "Paolo, I hope you can find the answers to your father's family. Dad would be very proud of you."

"Thanks, Mom, I'm sure the trip will be interesting, to say the least."

"Interesting?"

"Yeah, you never know what God has in store for me."

Lynn looked at him quizzically. "God?"

"I have no idea where that came from." Paolo shook his head, leaned over, and gave his mother a kiss on the cheek. "See you next month, Mom."

With a tear in her eye, she said, "Okay, be safe, Paolo."

"Will do."

* * *

Paolo arrived in Rome on a hot spring day. He hired a driver to take him to Amalfi. The passion within him to visit Italy tugged at his heart. He stayed in Amalfi for a week, searching for family, his mission to fill in the missing blanks of his elusive genealogy tree. The importance of knowing what made him tick drove him on his quest to find his ancestral origins. He felt the generations past gave insight to his being, his inner psyche. There was a thought that nagged at him: a truth was being hidden, an unrevealed truth about his family that might provide an explanation of his gift. While in Amalfi, Paolo successfully tracked the history of his two grandmothers.

His research completed, Paolo hired a local driver from Amalfi. Giacomo, a short, balding man with a paunch for a stomach, said he ate well. He was in his late fifties, old enough to be Paolo's father. The Italian spoke broken English with an animated style. Paolo couldn't help but like him.

"Sonny boy," Giacomo said, using his nickname for Paolo, "How long are you going to stay in Ottati?" Giacomo's English was clouded by his heavy Italian accent.

"Maybe four days."

"Ah sonny boy, you're going to fall in love, amore, amore. We will find you a nice Italian girl, how do you say, bella?" Giacomo kissed the tips of his fingers. "Bella, bella no bu ton for you, sonny boy." He continued to talk as he drove the winding roads of the Amalfi coast.

"Sonny boy, we are going to stop at my brother's. We will stay the night, we mangia, drink wine, and have some fun."

"Sounds good to me, Giacomo." A kinship developed between the two.

* * *

Giacomo drove on Highway A3 in the heavy weekend traffic. He maneuvered the car along the curves of the coastline. The stop-and-go jerk of the car took a toll on Paolo. His mind needed a rest and he fell asleep. He dreamed of a woman with blonde hair and green eyes, the recurring dream he'd had since childhood.

She floated toward him, her eyes focused on his. Mesmerized, he could not move. She began to speak, but he heard no words. Tranquility engulfed the two. Paolo knew he was dreaming; his heart began to race. She touched his face, her hand smooth; she looked in his eyes, her head tilted. Her hand dropped to his chest. He took her hand and placed it within him. She clutched his heart, withdrew her hand; she placed his heart onto hers. Their two hearts beating as one, she kissed him and disappeared. He awoke to the smell of the sea wafting across his nostrils.

"Sonny boy, you sleep well?"

"Yes, I did," he replied as he stretched his legs. "Where are we?"

"We are about five kilometers from Vittorio's hotel, we will be there real soon." Giacomo went on to tell him that the hotel was a lifelong dream of Vittorio's.

Chapter 9

PAOLO AND GIACOMO arrived at the seaside village of Pontecagnano at midday. The mountains rose in the distance. The hotel was located across from the beach with magnificent views of the Gulf of Salerno.

The Maserati's engine roared. Giacomo made a left turn into the entrance of the hotel and beeped the car horn to announce his arrival. The few vacationers who sat on the balcony enjoying the day showed their displeasure. One particular guest displayed a familiar Italian hand gesture. A portly man with an uncanny resemblance to Giacomo walked out of the hotel entrance. Judging by the snarl on his face, he seemed quite angry. Who was the jackass making all the noise? When he realized who it was, the innkeeper's eyes ignited into a look of joy, as if the prodigal son had returned home. He ran back into the hotel, stood in the doorway, and shouted for his wife.

"Isabella, Isabella, veni, veni. Giacomo is here!" The car screeched to a halt in front of the hotel. As if he were a fit teenager, Giacomo jumped out. With tears in his eyes, he ran to his brother; they embraced and kissed each other. Isabella came out of the doorway, a kitchen towel in her hands, wiping as she neared the two men. Giacomo turned to Paolo, who was still in the car watching the two cousins embrace, and said, "Sonny boy, sonny boy, veni, veni. Come, come."

Paolo exited the Maserati and placidly approached the three. His long hair disheveled from the two-hour drive, Paolo stretched his well-trimmed body; he could easily pass as a native Italian. Isabella leaned over to her husband and whispered loudly in his ear.

"Vittorio, he reminds me of you when you were young, what happened?"

"It is your cooking, my principessa, do not blame me."

Paolo listened as husband and wife bantered back and forth. A truth struck the young man. This husband and wife were united in the true bond of love, a love his heart longed for.

"Sonny boy, this is my brother Vittorio and his wife Isabella."

The couple greeted Paolo with hugs and the customary kiss on the cheeks. Isabella's embrace lasted longer. The two escorted him into their house. Paolo understood some Italian; he overheard Giacomo and Isabella as they spoke about him. Isabella wanted to know if he was married or had a girlfriend. She couldn't help but think of the possibilities of him with one of her nieces. Giacomo politely told her to leave him alone.

Excited that a guest from America was visiting, they treated Paolo like royalty. Sergio, the son of Vittorio and Isabella, carried Paolo's luggage to a room overlooking the plush gardens surrounded by cypress trees. Two French doors led to a small balcony with a table and two chairs. The room was decorated with picturesque scenes of the Amalfi Coast. A blue swirled pitcher filled with water and a matching basin sat on a brown four-drawer dresser. A nightstand next to the single bed completed the simple, peaceful room.

The hotel had a classic Italian charm and beauty, the courtyard surrounded by lush gardens with a swimming pool in the center. The smell of the sea coupled with the aroma of the gardens overwhelmed Paolo's senses. Peace came over him, a feeling of home, family, and safety.

Sergio said, "You can unpack later. Let me show you our house."

The young men walked into the residence separate from the hotel. The furniture reflected past family hand-me-downs. Photos of family outings hung on the walls: a series of photos of Vittorio and Giacomo when they were young, a wedding picture of the husband and wife. Overall, this modest home was a pleasant one.

Isabella went off into the kitchen. Known for her culinary delights in and around Pontecagnano, she cooked a sumptuous late-afternoon meal of fish and pasta. Isabella served the feast under a canopy of grape vines. The portico overlooked the gardens of the hotel. Paolo was enthralled at the scene that lay before him—the ocean, the cypress trees, and the gardens. He was oblivious to the Italian conversation taking place. Eventually the conversation encompassed him.

Isabella questioned him about America. What was it like? Had he ever met Frank Sinatra? How many brothers and sisters did he have? Did he have a girlfriend? Was he looking for a girlfriend?

Finally, Vittorio chimed in, "Isabella, basta, basta. Let him enjoy his food, we have plenty of time to talk."

"In life sometimes we don't have plenty of time," Paolo replied to Vittorio. "It's okay, Isabella, whatever you ask I will answer." He spoke with a smile and sincerity.

Vittorio seemed impressed that the young American understood his statement. After the question-and-answer period was over, Isabella stood and began to clear the table.

"Come, let us men go and enjoy the gardens with some wine and fruit." Isabella was some distance away. Vittorio yelled, "Isabella, bring us some wine and fruit, we will be in the terrace garden."

"Yes, my darling husband."

Paolo perceived the mutual tone of respect between husband and wife. Isabella and Vittorio had a natural form of communication, seen and unseen. They were two people who had come to realize through their own life experiences the meaning of love and respect.

The three men stood and began to walk to the gardens. Giacomo and Vittorio, their arms interlocked, walked ahead of Paolo. He had never seen two men walk together in this fashion. Paolo wondered about their closeness. There was a bond between the two, a life experience held them together. He imagined they would die for each other.

The sun, well past its zenith, laid its late afternoon shadows. The cypress trees showered their green hues upon the bright ocean-blue sky. A gentle sea breeze came from the east. They sat around a picnic table underneath a pergola lined with purple grapes.

"Your hotel is beautiful."

"Thank you, Paolo." Vittorio reached up, grabbed a grape, and popped it into his mouth.

"Giacomo told me you almost became a priest?"

"Yes, when I was a young boy my life changed and I began to look at life differently." Paolo could see a sadness in Vittorio's eyes.

"My parents died when I was young."

Giacomo chimed in, "That's how we became brothers."

Paolo was confused, "I see."

"Tell him the story, Vittorio."

Vittorio's eyes fixed on a point beyond the cypress trees; a blank stare overcame his face as he recalled the painful memory, a memory with no escape, a reality in a young boy's life, the nightmare that crept into his dreams. Vittorio began to tell his story . . .

Chapter 10

VITTORIO WAS BORN in Rome in 1917 to Anna and Paolo Esposto. At the age of eight, he walked the sidewalk along Viale Dei Parioli in the town of Pinciano. Carefree, he strolled by a row of three-story yellow stone apartment buildings hung with orange shutters. The fragrant aromas of the evening meals filled the air.

Vittorio turned the corner to find three black cars parked by his house. He cautiously walked closer, a bewildered look on his face. The street was deserted. People stared out their windows, hiding behind curtains as if evil lurked close by. One of his neighbors, seeing him, tried to wave him away. He waved back as he walked a path that forever changed his life.

As Vittorio approached his house, Mr. Parisi, his next-door neighbor, ran out and swept him off the sidewalk. Taken by surprise, the eight-year-old began to fight; he kicked his little legs and tried to scream. Mr. Parisi covered Vittorio's mouth with his hand and whispered, "Keep quiet, little one, the Squadristi." Cradling Vittorio in his arms, he ran back into his home. He placed the young child on the floor.

"Pietro," his wife whispered, "the Squadristi are leaving."

"Giacomo," he called softly to his son. "Take Vittorio to your bedroom."

Pietro and his wife, Christina, stared at one another, their faces ashen with fright. They had heard the blood-curdling screams of their neighbors.

"Christina, I am going over there. Go be with the boys and make sure they stay in the bedroom."

"Be careful, my husband, maybe it's best that you don't go," the panic-stricken wife said.

"I have to," Pietro's voice hardened.

"Why do you have to?" Her voice filled with fear. "Don't get involved, they will kill you as they did them."

He said to her in a loud whisper, "I have to, they are our friends." Pietro walked through the door to face the brutality of man.

Giacomo, four years older than Vittorio, guided him down the dimly lit hallway to his bedroom. Vittorio, frightened, almost in tears, asked, "What is happening, Giacomo?"

"Shh, shh." He held his finger to his mouth. "You must be quiet."

"But why? Why did your father bring me here? I want to go home to my mother and father," his voice started to tremble.

"I don't know, Vittorio, now be quiet. The Black Shirts were in your house."

Not knowing who the Black Shirts were, Vittorio began to ask questions. He stopped abruptly when he looked out Giacomo's bedroom window.

Chapter 11

AN EERIE SILENCE echoed throughout the neighborhood. Pietro ran into the house, yelling out the names of his two friends. He searched the bedrooms, then entered the library where his friend wrote editorials for the newspaper he owned, his pen his only weapon. Desk drawers lay on the floor, overturned books were strewn about, picture frames had been broken. The silence was overwhelming.

Like a madman, Pietro searched the rooms until he came to the kitchen door. A sick feeling overcame him. Bloodstained footprints mixed with larger smears from the dragged bodies of the two tormented souls. The rancid smell of vomit and bile conflicted with the aroma of that night's dinner.

Pietro swung open the kitchen door. He stared in disbelief at the two naked bodies that hung from the kitchen ceiling. The macabre scene unfolded before his eyes. Blood ran down the bodies, dripping from the feet of his dearest friends. The pooled blood, the torn flesh, the devastation of the human bodies caused Pietro to be violently sick. Bent over, he retched and cried. Finally, he mustered the strength to stand up.

Tears ran down his face, the baptismal water of death dripped from his chin. Pietro struggled to get a chair to stand on so that he could free the innocent bodies from the nooses tied around their necks. A neighbor who followed Pietro into the house passed out at the sight.

Pietro stood on the chair with a knife in hand and cut down

Vittorio's mother, Anna. He caught her bloodied, swollen body and gently placed it on the floor. A neighbor covered the body with a blanket, and then blessed herself with the sign of the cross. Covered in blood, Pietro cut loose his close friend Paolo, Vittorio's dad. He sobbed like a child as he held him under his arms and gently put him down next to his wife. Standing up, he heard the scream of a young boy.

Vittorio clawed at Giacomo's bedroom window. The horror-stricken face of the child, his eyes wide open, his nose running, the muffled scream, "Papa, Papa," was forever etched in Pietro's mind.

Giacomo ran over to the window. Witnessing his father freeing Vittorio's dad, he began to scream uncontrollably. Giacomo pulled Vittorio from the window. The two friends clung to one another, sobbing. Giacomo held his friend, saying, "We will kill you, Mussolini . . . we will kill you." From that day, Vittorio and Giacomo would become brothers over the spilled blood of Vittorio's parents.

The newspaperman had realized his words would one day inflame Mussolini. He took the necessary steps to protect his son and his fortune. His life always at peril, he arranged for Pietro and Christina to adopt Vittorio if anything happened. Throughout the country, the disappearance and death of the media became a common occurrence. Paolo understood at some point he and Anna might die for the words he wrote. A secret bank account was established, Pietro its trustee. Vittorio became Pietro's adopted son the day after the tragic deaths of Paolo and Anna Esposto.

Surprisingly, no repercussions took place against those who knew the newspaper editor. The Italian people resigned themselves to Mussolini's rule. He now controlled the media, its content and its delivery—the sole power of the printed word—or so he believed.

In the years from 1922 to 1943, life for the Italians—specifically, for those who opposed the Fascist regime—was hell. The hand of the Squadristi, or Black Shirts, struck down those who opposed the Fascist state with deliberate cruelty.

Chapter 12

VITTORIO CONTINUED HIS story in fluent English. He studied philosophy at the University of Rome La Sapienza, the most ancient university in Italy, founded in 1303 by Pope Boniface the VIII. He spoke with pride about the school, its influence on his life, and his desire to be a priest.

Vittorio was twenty-six and in his sixth year of seminary when World War II ended. Giacomo, who graduated two years earlier, worked for his father in the Italian underground. He kept a watchful eye over his younger brother.

One day in April 1945, Giacomo knocked on the apartment door.

"Come in."

"Vittorio, Vittorio, my brother, come, we need to take a trip," Giacomo said.

"Where to, my brother? I have too much work to do."

"Papa wants us to be in Milan by tomorrow morning. They arrested Mussolini by Lake Como and he and some others were executed. The bodies are on their way to Milan."

"Arrested Mussolini? Dead? How much wine did you drink?" Mussolini's name always stirred an inner anger in Vittorio, a hatred he tried to repress.

"No, no, I am serious. Let's go." Giacomo reached over, grabbed Vittorio, and shoved him out the door. "Come, we will drive through the night."

"Alright, alright, I'll go. And can you tell me why I would want to be near that bastard?" Anger seethed through Vittorio's words.

"It is important. Hopefully your nightmares will finally stop."

"I don't have nightmares," Vittorio replied.

Of course, they both knew he did. Vittorio would wake in the night screaming, drenched in sweat. The memory of the murder of his parents never escaped his tormented mind.

"Well, hopefully my nightmares will stop," Giacomo said with sorrow in his voice.

A car waited for the men as they walked into the spring twilight. After resting for a couple of hours along the way, they arrived in Milan in the early part of the next day.

They parked on a side street, not able to travel any further due to the congestion of cars and people on the road. In the distance, the muffled yells and screams of a large crowd filled the morning air. It sounded like a sports event. The two brothers walked and then began to trot toward the multitude surrounding the Piazza Loreto. As they got closer, they heard people yelling. "Down with the Fascist pig Mussolini! Morte, morte! Death to the pig."

Giacomo ran ahead and stopped dead in his tracks. He turned, with tears in his eyes, grabbed his brother, and said, "It is over, the nightmare has ended. Vittorio, the nightmare has ended!" His voice filled with joyful exuberance.

Across from the village square, at a Hess gas station, Mussolini and his mistress hung upside down on meat hooks, to show the world—and most of all, the Italian people—the dictator was dead. Vittorio was stunned at the sight. Memories filled his mind of his mother and father hanging in the kitchen. A deep sense of remorse came over him as he knelt and, before the eyes of God and his brother, the priest-to-be asked God for forgiveness. A wave of peace engulfed him, the hatred was gone, and his mind was blank. He sobbed like a child. Pietro and Giacomo lifted him.

"The nightmare is over, my child, revenge is ours. Soon our country will be liberated," Pietro said as he consoled his adopted son.

* * *

Vittorio finished the story. He told Paolo how he decided to leave the seminary, and how he met his wife. “I believe, Paolo, my wife is a gift from God. So I would understand the love of a man and a woman.” Vittorio stared deeply into Paolo’s eyes. “It is not often I talk about my life. For some reason I told you. Maybe I told you because you have the same name as my father, I don’t know.” Vittorio grabbed hold of Paolo’s shoulders. He continued, “What you must understand, my young friend, the day I felt the love of God was the day when I asked God’s forgiveness. The hatred within my heart darkened my soul. Paolo, love is the key to life. You must love, and you must forgive. Without forgiveness, you can’t love. Life will always continue in death, in sadness, in joy. Without love in your life, you merely exist, a puppet to society’s wills and ways.” He paused, still holding Paolo’s gaze. He said, “I can see the love in your eyes, Paolo . . . a love so deep that when the day comes, your words will touch many hearts. You will break down barriers.” Vittorio leaned over Paolo and kissed him on the cheek. With a tear in his eye, he said, “I must go and help my wife. May you have a great life, my friend.” He walked away.

Paolo, stunned, said to Giacomo, “Holy shit, is that true?”

Giacomo wiped a tear from his eye. “I am afraid so. But all this love and forgiveness stuff, I don’t know; I still hate the son of a bitch Mussolini.”

Paolo stood, stretched his legs, and said, “Giacomo, I’m going for a walk along the beach.”

“Okay, sonny boy, looks like there will be a beautiful sunset. Look to the mountains, my friend.”

“I’ll be back,” Paolo said, bewildered and disturbed by the story Vittorio had told.

Chapter 13

PAOLO CROSSED THE street to the beach. He felt sorrow in his heart for Vittorio. Listening to the horrific events of Vittorio's tragic childhood, Paolo sensed the pain in every word. *How can man be so cruel? What is it in the mind of man so dark, so hideous, to destroy life?*

Paolo approached the seawall. He took a deep breath. The smell of the salt water settled his mind—the cerulean blue of the Mediterranean, the mountains of Sorrento to his right. Paolo took off his sneakers. He looked for a place to sit to view the sunset. The beach was nearly empty. A young couple held hands as they walked the shore. He found a spot on the seawall, sat, and watched. The lovers walked in and out of the water, splashing each other. They embraced with a passionate kiss. The man whispered in the girl's ear, she giggled. The evening would unite them as man and woman. How he envied them.

Paolo jumped off the seawall and sat in the cool sand. He gazed at the sun setting over the horizon. The sun gave the illusion of molten iron dropping into the cooling bath of the sea. The steam enveloped the twilight sky, a red aura spread across the horizon. Paolo sat in peace, one with nature, awed at its beauty. Tranquility enveloped him. His mind filled with thoughts and desires for his life. At the young age of twenty-one, he reminisced about his father, who had died the previous year. "Pops, you would have loved this place," he said aloud.

“Paolo, Paolo,” someone called to him. He looked up.

“Sergio, how are you?” He stood to shake Vittorio’s son’s hand.

“So how do you like our beach?” the twenty-two-year-old asked.

“Bella, bella. It’s very peaceful.”

“Yes, it is. How did you like my father’s story?”

“I can’t believe what he experienced and endured. Your father is a remarkable man and then he forgave the bastard. That blew my mind, man.” Paolo shook his head in disbelief.

“My father is a great man. His dreams still torture him. Sometimes at night he will wake sobbing in his bed and in the morning, he won’t even remember the dream.”

“Wow.”

The two sat on the sand and talked about their different lives and their dreams. In the fall, Sergio would attend Columbia Law School in New York. They promised to keep in touch.

Chapter 14

THE FOLLOWING MORNING Paolo awoke well rested. He looked forward to the drive to Ottati. Vittorio's wife prepared a breakfast of eggs, cheeses, and dried sausages. Vittorio poured him a cup of espresso. After Paolo drank the strong Italian coffee, he said, "That will definitely put hair on my chest."

"Hair on your chest, what's that mean?" Giacomo asked.

"An American saying," he replied.

Vittorio and his wife walked Paolo and Giacomo out to the car. They said their good-byes. The husband and wife offered Paolo a place to stay should he ever come back. Vittorio walked up to him as he sat in the car. He placed his hands on the door and said, "Remember what I told you, Paolo. Don't ever forget love and forgiveness."

"I won't."

"Good, now Giacomo, get going." The brother tapped the car. Giacomo started the engine and they drove off the same way as they came, honking the horn.

The trip to Ottati was breathtaking. The beauty of the landscape filled Paolo's senses with excitement. They traveled along the cobblestone and dirt roadways. The tires kicked up dust in the warm early summer air. The top down, the late-vintage red 1950s Italian Maserati sped through the countryside.

The 350-horsepower engine roared as the car traversed the winding roads and hillside communities, at times reaching speeds in excess of

130 mph. Paolo prayed Giacomo would remain quiet while he drove. Several times, his young life flashed before him.

The everyday tasks of the Italian women hanging their clothes out to dry captured his imagination. The children played soccer. A freshly killed goat hung along the road, drying out for the evening's dinner. Paolo embraced the simple sights. He felt as if this country were his long-lost home.

They reached the hillside village of Ottati in the early afternoon. The heat of the summer day reached its peak. They drove the Via Sant Antonio, turned left on Via San Biagio, and passed the church of Saint Biagio. Paolo wondered what life in the quaint village was like eighty years ago. *What transpired in the lives of my descendants that caused them to pack up and leave this serene, tranquil village? What is the hidden truth of my family?*

The Maserati came to a stop in the Piazza Umberto. Giacomo had arranged for Paolo to stay with Antonio and Sophia Conforti. The couple owned a small café and spoke excellent English. They lived above the restaurant in a spacious three-bedroom apartment with their daughter Maria, who was studying in Rome.

Antonio and Sophia welcomed him with the customary kiss on both cheeks. The couple appeared to be in their late sixties. Antonio was five feet seven inches tall and rugged in appearance, handsome, with brown hair tinted with streaks of gray, and about thirty pounds overweight. Sophia was attractive—five feet two, thin, with the bluest eyes Paolo had ever seen. Someone once said the eyes are the portal to the soul. Sophia's eyes radiated peace and contentment. The couple provided Paolo a small room with a bed and dresser for fifty dollars a week. The price included breakfast, lunch, and dinner. His window overlooked the village square. The steeple of the Church of Saint Biagio was to his right.

"Sonny boy, I am going back to Amalfi, when do you want me to pick you up?"

"How about Friday, four days from now?"

"Very good, my friend, I will be here by one o'clock."

"Excellent, Giacomo. Do you know anyone at the Vatican?"

"Yes, my cousin is a Cardinal. If you like, I will take you there, maybe we can visit with the Pope."

"That would be excellent, my mother would be extremely happy. Ciao, Giacomo, be safe."

"Ciao, sonny boy."

The next day, Antonio introduced Paolo to the mayor. The mayor, who spoke little English, gave Paolo unrestricted access to the town's records. The village records had little information about the family, other than a record of their last names. He met the oldest person living in the village, eighty-five-year-old Mrs. Coseglia. The woman had dementia; she believed Paolo was her grandson. He spoke with several other villagers, with no success.

Early in the morning of his second day, after his morning walk, Paolo decided to visit the Church of Saint Biagio to look at the church records. The crisp, cool morning air and the cloudless sky amazed Paolo, who gazed at the top of the Alburni Mountains in wonderment. The white, rugged fascia with green pine trees loomed above him. The image was a reminder of the hard life endured by the inhabitants of the village.

In the short time Paolo was in Italy, the difference between the two cultures perplexed him. Life in the United States was about getting ahead, earning a dollar—in Italy, it was easier, simpler, and about food. His father had told him people in the States were more concerned about the almighty dollar.

"Life should be simple, enjoyable, filled with love and family," he said.

"That's all fine and good but love alone doesn't pay the bills," his mother said, angst in her voice as she put her hands on his shoulders and kissed the top of his head.

"You wait, Lynn, the people of our country are headed on a path of destruction. Drugs, money, no morals—evil is lurking. I pray I'm not here when it comes." Tony's prayer was answered. Evil attacked humanity like the bubonic plague. Evil so subtle no one knew it became a way of existence.

"Paolo, Paolo," he heard his name being called, awakening him from his reverie. Three men sat outside Antonio and Sophia's café, drinking their morning espresso. "Veni, veni! Come, come!" one of the men shouted.

Paolo walked across the cobblestone piazza and approached the three men. They stood to greet him. Their rough and weathered hands told Paolo these were hard-working people. Their powerful grips almost brought him to his knees. Paolo gazed into their eyes and noticed something else—a kindness, a tranquility, an inner beauty and peace. *Only after you have opened the bottle and experienced the taste do you know the wine's true value.*

The three men invited him to sit down and he graciously accepted. Vincenzo and Luiggi understood and spoke English fairly well. The third man, Sabatino, listened while Luiggi translated for him. They appeared to be in their late sixties, thin and of medium height. Vincenzo was bald, while Luiggi and Sabatino had thick, wavy brown hair with hints of gray. Their faces were aged by the sun, a telltale sign they worked outdoors in the elements. Sabatino offered Paolo a cigarette, but he politely refused.

Antonio walked out of the café with a pot of espresso and put the strong Italian coffee on the table. He went over to Paolo, placed his hands on his shoulders, and welcomed him.

"Paolo, you have met my friends. I hope you don't mind I told them a little about you." Paolo shook his head no. "Enjoy, my friends. I have to go help Sophia in the kitchen."

A short time later, Antonio returned. He carried a plate of cheese, salami, bread, and olive oil. He grabbed a chair and joined them. They talked for over an hour, mostly about life in the United States. Vincenzo's brother lived in California. He had visited him several times. Antonio had no desire to leave his native country.

"Life in America is too complicated," Antonio said.

Sabatino and Luiggi loved their mother country too much to leave. Paolo guessed their desire to visit was hampered by their own financial inadequacy. They talked with animation, their hands moving with every word spoken. Paolo soon followed. His hands moved in like fashion. In the midst of their conversation, Sabatino (through Luiggi's translation) said he had never ventured outside of Ottati. Paolo, surprised, asked why. Luiggi translated.

"My friend," Luiggi began, "why do I need to travel? I have everything I could possibly want right here. I have a wonderful life. I work, I make love to my wife, I eat well, I pray to God. My children are grown, they bring my grandchildren to visit, and then they leave. I have no problems. I am healthy and I live a simple life. That gives me everything I need."

Paolo listened, focused on every word as he continued to speak.

"If I traveled, then my life would not be so simple. I don't have to see how others live, it is how my wife and I live that is important. My ordinary life is my desire." He sat back in his chair and with a smile of epiphany, sipped his espresso. He knew he had the answers.

"When do you leave our village?" Vincenzo asked Paolo.

"In two days."

Antonio chimed in, "Tomorrow night Sophia and I are going to have a party in your honor, Paolo. We will celebrate your coming home."

Paolo liked the sound of it, "Celebrate me coming home."

Then it occurred to him, he had brought the family name back to the small village. He decided at that moment to buy a home in Ottati someday when he had the money. He rose and offered his hand to the three Italians. He said, "I'm going to Saint Biagio, hopefully I can find information about my family by looking through the church's records."

Chapter 15

LOCATED IN A small plaza just outside the center of the village, the church was painted white and outlined in red. Two bells adorned the top of the roof to call the villagers to the celebratory Mass of Jesus's life, death, and resurrection. The appearance of the house of God was different from what Paolo had observed in Amalfi and at home in the States. The red outline of the windows, doors, and roofline puzzled him. *Why red? What did red signify?*

He walked up the short flight of stone stairs, opened the large wooden doors, and entered. The interior was understated in appearance—high vaulted ceilings designed with frescos of the Last Supper, Stations of the Cross depicted along the inner walls. Paolo genuflected in the aisle and entered the last pew. He knelt to say a prayer. Paolo remembered his mother's words from when he was a young boy. "Paolo, whenever you enter a church for the first time, say an Our Father, a Hail Mary, and a Gloria, and make a wish." Paolo said the prayers but made no wish.

He sat back and absorbed the atmosphere. A white wood altar stood covered in a white cloth with the Tabernacle to the side. He wondered if his grandfather had sat here. The old stone Domo echoed with the slightest sound. Paolo heard footsteps as he sat with his eyes closed. Someone touched his shoulder. He opened his eyes. It was a Dominican nun dressed in a white habit. She had a round face, with bright brown eyes—she looked like she was in her thirties.

"Paolo," she said in a quiet voice.

Does everyone know my name? "Good morning, Sister."

"I understand you are trying to find information about your family," she said, in almost perfect English.

"Yes, I am."

"I am Sister Mary. I might be able to help you, come with me. We will search the church's records."

He followed her down the aisle. She genuflected before the Tabernacle and turned her head to look at him. Paolo took her cue and genuflected as well. They entered the sacristy through a side door off the sanctuary. He followed her through a series of openings that eventually led to the basement. As Paolo descended the narrow staircase, he asked, "Sister, how far back do your records go?"

"At least two hundred years. We must be careful, the papers are fragile. Over the past few years, we have been able to enclose them in plastic to help preserve them."

"Interesting."

They entered a large cavern-like cellar with rows of shelving filled with dated and numbered boxes. Paolo counted at least ten rows. The room measured forty feet by thirty feet, the shelving seven feet high. He noticed the room was well lit and dry.

"Paolo, do you know what year your grandfather was born?"

"All I know is he emigrated to the United States in 1911. He was sixteen years old at the time, it would've been 1895. His birthday was March twentieth."

Sister Mary easily found the year of his grandfather's birth. Paolo took the box from the fourth shelf and gently placed it on the table. Within thirty minutes, they found his grandfather's birth certificate and baptismal certificate. *Antonio Roberto DeLaurentis*. By the end of the afternoon, he discovered his grandfather had eight brothers and sisters. All the siblings but one emigrated to either Argentina or the United States. His grandfather's sister Teresa stayed behind. She was married at the time and her husband refused to move.

"Sister, thank you so much for your help. Can I ask you a question?"

"Of course."

"The red doors and trim on the church . . . why red?"

"I thought you would never ask."

Paolo looked at her, puzzled. There was something in her eyes that spoke to Paolo's heart—a truth to be revealed.

"Let's sit down over here." The nun pointed to a table with two chairs.

Paolo was at peace.

"The red symbolizes the blood that was spilled here many years ago, the blood of a husband and wife murdered but yet their son was left unharmed. The story I am going to tell you will answer your questions but will lead to many more questions in your life."

"I don't understand."

"You will."

Chapter 16

IT WAS WINTER of 1849. The Roman Republic had been established. Victor Emanuel had succeeded the throne and signed the armistice at Vignale. The French troops at Civitavecchia restored the Pope.

Franco and Lucia DeLaurentis gently placed their three-month-old son Vincenzo in his crib. They each blessed his forehead with the sign of the cross and kissed him. The child, covered in a blanket made of sheep's wool, slept peacefully in the homemade cradle. The parents lay next to the child on a mattress filled with straw. The husband and wife made love and fell asleep to the rhythmic breathing of the child.

Franco rustled in his sleep. Awakened by the mountain wind, he rose to close the wooden shutters. He opened the window; a cold breeze filled the room. He reached for the burnt-orange shutter and pinned it to the windowsill. In the dark of night, something caught Franco's eye, a movement on the street. He thought nothing of it, and went back to sleep.

His family's house sat on the outskirts of town off the Via Sant' Antonio, in the small mountain village of Ottati, an ancient town located southeast of Amalfi in the province of Salerno, Italy. It rested on the side of Mt. Alburni, nestled within the Cilento and Vallo di Diano National Park. To the north were green forest-filled mountains; the summer's vibrant rolling green pastures lay to the west. The top of the mountain was now covered in snow. The mountain protected the medieval village from the harshness of the winter cold but not from the callousness of man.

The unassuming community consisted of three hundred and fourteen families, mainly farmers and shepherds. The town was impoverished but self-sufficient. Folklore said the ancient city dated back to the beginning of the second millennium, the first house built by the Greeks who fled Civita as early as the year 1000. Historians placed the city's origins at some point in the middle ages. The quietness of the village and its charm drew religious orders. In 1484 and 1602, the Dominicans and the Capuchins established monasteries. For the religious, it was a sincere and contemplative life.

* * *

The assassins approached from the north. They walked in silence past the Church of Saint Biagio. The darkness of the night hid the men as they traveled along the Via Deodati to their target. The squalid darkness encircled the killers as they walked, the evil black tendril of the evening swallowed the assassins' souls. The town was all but silent except for the few noises of the animals that lay nearby.

They were clothed in black, anonymous to one another, joined only by the fellowship of their career. Faces covered, they communicated using hand signals. For four days, they lay hidden in the Cilento Forest as they waited for the moonless night. The leader would walk into town during the day mapping the roads to their destination. Together they hid from the world but not from the eyes of God, for no one can escape the eyes of God.

The men gathered their belongings. A night owl hooted as they left the darkened forest. Their footprints tracked through the snow. The job was to kill the parents and take the child. They would meet up with their employer and hand over the baby. The boy would disappear into a world where he would be brought up in such a way that the prophecy of old would not come to fruition—the prophecy that one would come after him, a prelude to the savior that will appear before man in the skies above. This warning to humanity was the saving effort of the man they would call the Star from the West. Those who listened would be saved; those who did not believe would die.

They walked around the house as they looked for the easiest way to gain entrance. There was no need to lock one's door, for crime didn't exist in the small mountain village. One of the men swore under his mask as he stepped in goat manure. The smell stayed with him until he had what you might call a change of heart, a spiritual epiphany.

Two members of the group climbed the wooden stairs to the second-floor apartment. A tiny squeak emitted as they reached the last step. Their minds numb, their consciences dead, the killers approached the apartment door. The leader of the group and one other assassin would perform the execution of the couple. The other two would stand guard, discreetly hidden.

The two entered the three-room apartment; an eerie silence filled the home. The leader of the group was unsettled, the hair on the back of his neck stood up. For the first time he felt fear, but fear of what? Franco and Lucia slept still in their bed; both lay on their backs as they waited for death, a new birth, a new life in heaven. Their arms were folded across their stomachs, a peaceful grace on their faces. An orange glow from a flute-covered candle filled the bedroom, highlighting the family of three.

The assassins' act was quick. They stood over the couple and plowed their daggers deep into the sleeping couple's chests. As the blades entered, the couple's eyes flashed open, staring their executioners in the face. Their eyes filled with sorrow—not for their premature deaths, but instead sadness for the men who sent them to the heavenly hands of God. Their death instant, the two felt no pain.

Time stopped, hand movements traveled in slow motion. The leader's assistant began to cry, a deep dread overcame him. Not able to withdraw the dagger from Lucia, he fell to the floor. The leader, paralyzed, stood by the bedside. A white globe of light surrounded Vincenzo and his cradle. The innocent child's eyes were open and a tear ran down his little cheek. His tiny hand reached for something invisible.

A driving wind rattled the house. The shutter doors swung open, the windows imploded. A jagged shard of glass sailed through the room, inserting itself in the neck of the leader, severing his carotid artery, his death slow and painful. The second assassin, still on his knees, heard the words, *Follow me, and seek my forgiveness.* He gathered himself and ran out of the building; his two compatriots who had been standing guard ran after him.

The trio traveled in silence, afraid to speak. They arrived at the rendezvous point three hours before the rising sun. Two horses were tied to a tree. Two men sat nearby, huddled over a small fire, their faces hidden. "Senor," the killer cried out. "Senor," again no answer.

They approached the two still bodies. The killer leaned forward and removed the hood from one of the men. The glow from the fire highlighted his face. The killer jumped back in horror, turned and vomited on the fire. The other two men stood paralyzed, staring at the charred faces of the two men. The two soiled their pants. A vision of hell flashed through their minds, their lives changed forever. One would become a priest, asking for God's mercy on his soul until the day he died. The other two sought forgiveness by rationalizing their involvement. Both committed suicide several years later.

The following day, neighbors found the family of three. Husband and wife lay at peace in their straw bed; the child lay peacefully in his crib. The murderer's body was found a quarter of a mile away, lying in a heap of manure, his face contorted, grimacing in agony and fright. His judgment came and went, no mercy shown.

The murder of Franco and Lucia threw the village into a frenzy. The questions: Why Franco, an ordinary shepherd and loving husband? And why did little Vincenzo live? The answers were never found. The population of Ottati relied on God to ease their pain. Franco's brother Antonio and his wife Caterina adopted Vincenzo. Vincenzo never knew about his parents. He lived a peaceful life, marrying Arabella Deodati. He fathered eight children and died peacefully in his sleep in 1910. He was Paolo's great-grandfather.

Chapter 17

THE NUN RELEASED Paolo's hands, sat back, and said, "Paolo, I have a strange question to ask. Did a globe of light ever surround you?"

Paolo was speechless. In a quiet voice, he said, "How did you know? Yes, when I was in third grade. I, I . . ." He stuttered, "I had a high fever; my parents placed me in the bathtub to cool me down. They said out of nowhere this bright light surrounded me, and my fever disappeared."

Sister Mary looked into his eyes. "You are a child of God, a messenger of hope."

"A messenger of hope? I don't understand."

"You will be God's messenger to mankind. Your words, the love that is within you, and your ability to forgive will cause many to fall to their knees and seek God's forgiveness. Don't be afraid to use the gift. You will witness many events in your mind, and your senses will lead you to places that very few have been. At times, you will not be able to explain the love in your heart. Many will question you and not understand you, but you will know it is true. Live by faith with no explanation. This is who you are—a child of God, a gift to man."

"I am?"

"You are. Your soul will never forget who you are. Your senses will tell you what is right, what is wrong. You won't know the reasons why, you will just know. God will take care of the rest. Your heart will guide you. And remember what will be revealed to you will be revealed in God's time, not yours. For now, live your life, use your gift wisely, and know you are human—fallible, not perfect. Every time you fail, God will pick you up and carry you to another door to make right the wrong. You must also be mindful of the Evil One, for he too will try to persuade you in subtle ways, for he knows the truth, as well. Most of all, be at peace in knowing God loves you as he loves all mankind."

Paolo sat back, his mind blank. "I'm speechless, what do I do now?"

"Enjoy your life, you will soon forget we talked."

"I see." Paolo stood, leaned against the wall, placed his hands in his blue jeans pockets, and cried.

"Paolo—may I suggest you travel to the outskirts of town and visit the cemetery? I am sure you will find some of your family members there."

Through his tears, he said, "Thank you, Sister, I'll do that." He walked over to the table, lifted the box, and returned his family's history to the fourth shelf. "Is the cemetery far from here?" Paolo turned around for a response. The nun had disappeared. "Sister, Sister," he called out. No response. Spooked, he left the cellar the way he had come.

Paolo DeLaurentis walked along the roadside, complete and at peace. The missing part of his family history was finally put to rest, the unknown truth revealed. Puzzled at the sudden disappearance of the Benedictine nun, he continued his walk to the cemetery. A goat grazed in a nearby field. He came upon the stone-walled cemetery, the gravestones littered amid the overgrown grass. Paolo began his search for his dead relatives. On the gravestones were pictures of the dead etched in the stone. "How bizarre," he whispered to himself. Paolo went from row to row. An hour passed before he found a gravestone with his surname.

Teresa DeLaurentis Ricci and her husband Alphonso died in 1952. Next to their grave lay their son Franco, who succumbed in January 1964. His headstone was covered in tall grass. Paolo began to pull the weeds from the sacred ground of his ancestors. The images of his grandfather's sister and husband appeared, etched into the gray marble. Paolo stopped and stepped back. On the right side of the gray monolith was a picture of his cousin Franco. Overwhelmed, Paolo stared at the picture. His cousin bore an uncanny resemblance to his brother Anthony. He smiled, filled with pride—*he knew who he was.*

Paolo headed back to the village, his head held high, his gait brisk, almost a trot. Paolo's mind focused on the revelation of who he was, and an inner joy grew within his heart as if he had opened a Christmas present and received exactly what he asked for. "Wow," he said in a whisper. "Wow."

He entered the apartment above the café, and went to his room to take a nap. Paolo slept through the night like a rock, oblivious to the outside world, not hearing Sophia knock on his door for dinner.

* * *

The night before his departure, the Conforti family gave Paolo a party. He felt as if the entire population of Ottati came to Piazza Umberto. Paolo was awed by the number of people that gathered.

The villagers brought food and homemade wine. Tables were arranged in the piazza under strings of colored lights. A mandolin player and accordion musician roamed the plaza, singing and playing their music. At one point, the wandering musicians tried to sing a Beatles song in Italian. Paolo saw Antonio and gave him a hug. "Antonio, thank you so much. I met a nun yesterday, Sister Mary. She was extremely helpful."

Antonio looked at him in astonishment. "Sister Mary?" Antonio reached in his back pocket, pulled out his worn black leather wallet, and withdrew a picture. "Is this the nun?"

"Yes, that's her."

Antonio stepped back. His eyes welled with tears. "Paolo, Paolo, that's my sister, she died five years ago."

"How could that be, Antonio? I was with her, I talked to her, she touched my shoulder, she was real." Paolo's voice rose in confusion.

"You, Paolo, are he, yes, you are the one she talked about the day she died."

"What do you mean?"

"My sister Mary was stationed in Rome for twenty years. She was diagnosed with cancer and moved back home to Ottati to live out the remainder of her days. When she was well enough, she would help organize the church records. That lasted two years before the cancer affected her mind. She would have visions of God, Jesus, the Blessed Mother, and the Holy Angels. We all believed she was doozie-pots—crazy. On the day she died, she told me she would come back when the youngest child of the DeLaurentis family came home. Paolo, are you the youngest in your family?"

Bewildered and in shock, he nodded yes. "Yes, I am. Antonio, what does this mean?"

Antonio said, "You are blessed by God and at some point in your life, he will use you. What did she tell you?"

Paolo paused for a moment, his mind blank. "I don't remember," he scratched his head in bewilderment. He knew, but yet he didn't. "Something about God's time . . . I'll just know . . . Wow, we talked, but I can't remember. We did find my family's records, and I went to the cemetery."

"And tell me, my friend, how do you feel?" Antonio looked at the young man.

"Great, I feel great."

"Bene! Now tell me, how did my sister look?"

"She was beautiful, Antonio, alive and beautiful."

"That makes me happy, she is no longer in pain," he said, a tear in his eye. "And you, Paolo, brought her back. I am at peace now; my sister is with God. Come, come, my son, let us enjoy this festival." Antonio took Paolo's arm and introduced him to the town residents.

The party lasted through the night; the townspeople danced and laughed, drank the homemade wine, enjoyed life. Paolo wondered if the feast was for him or an excuse for the village residents to come together. His conversation yesterday with Antonio's sister still baffled him. Tired, he left the gathering and went to his room and fell asleep.

She floated toward him, her eyes focused on his. Mesmerized, he could not move. She began to speak, but he heard no words. Tranquility engulfed the two . . .

* * *

Paolo awoke the next morning well rested. He showered and went downstairs to find Sophia in the kitchen cooking breakfast.

"Paolo, how are you today? My Antonio told me what happened. Come, come sit down. I will pour you some espresso." She pulled the chair from under the table.

"Thank you, Sophia, I'm peaceful. I came here to find out who I am and I think I found out." He continued, "You and your husband have been extremely kind to me. I cannot thank you enough. I hope I'll be back to visit in a couple of years."

"Well, when you decide to come back, you call us. You can stay here for as long as you like. Our home is your home."

"Grazie. By the way, Sophia, where did you learn to speak English so well?"

"Before I met Antonio, I lived in Rome. My father taught English at the University."

"Do you regret leaving Rome?"

"At first I did, but now my life is uncomplicated. Antonio takes care of me, and we enjoy life."

"I find it amazing that everyone I meet says the same thing. In America, we have forgotten the simplicity of life. We're more concerned with money and possessions."

"Paolo, as you get older, life becomes more enjoyable when it is simple. You are a young man, hopefully you will discover the simplicity of life before you grow too old to enjoy life." Sophia said this as she wiped her hands on a kitchen towel. She folded the towel neatly, placing it on the countertop next to the stove. "I need to go to church now to help the priest. Antonio will be right back; he had to go to the store. Enjoy your breakfast. I hope we will meet again before I die." Sophia walked out the back door.

Paolo sat at the wooden table with its white tablecloth and ate his breakfast of homemade bread toasted over the open flame, cured meats, freshly squeezed orange juice, and of course, espresso. *Antonio will be here soon.* The back door opened and a smiling Antonio entered the kitchen.

"Ciao, Paolo, how are you this morning?"

"A little overwhelmed," Paolo said.

"And why is that, my friend?"

"Antonio, these last two days have been most heartwarming. The acceptance of me by you, Sophia, and the people of my grandfather's birthplace touches my heart. I feel like I'm home."

"It is home for you, my son. This is where your lineage begins. Your life was set in motion here in Ottati. Now you can take your story home to the United States ever entrenched in your heart. You will share this short stay with those you will meet and those you have known as you walk life's journey. Remember this," he pulled out a chair and sat across from Paolo. "Remember this, Paolo, tomorrow waits for no man. Life dwindles away every day. There is no way you can reclaim yesterday but tomorrow is in the palm of your hands. One cannot escape from tomorrow's grasp—for there will always be a tomorrow. Even in death tomorrow still comes for it waits for no man. Now you must excuse me." With a tear in his eye, he added, "Paolo, you are a child of God." Antonio rose from the chair, placed his hands on the table, and said, "I should start preparing for the lunch crowd. I heard there is a bus of tourists on the way. This should be a very profitable day. When Giacomo arrives, bring him downstairs to the restaurant for lunch."

"I will."

Paolo sat contemplating Antonio's words. A warmness and sense of peace traveled through his body. Someone touched his arm. Startled, he turned. No one was there. Sister Mary came to his mind. Paolo cleaned up, went upstairs, and packed.

Giacomo arrived right on time. They had lunch at Antonio and Sophia's café, eating outside in the piazza. A blue-and-red Cinzano umbrella placed in the center of the table protected them from the heat of the sun. They said their goodbyes just as the small tour bus arrived with the twenty potential customers. Paolo and Giacomo jumped into the Maserati, Giacomo tooting the horn as they drove the winding road. Paolo looked back at his grandfather's hometown nestled in the Alburni Mountains, the jagged cliffs embraced by the bright blue sky with the serene village located at the base of the mountain. As they passed the Church of Saint Biagio, painters began painting over the red doors with white paint, while others erected scaffolding. An unexplained tear trickled down Paolo's face. With a lump in his throat, he said goodbye to the village of his ancestors.

Chapter 18

BACK IN NEW Haven, Paolo climbed the steps to his cousin Franco's restaurant. A Christmas wreath with its passion-red bow hung on the brown wooden door. The ornamental fixture covered the oval-shaped window. The scent of evergreen was present in the chilly evening air, while Mother Nature waited to display the first snowfall of the season.

Paolo was of medium height and build. In good shape, five feet ten and one hundred and seventy-five pounds, the Italian was attractive more than handsome. He had the classic Italian ethnic appearance: olive-colored skin, a Roman-shaped nose, a rugged, square-jawed face, wavy brown hair, and penetrating brown eyes. He was still single, the last of his siblings to get married. He sat patiently at the bar and waited for Franco. The bartender, a girl named Victoria, waited on him.

"You're Franco's cousin?"

"Yes, hi. My name is Paolo, and you must be Victoria?" Paolo pointed to her nametag.

"Yeah, that's me."

"Glad to meet you, Victoria."

"Same here, Paolo. Can I get you something to drink?"

"Sure, how about a rum and Coke?"

She poured the drink and asked, "Can I get you anything else?"

"No, thank you, this will be fine." He lifted the glass in salute.

Victoria was a pretty woman. Her face was thin and symmetrical;

she stood five feet five inches. She had a skinny waist, shoulder-length brown hair, bright brown eyes, and an infectious smile. For some reason, Paolo remembered a saying his mother had told him, "You can't judge a book by its cover."

"Paolo, Paolo, a sight for sore eyes." Paolo stood and the two hugged each other. Paolo kissed Franco on both sides of the face.

"Sorry it took me so long to get here. I've been busy in the city."

"No problem. So tell me, how was Italy?" Franco asked with excitement in his voice.

"Unbelievable. I can't even describe it. The mountains, the little villages, and the food—oh my God, the food was out of this world. You and Francesca definitely have to go."

"Glad you came by. You wanna eat? I'll get you a table."

"No, I'm fine. Steve and Tony are going to meet me. I think we'll eat at the bar."

"Your friend Tony, the writer? And Steve has the deli. Right?"

"Yep, Tony's trying to be a writer. And Steve's deli has excellent food, you gotta try it."

"Yeah, I will. Victoria, how about some menus for my cousin?"

Victoria served a beer to a customer, picked up a menu, and gave it to Paolo.

"Thank you."

"You're welcome," she said with a smile.

Paolo's eyes met hers. Distracted, he said, "Franco, did you get the recipes I sent you?"

"Yes, they're on the menu and our customers love the food. So tell me, what did you find out about our family?"

"I found where Poppie lived. I saw a picture of our cousin and he looks just like Anthony."

"Where is he? Does he still live in Ottati?"

"No, sorry to say, he died. There was a picture of him and Poppie's sister on the gravestone."

"On the gravestone?" Franco grimaced.

"Yeah, it was kind of freaky. All in all, it was an awesome experience."

"That's great." He put his arm around Paolo and quietly said, "The Giants and the Eagles are playing tonight. You wanna make a bet?"

"No, thanks."

"Smart move. Now if only I can have a winning streak like your father had. I could retire."

"Yeah, that was some streak." Paolo briefly recollected the memory and pushed it back to his subconscious.

Franco placed his hand on Paolo's shoulder and stood. "Listen, I have to get back to work. Enjoy your dinner with your friends. Oh, speaking of friends, your old roommate Rami was here. He looks good all dressed up in his Army uniform."

"Yeah, he told me he stopped by. I spoke to him when I got back. Wish I could've seen him. Hey, what's the story with your bartender Victoria?"

"Victoria, I'd be careful with that one. A good person, but a hot temper. She's a hard worker, put herself through college, lives on her own. She's a nurse at St. Raphael's Hospital—works here part time."

"She dating anyone?"

"Not that I know of. Do you want me to put in a good word for you?" Franco asked.

"No, I'll take care of it."

"Be careful, Paolo, remember what I told you."

"Yeah, yeah, I know. Go, your customers are waiting." In his mind, he heard the words, *stay away*.

* * *

Over the next several weeks, while on vacation, Paolo would come to the restaurant almost daily with the exception of Christmas Eve and Christmas. Finally, he asked Victoria out for New Year's Eve. He had his doubts about her. His intuition said, "Walk away from this."

The day before their first date, he had considered cancelling. Paolo pushed his senses aside, not wanting to consider his thoughts or his feelings. For how could his senses be right all the time? His childhood memories, the prodding of his mind by Dr. Payne and his dad, swept over him like a cold winter wind. He shook off the memories only to revisit them at another time.

He kept his date with Victoria. The adage "opposites attract" was true in their case; they were complete opposites in every respect. Victoria was all about justice, an eye for an eye. Paolo was passive, his ability to see goodness in everything and everyone was a total contrast to Victoria.

They dated for a year before Paolo asked her to marry him. By this time, Paolo commuted daily by train to New York City, where he worked. Paolo was hired as a business mediator. His primary job was to mediate between the buyer and seller of Fortune 500 corporations. Paolo had recognized it wouldn't be long before he had a family. The daily trek to and from the city gnawed at him. *How can I have a family and commute? I'll never be home early enough to be with my children.*

Two nights before their wedding, Paolo picked up Victoria at her apartment for dinner. For their last date as singles, they agreed to eat at Leon's, a local Italian eatery near the New Haven train station, at the time not a particularly safe neighborhood. A mandolin player roamed the interior of the establishment singing traditional Italian songs. They shared an appetizer of mozzarella en carozza. Paolo had veal parmigiana while Victoria ate half of her zuppe de pesce.

Paolo held Victoria's hand and spoke. "Are you nervous about Saturday?"

"No, I just want to get it over with and start our new life together."

He held up his glass of Chianti and stared deeply in her eyes. "May our marriage together be blessed."

Victoria wasn't able to hold his gaze. She turned away.

"What's wrong?" He let go of her hand. "Do you have doubts about us?

"Sometimes."

Paolo sat there, dumbfounded. "What do you mean?"

"Ignore me. Forget I even said anything."

"What do you mean, 'forget I even said anything'?"

"Just forget it, I don't want to talk about it."

Paolo was puzzled and taken aback. “Listen to me, Victoria, if you have any doubts, we don’t have to get married.” Paolo’s eyes penetrated hers; he looked deep within her, touching her soul. An eerie awareness overpowered him. Paolo sat back in his chair as if zapped by a stun gun. Bewildered, he tried to process what had just taken place.

“Paolo, Paolo, are you alright?” Words he did not hear sucked into the void of his subconscious. “Paolo, Paolo.” A cold hand touched his face.

“What?” he snapped back.

“Are you alright?” she said with alarm in her voice.

“Yes, I’m fine, fine. What the hell happened?” His voice rose in anger.

She began to laugh, “I don’t know. Your face went white, then red.” She took his hand. “Forget what I said, it’s my nerves, and it’s getting close to that time of the month.”

Boy, did he understand that comment. Almost every month, there was a contentious moment between the two. Victoria’s hormones raged with unbridled intensity. A week before, she was a hungry lion devouring everything in her sight. She was extremely vocal, even if it was irrational and cruel. Paolo believed he could live with the situation. He learned early on to adapt. Paolo’s father often told him that no matter what life throws at you, you either fight it or accept it. He adapted.

He gazed at Victoria as if he saw the darkness of man. A cold bead of sweat appeared on his forehead. Paolo tried to shake off the emotion. He said, “I guess I drank too much wine.”

“Paolo, you had one glass.” Victoria touched his hand. “Let’s go to your place and practice making babies.” She used her most seductive voice. “I’ll give you a backrub, and we can forget this ever happened.”

“Yeah, sure, sounds like a good idea.” His voice was less than enthusiastic. He leaned over and kissed her. They walked out of the restaurant into the dark, chilly spring air.

* * *

Paolo DeLaurentis and Victoria Trapani were married on an overcast day in May. Two hundred guests gathered at a local country club—the majority from Paolo's family. Victoria's guest list was shorter—the Trapani family and several friends from the hospital where she worked. They honeymooned on the pink sands of Bermuda.

Within a year of their wedding, Victoria became pregnant with twins and Paolo resigned his $150,000-a-year job. The New York City consulting firm Abrams, Sheehan, and Mylott tried in earnest to keep him, to no avail. As was his plan, Paolo ventured out on his own and started Ottati Consulting. New York provided Paolo a unique opportunity to network. He constantly made contacts and solidified relationships. His innate ability to understand and look ahead gave him an unequaled advantage over his co-workers.

Paolo called upon his associates in Italy—in particular, Vittorio's son Sergio, who became the prime minister—as well as the contacts he developed in New York. Ottati Consulting flourished. Within five years, he became a multi-millionaire. Paolo used his gift to speculate on gold futures, as well as to develop a niche market that many tried to emulate. The company became one giant think tank, providing businesses and governments with problem-solving ideas. A prospective client could seek advice on any number of issues, ranging from acquisitions and mergers to the selling of company assets and the restructuring of the corporate hierarchy.

Paolo's business was growing, but his marriage to Victoria was disintegrating. After the birth of the twins, Giacomo Anthony and Rio Marie, Paolo noticed a change in her. At first, he accepted the mood swings. After all, she was home with the children all day long while he "sat on his ass all day at work," a comment he heard more than once. Their relationship became extremely turbulent. Victoria's emotional outbursts, coupled with irrational thoughts and actions, destroyed the fabric of their family.

Paolo tried to get Victoria help. "I've taken care of my issues in my life. I don't need any more damn psychological help. This is the way I am. If you don't like the way I am, leave."

How he wished he could. Instead, Paolo wrapped himself in his work and defended his children against her tirades. After two years of verbal abuse, he gave up. Paolo hid within the peace and solace of his mind.

* * *

In 1987, Paolo moved the company headquarters to the Gold Building on Whitney Avenue in New Haven. The fourteen-story building got its name from the gold-mirrored windows that encased the offices. It was also befitting when one considered Paolo's investment in gold.

With the help of his friend Bill Conti, Paolo purchased an array of electronic equipment. Bill was now a commander in naval intelligence.

"Pard, I don't understand why you need this equipment. Damn, you know just about everything before it happens. What the hell do you need this shit for?"

"I need this shit, as you say, to mask my gift. I can't allow people to know, not even my lunatic wife knows. And to be honest, Pard, the gift has been absent. Besides, it would be too controversial and would cause a media frenzy. And I would be a freak again like . . ."

"I know, I know, when your father used you to bet football games." Bill's voice was exasperated; he had heard the comment way too many times. "But why is the gift absent?"

"I don't know . . . other than an occasional glimpse. I couldn't tell you why."

"But everything you touch turns to gold, no pun intended."

"None taken. I don't understand it either, Bill. I just make the right decisions. Besides, this equipment will help my people if I'm not here."

"Yeah, as if that would actually happen."

"True, my friend, true."

"Did you hire Mike Quinn?"

"Yep. Thanks for the intro. I'm going to use him to lead a team of analysts to research and investigate potential clients."

"He's a good man, very thorough. He's better than all this technology."

"We'll see."

Ottati Consulting housed two conference rooms, both adjacent to Paolo's office. Over the years, they came to be known as the war room, where all the business deals were consummated, and the spy room.

The war room, or client conference area, had a total of fifty hidden cameras and microphones. It held a twenty-foot, varnished, high-gloss cherry wood table surrounded by eighteen high-tech brown leather chairs. An elaborate medical monitoring system measured the occupant's blood pressure, heart rate, and body temperature; miniature sensors tracked body movement to the minutiae. The technically advanced cameras scrutinized facial reactions and idiosyncrasies. The video and audio equipment recorded every nuance in the state-of-the-art room. The data was sent to a computer software program, analyzed, then spewed out on monitors in the spy room.

The technology provided Paolo a hidden snapshot of his clients' behavior. Paolo and his analysts could determine if someone was hiding, lying, or omitting key information. All meetings were videotaped and filed in a secure fireproof safe. The room was soundproof—nothing in, nothing out—and constantly swept for non-approved electronic devices. Media hookups for video conferencing provided the company a global stage.

* * *

The following year, Paolo acted as the mediator between Point Media—a Fortune 500 corporation that specialized in the acquisition of communication companies—and Grosseto Stilografica—a large Italian pen manufacturer. The CEO of Point Media, Robert Taft, contacted Paolo and asked if he would mediate the sale as well as perform a due diligence investigation of the board of directors and top management personnel.

Paolo expected problems to crop up even though the deal seemed to be straightforward. The only time he used his paranormal gift for business was when a deal went sour or a legal issue was made known. There was one other time: when he invested in gold.

Point Media was paying seventy-five million in cash to Stilografica. Paolo's firm would earn seven million. He dispatched his team of private investigators to Italy.

"Paolo?"

"Mike, how are you progressing in Italy?" Mike Quinn was Paolo's private investigator, who also headed the fifteen-member due diligence team in Italy.

"Fine, but we have a little problem."

"Doesn't surprise me. What did you uncover?"

"Well, Giuseppe and Rocco, the CEO and CFO of Stilografica, were never consulted by the board members on the sale of the company. Apparently, nine board members—all related, by the way—decided over a family dinner to sell the company. When the board convened the following week, the chairman called for a vote to sell the business. Apparently the CEO and CFO nearly shit a brick."

"Why?"

"That's where the story gets interesting. Our accountants found a discrepancy in the balance sheet."

"How much of a difference?"

"Ten freak'n million dollars."

"Damn, that's a lot of change."

"Sure is. So, I approached Giuseppe and Rocco. I said, 'You two, what are you, crazy? Where's the money?' Are you ready for this one?"

"Yep."

Mike repeated himself, "I say to the little shit Rocco, 'what are you, crazy?' He says, "screw you.' Well, I just about leaned over and pulled his esophagus out of his throat."

"You didn't do that, right?"

"No, but he sure pissed me off. Then they both tell me they're not going to return the money. Paolo, those two have a set of balls. What do you want me to do?"

"Do nothing, I'll take care of the problem."

"Okay, you're the boss. Everything else was okay, I'm sure you saw the report. Point Media is getting a bargain even with the ten million missing."

"I agree. Nice job, Mike. When you get back, I'll take the team out for dinner."

"Sounds great. Goodbye, Paolo."

"Bye, Mike."

Paolo informed both chairmen of the discrepancy in the balance sheets of Stilografica and assured the two he would recover the embezzled funds. Giancarlo Venti, Stilografica's chairman, wanted to arrange the disappearance of Rocco and Giuseppe. Paolo assured the Italian that killing the two would not be necessary, justice would be served.

The next day when Rocco and Giuseppe tried to access their hidden bank account, to their surprise, the ten million in embezzled funds were no longer there. At the same time, the polizia arrived and arrested the two.

"Paolo."

"Hello, Mike."

"Paolo, Rocco and Giuseppe have been arrested. The worst part is the money is missing."

"I see," Paolo paused for a moment. "Mike, I transferred the money back to Stilografica."

"How did you do that? I mean I couldn't even find the bank account until the police told me and that was like pulling teeth out from a charging bull."

"Nice analogy."

"How did you do it?"

"Mike, do I ask you how you accomplish certain tasks?"

"No."

"Trust me on this, you don't want to know."

"Okay, you're the boss."

"I'll see you back in New Haven, Mike."

Bewildered, Mike said, “Okay, see ya in a couple of days.”

“Ciao.” Paolo hung up the phone. Rebecca had walked into his office.

“Why are you smiling?” she asked.

“No reason.” *Sometimes I love this gift I have.* “What can I do for you?”

* * *

Two weeks later, at the closing, the chairmen of both companies and their attorneys sat in the opulent conference room. Paolo watched the monitors and body rhythms with three of his analysts. Paolo’s attorney walked in to greet the two men. Paolo had prepped him on what to say.

“Good morning, gentlemen. How are you?” The men stood to greet the attorney. Shaking hands, he said, “I’m sorry for the delay, Mr. DeLaurentis will be with us shortly. Please sit.”

“Will Paolo be long?” Giancarlo said.

“No, I just saw him. He’s on the phone with your prime minister, they’re long-time friends.”

An analyst who sat next to Paolo in the war room said, “did you see the spike in Giancarlo’s heart rate and blood pressure?”

“Sure did, Matt.” Paolo pointed to the monitor, “Look at Taft, he’s starting to sweat. I wonder what these two are up to?” Paolo reached for the phone. “Rebecca, call Sergio back for me. I need to talk to him again right away.”

“Yes, sir.”

“I hate it when she calls me sir,” he said to no one in particular.

The intercom buzzed. “Sergio, line two.”

“Thanks, Rebecca.” Paolo picked up the phone. “Sergio, what did you find out?”

“Paolo, I have the information for you.”

“Excellent.”

“Our government is not investigating Stilografica. We were investigating the chairman and his American partner, Robert Taft.”

"Partner? That's interesting. Anything I need to worry about?"

"No, we've stopped our investigation. Apparently, Venti's brother made a complaint. Our investigation found no illegality."

"Do you have a problem if I tell them the investigation is over?"

"No, not at all. By the way, how did you know about the investigation?"

"I didn't, my attorney mentioned to them I was on the phone with you, and they got very nervous."

"They play with the diavolo, Paolo. Be careful."

"I will. The devil can't touch me."

"That is true, my friend. Say hello to your beautiful daughter for me, I have a ministry meeting I have to attend. Ciao."

"Ciao," Paolo hung up the phone.

Paolo opened the conference room door and walked in. He held two copies of an updated invoice. "Gentlemen, I'm sorry for the delay." The men stood. He approached the two principals and shook their hands. "Why don't we take our places and we'll complete our business," Paolo's voice was stern. He sat at the head of the conference table, the Point Media team to his left and the Stilografica group to his right. Paolo's attorney sat opposite Paolo. Paolo took the two updated invoices and gave them to Taft and Venti. "Gentlemen, you will notice that I've added an additional four million dollars to my seven-million-dollar fee." He paused and looked sternly at the two men. Their attorneys jumped up as if they were objecting in court.

"This was not part of the deal," Point Media's attorney said.

"Sit down and be quiet," Venti said.

Taft watched.

"Mr. DeLaurentis, could you explain the additional cost?"

"To be candid, I recovered your missing ten million dollars, and you haven't been honest with me. You'll be interested to know that the Italian government is no longer investigating your partnership with Mr. Taft."

"My client is not a partner of Mr. Venti," Taft's attorney said.

Taft placed his hand on his arm and said, "Shut up."

There was a long silence in the room. Paolo stood to leave.

"Mr. DeLaurentis, may I borrow your phone? I will make sure your eleven million dollars is funded into your bank account. I believe your fee is fair. Would you not agree, Bob?"

"Absolutely, Giancarlo."

"Well then, with that said, I'll leave you to my attorney, who will guide the closing process. Gentlemen, I'm sure we will no longer be doing business together. My attorney will give you the name of someone who can help you if the need arises." Paolo abruptly walked back to his office.

"Rebecca."

"Yes, Paolo," came the reply over the intercom.

"Check our bank account and let me know when the eleven mil is transferred."

"Will do."

"Oh, Rebecca, donate seven million to the Children's Hospital—anonymously."

"Okay."

* * *

With the money from the Point Media negotiation, Paolo purchased a five-thousand-square-foot English Tudor with an au pair apartment in the most western part of New Haven. The house, built in the late 1920s, had a classic library, with maple bookcases and a bowed multi-pane window that overlooked a fenced-in swimming pool surrounded by large evergreen trees. The library became Paolo's escape in the seventeen-room house. His desk faced forward, with the backyard to his back. Two brown leather couches opposite each other guarded the fireplace to his left; he was surrounded by books to his right. A TV sat in the corner.

The house was within walking distance of the Yale Bowl. He often took his children to the Yale football games. Giacomo especially liked the Yale-Harvard game. The high-spirited child would run ahead and hide in the bushes to ambush his father and sister as they walked past. Saturday afternoons were a reprieve from their dysfunctional home life. Paolo didn't live an extravagant lifestyle that matched his wealth. Giacomo and Rio knew they were well off but never asked for anything other than the love of their father. They grew to be mild-mannered and respectful to both their parents.

A close friend, Jayne, a psychologist, aware of the household turmoil, told Paolo that he needed time for himself. She suggested he write down his thoughts. Paolo took his friend's advice and tried. He remembered what Vittorio told him when he was in Italy. "Love is the key to life."

Paolo wrote: *So absent is love in my life, I have nowhere to turn. My children are my life, are my love, and when they are grown and gone, I will be all alone, love absent from my heart, the key to my life locked in the pain and misery of my existence.*

Paolo closed his journal. He didn't want to relive the present: the pain in his heart, love absent, the love of a woman gone. At thirty-two years old, he engrossed himself in his work and his investments. In the eight years that followed, his paranormal gift was an inherent knowledge of making the right choice. Sometimes he had the ability to remote view. The words *In God's time* continually echoed within him. On occasion, his mind would take him to some future event in his life. He would write what he saw in his journal and sometimes those events were ripped from the book and placed in an envelope to be opened at a later time . . . in God's time.

Chapter 19

PAOLO AWOKE, STARTLED, the dream a reality in his mind. *The gray ashen soot fell from the sky, the black melted steel girders in the distance.* The vision was so clear he awoke in a sweat. He looked at the clock. Six-thirty. He would be late today. Last night's argument with Victoria had wiped him out.

"You're such a moron, Paolo. I can't believe you donated a hundred grand to some stupid halfway house. Those people aren't going to change. They're all drug addicts. You're wasting your time and our money."

"Vic, it was for a good cause."

"Good cause my ass, you're just a stupid fool."

"Thanks for the compliment."

Her face was red with anger. "By the way, when you come in the house, take off your shoes. I'm tired of cleaning up after you."

Paolo, his nerves stretched to the limit, whispered, "Kiss my ass."

"What did you say?"

"Nothing."

"What's the matter, you don't have the balls to say it to my face?"

Paolo ignored her.

"Yo asshole, didn't you hear what I said?"

"Yeah, I heard. I'm going to bed."

"Not with me, you're not."

Paolo slept in the au pair apartment.

* * *

Paolo walked into the large floral-papered bathroom, an old-fashioned bathtub on the far right side, and a separate shower stall with multiple heads in the corner. He tried to shake the cobwebs from the night before and his dream. He turned on the shower and went back to brush his teeth. He leaned on the white porcelain sink and looked into the mirror, his hair disheveled; he rubbed the bristled stubble on his face. In the reflection, Paolo focused his eyes behind him out the window. The pine tree in the back yard with its large green branches waited to become the bed for the first fall of snow. The sun was beginning to rise. He wondered what this day would bring. Would it be a contrast to his dream, to his vision . . . a nightmare for humanity? The water finally warm, he opened the tinted glass door and entered.

"Hey, asshole?"

Ah, the charming voice of my wife. "Yes, dear?"

"Are you driving Rio to school?"

"Sure. What about Giacomo?"

The response was quick and to the point. "He walked. And don't cook in my kitchen anymore; you left a mess around the stove." The bathroom door closed.

Paolo used cooking as an outlet, to show his love for his friends, to unite people through food, drink, and conversation. Paolo loved to hear how tasty his food was. Paolo's friend Alicia, a true connoisseur, often remarked after she tasted his culinary delights, "Oh my God, this is so good." An ego booster for Paolo, cooking made him smile.

* * *

"Good morning, principessa." He walked over to his fifteen-year-old daughter as she ate her breakfast and kissed her on the forehead.

"Morning, Dad."

"And how are we today?"

"We are fine."

"Cocoa Krispies?"

"You want some?" Rio handed her father a spoonful of chocolate morsels.

"No, thank you, they're too soggy."

"Yeah, okay Dad." Rio rolled her eyes. "Dad, you're going to be forty next month, you old man." She laughed.

"Very funny, Rio."

"Do you want anything special?"

"Just you and Giacomo."

"You will always have us, Dad. You taking me to school?"

"Sure am."

"Good, Mom's being really weird today."

"Tell me about it. Are you almost finished?"

"Yep." Rio picked up her dish, rinsed it, and placed the bowl in the dishwasher.

Paolo DeLaurentis sat in his executive suite. It was just after eleven a.m. He sipped black coffee as he prepared for his one o'clock appointment with Sydney Hill. He read the detailed forty-two-page report on his future client, then looked at his Rolex.

Paolo pondered the idea of retirement. He was tired of playing the game. His company was sought out by almost every significant corporation and government body in the free world. Paolo DeLaurentis now picked and chose the clients he wished to work with. He held the cards. It was his game, his rules. If a client didn't like it, tough. *Maybe it's time to retire? Hand over the reins to somebody else. Life has more to offer than money and personal achievement.* His mind faded into recollections of his life.

His corner office was surrounded by windows, a vintage cherry wood desk with matching bookcases filled the room. File cabinets sat in the corner. Pictures of his children were placed on his desk. The suite overlooked picturesque New Haven Green. The hallowed halls of the Yale University campus provided the backdrop.

Ottati Consulting Ltd. encompassed the entire fourteenth floor of the Gold Building. The majority of his employees had worked for Paolo since the company's inception in 1980. Early on in his career, Paolo identified the need for motivated individuals who had a work ethic that exceeded national norms. He provided an inimitable work environment that assured loyalty and hard work. Paolo used his gift to expand his business and invest in gold. In his heart, he knew it was the right thing to do. He also knew there was a time coming when his gift would be used for something else.

Paolo's sense of humor annoyed most of his employees, for the simple reason that he turned it on and off, like a water faucet. Those who knew him or believed they did left him alone until spoken to. Paolo's ability to focus on a problem was so intense, he was often found at his desk staring into space. The uncanny look in his eyes bewildered those who happened to witness it. He played chess in his mind, moving the game pieces quietly. He manipulated business solutions, at times using his gift for his advantage.

Rebecca, his trusted long-time secretary, entered his office and placed a document on his desk.

"Paolo, here is the deed to the Gold Building. Do you want me to put it in the safe or will you take care of it?"

Paolo picked up the document. "I'll take care of it. We've come a long way since we moved in here eight years ago."

"You sure have, Paolo."

Opposite Paolo's desk was a collection of photographs of world leaders and corporate magnates shaking hands with Paolo, each autographed with a thank-you. He disliked them. Paolo never wanted to bring attention to himself. In the center of the 8x10 photos stood a 24x24-inch photo of him and his friends at Warren's pig roast, an annual event he never missed. The image, in contrast to those around it, showed true love and friendship.

As Rebecca exited the office, she straightened the other photo that Paolo held dear to his heart—the picture of him with the Italian prime minister. "Oh, I almost forgot . . . the prime minister left a message on your voicemail. He said he would call you back."

"Did he say what time?"

"Should be within the next fifteen minutes. And don't forget about your meeting with Mrs. Hill."

"Very well, put him through when he calls. Oh, Rebecca?"

"Yes?"

"Have I told you how much I enjoy that you are my assistant?"

"Yes, Mr. DeLaurentis, many times," she chuckled.

"Thank you, Rebecca. Now go back to work."

He looked at the pictures. *How did I ever do this?*

"Excuse me, boss?" Rebecca said through the intercom.

He hated when she called him boss. "Yes?" he said, drawing out the word.

"Your pictures of Amalfi, Messina, and Ottati are here."

He stood up. "They are," he exclaimed. "Well, bring them in, woman." Happiness resonated in his voice. Rebecca carried the three wood-framed pictures into his office and placed them against the wall. Paolo was awestruck at the beauty of the towns and villages of his grandparents' native Italy. He longed to live in the ancient country of his ancestors. He had the resources and enough money to do so, but his wife Victoria hampered him. The only time he got to Italy was for business, rarely for pleasure. Paolo stood admiring the pictures.

"Rebecca, there is my passion—to be back in Italy again."

"When are you returning?"

"Soon, I hope."

She left him as he gazed at the pictures.

Paolo walked back to his desk. He decided to hang the pictures in the client area. They would provide excellent topics of discussion.

* * *

Prior to accepting a new client, Paolo had Mike Quinn do background checks. Akin to an FBI investigation, no stone was left unturned. Paolo wanted to know every facet and fact about any new customer. He refused to waste his time as he had seven years earlier with Point Media. Bill was right—Mike was better than the technology.

Paolo sat in his tall leather ergonomic chair and continued to read the biography of Sydney Hill's husband, Peter. The report listed Peter's exploits in detail. Peter grew up with a silver spoon in his mouth. An only child, he enjoyed the finer things in life. He attended Choate, one of the most elite private high schools in the world, then Cornell, where he majored in Economics. Peter, the definition of a spoiled brat, received anything he asked for, including a new Corvette when he was sixteen. His vacations were spent with his mother, on the Vineyard in the summer and in the Bahamas or Aspen in the winter. Occasionally, his father accompanied them. When the old man was present, it was all business, no time for the family. Peter saw his father on the weekends during the summer. By the time he reached the age of fourteen, he had begun to loathe his parents. His mother, taking out her anger on him, became an alcoholic. She died of liver disease when he was a junior at Cornell.

Peter's life became centered solely on his own selfish needs. This was his way of dealing with the pain that laid waste his heart. The years of rejection, the death of his mother, and the absence of his father unconsciously strengthened his resolve to destroy his life. Peter became a train wreck of pain and misery.

The report continued to describe his various indiscretions, including a one-night stand the night before his wedding to Sydney. After he graduated from Cornell, he cut off all ties with his father. Peter wanted no part of his father's money or his life. In April of the following year, an article about his father's financial and legal problems appeared in the *Wall Street Journal*. It portrayed his father as a dimwit. Peter had no pity for his father and reveled in his misery. Within six months, his father filed bankruptcy and committed suicide.

Paolo's intercom buzzed. "Yes, Rebecca."

"The prime minister is on the line, and your appointment with Sydney Hill is in one hour."

"Thank you, Rebecca." A moment later Paolo's intercom beeped.

"Sergio, my friend. How are you?" Paolo asked with a smile.

The prime minister's voice was somber. "Fine, Paolo, but I have some sad news."

Paolo sat and listened as a wave of sadness crept into his heart.

"My father died, he had a heart attack this morning."

Paolo, his eyes filled with tears, said, "I'm so sorry, Sergio. How is Isabella?"

"My mother is doing okay. She cries a lot. As you know, they have been together for a long time." A crack in his voice, the prime minister paused, "I pray dad is finally at peace."

"I think your father made his peace a long time ago," Paolo said.

"I thought so, as well. My mother told me recently that the last couple of years the recurring nightmares of when he was a child had returned. I don't think he ever got over the death of my grandparents. Then again, would any child?"

"You're probably right, Sergio. I'll never forget that day at your hotel those many years ago when he told me the story and how he forgave Mussolini in the Piazza Loreto. Forgiveness saved his soul and that lesson stays with me always. It's easier to forgive than to hold a grudge." There was a moment of silence. "Sergio, is there anything that I can do? I can get a flight out tonight and be in Rome tomorrow."

"No, no, my friend, we are fine. If you can come to the funeral . . . ?"

Paolo interrupted him. "Sergio, you're a brother to me. My own death couldn't keep me from attending the funeral. When is it?" Paolo's voice cracked.

"A week from today."

"I'll be there; I'll give your mother a call."

"She would love to hear from you."

"I'll call her later. Ciao."

"Ciao, Paolo."

Paolo hung up the phone. He wept at the loss of his old friend of thirty years. He sat back in his chair and gazed out over the New Haven Green. Tears slid down Paolo's cheeks as he reminisced on the first time they met.

Chapter 20

THE PRESIDENT AND founder of Ottati Consultants Ltd. sat in the reception area of Sydney Hill Enterprises. Paolo was not the typical brash, egotistical CEO. This man was gentle and realistic; he pulled no punches. When he walked, heads turned—both men and women alike. He exuded an air of authority yet was unpretentious, kind, and thought-provoking. Wherever he went, he was recognized. It appeared everyone was attracted to him. There was something within him, a distinct quality that set him apart. His charismatic personality allowed him to speak with a genuine frankness. When Paolo communicated the truth and it was contrary to popular opinion, a cold shiver would travel down the recipient's spine. His gift spoke for him.

Paolo heard the elevator doors open on the tenth floor of the high-rise office building. His potential client, Sydney Hill, walked into the plush oriental-carpeted waiting room, its built-in cherry bookcases and Louis XIV furniture giving the impression of a private library. The warm, comfortable environment radiated peace and tranquility.

She was anything but peaceful. Her twelve-year-old daughter, Lisa, walked closely behind her.

"It will be okay, Mom. Don't cry."

"I'm not crying, it's my allergies."

"Oh."

Paolo overheard the conversation. He knew differently. Lisa was the last child to leave Sydney's womb. Her husband had demanded she tie her tubes immediately after the child's birth. For Peter, the children and her business were taking up too much of her time. Torn between motherhood and career, she decided the time was right to sell her company.

The thirty-nine-year-old woman was dressed in a black pantsuit; the V-neck jacket accentuated her curves. Her neck was adorned with a classic pearl necklace. Her striking greenish-blue eyes were so beautiful that even through her tears they captured Paolo's soul.

She stood five feet four inches tall. Public opinion classified her as Hollywood gorgeous. Petite in size, proportioned by Mother Nature, her good looks grabbed the imagination of every man she met. Sydney's beauty was intimidating. Her angelic face was surrounded by shoulder-length natural auburn hair streaked with hints of blonde. Eyeliner stained her face, the telltale sign she'd been crying for some time. Paolo was not at all surprised.

Sydney Hill walked through the lobby. Paolo stared as the beautiful woman walked past him. His mind ran away in a daydream of her. Her attractiveness aside, something inside him spoke to his soul. A warm sensation overcame him. Paolo noticed her backside. He made a mental note to tell his private investigator, Mike, his eyes should be examined. *This woman is gorgeous. Sydney Hill is downright gorgeous.* His breath taken away, he fell instantly in love.

"Good morning, Ellen," she said to the receptionist as she entered the French doors into the office suite.

"Good morning, Sydney." The receptionist looked up and then went back to work.

Sydney had amassed a small fortune with an innovative software concept. Many suitors over the years tried unsuccessfully to buy her business. She decided the time wasn't right and instead invested her time and energy in the growth of her company. Sydney Hill made a name for herself as a tough negotiator and a no-nonsense executive. She spoke at various conventions and conferences; she became a spokesperson for Women in Corporate America. Sydney's life journey would take abrupt curves and winding paths. The journey tested her resolve and awakened a hidden love deep within her.

She juggled her family and work, at first out of necessity, then practicality. Little did she know she would be so successful. She received no help from her husband, Peter. She'd been married for fifteen years to a man who needed her attention every waking minute of the day.

Motherhood is a funny conundrum. The nine-month gestation period forms an intrinsic bond between mother and child, a bond a man cannot have or even understand. This natural bond can sometimes get in the way between husband and wife.

The children are the mother's sole reason for living. The children are first, the husband second. Often the man was last in the mother's world. Not because she didn't love him, it was simply the way it was. When the time finally came for the man to be first, it was often too late.

The hectic years of growing her business and being a mother put a wedge between her and Peter. The communication between husband and wife stopped. Peter buried his life in his work and extracurricular activities. Sydney gave her life to her children and her career. They both did what they had to do, their marriage long over.

Chapter 21

"HELLO, MR. DELAURENTIS, I'm Amanda, Mrs. Hill's assistant. Will you please follow me? Mrs. Hill will meet with you now."

Paolo stood, grabbed his leather briefcase, and placed the *Wall Street Journal* on the coffee table. "Of course. Please call me Paolo." He smiled at Amanda as he gazed intently in her eyes.

"Would you like a cup of coffee, Paolo?"

"Yes, please. Black, no sugar."

They walked past the receptionist. He followed Amanda along the carpeted hallway. A bank of window offices were on his left, the usual corporate gray fabric cubicles were to his right. The atmosphere was pleasant; people seemed to be enjoying the work they were doing. Paolo felt the stares of Sydney Hill's employees, the majority of whom were women.

He was dressed in a blue pinstriped Armani suit, a white shirt, and a power red tie. His cuffs were clasped with black pearl cufflinks and his black Italian leather tasseled shoes were shined to perfection. Paolo DeLaurentis walked the hallway with a confidence recognized by Sydney's people.

As he entered the corridor, he acknowledged those nearby with a "Hello, how are you?" He looked deep in their eyes, identifying personality traits. What others would miss, he observed—their loyalty, concern, and passion. Amanda escorted him to Sydney's office. The door open, she knocked on the molding.

"Syd, Mr. DeLaurentis is here."

"Thank you, Amanda."

She stood up and walked toward Paolo. "Mr. DeLaurentis, please come in." They shook hands—her hand soft, gentle; his hand surrounded hers. It was more than a handshake, it was a connection of two people. Paolo's heart jumped, he felt his face blush. He was speechless for the first time. He tried to speak, awed at the beauty of the woman who stood before him.

"Please, call me Paolo."

"Okay." She paused, "Paolo." He released her hand. "Call me Syd."

There was a momentary silence as the two gazed at each other. Sydney caught herself. "It's a pleasure to meet you, Paolo. Please." She pointed to two dark-blue leather chairs separated by a glass coffee table. She sat opposite Paolo as her secretary walked in and placed his coffee and her green tea before them.

"Thank you, Amanda," he replied.

"Yes, thank you, Amanda," Sydney said.

"Amanda has been with you for a while?"

"A long time, in fact, from the beginning."

Paolo nodded, "Yes, from the beginning."

Her office was modestly decorated—pictures of her children on the wallpapered walls, a blue oriental rug on the hardwood floor. Her desk faced the door, positioned in front of the six-foot-high windows that overlooked the city of Stamford. A Dell laptop was open and the standard black office phone was positioned neatly to the computer's left. A stack of manila folders lay on the black, decorated blotter. Paolo scrutinized the surroundings. He absorbed everything. He tried to find commonality that would ensure a comfortable conversation and working atmosphere.

Paolo learned early in his career that without a mutual synergy of ideas, the business relationship would be doomed to failure. He studied the traits of human nature—how clients treated themselves and others. Paolo couldn't tolerate the egotistical bastard, the arrogant owner or CEO who believed he or she was God's gift to the world. When they called for help, he politely refused their lucrative offers.

In order to be a client of Paolo's, you had to follow his game plan—no agenda but his. If you accepted his terms, then and only then did he agree to the contract. Paolo had a one hundred percent success rate. He methodically removed the cancer from any organization he worked with. Paolo refused to be trapped in the plutocratic bullshit of the so-called who's who in corporate America, even though he was the go-to person, the who of who's. He kept his autonomy.

Sydney Hill, who sat before him—beautiful to his eyes, perplexing to his mind—excited him intellectually and physically. Subconsciously, he realized she was the girl in his dream, the one who took his heart. *Yes, this is the woman I dream about.*

A vase with a dozen long-stemmed yellow roses sat in the middle of a small conference table. He knew the roses were not from her discontented husband, but said, "I love the roses, your husband must be quite the romantic."

"No, they're not from him. I love yellow roses," she said.

"And the passion of red roses?"

"Definitely not, who has time for passion?" She avoided his gaze.

"Yes, passion has gone by the wayside," he said reflectively. "So tell me, Sydney Hill, are you passionate about your business?"

"I love my business. The problem is, my company has grown to the point where I am overwhelmed. Our profits are smaller, and my children are getting older." She paused, "I believe it's time for a change."

"Change?"

"Yes, change. Life is too much of a roller coaster for me right now. I need to stabilize, or as my nephew Blake says, chill. It's time to chill."

"I understand." His penetrating eyes gazed deeply into her green eyes. "What can I do for you?"

"I want to sell my company, and ensure all my employees are protected and no employee terminated due to the buyout. Of course, I want to be able to get the maximum value for my company."

"I understand. So what is it that you want from me?"

Sydney stared at him for a moment.

"Sydney?"

Embarrassed, “Oh, I’m sorry. I was thinking.”

And what were you thinking about, Sydney Hill?

She responded, “What I want is for you to analyze my company. Determine if the company is viable to sell and handle the negotiations between the buyer and myself.”

“I understand. How soon would you like this to happen?”

“As soon as possible, but I don’t want to do a fire sale,” she said with authority.

“Okay.” Paolo continued, “I’m sure you are aware I am not cheap. It will cost you.” Paolo paused. “I can assure you that by the time the contract is fulfilled, the value of your company will rise twenty percent from what your accountant values it today.”

She stared at him as if to say, “Is this guy full of shit?”

“Twenty percent, that’s a steep number,” she said.

“Absolutely.” Paolo replied with an edge of cockiness.

“Well, Mr. DeLaurentis, what will it cost me?”

“Before I make a proposal, will I be working directly with you or with someone else?”

“No one else, you’ll be working directly with me.”

Interesting. He started asking her a litany of questions, even though he already knew the answers. Their meeting seemed to last minutes; in actuality, their conversation lasted two-and-a-half hours. Paolo’s BlackBerry chimed. “Excuse me,” he said as he read the information on the screen. “Sydney, if you don’t mind, I have another appointment. I need to pick up my children in an hour.”

“Not at all, I completely understand. I appreciate the fact you spent this much time with me.”

They both stood and faced each other. “I’ll instruct my attorney to send you a contract. Have your accountant value the company.”

“How long do you think it will take?”

“From what I know about your company and what I think needs to be accomplished, about two to three years,” he said as a matter of fact.

“Two to three years?” A hint of disappointment was in her voice.

“If you don’t want a fire sale or if you don’t want to pay me twenty percent of the sale price, two years. If we work hard," he paused, "maybe two and a half." Paolo recognized the disappointment in her eyes. "Believe me, Sydney, these next years will go by quickly." A look of resignation crossed her face. "The contract will explain all the details involved. Besides, I think you and I are going to enjoy ourselves. I won't let you down. By the way, my name is Paolo, enough with the Mr. DeLaurentis."

"Okay, Paolo." Sydney moved forward as if to give him a hug. She seemed to realize what she was about to do and pulled back instead, and stretched out her hand. Paolo took it in his and laid his other hand on top.

"I believe this will be a fruitful endeavor, Mrs. Hill."

"Sydney." She smiled.

"Yes, Sydney," he smiled as he said her name. "I'll be out of the country for the next ten days."

"A vacation?"

"A little of both. A friend of mine passed away. The funeral is in Rome. I rented a small villa in the Tuscan countryside, so I'll spend some time there as well."

"I'm sorry to hear about your friend. I do love Italy."

"When was the last time you visited?"

"Quite a few years ago, we visited Milan."

"When I get back, we'll talk about Italy." Paolo looked at his Rolex. "Right now I've got to get going. My daughter will have a bird if I'm not there to pick her up on time."

"How old is your daughter?"

"Fifteen going on thirty."

"Good luck with that."

"Tell me about it." They both laughed. "Teenagers," Paolo said as he shook his head.

As Sydney escorted him to the elevators, they talked about his two children. They walked side by side down the corridor as if they were long-time friends. The chime of the elevator and the hiss of the doors opening marked the dawn of their relationship.

"Have a great day, Syd."

“You as well, Paolo. I’m sure we’ll be talking again soon,” she said, smiling.

“I’m sure we will.” He entered the elevator and turned around to face the door. Sydney Hill stood in front of him, her majestic green eyes dazzling, penetrating his soul.

“Have a nice time with your children, Paolo.”

“Thank you, Syd,” he said as the elevator doors closed.

He stood in the emptiness of the elevator, surrounded by mirrors. A euphoric sense overcame him, a broad smile across his face. The elevator doors opened again. Sydney, her back to the elevator, turned. Paolo stood with a puzzled look on his face.

“Paolo, did you forget something?” Her eyes twinkled.

“Yeah, I forgot to push the floor button,” he laughed. “We are going to have an excellent time, Sydney Hill,” Paolo said as he leaned over and pushed the lobby floor button.

She giggled as the doors closed. “I hope so, Mr. DeLaurentis, I hope so.”

Chapter 22

After Paolo had returned from Vittorio's funeral, he arranged for Sydney and their attorneys to meet at a local Italian bistro to sign the contracts. Paolo noticed her gaze as he took his Mont Blanc pen from her hand. Their hands touched ever so slightly, her eyes fixed on his, an unspoken word, a momentary union of souls.

Paolo raised the fluted glass of Chardonnay. "To a happy business relationship." He paused, "May we work together well."

"I'll drink to that, Mr. DeLaurentis."

The attorneys excused themselves and left Sydney and Paolo to talk.

* * *

The agreement lasted just over three years. Within that time, Paolo and Sydney became close friends. Their friendship was one of mutual respect. Paolo was at her place of business a minimum of three days a week. A conference room adjoined her office, where they'd share lunch together. They discussed corporate strategy and other business matters. Most of all they talked about their lives and their children. They both acknowledged their marriages were frail. Each made a silent conscious effort not to cross the boundaries of friendship.

As they talked, Paolo would gaze into her eyes. He read the inner secrets of her being. Sydney, captivated by his intense look, held back her desire, seemingly embarrassed at times by the way he looked at her. Sometimes he'd catch her daydreaming. Paolo couldn't help that he was falling in love with her. He understood—they were both married, and he would not cross the line, though he wanted to. The love he had for Sydney nagged at his heart.

Paolo successfully implemented new product lines as well as negotiated the sale of her business to a close friend of his. Sydney's business tripled in size while her profits quadrupled. Paolo walked away with two million dollars. Sydney, for her part, was now a multimillionaire who could now spend the time she so desperately wanted with her children and possibly reconcile her marriage.

"Hello, Sydney."

"Hello, Paolo

"What's up?"

"I just wanted to say thank you again and I hope we'll stay in touch."

"I most certainly will, Ms. IIill."

"It's Mrs. Hill."

"Oh yes, how stupid of me."

"You're too funny. Thanks again, Paolo. Oh, I almost forgot—have a happy forty-third next month."

"Thanks, Syd. Hopefully I'll speak to you before then. Have a great day."

"You, too. Bye."

"Bye." Paolo ended the call with a smile on his face.

Chapter 23

PAOLO AND VICTORIA'S marriage was ending. Paolo dreaded the idea, but sometimes in life no matter how you try, opposites don't attract. The magnetism of their lives repelled them from each other. They were absorbed in their own personal problems, their own issues of rejection—a self-imposed rejection, controlled by generations of familial genetics passed on to the unsuspecting couple.

The conflict between Victoria and Paolo became obvious to those around him; his friends and family witnessed it firsthand. The public outbursts, the put-downs, the early-morning arguments, the middle-of-the-night diatribes—he had nowhere to run. He told his friends he was always in a catch-22, he could do no right.

One evening at a sit-down dinner with his childhood friends Tony and Steve, they suggested Paolo leave her.

"How can you allow her to treat you the way she does?"

"Be a man, who wears the pants?"

"You can have any woman you want, you don't need her."

Paolo felt as if he were Johnny Fontaine in *The Godfather*, hearing Vito Corleone's raspy voice ordering him to "be a man." His friends finally shook their heads and said, "It's your life, and we'll be here for you if you need us."

Finally, a straw broke the camel's back. After an early-morning argument in which Paolo was so berated he began to tremble and shake involuntarily, he called a marriage counselor.

Once again, Paolo and Victoria attended marriage counseling, this time for two years. The decision to enter therapy was Paolo's, but Victoria soon acquiesced as she knew she was destroying herself mentally. After eighteen months, Victoria stopped attending the sessions, not wanting to explore the pain of her childhood anymore. At forty-two, Paolo still wasn't ready to leave her, but he realized if he was to remain sane he needed to adapt; he continued to see the psychologist. He came to understand how he was impaired. The doctor diagnosed him as a victim of Stockholm syndrome. Paolo was a hostage in his own home and didn't have the balls to call it quits. Paolo began to fight back, to restore himself to the nice-natured man he was, no matter what she said. All he wanted was some peace in his life, a woman to love, and the love of a woman.

* * *

One Saturday afternoon in October, a week after Paolo's forty-third birthday, he sat in his sanctuary, his library, reading a poem he had written. Victoria abruptly opened the door. She stood before him, her eyes seething with anger.

"What the hell is wrong with you, you stupid idiot!" she yelled.

He sat in his high leatherback chair. His hand started to shake. "Victoria, what are you talking about?" He made sure his tone of voice didn't match her anger. Her nostrils flared, a sure sign she had gone over the edge.

"You know what I'm talking about."

"Honestly, Vic, I don't know why you're so angry?"

"I'm not a fool, Paolo, tell me, where'd you put the fucking money?"

"What are you talking about?" At that moment, something snapped, and for the first time in their marriage, Paolo grew a set of balls.

"The money in our checking account?"

Still, he refrained from getting into a head-on collision. He said calmly, with a stern look, "Sit down, Victoria."

Victoria's anger became so intense, a vein in her forehead popped out. Her face turned red. She realized she had crossed the line, a line drawn in the sand for the last ten years, a buffer zone.

Paolo said nothing and listened to the sobs.

"I can't take this anymore, Paolo, I can't go on this way." Paolo handed her a tissue and came around the desk. He sat beside her and held her hand, with his other hand he wiped her tears.

"Victoria, look at me." She lifted her head and her eyes met his. "Both of us are unhappy. We haven't been happy for a long time. Who are we kidding, Vic? The time has come for us to stop playing the game of husband and wife. I moved the money to another joint checking account, I forgot to tell you, and I apologize," he said with deep sincerity. He continued, "Whatever you want, I'll give you. Money is not an issue. The issue is our sanity—your well-being and mine—just like our therapist has being saying for the past two years." Two days later, the divorce papers were filed.

* * *

A week later, Paolo boarded his Gulfstream Five and flew to Salerno, Italy. He rented a car and drove to his grandfather's hometown of Ottati. He arrived just after eleven in the morning. He stood, his hands on the black railing of the Piazza Umberto, and looked out over the rolling green valley and the mountains to the west. The orange-roofed dwellings of Ottati lay below him. He took a deep breath, filling his lungs with the fresh mountain air. He turned and leaned against the fence and gazed across the Piazza . Antonio and Sophia's restaurant was still there. Little had changed in the village in the last twenty-two years.

He walked into the eatery. Inside was a bar to his right and a row of tables to his left. A pretty woman was sweeping the floor toward the back. A collection of photographs was taped to the wall by the bar. To his amazement, there was a picture of him, Antonio, Sabatino, Vincenzo, Luigi and Sophia sitting around one of the outdoor tables. *I wonder if they're still alive.* Paolo smiled as he remembered that day.

"You like the pictures?" the woman with the broom asked.

"Yes." Pointing, he said, "That's me."

"You must be Paolo."

"Yes, I am. Do I know you?" He paused for a moment. "You're Maria. Antonio and Sophia's daughter."

"Yes."

"Are they here?"

Maria hung her head. "No, they passed away a few years ago."

"I'm sorry. I loved your parents."

"They loved you. They talked about you all the time. My father said you were the lost son of Ottati."

"Yeah, he said that to me as well. I wish I'd come back sooner. Sometimes life takes you in a different direction."

Maria was a pretty woman with dark brown hair, a thin face, and beautiful, sparkling light- brown eyes. Though she didn't have her mother's blue eyes, she had Sophia's smile.

"Can I get you an espresso?"

"That would be great. Are the men in the picture still alive?"

"No..."

"Buongiorno, Maria?" the voice came from the doorway. A man in his early thirties with wavy brown hair entered the restaurant.

"Buongiorno, Sabatino. Espresso?"

"Grazie." He stood next to Paolo.

"Sabatino, this is Paolo DeLaurentis." She pointed to the picture.

"You knew my father?"

"Briefly, he was a nice man."

"Grazie, what brings you back to Ottati?"

"I came to buy a house."

Maria looked at him. "So you are coming home?"

"I guess so."

* * *

Paolo stayed in Ottati for three days. Maria provided him with a room above the restaurant. He spent his days walking and contemplating his life. In the evenings, he enjoyed dinner with Maria; being the same age, they had a lot in common. Sabatino showed him several houses. He purchased a three-floor stone building that overlooked the valley and the mountains to the west. Paolo hired Sabatino to manage the remodeling of the centuries-old building.

* * *

The following year Paolo visited his home in Ottati two more times—once in the spring and again in late August. He enjoyed the quietness and the serenity of the village.

"Sabatino, I don't know when I'll be back. Keep an eye on the place."

"Sure will, Paolo."

Chapter 24

PAOLO EXITED THE parking garage of his office building and turned left on Whitney Avenue en route to meet Steve and Tony at the Brewster Estate.

His cell phone rang. He looked at the screen no number was displayed. "Hello, Sydney Hill, how are you today?"

"Good morning, Paolo. How did you know it was me?"

"I just knew. How are the children and Peter?"

"The children are fine. As for Peter . . . well, we were divorced yesterday."

"Divorced? Shit, Syd, why didn't you tell me?"

"I couldn't talk about it; Peter had filed the papers and his lawyer got the court to agree to silence the parties."

"Oh, I'm sorry to hear that. Are you okay?"

"Yeah, I'm fine. It's been pretty bad these last several months. Sorry that I didn't return your phone calls."

"No problem, I understand. The stress can be unbearable. Believe me, I know."

"I'm sure you do. How are you? What have you been up to?"

"Just got back from Italy and still living in the maid's quarters, as my friend Bill would say. I negotiated a piece of property where I plan to build a new house. Just waiting for zoning approval."

"That sounds great! You must be excited."

"I am."

"How was Italy?"

"Nice and relaxing. Went by myself."

"Sad."

"No, it was perfect."

"And the ex, how is she?"

"She's almost my ex."

"You mean the divorce didn't go through yet?"

"Nope, I have too much money, and the lawyers want their share. It's not us, it's the attorneys. We want it over with. Could be another seven months or so, but it's okay."

"You have more patience than I do. How are Giacomo and Rio?"

"Doing great. Giacomo will be graduating soon from West Point and Rio from Yale. It will be a very busy month."

"Wow, you must be very proud."

"Yep."

"Can you believe it's been five years since we met?"

"Time flies. We did have a good time, Sydney."

"Yes, we did. I just wanted to call to apologize for not returning your phone calls. Hope to talk to you again soon."

"Me too, Sydney. I miss our talks."

"Have a good day, Paolo."

"You too, Sydney."

Paolo placed the cell phone in the cup holder between the seats. *"I miss you, Sydney Hill."*

* * *

A local industrialist by the name of James Brewster purchased a twenty-two-acre piece of property in the mid-1800s. The parcel, surrounded by a ten-foot-high, three-foot-wide stone wall, encompassed three city blocks. Within its walls were rolling hills, a man-made lake, and Brewster's thirty-room mansion in the center. The two entrances to the estate were dwarfed by servant quarters.

A philanthropist, Brewster had donated the land to the City of New Haven for a park. The only stipulation was that his house would be demolished within ten years. The destruction of the mansion never occurred, and during that time, the terms of Brewster's will were forgotten. The city, unable to continue to pay for the increasing expense of maintaining the park, approached Paolo for a donation. Paolo was made aware of the city's failure to abide by Brewster's wishes. He offered the city a swap plus an additional cash settlement. The deal was a win win for the city and allowed Paolo the opportunity to isolate and protect himself.

* * *

Paolo walked through the black wrought-iron gates of Brewster Park. Multi-colored autumn leaves dotted the park. The warm October sun enhanced the bright fall day. Paolo saw Tony and Steve. "Gentlemen! And I use the term loosely."

"Paolo," Tony yelled out.

The three childhood friends embraced, patting each other on the back.

"Glad you guys could meet me here."

"Hey, happy birthday," Tony said.

"Yeah, happy birthday, Paolo."

"Thanks, guys. Forty-four and I still look like I'm twenty-five."

"Yeah, okay." Tony laughed.

Steve looked around the property. "It's been a long time since I was here."

"It's been a while. I used to bring Anthony and Dominique here when they were younger," Tony said.

Steve took a final drag on his cigarette, and then threw the butt on the ground. "So what's up?" Steve was always direct, to the point, and in a rush. A restaurateur, he found life extremely busy. Tony, laid back, was a popular author who enjoyed life, food, and airplanes.

"So what's going on? I have a deadline, I have to get back to work."

"Work? You call that work? You should have a restaurant—*that's* work."

"Really funny, Steve. Every time I go there, you're gone."

Paolo looked at his two childhood friends and shook his head. "You two are like husband and wife." The three men laughed.

Tony placed his hands in his denim jeans. "Rumor has it you're buying Brewster Park?"

"Yep, somewhat. Let's take a walk."

Steve tapped on the bottom of the pack of Marlboros, took out a cigarette, and reached inside his pants pocket for his orange Bic lighter. He lit the cancer stick. "What do you mean, 'somewhat'?"

The men walked side by side as they entered the park. The only person missing was Bill. United by the tragic incident of fifth grade, the men enjoyed their companionship. Paolo could be himself. The two friends pulled no punches, especially Steve. They treated Paolo as if he were just a regular guy, not a member of the wealthy elite whose ass should be kissed every time he walked through a door. Paolo trusted the two men; he could be honest and not be concerned with betrayal. Both men were aware that Paolo had an uncanny sense of knowing things before they happened. Rumors had circulated about Paolo since he was a child. Though never able to confirm their suspicions, the two men valued Paolo's insight and advice. He was never wrong.

They walked along the black-tarred pathway toward the mansion. As they sat on a park bench, Tony asked, "Paolo, how are you doing? We've been concerned—you don't seem yourself. We hardly hear from you."

"I'm fine. I've been busy at the office." He paused, "Making some life changes, so a lot of my time is tied up. That is one of the reasons I asked you to meet me today. I need your help."

"You need our help? Yeah, and I need a hole in my head."

"Steve, give the guy a break, he needs us, though I don't know why with all the money he's got."

"Sorry, Paolo." Steve lit another cigarette.

"No offense taken, and when are you going to stop smoking that shit?"

"When I die."

"If you keep on smoking like a chimney, it's going to be very soon."

"Yeah, yeah, yeah, you sound like my wife." Steve stood up. "So, Mr. DeLaurentis-who- can't-do-anything-wrong-except-for-love, what can we do for you?"

"Sounds like a song," Tony said.

"How would you like to own Brewster Park?"

The two men looked at Paolo.

Tony stood. "Paolo, we might have money, but we don't have that kind of change."

Steve threw his cigarette into the fountain. "Why us? You can easily purchase it."

"You're correct. I can."

Tony looked at his longtime friend. "You want to stay under the radar."

Paolo nodded. "Guys, listen, I know you're not stupid. We've been friends for a long time. You've never asked me for anything, and you've accepted me as I am." Paolo paused and stood, the three men in a circle. "The truth is, I need a place to live. If I'm the purchaser, it only brings me into the limelight, and I don't want that type of recognition. I need someplace where I can be a chameleon."

Steve said, "But everyone knows you're buying the property. It was plastered all over the news."

"After today, I'll back out of the deal and you two will, so to speak, fill my shoes. So, are you on board?"

They both nodded. Paolo reached in his pocket and pulled out a bank check for twenty million dollars made out to both men. "Now you can buy Brewster Park."

Paolo outlined the deal. The two friends would purchase Brewster Park for eight million, and use the remaining funds to subdivide the property into twenty-one lots consisting of individual townhouses, with an exclusive condominium complex situated in the northeastern part of the park. The complex would house fifty-two private residences. A contractor under Paolo's supervision would build Paolo's townhouse. Paolo would pay for all security enhancements as well as the personnel necessary to protect the complex.

"Sounds like you've been thinking about this awhile," Tony said.

"Sure have. Now for the best part—for helping me out, each of you will receive ten percent on the sale of the residences, which should net you guys approximately two million each."

Steve lit another cigarette. "Paolo, this is very generous, but what's really going on here? You need us like you need a hole in the head."

"You're right . . . as I said, I don't need you financially. But I do need to stay under the radar." Paolo's gaze caught Steve's. "I need to stay under the radar. I need autonomy and privacy."

"Why? Are you in some type of trouble?"

"No, Tony. For whatever reason, I just know I have to do this. Besides, this place is beautiful."

The two friends looked at each other and kept their thoughts to themselves. "I understand," Steve said.

"No problem on my part, either. Forgive me for being an ass."

"Don't worry about it, I would've asked the same if I were in your shoes. Thanks, guys, I knew I could trust you."

The three men walked back toward the wrought-iron gates. They stood outside the park and shook hands.

Tony said, "Have you heard from Bill?"

"No, not yet. Like you guys, he always calls on my birthday. So I'll probably talk to him tonight."

"Make sure you tell him I said hi."

"Yeah, tell him hi from me, too." Steve lit up another cigarette. "What? It's only my second one."

Tony and Paolo laughed. "The second one, my ass," Tony said.

Tony walked up to Paolo and gave him a hug. "Have a happy birthday, Paolo."

Steve did the same.

Paolo walked back to his car. He looked at his cell phone. *Shit, a missed call from Sydney.* Paolo dialed his voice mail.

"Paolo, I'm sorry I forgot to wish you a happy birthday. I hope you have a great day."

Paolo drove back to his office with a smile on his face.

* * *

For the next twelve months, Paolo lived in a world of contemplation and writing. Inexplicably, he began to witness visions of future events. He detailed them in his journal.

Chapter 25

VICTORIA AGREED THAT Paolo could live in the au pair apartment and use the study until his house was built. Paolo sat and looked at the aerial photos of the Brewster Estate. The doorbell chimed, and a few moments later the study door opened. Paolo smiled. There stood his childhood friend, Bill Conti, in faded blue jeans and a blue blazer. The imposing six-foot-tall man of muscle said, "Pard, how the hell are you?"

Paolo rose from his desk. "Pard, come on in."

The two embraced and patted one another on the back.

"How have you been, Bill? God, when was the last time we saw each other?"

"Rio's birthday, seven years ago."

"Shit, that's too long. At least we talk on the phone."

"Yeah, thank God for cell phones. Happy birthday, by the way. Forty-five. Shit, man, you're getting old. How was the party last week?"

"It was nice, nothing special."

Bill pointed to the photographs. "Is that the property?"

"Sure is. Should be completed in another six to nine months, I'm hoping by the end of June."

"I still can't believe you got the city to sell you the property."

"Money helps, my friend." The two walked over to the two couches and sat across from each other.

"Victoria looks terrific . . . she was pleasant when she answered the door."

"Once we decided to get divorced, the pressure was lifted off her shoulders, and to be honest, off mine as well. We actually get along better now. The divorce will be final next Wednesday."

"That's good. Still living in the maid's quarters?"

"Yep."

"How are Tony and Steve doing with the Brewster project?"

"Great, they'll have all the units sold by next year at this time." Paolo paused, his head bowed. "I know we don't like to revisit the past. Specifically, the sand pits. As I told you a couple of weeks ago, that experience has bound the four of us. I should've been there. At times, I feel guilty that I wasn't."

"Pard, you're talking like an ass. Thank God you weren't, none of us would be here today."

"Yeah, but.."

"Yeah, but nothing. Stop it."

"Alright. Anyway, I know they wouldn't take any money from me, so I thought I'd give them a business opportunity."

"Sounds great. How long before your house is built?"

"It's almost done."

"Wow, that's pretty fast."

"Money can move mountains, my friend."

"I guess so."

"Let me show you what they've done." Paolo reached over and pulled the blueprints from his desk to the coffee table. "My townhouse is here," Paolo pointed to the northwest corner. "For security reasons, I'll have a separate-access driveway by the guard house for my personal use. Anyone who comes to visit me will use the common road."

"Security? Why do you need security?"

"I don't know. I just know."

"Okay, so you'll live here until the house is built?"

"Yeah. I'll be doing some traveling, so it won't be too bad. I'm hoping to be in by May. The security system was put in last week. Pard, I can now monitor all the activity around my house from my computer." Paolo's voice filled with excitement. "All the intruder detection systems and facial recognition software will be up and running by next week. The Brewster Estate will be the best-protected community in the country. I have a three-acre secured perimeter around my house. It's amazing."

"But why?"

"You know why, Bill." Paolo changed the subject, "Well, it looks like retirement is doing you well?" Paolo chuckled.

"Retirement my ass, I'm a liaison to a clandestine unit of the government."

"Really?"

"In fact, I work with an old friend of ours."

"Who?"

"Rami."

"Rami, long time since I spoke with him. How is he?"

"Doing great. He says hi."

"I have to give him a call. It's been a long time, we've lost touch over the years. He's a general now, isn't he?"

"Yeah." Bill paused. "I have a question for you."

"Shoot."

"Do you ever talk with Dr. Payne?"

"That's a strange question to ask."

"Well, do you?"

"No! The last time I spoke with him was when he threatened to disclose my gift." Paolo gazed at his old friend.

"Shit, Paolo, stop looking at me like that. I hate when you do that. Just like when we were kids, trying to do that hocus-pocus shit on me."

"Yeah, I know, that's why I'm doing it. You need my help. What's going on with the Russian?"

"Shit man, you really freak me out when you do that. How do you know?"

"I knew it when I first saw him when I was a kid. Mom slapped me in the back of the head for being rude to him."

"That's pretty funny."

"I didn't think so at the time." Paolo chuckled as he rubbed the back of his head.

"You know that clandestine unit that I just told you about?"

"Yep."

"Well, Rami is the commander of the unit. We worked together when I was with naval intelligence. After I retired, he asked me to sign on with him to head his intelligence group."

"Is that good for you?"

"Yeah, I enjoy it, I'm out of harm's way, and Rami and I get along very well."

"Does the unit have a name?"

"Sure does. BOET. For you laymen, Black Operations Elite Team."

"Ooh, I'm impressed."

"Asshole."

"Thanks. So, what do you need from me?"

"As you already know, Payne is a Russian." Bill reached inside his blazer, pulled out a two-page document, and gave it to Paolo. Paolo unfolded the paper and read the words "Classified Top Secret."

"Can I read this?"

"Yes, Rami cleared you."

Dr. Colin Payne: neurologist, paranormal expert, and now member of the National Security Council, Director of Intelligence. Real name: Anton Polzin. Born 1938, in Philadelphia. Son of Leonid and Alina Polzin.

"I told you he was a Russian."

"Read on."

Father, a professor at the University of Moscow, taught English. He and his wife immigrated to the United States in the late '20s. In 1948, the family moved to New York City. The father, with the help of the Russian government, was hired by the United Nations as a translator.

In 1954, the body of Leonid Polzin was found floating in the East River, his neck sliced to the vertebrae. The FBI believed Polzin was a Russian spy assassinated by his Russian handler, Boris Kavlov. The Bureau interrogated Alina for three days while they kept Anton in a boys home, secluded from the population. Alina died of a heart attack while in FBI custody.

"Wow, this is sad, I feel sorry for Payne now."

"Don't. Finish reading the freaking report. I don't have all day." Bill laughed and stood. "The bathroom in the same place?"

"Yep." Paolo continued to read.

Anton lived in a boys' home for two months. A wealthy family with ties to the government offered to adopt him. His name was legally changed to Colin Payne. The adoptive parents provided his education, and helped him advance to a place of prominence.

The adoptive parents died in a tragic plane accident while Payne was in medical school. During the autopsy, matching dental records revealed that the father was Boris Kavlov.

"Holy shit, the Russian spy?"

Bill walked back into the study. "I see you've finished."

"Damn, Bill, wasn't it Kavlov who killed his father?" He folded the paper and handed it back to Bill.

"That's what the FBI report says. The truth? It was the CIA."

"The tragic plane accident . . . also CIA?"

"No, that was real."

Paolo sat back on the couch and put his hands behind the nape of his neck. "So, you want me to cozy up to Payne?"

"Yeah, sort of. We need you to do that hocus-pocus stuff to see what you can find out. We believe he's an agent for Russia and is passing secrets."

"Does the president know?"

"Not yet. We have to get the proof, and what we have now is circumstantial."

Paolo leaned forward. The men's eyes were locked on one another. "Pard, I have no problem in helping you and Rami. But like I've told you before, sometimes I don't have control of the gift."

"I understand. Whatever you can do, I'm sure it will help us. The best part, we won't ask any questions."

"No questions?"

"No questions. Believe me, Paolo, I don't want to know and neither does Rami."

"Okay. So, tell me about BOET."

"BOET is autonomous, and is under the direction of the president and the president only communicates with Rami. All the names of the members of BOET are classified."

"What is Payne's involvement?"

"None, he is trying to convince the president that the unit should be under his control."

"And the president?"

"The president is against it. Currently we are under the Secret Service budget. The unit's primary focus is to stop any aggressive behavior against the United States by any and all means necessary."

"Whoa, that's a strong statement. How does Congress feel about the group?"

"One senator told it to me this way: The fundamentalists on both sides of the aisle would say the organization was illegal. Those behind closed doors on Capitol Hill and the American people and the millions of lives saved would say otherwise. We operate within the laws of our country for our country."

"Ooh, should I break out the American flag?"

"You are an ass."

"Listen, you sold me. I'll help as long as I can quit anytime I want."

"You've got a deal."

"I'll call Payne on Monday and tell him I've had a change of heart and would like to help our country. I'll put additional security safeguards at Brewster, as well. I've got a feeling things are going to get dicey."

"Aw shit, just what I want to hear."

"I take it I'll communicate with you or Rami?"

"Yes. Only Rami and myself. And since you and I are childhood friends and Rami was your roommate, no alarms should be raised in the Payne camp. I have a secure satellite phone for you in the car. Always use that phone when we talk."

"Excellent, I'd love to help. It will give me something to do."

"What do you mean by that?"

"I haven't told you. I've decided to liquidate the majority of my assets. Right after I finish working with Sergio."

"Wow, liquidating. Should I do the same?"

"No, you're okay, hold on to the gold."

"Do your employees know?"

"Just Rebecca. I'll tell them in two months at the Christmas party. I have to make sure they'll be compensated properly. Believe me, they'll be very happy."

"I'm sure they will. But why? And what do you have to do for the prime minister of Italy?"

"Boy, you're full of questions. It's time, Bill. I'm tired of the business, I don't need the money. Maybe I can use the gift for something good. And to answer your second question, Sergio asked me to track down a money launderer. I leave for Paris next week."

"Paris?"

"That's where the trail is leading."

"Oh, does Sergio know about your gift?"

"Hell no. I'll use the company resources and Mike Quinn."

"So, in other words, you're going to use the gift."

Paolo said nothing.

"Are you still writing down your visions?'

"Yep."

"Do you think they'll come true?"

"Yep."

"In our lifetimes?"

"Maybe one or two."

"Shit, man, you scare me."

"You should be in my shoes."

The two talked for a while, discussing their children and Paolo's divorce. They met Steve and Tony at Sally's Apizza on Wooster Street and enjoyed a pizza.

* * *

That evening Paolo researched BOET. Just as Bill had said, the team operated on its own accord under the direction of the president. The only requirement was that the commander-in-chief was to be briefed daily. Members of the elite squad were fire-tested in a furnace, subjected to scrutiny in every aspect of their lives. A team of dedicated men and woman who understood the core values of the American people handpicked the members. The group came into existence in 1975, its funding part of the Secret Service budget.

The commander was General Tawten Ramirez. His friends called him Rami. Tawten, the president, and Paolo graduated from Yale together. The president and Paolo were acquaintances more than friends. Rami lived with Paolo for a year prior to his induction in the Army. The two roommates kept in touch with one another for the first several years out of Yale. The burdens of their careers and life's circumstances eventually eroded their communication to a Christmas card and an occasional phone call. Paolo had a desire to help the world before its inhabitants destroyed themselves. The more he wrote in his journal, the more he knew that helping Bill and Rami was the right thing to do.

* * *

Paolo arrived at his office late Monday morning. He looked out his window, pondering what he was about to do. *My gift is not just for me, some good must come from it. Please, God, don't let me do wrong.* He reached for his phone and called Colin Payne.

"Dr. Payne's office. How may I help you?"

"I would like to speak with the doctor, please."

"May I ask who is calling?"

"An old patient. Paolo DeLaurentis."

Two minutes passed. "Paolo, It's been a long time."

"Hello, Colin. Yes, it has."

"You've done well for yourself, young man. What can I do for you?"

"I've done okay. No sense in beating around the bush, are you interested in sitting down and discussing what I can do for our country? I'm sure you understand what I'm talking about." There was an unusually long pause. "Colin, are you there?"

"Yes, I am. To be honest with you, you caught me off guard."

"Well, let's just say the years have changed me."

"Yes. I would like to sit down and talk. When can you come to Washington?"

"I'm in the process of closing part of my business. How about the first week in January?"

"That sounds fine; I'll be out of the country in December, so that will work out. Give me a call on January 2 and we'll set up a time. Let me give you my direct number."

Payne gave Paolo his private telephone number and after some idle chat, the phone call ended.

Chapter 26

"HELLO, QUINN HERE."

"Good morning, Mike, sorry to wake you."

"No problem, Paolo. Where are you?"

"The City of Lights, my friend."

"Paris? Nice. What time is it there?"

"Ten in the morning."

"Four o'clock here in the States."

"Quick question, Mike, then you can go back to bed."

"I'm getting up anyway. What do you need?"

"Do you know an Arnaud Chambery?"

"Yes, I do . . . wealthy guy, was into heavy arms trading about five years back . . . made a fortune."

"Is he still in the business?"

"I don't think so, why?"

Paolo ignored the question. "Could you arrange a meeting?"

"Probably, I'll call you back."

"Thanks, Mike."

Two days later, Paolo met with the Frenchman at the Grand Couvert, one of two outdoor cafes in the Tuileries Garden. The November morning was unexpectedly warm. Arnaud was a handsome man with a round face and a bushy mustache that masked his rather large nose. A black beret covered his almost-bald head. He walked with a pearl-handled cane, although he had no noticeable injury. Paolo immediately recognized him from a photo he had. Paolo drank his coffee and tried to read a French newspaper, while Jim, his pilot-bodyguard, sat at a nearby table. The Frenchman walked up to Paolo. "Monsieur DeLaurentis?"

Paolo looked up, "Mr. Chambery, please sit down." Paolo offered him the seat.

"What brings you to the City of Lights?"

"I'm here because of you, Arnaud." Paolo gazed into the Parisian's eyes.

"Because of me?"

"Yes."

* * *

While investigating the corrupt Italian politician, Paolo was able to trace numerous hidden bank accounts to arms dealers in the Middle East. The Italian politician was a broker who laundered money for a small percentage; he used his influence as a member of the finance committee to facilitate his illegal activities. With the help of Rami, Paolo obtained a picture of the Middle Eastern men. The night before his conversation with Mike Quinn, Paolo remote-viewed the arms dealers. Present at the meeting, Arnaud Chambery.

Paolo looked at his surroundings; his mind took snapshots. He was in a large hotel suite. Three men were present—two Middle Eastern men and a third who had a white pearl-handled cane.

The man called Duman said, "Mr. Chambery, we understand that you are able to acquire weapons for a reasonable fee."

"Yes, I can—or I used to. I am out of the business."

Paolo looked about the room. He noticed the bedroom door was closed. He could see shadows under the door moving back and forth. He felt queasy.

"Abir, tell Mr. Arnaud Chambery what we wish to purchase, maybe we can change his mind."

"I am really not interested."

"Listen to my friend Abir. Believe me when I tell you." A noise emitted from the bedroom as if someone fell out of bed.

"What was that?" Arnaud asked. He stood and took his cane.

"Please, Arnaud, it is nothing but my stupid bodyguards. Please sit down." Arnaud sat as he held his cane between his legs.

"Abir, please." Duman pointed at Abir.

"We are in the need of a nuclear weapon? Two, to be exact."

"I'm sorry, I can't help you."

"We know you can. We will pay you very handsomely. Say, five million euros over the price of the product," Abir said.

"I'm sorry, I can't help you." Arnaud stood, his cane in his right hand.

"Sit down, Mr. Chambery," Duman said.

"Up your ass. Good luck on your quest."

Abir jumped up and raised his hand in an attempt to strike Arnaud. The Frenchman blocked the punch with his cane and struck Abir in the head. Abir fell to the ground. The double doors of the bedroom swung open. Two bodyguards walked out with guns drawn on Arnaud.

Duman held up his hand and the bodyguards stopped. "Please, Arnaud, this violence is unnecessary. If you wish to leave, go right ahead. No hard feelings." Abir groggily stood and sat on the couch. He massaged the bump on the side of his head. Arnaud began to walk toward the exit. Duman signaled one of the guards.

"Arnaud, before you leave . . ."

Arnaud turned. There stood Arnaud's sixteen-year-old daughter, Emily. The beautiful blonde-haired girl's mouth was duct-taped and her hands were tied behind her. Her frightened eyes stared at her father, tears ran down her face. A stunned Arnaud stood motionless.

* * *

"You are here because of me?" Arnaud repeated.

Paolo positioned himself and leaned forward. He pointed to the cane. "You're very handy with that cane. You did a great job in dealing with Abir two nights ago." Arnaud's face turned white. Paolo put out his hand and touched his arm. Police sirens echoed through the Rue de Rivoli. Jim stood and walked away from the table. “Do not worry, my friend.” Paolo’s eyes softened.

“How do you know about Abir?”

“I know about your daughter as well.”

Paolo noticed Arnaud as he clutched the cane. “You won’t need that.” Paolo pointed to the walking stick. He held Arnaud’s gaze. “I’m a friend; the men you met with have been arrested and if you turn around, Emily is running toward you.”

Arnaud stood and ran to his daughter, leaving the cane behind. Jim walked with two gendarmes behind Emily. Paolo stood and watched the reunification,

“Sometimes I love this gift, what a great Thanksgiving. Thank you,” he said to no one.

Chapter 27

PAOLO USED HIS annual Christmas Eve luncheon to thank everyone on his staff for their hard work and commitment to Ottati Consulting. This year the party was hosted at the Amalfi Grill, an Italian restaurant in New Haven, and a favorite of his.

After an hour of mingling, the staff moved to a private room. Paolo stood and addressed his twenty-one employees.

"Merry Christmas! And for our Jewish friends, Happy Hanukah! What a great year we've had. You have all performed above and beyond your job description. Thank you." Paolo clapped his hands in appreciation. "Thank you again. If it weren't for you and your efforts, Ottati Consulting would not be here today." Paolo paused. "For me, personally, this has been a difficult year, and I've made some tough decisions, decisions that will affect all of you." Paolo sensed uneasiness among the group. "I've decided to retire from the business world and devote my time to the needs of society. I've discovered over these last several years that we as a people have put too much emphasis on personal wants and greed. We've left the poor and the destitute to die in the streets of the world. As most of you are aware, I like to work behind the scenes, or as Rebecca says, I like to stay under the radar. Well, that's going to change to a certain extent. I realized our problems in society are not being addressed in our colleges and universities. I believe we have entered an era of change and disillusionment.

"As you know, I often lecture at Yale University's School of

Business and other area colleges. I've chosen to use that venue and enter the lecture circuit with the hope of sending a new message to our upcoming graduates.

"Over the years, our company has made numerous contacts in various world governments as well as many corporate connections. By utilizing these, I believe we can make small changes that will help the world. As of January 1, Ottati Consulting's mission statement will change. Instead of helping the wealthy, we will help the needy of the world."

The employees sat there with shock and disbelief on their faces.

"I can tell by the looks on your faces you are concerned. I'm sure you are asking yourselves, what does this mean? Under your placemats are envelopes." With his hands, he gestured to the astonished employees. "Please, open your envelopes."

"Holy shit," "Oh my God," his employees responded. Some stood, not believing what they held in their hands. Others had tears in their eyes. Mouths were open, speechless in disbelief. In each envelope was a tax-free check for five million dollars.

Paolo quieted the room of new millionaires. "I hope this Christmas present will help you. As to your employment, you are all invited to stay on and help or you can retire, the choice is yours. A word of advice and caution—spend and invest this money wisely. In addition, your vested retirement accounts will remain yours. I have placed financial safeguards on all of your accounts. You are protected against any economic disaster that will occur. I can assure you there will be an economic collapse within the next ten years." Paolo said this with absolute resolve, and nobody doubted his words. What they didn't know was that their retirement funds were backed with gold.

* * *

In early 1971, the United States deregulated gold. At the time, gold sold for thirty-eight dollars per troy ounce. Paolo knew that once gold was deregulated, the value could only increase. It was a no-brainer. Investing in gold was better than the stock market. In the years from 1972 to 1985, Paolo amassed over 150,000 troy ounces of gold. In

1980, gold hit a record price of eight hundred dollars per ounce. Without hesitation, he converted his investment into cash. Paolo's thirteen-million-dollar investment was worth one hundred and twenty million dollars. By 2000, Paolo's liquidity had grown to over a billion dollars in cash. He had another half billion tied up in real estate and gold. The employees' gold value exceeded two hundred and fifty million dollars. Paolo knew the value of gold would surpass the record price established in 1980. His employees' financial security was no longer a concern for the ex-billionaire.

* * *

After the Christmas party, Paolo went to his cousin's house for the traditional Christmas Eve dinner. For the first time since he was a teenager, he was at peace. He carried with him thirty-five envelopes. Each contained a five-million-dollar tax-free check. His gift to his family and employees totaled two hundred and eighty million dollars.

Paolo liquidated the majority of his assets into cash, financially securing his children and grandchildren. By year-end, Paolo's portfolio dwindled down from almost two billion dollars to one hundred million. His donations to churches and charities exceeded one billion dollars.

Paolo took his expertise, knowledge, and intuitive sense to another level. Besides the lecture circuit and his new role working with BOET, he donated his time to countries affected by natural disasters. His proficiency to chop through governmental bureaucracies allowed him to conquer those who hampered relief efforts.

Chapter 28

THE FIRST WEEK of January 2001 brought the New Year in with a cold blast. Temperatures hovered around zero with the wind chill factor registering minus ten. Paolo was scheduled to meet Colin Payne in the suburbs of Washington, DC, at a nondescript office building.

Paolo drove to Oxford airport where he would fly to Washington on his Gulfstream Five, the last flight on his own aircraft. He had sold the airplane to Tony at a price well below wholesale. As part of the deal, Tony had to keep Paolo's flight crew, and he would have access to the plane if need be.

"Hello."

"Hello, Sydney. Happy birthday."

"Paolo, thank you so much. You amaze me. You never forget my birthday."

"How is your day today?"

"Not too bad, I'm enjoying the day as a free woman."

"Good for you. You deserve it. You have plans tonight with the kids?"

"Yes, we're going out to celebrate my birthday. If you'd like, you can join us."

Paolo's heart skipped a beat, "Damn, I wish I could, but I'm having dinner with Rio tonight."

"Oh well, maybe next time. What are you up to today?"

"Business trip to Washington, DC."

"Sounds like fun."

"Yeah, a real thrill. Well, I just wanted to wish you a happy birthday."

"Well, thank you very much."

"You're very welcome. I'll call you in a couple of days."

"Okay. Have a safe flight."

"Thanks. Have a great day, Sydney."

"You, too. Goodbye."

"Goodbye."

Paolo's heart sank. Another missed opportunity to see Sydney. He focused his mind on his meeting with Dr. Colin Payne.

* * *

Paolo exited the private aviation terminal. A black Lincoln sedan was parked by the curb. The driver held the back door open.

"Mr. DeLaurentis?"

"Yes."

"I will take you to see Dr. Payne."

Paolo entered the back of the car. "Thank you. How long of a drive?"

"About twenty-five minutes, Mr. DeLaurentis."

"Please call me Paolo. And your name is?"

"Mark."

"Very well, Mark."

The car approached the five-story red brick building. A sign bordered the driveway: Center of Behavioral Studies. "Interesting."

"What was that, sir?"

"Oh, nothing. I was just talking to myself."

Paolo was escorted through three security doors to the reception area of Dr. Payne's office, where he was greeted by a woman who appeared to be in her late fifties. Her hair was pulled back in a bun, and she wore a gray suit with a ruffled shirt and low black heels. She reminded Paolo of the classic old librarian spinster.

"Please, Mr. DeLaurentis, come with me. Dr. Payne is expecting you."

Paolo walked behind the woman into Payne's office. The white walls were interspersed with red brick. Plenty of photographs of Payne and the president hung on the walls—playing golf together, having dinner in the private residence of the White House, shaking hands. When you entered Payne's office, there was no doubt about the power he believed he wielded. He had the president's ear, and through his pictures, he made sure everyone knew it. There was a black couch against one wall and a large-screen television against the other. In front of the windows was his desk, piled with papers and folders, some marked Top Secret. Paolo knew that this was all for him; Payne was saying, without words, *I'm the boss*. The doctor had changed since the last time Paolo had seen him, twenty years ago. His nose appeared bigger, no longer did he sport a full head of hair, and it looked as if he'd gained a good forty pounds around his stomach. He looked up from his desk over half-rimmed glasses.

"Thank you, Esther. Please make sure I'm not disturbed—unless, of course, *he* calls." Payne's voice still sounded nasal.

"Yes, Dr. Payne." Esther walked out of the office and closed the door.

Paolo walked to the desk and held out his hand. Payne stayed seated.

"Paolo, so good to see you. Please sit down." Payne pointed to one of two chairs opposite his desk. He took off his glasses and leaned back in his chair.

"Good to see you as well, Colin. I take it your reference to "he" is the president?"

"Yes. You two went to Yale together?"

"Yep. We traveled in the same circles until he went to Columbia—we lost touch. Make sure you tell him I said hi."

Payne ignored the comment. "You've done quite well for yourself. A self-made billionaire, international contacts, and nobody knows who you are. Until next week, of course, when *Time* magazine publishes your story about how you gave away all your money. Impressive."

"I like to stay under the radar. The *Time* article was a favor to the editor."

"Well, you've certainly stayed under the radar. I recall the last time we talked, you were not interested in helping. You were quite irate."

"So were you, Colin, with your threats of taking me public."

"How foolish we are when we're young and trying to make it in this world. As you can see, I've made my mark." He pointed to the pictures of him and the president.

"Yes, you have."

Colin leaned forward, his forearms on the desk. He twirled a Mont Blanc pen in his hand as he looked Paolo straight in the eyes. The time of truth had come. "How is the gift?"

"It's still there."

"Can you still remote view?"

"Yep."

"I will never forget that day when you and your mother called. It happened on a Sunday, if I remember, at your parents' house. Something with your cousin Carla, wasn't it?"

"Yep."

Payne diverted his eyes from Paolo's. "Have you remote viewed recently?"

"No."

"I see. Do you still have visions?"

"On occasion."

"Care to tell me?"

Payne reached in his drawer and pulled out a manila folder. He laid it on the desk and opened the dossier of Paolo DeLaurentis. He thumbed through a series of handwritten lined paper and withdrew a photograph.

Here we go, no turning back. "The vision that I continue to see is blackened steel girders in a pile of debris. I thought before we continue, we could lay out some ground rules—your expectations, my expectations, what I'll agree to and what I won't."

"Fair enough. Would you like to start?"

"No, you tell me what you want. If I agree, I'll say yes; if not, no."

"Wow, you've got some balls, kid." Payne's face was red. "Do you know who I am, son? I can be your worst nightmare. Why don't we start with what you are going to do?"

Paolo wanted to jump up and punch the bastard in the face. Instead, he remained calm and focused on the goal of putting this traitor in jail. However, he was not going to allow Payne to talk to him in this manner.

"Well, I guess our conversation is over." Paolo stood. "Have a nice day, Doctor."

As he approached the door, Payne spoke up. "Paolo, Paolo. I'm sorry the stress of the day overtook my emotions. Come, sit down. We'll figure this out."

Paolo turned. The red-faced doctor smiled. Paolo wanted to throw up.

"Come on, sit down." Again Payne pointed to the chairs.

Paolo stood behind one of the black leather chairs, his hands firmly planted on the back. "Okay, maybe I was a little jumpy, too. I'm not used to being talked to that way. If I wanted that, I would have stayed married."

"I'm sorry, Paolo." An evil smirk crossed Payne's lips. He stood and offered his hand. *Into the spider's web.* Paolo sat down. "Apology accepted. Don't let it happen again." He chuckled.

Payne stared at him with lifeless eyes.

"Alright, let's put all this shit aside. After all, it's about our country and our people, not about you and me."

"Agreed." Payne paused. "My country."

My country, that's interesting. What does he mean by that? "Agreed. First, I don't work for you. Second, I can quit whenever I want. And third, and most important, this is between you and me. No one else without my approval."

Payne leaned forward. "I see. Well, my friend, if you are to be paid, then you work for me."

Paolo laughed in his face. "What do I need your money for? I have my own. I'm volunteering my time to help our country. If you don't like it, I can always go to the president."

“The president will never believe you, I can make sure of that.”

“Maybe.”

Payne’s face was red, the tips of his ears white. Paolo knew he was pushing his buttons. “Okay, let me put it another way. You helped me when I was a kid, let’s just say I want to help you.” Paolo wanted to throw up, the bile caught in his throat.

The redness in Payne’s face began to diminish. “Okay, I can live with that. Are you willing to come here when needed?”

“Why?

“I want to use your remote-viewing capabilities; it would be easier to debrief you here in our offices.”

Paolo paused for a moment. “Sure, that will be fine. Give me a couple of days’ notice, I’ll make it happen.”

With a smirk on his face, Payne handed Paolo a photograph of a little blonde-haired girl and a man walking with a cane. Paolo recognized Arnaud and Emily immediately. He gave it back to Payne, saying nothing.

“You know what’s interesting about that picture, Paolo?”

“No.”

“You’re nowhere in sight. You’ve been erased from the picture.” His voice sounded like fingernails scratching on a blackboard.

“Interesting word choice—erased.”

Payne grunted. “Watch out who you associate yourself with. It might be construed the wrong way.”

“I have a few international contacts that I do business with, no concern of yours.”

“Let’s just say a picture can be worth a thousand words in the wrong hands—almost treasonous.”

Paolo stood, furious, his buttons pushed. He began to speak but was cut off by Payne’s intercom.

“Dr. Payne, the president is on the line.”

Payne picked up the receiver. Just before he pushed the button that would connect him to the most powerful man in the world, he said, “I have to take this, Paolo. I’ll be in touch. Thanks for stopping by.” He laughed. “Yes, Mr. President?”

Chapter 29

PAOLO WAS BACK in his office that day by four o'clock in the afternoon. He sat at his desk, opened his drawer, and pulled out the secure satellite phone. He pressed speed-dial. The call was answered immediately.

"How did it go?"

"He's an asshole."

"So you're tell'n me something I don't know?"

"Pard, I thought I was going to vomit twice. His face sneered of evil. I don't know, Bill, this guy is trouble. I feel it, I sense it, I know it. Are you sure you want to go after him? I guess that was a dumb question. We don't have a choice, do we?"

"Right now, no."

"During our talk, he gave me a retouched photo."

"Of who?"

"A Frenchman by the name of Arnaud Chambery and his daughter Emily."

"Why? And how do you know it was retouched?"

"Because I wasn't in the picture."

"Oh." Bill paused. "Pard, what were you doing with a known arms dealer?"

"I saved his and his daughter's life."

"What!"

"Remember when we met at the end of October and I told you I was going to Paris?"

"Yeah, you were helping Sergio find a money launderer."

"Exactly. Long story short, the bad guys held Arnaud's daughter hostage until he provided them with some nuclear arms. I happened to remote view the meeting. I anonymously made a phone call to the DGSE and the rest is history."

"Shit, Pard, the French secret police. Did they know it was you?"

"No, of course not. Anyway, back to Payne. He's playing his cards right now, letting me know that he's keeping very close tabs on me. I wouldn't be surprised if he always had. I was in his inner sanctum and can easily remote view him. The problem is, he knows my capabilities, and is very suspicious of my out-of-nowhere appearance. And if he's been keeping such a close eye on me, then our job is going to be very difficult. I hope you have another avenue?"

"We're working on it as we speak. We have an insider within Payne's organization. I'm surprised, Paolo, you're not pissed off. You're sounding rather calm."

"It's the calm before the storm, my friend."

"Shit, I hate it when you talk like that."

"Sorry, Pard. I was pissed and he did push my buttons. I wanted to slap him."

"Slap him?"

"You know what I mean. But as I was driving to the airplane, a sudden peace came over me and then I knew everything would work out."

"You're freak'n weird. If it were me, I would've kicked the crap out of him."

"We must learn tolerance, my friend. Forgiveness, not revenge."

"What are you, the Dalai Lama or something?"

"No, I'm serious. We must learn to forgive."

"Oh boy, you've lost it."

"Thank you. What do you want me to do?"

"Let me know if Payne calls. He will. It's just a matter of time, he's not going to let you pass by. I agree with you, he's just showing you who's boss."

"You're absolutely right, Bill. I'll talk to you next week."

Paolo sat back and closed his eyes.

Payne sat at his desk. He took his glasses off and rubbed his face. He opened the right desk drawer and took out a black-and-white photograph of a couple holding a baby boy. With photo in hand, he swiveled his chair around and grabbed his brown leather briefcase. He entered the combination code and inserted the photo on top of a file labeled "Paolo DeLaurentis."

Paolo opened his eyes. "Bill's right—he'll call. But when?"

Chapter 30

THE MORNING'S CRISP air waited for the warm spring sun to rise. Paolo arrived at his office earlier than usual. He looked at his watch as he set his coffee on his desk. It was five o'clock in the morning. Paolo felt refreshed from a good night's sleep, not haunted by the previous night's apocalyptic vision. He swiveled his chair and looked out the window. The streets were almost empty. A lone garbage truck traveled Church Street under the glow of the orange street lights. The offices of the Knights of Columbus Building twinkled in the early morning.

The conference call was to begin in fifteen minutes. Paolo opened his drawer and reached for his secure satellite phone just as the phone's warbled tone rang. He punched in the five-digit access code and was connected to Bill and Rami.

"Good morning, Bill, good morning, General. Of course, I assume we are all on the eastern seaboard."

"Good morning, Pard, not quite—we're in Europe."

"Good morning, Paolo, how are you?"

"I'm doing fine, Rami, and you?"

"Fine. When are we going to get together?"

"Soon, I hope. It will be great to see you again."

"It most surely will. I look forward to it."

"Okay, you two love birds—it's almost noon here and I'm getting hungry."

"Oh, poor baby."

"Thanks, Pard. What do you have?"

Paolo opened up his journal. "Well, guys, not much. It's been almost three months now and I haven't heard from Payne. I've remote viewed him every day at his office, his home, and even when he was at the White House. Nothing, squat, zero. If he's doing something, he's keeping it very close to his chest. I still believe he's on to us. I don't know how, but he is."

"We think so, too. Bill said you have a well-secured office, better equipped than most intelligence agencies."

"Yep, that's correct. Currently I'm in the process of updating it."

"Well, my friend, that's a good thing. The problem is, we've uncovered a detail of men who've been dispatched to watch you. We believe Payne has been watching you for the last ten years. We know through our inside man that he's tried numerous times to plant someone in your office. Without any success. This in itself is amazing."

As Paolo listened, his blood began to boil. His face turned red as he repressed the hidden anger that was within him. He interrupted Rami, "Shit, I knew it. I knew twenty years ago when I told him to go take a hike, he wouldn't let go. What do I do?"

"Pard, do nothing. We have you protected. It was a good idea to have Tony and Steve take over the Brewster project. We can insure that all your security measures will be in place and not tampered with. There is one issue."

Paolo said nothing. He closed his eyes. A tear trickled down his face.

"Pard, you there?"

His teeth clenched, his reply was curt. "Go ahead."

"Payne tried to approach your son. We're lucky we got hold of Giacomo first."

"What happened?"

"A number of our new captains who show the qualities of potential good agents are hand-picked by their commanders for the intelligence agencies. Giacomo was one of those picked."

The general interrupted, "I happen to be on the committee. After the vetting process, the files come to me at the Pentagon for my review and approval. Since I'm also the commander of BOET, I get first pick. Anyway, I spoke with Giacomo. I told him that it would be in the best interest of the Army that he'd be unavailable to meet with any other intelligence agencies."

"How did he respond?"

"Like a dedicated Army officer, he was conveniently unavailable and asked to be removed from the list."

"I have a smart son."

"Yes, you do, Pard, but that didn't stop Payne from trying to contact him."

"We intercepted a phone call from Payne directly to your son's cell phone. The interesting point here is that Giacomo had already been removed from the list of eligible captains."

"So, in other words, Payne had no idea that my son was selected for the interview process."

"Exactly. We sent Giacomo overseas to prevent any potential contact."

Paolo was enraged. "Okay, guys, let's stop right here for a moment. I'll take care of the asshole Payne. He's not going to bring my son into this . . ."

Bill interrupted him, "Pard, before your Italian anger blasts off into outer space, listen to us."

"No. He will not interfere with my son! And I'll call that son of a bitch and tell him."

"Paolo, calm down and listen."

"Listen my ass, Rami. All Payne wants to do is get to me through my son. I will not allow that to happen!"

"Okay, Paolo, I understand, now calm down. First, your son is a member of the United States Army, we'll protect him as we will protect you, but you have to allow this to play out. Don't say anything to Payne. It is important that he thinks he can use his political power to manipulate you for his own agenda, even if that includes your son." There was a long pause. "Paolo, do you understand?"

"Yep. I just don't like it, Rami."

"I understand. Okay, now that is taken care of. We did uncover some information about Payne's Center of Behavioral Studies. Were you able to find anything out?"

"No, I believe it's a front for something other than NSC. My investigator, Mike Quinn, was able to track down some info but nothing concrete. What did you find?"

"You're semi-correct, it's a front for something. We don't know what yet. But it's also part of the NSC, with government employees."

"What do you mean, semi-correct?"

"Our man inside discovered something out of the ordinary. Payne's budget is non-reportable. In other words, he's operating similar to BOET, with the caveat that the president knows nothing about it. The other interesting point is, we can't establish where he gets his money."

"Interesting, Could that be for the president's own protection and deniability?"

"It could be. We doubt it, though. He's operating a secret agency within the NSC, without the knowledge of Congress. Totally rogue."

"Pard, the people that are following you don't work for the NSC."

"How do you know this?"

"Remember the driver who picked you up at the airport the day you met Payne?"

"Yeah, his name was Mark."

"Very good. After he dropped you off, we had him followed. On the morning of the second day, on his way to pick up Payne, he discovered our people. In an effort to avoid the tail, he made a sharp one-eighty turn to try to lose them. He must've thought he was in a movie. Well, it didn't work. His car was sideswiped by the oncoming traffic. He was killed instantly. Our agents ran to the scene under the guise of medical personnel. Before the police arrived, we were able to get DNA samples as well as fingerprints."

"And what did you find?"

"Go ahead, Rami, tell him."

"Mark's real name was Alexander Trotsky. His father was a Russian diplomat during the Cold War. He was attached to their embassy in

Washington until 1967, when he disappeared. His wife and children stayed in the United States. Alexander, or I should say Mark, grew up in Baltimore and eventually joined the military. Early on in his military career, he was given a dishonorable discharge. Somehow he came to know Payne and became his personal driver and bodyguard."

"Whoa, sounds kind of familiar—like Payne's story."

"Sure does. We tracked down his bank account. All his deposits were from an offshore account in Cancun. The man was well paid—every month a deposit of fifty thousand dollars was made."

"That's some serious money for a driver slash bodyguard."

"Sure is. Just two days ago, our investigators found out he was in Paris in November."

"So he took the pictures of me?"

"More than likely, Pard."

"So what do we do now?"

"I have a close friend within the Soviet government that I can trust, we met with him four days ago. Yesterday he briefed us on his findings."

"With all that's going on, can you trust him?"

"Yes. Paolo, I trust him with my life."

"That sounds kinda strange, Rami. And what about you, Bill, you trust this Russian as well?"

"Sure do, Pard."

"Sorry, guys, for being skeptical, it seems a little strange."

"We understand. Trust us on this one, Paolo."

Silence. Paolo closed his eyes. As he slipped into the darkness of his consciousness, peace fell over him.

"Pard, are you there?

"Yep, just had to think for a minute."

"Shit, you're doing that hocus-pocus crap again."

"Yep."

"And?"

"You and Rami are right. Sergei can be trusted."

"How the hell . . ."

"Rami, don't question him, he knows. He just knows."

"Shit, that's amazing. Anyway, the report was given to us with the direct knowledge of the premier and certain members of the politburo."

"Really? Why?"

"Very simple. In a nutshell, missing nuclear arms and the Russian mob."

"Do they know about Payne?"

"No."

"What did you tell them?"

"Our inside guy found out that Payne has been using his resources to track Russia's lost nuclear weapons, without our president's knowledge. So when Bill and I met with Sergei, we told him that we've found someone in our government who was using an outside network to track their missing bombs. Needless to say, some eyebrows were raised."

"I see, so the Russian government is concerned that Payne, even though they don't know it's him, will try to sell the arsenal to a terrorist group. And no matter how the ideologies of our countries disagree, they don't want a nuclear detonation, especially with one of their weapons."

"Exactly, Pard."

"How many bombs are missing?"

"The Russian government suspects ten. Their concern, of course, is that the Russian mob will get hold of them and sell them to the highest bidder."

"Makes sense. How did our president take it?"

"How do you . . ."

"Rami, how many times do I have to tell you? He just knows."

"Bill and I met with him before we left for Europe. We didn't mention Payne. We told him that since we are tied to the Secret Service, our findings couldn't be discussed with anyone because of a possible threat to his life."

"How did he take that? And will he keep quiet?"

"To answer the first part, he wasn't happy. He wants answers, and he wants them yesterday. Will he keep quiet? Let's hope so."

"Alright, what do you guys want me to do?"

"Keep on doing what you're doing. Continue to remote view him and see what you can find."

"Okay, will do."

The phone conversation lasted forty-five minutes. Paolo placed the secure phone in his drawer. The sun was cresting over Long Island Sound. A commuter aircraft appeared in the sky on its way to Tweed New Haven airport. *What am I doing? The anger I feel isn't right. I'm at peace, though, so I know it's the correct thing to do. But why? My life feels empty, my children are doing their own thing, and I'm alone. Where is the love in my life?* A tear trickled down Paolo's face as he gazed out his window. He wanted to go home and go to bed but even that he couldn't do, for he had no house that he could call his own.

Paolo walked out his office. It was still early. He decided to get some more coffee. As he passed Rebecca's desk, his private fax machine rang. He waited for the transmission to end. The fax, from Sergio, was a request from the Italian government. Paolo shook his head. *When is this guy going to get email?* He read the message.

"Paolo, the government here is asking our help in developing a monetary relief plan. Their concern is a catastrophic volcanic eruption on the island of Sicily. Specifically, how to acquire United States funds for rebuilding in and around Mount Etna. Call me so we can discuss. Ciao, Sergio."

Paolo didn't find it an unusual request. The Italians had employed Paolo on several occasions. The government hedged its bets on a man who disseminated, and cut through the bullshit. Paolo knew better; this wasn't a coincidence, time was running short.

The vision of two nights ago disturbed him. He opened his journal and reread his description of what he had seen. *I am alone, and I see the Earth, its blue waters, the land masses. I see the planet collapse, then expand, sprouting volcanoes across the lands. The volcanoes disappear, and then I see the eyes of hurricanes in the oceans. Land disappears into the depths of the sea. Then the earth shakes violently, and the lands become divided. I awoke in a cold sweat. A feeling of peace settled in my bones and I fell back asleep.*

Paolo had seen a series of unprecedented natural events that could only be described as biblical in nature. In his vision, within ten years, the world would experience seven significant earthquakes. Each quake would exceed 7.5 on the Richter scale. The relentless fury of Mother Nature would also slam the earth with four tsunamis and three Category 5 hurricanes. In total, close to three million people would die and seven million would lose their homes. Relief efforts would be stretched to the maximum and the financial burdens of recovery would be placed on the governments of the world. Earth would experience constant spasms, as if it had irritable bowel syndrome—a planet trying to get rid of the waste that humankind had thrown upon it.

Paolo left work early and had dinner with Rio. That night he slept restlessly. He dreamed once again of the cataclysmic times to come.

Chapter 31

PAOLO ARRIVED AT his office at his usual time—six o'clock the following morning. He tried to forget about the dreams and the conversation with Bill and Rami. He immediately went to work on the Italian request. He made a quick phone call to Sergio to discuss the particulars. He wrote a detailed letter to the State Department. A copy was sent to the Italian prime minister.

He sat back in his chair. The time was nine o'clock. *I need a cappuccino before I speak.*

Paolo walked out of his office and stood by Rebecca's desk. She looked at him with a smile.

"Off to your lecture?"

"Yep, but first I'm going to get a cappuccino and review my notes. It's a beautiful spring day, Rebecca, and I have to take advantage while I can."

"While I can?" she asked quizzically.

"You never know, Rebecca, you never know." As he left the office, he straightened his navy blue blazer and said, "What a beautiful day."

Paolo exited the elevator into the burgundy-and-gray-marbled reception area. The attendant opened the door for him. "Excellent article in *Time* magazine, Mr. DeLaurentis."

"Why, thank you, Matt. Have we had any more visitors?"

"No sir, all quiet here."

"Excellent. It's a beautiful day today, Matt. I hope you get off early."

"Me, too. Have an excellent day, Mr. DeLaurentis."

"You as well, Matt."

Outside in the fresh air, Paolo looked up at the blue sky, took a deep breath, and said, "What a beautiful day."

He walked down Church Street toward the center of New Haven. The downtown district bustled with traffic. He took a right on Elm and a left on Temple. The New Haven Green was to his left and the Yale dormitories were to his right. University students sprawled out on the grass enjoying the fine April day. The bright sky was dotted with geese flying home after the long winter.

Paolo was scheduled to speak to the undergraduates who were majoring in ethics, politics, and economics, a Bachelor of Arts program offered by Yale University... As he walked, he absorbed all the smells of spring. Freshness was in the air. The trees had started to bud. The sun warmed the day after the crisp chill of the morning. In the distance, Paolo heard the faint sound of an ambulance siren as it rushed to the University hospital. The sounds of conversations filled the air. "Yes, a beautiful day," he said to himself.

The Café Espresso was located on the corner of Chapel and York, surrounded by the gothic architecture of Yale University. The coffee shop was a gathering place for students and professors. Paolo held open the door for several Yalies. They walked by, discussing the events of the year and their upcoming graduation. Their ideology and innocence would be rudely shattered in the years to come. Some would lose their lives to terrorists, in a war that would last twenty years, destroy cities, and devastate hundreds of thousands of American lives. Yes, it was a time to live, a time to die, and a time to love.

"Good morning, how can I help you?" the smiling counter girl asked.

"I'll have a large cappuccino with three sugars, please." *How many times have I walked in here and still you don't know how I like my cappuccino?* Paolo paid his $5.00 with tip. He maneuvered between the outdoor tables while patrons read their daily newspapers, choosing a seat close to the street corner underneath a green light post. A loving couple bit by cupid held hands and stared at one another. He overheard someone say, "Hey, isn't that the guy who was on the cover of *Time*?"

"I don't know."

"The man who gave away all his money?"

"Yes, I think it is."

"What a fool," someone at the table retorted.

"The world needs more people like him."

"Yeah, maybe you're right."

The media found out that Paolo had donated his fortune away. In short order, they came knocking on his door. At first Paolo shied away from the publicity, but he had several contacts on the editorial staff at *Time*. Approached by the senior editor, Paolo agreed to the interview. The title of the article was: "Sometimes You Just Have to Do What Is Right."

Paolo sat on a black wrought-iron chair. As he read his notes, his left hand twirled his wavy brown hair above his forehead. He wondered if anything he was about to say would touch the hearts of those students listening. His cell phone rang to the tune of "Für Elise."

"Hello."

"Hi! What are you doing?" It was Sydney's morning call to him.

Paolo's relationship with Sydney Hill had continued to grow. Sydney's life had changed, now she was divorced and her children were older. Andrew was in college and Lisa was a senior in high school. The family had adapted to a new life without their father, who had left the state. Sydney's psyche was damaged, and her belief and trust in men had dwindled to nonexistent. To her, Paolo's friendship was safe, for Paolo wasn't like any other man.

Paolo continued to write about Sydney and held on to the memories of when they worked together. Paolo lived in a life of dreams and words. How he loved it when she called him.

"I'm sitting here drinking my cappuccino. I have to speak at Yale today. What are you doing?"

"I just dropped Lisa off at school. I'm on my way to my office. I was wondering if you could meet me today?"

"Sure, everything okay?"

"Everything is fine, I just need to talk with you."

"Okay, no problem—how about 1:00?"

"That would be good, I appreciate it," she said.

"I will see you then." Yes, what a beautiful day.

* * *

"Good morning," Paolo said as he stood at the lectern before the Yale students. "As I walked here today from my office, I couldn't help but notice the unhurriedness of this spectacular spring day. It brought back many memories of when I was a student at Yale.

"What struck me was that in just six months, the bright autumn colors of fall will begin to fade away. Gray squirrels will scamper among the fallen leaves, hoarding their acorns for the winter cold. My analogy of the seasons represents the seasons of our lives and our world. What season are we in? Have we—the inhabitants of this world—entered into our final season, the season of winter? Will we be able to awaken in the spring, to a new birth? Or will the cold and darkness of our society keep us in the dregs of winter?

"Are we, as one of the leading societies of the world, entering an era of winter cold? Is our society fading away? Are we preparing ourselves for the repeat of history, a prelude to a disintegrating society concerned with self? Are we ready for the trials and tribulations or will we be surprised, as were our ancestors? I propose these questions to you in the hope your minds will be open to the possibilities and the simplicity of life.

"Human mores are crumbling. Our souls are disintegrating into blackness because of our disregard for one another. Does our world's population mimic the ancient Roman and Greek cultures? Have the cities of Sodom and Gomorrah been brought back to life? Have they?" Paolo paused.

"Greed for the almighty dollar is feeding this presumed global economy. Right-wing prognosticators will not be disappointed in the future, as their prediction of an economic collapse will occur.

A cloud of darkness shadows the human race—darkness defined as selfishness and pride.

"America, as well as many European nations, has placed individual selfishness first. I have come to realize that life is not about money, personal possessions, or being number one. No, life is about giving back, it is about family, love, and God. In our society today, family is almost nonexistent, and God . . . well, where is God, many ask. Faith and belief are stretched to the limits of human boundaries. Priorities are skewed, simplicity and innocence gone." Paolo paused, as the students started to move uncomfortably in their seats, the sign that what he said had hit a nerve.

"A world culture has evolved that prides itself on individual accomplishment, success, and choice—a culture that appears to have total disregard for the poor, total disregard for the old, and total disregard for the destitute. A two-class society is emerging.

"The Islamic nations blame the United States for the moral degradation of human society, and truth be told, they are not too far off. Islam fights for God to destroy the infidels of the world, the non-believers. The Koran will fuel sociopaths who use Islamic culture to feed their hate against modernity. We've already experienced Islamic terrorism and soon—frightfully soon—terrorism will take its toll on the nations of the world and our country will not be exempt. The bewitching midnight hour has arrived." Some of the students leaned forward, some began to whisper.

"Should history repeat itself, this is what we can expect: natural disasters, economic collapse, and wars. The Christian right will say the wrath of God has arrived. The truth? It was humanity's decision to leave the simple life. The question of 'Why would God allow natural disasters, illness, and death to take place?' shadows the choice of man. We will come to realize that God allows these things because we as a people chose them.

"Life is becoming a menu of choices, with total disregard for the truth. The truth today is man's rationalization of perceived fact. The world walks in a state of fog on a precipice, humanity's vision obscured. There is no longer right and wrong, our societies continue to walk a path of degradation until the time comes when we get slapped in the face and the truth becomes known.

"The governments of the world have become unglued. World leaders are presenting their own agendas of what is true, what is wrong. The irony is that our titular leaders—the dictators of the world—say the nations are at peace. The reality is that a turbulent time for all humankind lies ahead. The consequence of man's decisions will come to a sad ending, with peace and harmony thrown out the window, cascading to a cataclysmic thud. Time will continue to move forward, and history will continue to be made. What will history say about us as a people?

"Today I have proposed hard questions with extremely difficult answers, and I know they have made some of you uncomfortable, but I am not here to blow smoke up your asses. I am here to make you think, to think about our country, our world, and most of all, our co-inhabitants of this planet. Life will become difficult if we stand still and do nothing. My generation has stood still. We have allowed our greed and selfishness to destroy the basic principles of life. Will you, the next generation, be the ones that will make our world right? Will you choose a world of peace and harmony? Will you put selfishness and greed out to pasture? The point is, you can make a difference in our ever-changing world with a simple decision—to help one another. For I fear the angels in the vestibule of heaven are waiting for God to give the last eulogy for the human race. Thank you."

There was a long silence. Paolo turned away from the podium. A student in the back of the lecture hall stood and began to clap, then another stood, then another, until finally the entire assembly gave a standing ovation. The clapping continued even after Paolo had exited the room.

As Paolo walked back to his office, he basked in the late morning sunlight. The lecture left behind, his thoughts moved to Sydney. He hadn't seen her in almost five months. Paolo loved every minute he spent with her, it didn't matter where or with whom. Paolo loved her company. He loved to look at her, talk with her, see her move, watch her smile, and yes . . . gaze into those beautiful green eyes. When he was with her, an incredible joy overcame him, joy he could never explain other than to say it was a gift from heaven.

The two friends chatted almost daily—to his satisfaction, sometimes more than once a day. Paolo missed her. Sydney had her life with her children, and she wasn't ready for another relationship. Paolo's picture on the cover of *Time* only made matters worse. Sydney shied away from any type of publicity and limelight. She never wanted that type of intrusion in her life. Sydney valued her privacy.

* * *

As he drove the Merritt Parkway toward Stamford, Paolo listened to the '70s station. He took in the beautiful spring afternoon. The four-lane road was lined with trees soon to be fully blossomed. He loved this drive, especially in the fall. The vibrant colors of orange, yellow, and red leaves encased the turnpike. The Merritt was one of the most picturesque thoroughfares in the United States. Paolo daydreamed of being with Sydney Hill.

The Bay

I walk on the moonlit dock
The full moon captures my mind
In my heart you are here
The desire for me to hold you overwhelms me
The light of the moon dances on the water
The erotic sounds of the waves against the dock
Makes me dream of you and me

Then I awake and you are not here
The loneliness creeps in
How I hate the loneliness

Chapter 32

Every time I think of you
My face smiles
Every time I think of you
My heart skips a beat

I count the days when I will see you again
When our hands will touch and our lips will meet
I will hold you in my arms not wanting to let go

Every time I think of you
My eyes light up, my heart skips a beat

AS PART OF the deal when Sydney sold her business, she kept an office where she could spend part of her day doing philanthropic work and assisting women's causes. Paolo arrived there just after noon. He sat in the small reception area and watched her walk down the short corridor to meet him. Mother Nature had been kind to Sydney Hill over the past six years. No one would guess she was forty-five. Her beauty withstood the stress of her divorce, the sale of her business, and teenagers. She still had the fine curves Paolo noticed when he first met her. Except for a few wrinkles around the eyes, Sydney Hill was still a captivating, gorgeous woman.

Sydney wore tight, oak-colored corduroy trousers with a belted graphite sweater over a ruffled print shirt. Her espresso-colored high heels highlighted her perfect curves. She greeted him with a smile and a kiss on the cheek.

"How are you? Looks like you lost a couple of pounds?"

"I did. I think it's stress."

"What stress can you possibly have?" she said sarcastically. "You have no money."

"Aren't you funny." They laughed.

They walked to her office, chatting about their children. Paolo walked in and went to the windows. The sun peeked through the clouds and penetrated the trees, highlighting the colors of spring.

"Beautiful view."

"Not as nice as the view from your office in New Haven."

"True, but still beautiful."

Sydney shut the door behind her and walked toward Paolo.

"So Sydney, my friend, what can I do for you today?"

"Thanks for coming. I thought we could talk."

"No problem. Is everything okay?"

"Everything is fine."

Sydney stood unusually close to Paolo. His heart began to race. He stared intently into her green eyes that remained transfixed on his. Paolo's mind became clouded. *What's happening?* Sydney moved forward, wrapped her arms around his waist, and hugged him. She placed her head on his chest. The hug surprised the hell out of Paolo. Sydney had hugged him before, but this was different. Their bodies touched and he started to become aroused. *What's happening?* Paolo had often dreamed and written about this day. His heart beat in time with Sydney's heart; they synchronized with one another. Sydney stepped back and leaned against the window as she held his hands.

"You are the most compassionate and understanding man I've ever met. I wanted you to know this, because you mean so much to me."

Befuddled, Paolo was at a loss for words. "Thank you. I don't know what to say."

"You don't have to say anything. I've known for a while how you feel about me."

"That obvious?"

Sydney shook her head, "Just a little." She paused, "Many times when we worked together or sat and talked, I wanted to lean over and touch your hand or give you a kiss. I just couldn't cross that line even though my marriage was ending. I couldn't cross the line." With tears in her eyes, she added, "Thank you for being my friend."

Paolo had no words. He was stunned. An awkward silence set in. *What do I do next?* They stared deeply into each other's eyes. Together they leaned forward, their lips about to touch. Sydney's cell phone rang.

"Sorry." She answered her phone. "Hello? . . . Okay. I will . . . Love you, too." She closed the flip-top phone. "Sorry about that. My daughter Lisa needs to be picked up earlier."

Paolo was astonished. The kiss he so longed for was about to happen and the phone had to ring. *Just my luck.* "It's okay," he replied. "Is it my imagination or were we going to kiss?" He stared at her intently. Sydney reached up, grabbed the lapels of his blazer, and pulled him closer. A slight hesitation occurred as their lips touched. The smoothness and softness of her lips and the sweetness of her breath was intoxicating. Paolo held her close. Lost in time, a memory etched in his heart. Slowly she pulled away.

"Wow, you are a wonderful kisser." She patted the blazer's lapels with her hands and made sure nothing was amiss.

"So are you."

"We'll have to continue this at another time. Right now, I have to go and pick up my daughter. Call me later on my cell phone. Oh, by the way, those pants look superb on you, nice butt. Now leave before my 'mother' walks in," as she jokingly referred to Amanda, her secretary.

Paolo looked deeply at her. "You made my day today. I'll call you later."

"Okay. Paolo?"

"Yes."

"You can kiss me again if you'd like."

Without hesitation, Paolo gently kissed her, savoring the moment.

Paolo walked out of her office past Amanda's desk with a bounce in his step. He flashed her a smile and said, "It's a beautiful day, Amanda. Have an excellent afternoon."

She replied, with a smile on her face, "You too, Paolo."

Paolo left Sydney's office in a euphoric state. He drove home with the radio blasting, a happy smile plastered on his face.

* * *

Rebecca had left early by the time he returned to his office, but she had taped a copy of the phone log on his door. Three messages, one from his daughter. Rio explained why she couldn't meet him for dinner this weekend and asked if she could borrow some money. The best part of the message was, "I called to say I love you." Little did Rio and her brother know they were multimillionaires. Only after Paolo died and his will was read would they understand the true extent of their wealth.

Paolo reviewed the last two phone calls on the list. One name caught his eye—Dr. Colin Payne. *Wow, he finally called. I'll call him tomorrow.*

He opened his desk drawer, pulled out the secure satellite phone, and punched the button.

"Hello, Rami."

"Hi, Paolo."

"He called."

"We know."

"Any idea why?"

"No."

"Bill wants to meet you in Venice within the next two days. Can you do it?"

"Sure can."

"Good. Talk to you when you two get back."

"Okay."

Paolo, still excited about Sydney, tried to remote view Payne. For the first time, he was unsuccessful. He sat on his office couch and relived the afternoon's events in his mind. Paolo tried to rationalize his feelings. As if he were a teenager, his hormones raced, kicking off the adrenals winding him up. The serotonin in his brain was in high gear; he felt happy.

After dinner with a couple of his employees, he drove to Victoria's house and entered the au pair apartment through its private entrance. He sat in his recliner and reached for the phone.

"Hi, it's me," he said.

"Hi, me."

"Can you talk?"

"Not right now, I'm helping Lisa with her homework."

"Okay, real quick—I have to go to Venice, Italy. I'll call you when I get back. Thanks again for today."

"No, thank you. Say hi to Sergio for me," Sydney replied, joy in her voice.

"No. I'm meeting Bill."

"Well, tell Bill I said hi."

"Okay. Bye."

"Bye. Be careful."

He sat back in his recliner and fell asleep . . . She floated toward him, her eyes focused on his. Mesmerized, he could not move. She began to speak, but he heard no words. Tranquility engulfed the two. Paolo knew he was dreaming; his heart began to race. She touched his face, her hand smooth; she looked in his eyes, her head tilted. Her hand dropped to his chest. He took her hand and placed it within him. She clutched his heart, withdrew her hand; she placed his heart onto hers. Their two hearts beating as one, she kissed him and disappeared.

Paolo awoke, startled. *The woman in my dream is Sydney! It's Sydney!* He fell asleep, content in his mind and soul.

* * *

"Dr. Payne, please?"

"I'm sorry, he's out of the office for the remainder of the week. May I ask who's calling?"

"Paolo DeLaurentis."

"I'll tell him you called."

"Thank you."

Chapter 33

PAOLO ARRIVED IN Venice on April 10 and awoke the following morning to the sound of sirens warning of the Alto Aqua. The Canale Di San Marco flooded San Marco Square and the high water dispersed throughout the city. Gondolas and motorboats were unable to traverse the tributaries, which forced residents and tourists to travel by foot. Over one hundred and twenty islands made up the city of Venice. Each island had its own set of hidden alleyways, walking bridges, shops, restaurants, and hiding places. Paolo exited the hotel. To his left were red barber poles, which flanked the dock and the flooded sidewalk. A white stone walking bridge lay across the Rio di Fisari. Paolo imagined the thousands of people who over the centuries had crossed the same bridge he was now on. He stopped and looked at the ancient city, empty of cars, its pink concrete apartments lining canals full of green water. Paolo was originally going to meet Bill at San Marco Square, but the morning's floods forced them to change the meeting spot to the Rialto Bridge by the Canal Grande, where it was less flooded.

Paolo weaved his way past the shops and cafes. When he arrived at the Rialto Bridge, the sky was a picturesque blue dotted with white clouds. A cool breeze brushed against his face. He looked at his watch. *Bill should be here any minute now.* Venetians waded through the water in colorful knee-high boots. Two-foot-high platforms surrounded the docks, which allowed the pedestrians to keep their feet dry. Paolo watched the motor taxis and the vaporettos, Venice's version of a bus, maneuver in and out of the docks as they picked up and dropped off their fares.

Paolo's spirit was unsettled. An uncomfortable, uneasy sense overcame him. He looked forward to seeing his longtime friend but secretly he wished Sydney were here.

"Pard!" Paolo heard his name. Bill walked up the bridge with a manila envelope in his hand. The two embraced each other, then turned and looked out over the Canal Grande.

"Beautiful sight, isn't it, Pard?"

"Sure is, Paolo. I love it here."

"I know what you mean. I should retire and move here."

"Here or Ottati?"

"Ottati, of course. I just can't seem to let go of the States."

"You mean let go of your dream—Sydney Hill."

"Ah, my friend, you know me all too well." Paolo often talked to Bill about his friendship with Sydney. It was evident that the relationship was more than what Paolo made it out to be. Paolo changed the subject. "Come on, let's go get some espresso. I'm dragging my ass."

"Sounds good. I've got something to show you." Bill held out the manila envelope with Paolo's name written on it. "I know of a place not too far from here, a courtyard restaurant behind a church. A nice, quiet place where we can talk."

"Great, lead on, my friend." Paolo placed his hand on his friend's shoulder. "I'm glad we can meet, Bill. We don't see each other as often as I'd like."

"I know what you mean, Pard, I know what you mean."

As they walked, Paolo added, "Before I forget . . . I met with Tony and Steve last week. They wanted me to say hello for them."

"Tell them I said hi. How's the Brewster project going?"

"Why are you asking me, you know damn well how it's going. Your men are there."

"True, my friend, true. You're keeping yourself under the radar."

"Yep."

"Looks like you'll be in your new house soon."

"Yep, hopefully by the end of June or early July. The contractors are working around the clock. They get a bonus if they finish by September. I've got to get out of Vic's house. I'm going stir crazy, I need my own place. I thought I'd be in it by now, but we ran into some minor glitches because of my new security system. Before you even say anything, I'm not paranoid."

"Yeah, right."

"I'm not. You heard that Payne called me?"

"Did you call him back?"

"I tried, but he didn't answer. Another one of his control tricks. I have a really bad feeling about good ol' Dr. Payne. He knows every move I make."

"Well then, you'll be very interested in this package I have for you. Turn left over here." Bill pointed to an alleyway between a church and a row of clothing and memorabilia shops.

The two men sat at a table under a green awning. The empty restaurant waited for the afternoon lunch crowd of tourists and Venetians. Bill placed the manila envelope to his left. Pigeons walked quietly on the stone courtyard looking for tiny morsels of food, their coos echoing in the small piazza. A waiter approached and Bill held up two fingers. "Due espresso."

Paolo noticed his friend's eyes showed a greater intensity and sadness from when he last saw him. The ex-Navy Seal was always on the lookout—his eyes darted back and forth, always capturing the scene. Nothing escaped his eyes. He was keenly aware of his surroundings.

"How is my beautiful goddaughter Rio?

"Rio is Rio, enjoying Yale."

"Did Rami tell you they're going to fast-track Giacomo to major?"

"Yep. I was surprised, that doesn't happen too often."

"According to what Rami told me, Giacomo shows great leadership and promise."

"As long as it's not because of me. He leaves for Germany in a couple of weeks. He just completed Ranger school."

"Tough program. Not as tough as the Seal program."

"Naturally, only real men can become Seals." Paolo smiled at his friend.

"You're an ass."

"Thank you very much."

"And your ex-wife?"

"She's fine. I told Steve and Tony that we actually get along better now than when we were married."

"And your friend, Sydney Hill?"

"Didn't you already ask about her?"

Bill said nothing.

"I guess she is okay. I talk to her occasionally."

"Occasionally?"

"Alright, a couple of times a week."

The waiter carried the espresso to the table and placed the tiny white cups in front of them.

"Grazie." Paolo changed the subject again and pointed to the manila envelope, "So, what's in there?"

Bill took a sip of his espresso and sat back. He looked around and slid the envelope to Paolo. "You tell me?"

Paolo opened the envelope and pulled out two photographs. The first showed a man and a woman having dinner in a restaurant. The bearded, bald-headed man held hands with the attractive woman. Paolo recognized the man immediately. "Shit, that's Payne. Where did you get this?"

"I have my ways."

"Oh, so he's having an affair, big deal. We're now stooping to blackmail."

"No, my friend, you have it all wrong."

"I do?"

"You see that woman?" Bill took the picture and pointed. "We believe she's a Chechnyan assassin."

"Assassin? Pard, the guy works for the NSC. He's probably on a mission or something. And he knows we're watching him. He's not that stupid. Is he?"

"I think he feels infallible. And that, my friend, is stupidity. So I guess the answer is yes. Now look at the second picture. Do you recognize that man with Payne?"

"Holy shit, that's Duman. That's the guy who tried to buy the nuclear weapons from Arnaud."

"Are you sure?"

"Absolutely positive, without a doubt. When was this picture taken?"

"Two days ago."

"Two days ago? I thought he was in custody of the DGSE?"

"Apparently not."

"Where is he?"

"In Russia with Payne."

Angered welled up in Paolo. "My face red?"

"Sure is. What's the problem? You knew Payne was no good."

"Yeah, but we can't prove anything, and maybe I didn't want to believe it."

"Pard, I don't understand?"

"Because I just realized what a moron I am." Paolo pointed to the pictures. "To think I actually thought of going to work for him."

"You did?"

Paolo hung his head. "Yeah, he almost had me convinced, all those years ago, that I would be helping the government. He fed me a bunch of crap like an insurance salesman. Bullshit. He wanted me for his own purposes, not to help our government but to help him, to snare me in his web of deceit." Paolo leaned forward. "The baloney of me helping the government and his constant recruitment was a bunch of bullshit."

"But Pard, you knew that."

"I know! I know! Damn it." Paolo's voice rose in anger. "I should've done something about it, I could have used the gift to stop him. Instead, I became a rich man. I'll show you, Payne, I thought. I'm nothing but a freak, like when I was a kid."

"Remember, Pard, that freaky shit saved my life."

"I know! I know! Damn it. That's my point! This guy is trouble. I knew it when I was a kid, and did nothing about it."

"Pard, you're talking like an ass."

"Yeah, yeah." Paolo stopped talking and stood. As the backs of his legs pushed the chair across the ground, an irritating screech echoed through the courtyard. Pigeons briefly flew into the air. He walked away from the table, rubbing his head.

Bill sat silently. With a wave of his hand, he called the waiter over. "Due espresso."

Paolo reached the end of the courtyard near the church. He spoke to himself, "What do you want from me? I gave my money away, I've helped the poor, what, what do you want me to do?" Angry and frustrated, he went back to the table and sat.

"What do you want me to do?"

"See if you can do your hocus-pocus stuff and find out where she is and what Payne is doing?"

"Maybe this is why?" He said it to himself but loud enough for Bill to hear.

"'Maybe this is why?' What do you mean, Pard?"

"You don't know the half of it, Bill."

"You're losing me, Paolo. You're not making any sense."

"The gift has gotten stronger. I'm flooded with visions of catastrophes, I can remote view longer and bi-locate to the point I can make my presence felt."

"What do you mean?"

"I can move objects."

"What you're saying is you could be sitting in your office, bi-locating somewhere in the world, and move a piece of paper there?"

Paolo nodded. "Yeah, how do you like that shit? I'm a real freak of nature now." Paolo sat back, turned sideways, and crossed his legs. He rubbed his right temple, then took a sip of his espresso.

"Paolo, you're not a freak of nature. Remember what you told me when you got back from Ottati? In God's time. I have no idea what that means, you know me, I haven't been inside a church in twenty years, but it means something." He paused, "Maybe it's God's time now."

Paolo was sullen. "Maybe." He lowered his head, then looked Bill in the eyes. "I see things, Bill. I have visions of planes hitting buildings, nuclear explosions, hurricanes, tsunamis, earthquakes—you name it,

I've seen it. And let me tell you, there's nothing I can do to stop any of it. Our world is in turmoil. I know it, you know it, and there is nothing we can do about it."

"That might be true, Paolo, but you're going to help us and with your help, we'll save many lives. You might think you're a freak, but you're not. Remember, you saved my life, and look what you've accomplished and all the people that you've helped. Damn, Paolo, there are not many who would give away their fortune like you have. Don't let this piece of shit Colin Payne bring you down, you have to turn it around."

"Yeah? How?"

"I don't know yet, a door will open and you will walk through it." Bill paused, "Damn, I sound like a preacher."

Paolo chuckled.

Bill reached out, touched Paolo's hand, and looked him in the eyes. "We have to be careful of Payne. He knows about our surveillance in Russia."

"How?"

"He saw me."

"Oh, that's great."

"Not to worry. He immediately called the director of the CIA and gave him a cover story of trying to convert an asset to our side. We think he's full of shit."

Paolo heard a noise coming from behind Bill. He turned. This time he wasn't able to yell at his friend to get out of the way. The bullet entered the top of Bill's head and exploded inside his skull. Blood and gray matter splattered the table and Paolo. The few people in the courtyard ran for their lives.

Paolo stood and yelled, "Come on, you chicken-shit bastards! Shoot me, too!" An aching pain shot through his heart like a freight train running into a brick wall. He clutched his chest. There before him, his friend lay, face down on the table, a hole where part of his brain should have been, his skull obliterated. Pard had entered the realm of eternity.

Chapter 34

THE WAITER RUSHED out of the restaurant and ran to Paolo. "Mr. DeLaurentis, come with me now. I'll get you out of here."

Paolo was stunned. "Who are you?"

"A member of BOET, sir, we have to get you out of here." Another bullet hit the ground by Paolo's feet, ricocheting into the metal table. "Now, Mr. DeLaurentis!" He grabbed Paolo's arm and together they ran back into the restaurant.

* * *

A week later, the sounds of the twenty-one-gun salute broke the eerie silence of the cemetery. The lone bugler off in the distance played "Taps" as Paolo sobbed. His son, Major Giacomo DeLaurentis, stood by his side, a tear running down his face. Paolo wrapped his left arm around his daughter as she cried on his shoulder. Victoria, tissue in hand, wiped away tears as she rubbed her daughter's back. Rio patted her father's chest with her left hand.

"It'll be okay, Dad. Pard is in heaven."

Paolo nodded and said, through his tears, "I know." The four stood next to Bill's wife, Lea, and their two children, Paolo and Bill Junior.

The priest said, "And forever may Bill rest in peace with our Lord and Savior Jesus Christ. In the name of the Father, the Son, and the Holy Spirit, Amen."

The abnormally cold April day came to an end. Daylight diminished into the twilight of the night. Paolo sat in his study and looked out at the stark back yard, where a lone squirrel scampered through the leaves. His mind a flurry of conversation and ideas, he reached into his desk drawer, pulled out his journal, and wrote.

Where was the love, the love for mankind for one another? This gift, these visions, is it God's twisted way of abusing my mind? How am I to use this gift? I can't even save my best friend's life. Paolo threw the pen down as a tear trickled down his cheek. He took his hands and covered his face; he became lost in a moment in time. A picture developed in his mind. *A ruined building, charred steel, gray ash floating from the sky.*

He wiped the wetness from his face and picked up the pen. *What do I do with these visions? I can't control them; I don't know where they are in the world other than knowing that they will happen. I feel cursed, I'm a freak once again. The visions are increasing, I can't seem to get away from them. I take a shower, I take a walk, and out of nowhere they appear. God has opened the floodgates of the future in my mind, and I can't do anything about it! Paolo felt himself getting angry.*

The door to his study opened. Rio stood in the doorway. "Dad, you okay?"

Paolo looked at his daughter and a smile came to his face. "I guess I've had better days." He closed the journal.

Giacomo walked in behind her. The two children sat on the couch. "How are you, Dad?" the army major asked.

"I'm okay, I guess. I'll miss Pard."

"We all will, Dad. General Ramirez asked me if you would call him in a couple of days."

"Thanks. I'll give him a call."

Rio stood, walked behind her father, and started to massage his shoulders. "Any idea who killed Uncle Bill?"

Giacomo looked at his father. Paolo looked at his son. He sat quiet for a moment and finally said, "No, but we have a couple of ideas."

Rio released her father's shoulders. "Who is we?"

Paolo looked at Giacomo, his face hidden from his daughter. "Rami."

"Oh, I hope they find the son of a bitch."

"We will, Rio, we will."

Rio placed her hands on his shoulders. Paolo took his hand and placed it on hers. "I'm a very lucky dad to have you two." He paused, and then added, "I think I need some alone time right now. You don't mind, do you?"

"Not at all, Dad." Giacomo stood.

Rio leaned over and kissed her father on the cheek. "Sleep well tonight, Dad. Love you."

"Love you, too." The brother and sister walked out of the study. Paolo sat behind his desk, his eyes welling with tears. His head ached and he rubbed his forehead. *Justice must be served. Wrongs must be made right. Bill's murderer must be found, Payne has got to pay.*

Chapter 35

I awake in the morning
Will we meet today?
Great friends we are
So much more to me
My days overcome
With thoughts of you
Will our lips ever touch?
Will we ever become one?

I await the day
When I can hold your hand
A date; dinner for two,
Just you and me
Why so much desire in my heart for you?
So far away is our love from one another
So far away
Someday, someday
I will hold you in my arms
Friends we will always be
Lovers yet to be

PAOLO SAT IN his study. Bill had been buried three days ago, Giacomo had left for deployment in Germany, and Rio had gone back to her classes. He wondered when he should go back to work; a deep, unsettling anger brewed within him. He recalled the words of Sergio's father, Vittorio: "You must forgive to achieve true peace." Paolo found it difficult to forgive those who'd killed his best friend—especially Dr. Colin Payne. *I'll catch you, you bastard.*

His cell phone rang and he answered, his tone angry. "Hello."

"Paolo, I'm so sorry to hear about your friend Bill. I just read about it in the newspaper."

A calmness settled over him. "Thank you, Sydney," he said.

"I would've attended the funeral, but I didn't know. Did you get the messages that I called? I haven't heard from you . . . I hope I wasn't annoying."

"No, not at all. I should've called you when I returned from Venice."

"Were you with him when he died? The paper said he died of natural causes, was it a heart attack?"

Paolo, not wanting to lie, said, "Yes, I was with him. His death was very sad. I find it very difficult to talk about."

"Oh, I'm sorry. We don't have to talk about it."

"Thank you, Syd." His voice cracked.

"My heart aches for you. Let's change the subject."

"Sounds good to me."

"I think we have some unfinished business to attend to since our last meeting."

Paolo smiled. Sarcastically he asked, "And what would that be?"

"Oh, you're funny. Maybe I won't kiss you again."

"You can't do that."

"Woman's prerogative."

"Okay. I'm sorry and yes, we have some unfinished business."

"Oh, and what would that be?"

"For me to give you a passionate kiss and hug."

"Ooh, sounds nice."

"How about dinner Saturday night?"

"That would be great. I know of a great French restaurant in Stamford. I'll make reservations."

"Excellent. I'll pick you up at seven."

"Paolo?"

"Yes."

"Again, I'm really sorry to hear about Bill."

"Thank you, Sydney. I'll see you Saturday."

"Call me if you need to talk."

"Okay, bye."

"Bye."

Paolo swiveled his chair, looked outside at the yard where his children used to play, and reminisced about Sydney Hill.

From the very first day Paolo and Sydney met, a magical, surreal sense enveloped the two. For Paolo, time didn't exist. He would become so engrossed in conversation with her that he would often forget they were friends. His eyes betrayed the love he had for her. They talked about everything; they had no secrets—except for how they truly cared for each other, and Paolo's paranormal ability. He understood the relationship—they were friends. He accepted the situation. He adapted. Paolo's life was all about adapting. It never stopped him from thinking *what if*. . .

Paolo's heart would race with excitement every time he was with her. Filled with a love that was divine by nature, the feeling reached beyond the depths of his earthly existence, beyond all reality. He'd recall the times when they worked together—the slight touch of her hand on his back, the laughter they shared, the scent of her perfume, the look of affection and kindness she showed him. Paolo understood the love between them conquered and transcended all evil—it was eternal. For Paolo, the friendship was so strong that his heart ached.

Paolo DeLaurentis had fallen madly in love with Sydney from the moment he gazed into her beautiful green eyes. His only outlet became the pen and paper. As in the story of Dr. Zhivago, Sydney became his Lara, a source of immense joy and sorrow. He was a man who had everything, except for the one thing he longed for.

Your love awakens my heart
So ever in love with you
Be my friend
Be my lover
Together let us walk along the path of our love
The desire of my heart is you
No other shall enter

Grab my hand and let us walk, as if we were on a beach
The sun setting over the horizon
Our feet burrowing in the cool twilight sand
Embraced by the love for one another

Your love awakens my heart
So ever in love with you
Be my friend
Be my lover

Chapter 36

PAOLO'S LIFE NOW traveled an endless pursuit of love and happiness. He longed for true love—love that could make him laugh, cry, and jump for joy.

Paolo arrived at Sydney's house. He rang the doorbell and wondered if the video cameras still worked. Careful not to do anything stupid, he stood with his hands crossed in front of him. The door opened and Sydney's daughter, Lisa, stood in the doorway.

"Hello, Lisa."

Lisa was a little smitten with her mother's new boyfriend, the only one since the divorce.

"Hi, Paolo! Come on in."

"And how are you tonight, Lisa?"

"Great, thanks."

"What are your plans for the evening?"

"Oh, a couple of my girlfriends are coming over."

"Sounds like fun."

"Should be. I'll get mom."

"Okay, thanks.

Lisa walked to the bottom of the staircase and yelled for her mother. "Mom, Paolo's here!"

"Thank you, Lisa." Sydney shook her head as she walked down the semicircular staircase, her hands by her side. She wore a black sweater-dress that hung just above her knees. Her glistening green eyes made Paolo's heart skip a beat. Paolo wore an Yves St. Laurent white shirt with blue pinstripes, a blue jacket, and khaki pants.

"What a couple. No PDA," Lisa said as Sydney entered the two-story foyer.

"Shouldn't you be doing something?" Sydney said.

"Whatever, Mom, whatever." She giggled out of the room.

Sydney said, "You look so handsome."

"And you, totally captivating."

"Why, thank you. Shall we go?" she said as she kissed his cheek.

"Ugh, no PDA." Lisa stood in the archway between the foyer and living room.

"Goodbye, Lisa."

"Goodbye, Mom. Be home early," Lisa chuckled as she walked into the living room.

"Teenagers."

They walked to Paolo's car. He opened the door for Sydney. "What the hell is PDA?"

"When you get in the car, I'll tell you."

"Oh, okay."

As he was about to put the car in gear, Sydney said, "Look at me." She leaned toward him and kissed him passionately and deeply.

"Okay, now I need a cold shower."

Sydney replied, "That is a PDA—a public display of affection."

They ate at a local French restaurant in Stamford. The owners, friends of Sydney's, gave them a quiet table in the corner. They enjoyed a sumptuous dinner—veal for Paolo and duck breast with foie gras for Sydney.

The waiter cleared the table and asked, "Would you like some dessert, coffee, or tea?"

"What would you like, Syd?"

"No dessert for me, I'm so full." Sydney touched her stomach. "Dinner was excellent. I will have some decaf tea."

"And you, sir?"

"Decaf tea as well, please."

"Very well. Two decaf teas. I'll be right back."

"I can't believe that at forty-five, my emotions are running away. I keep reminding myself, I'm not a teenager." Sydney's eyes twinkled.

"I know what you mean. Every time I hear your voice or see you, my heart skips a beat."

Sydney placed her hand on Paolo's. "That's so sweet."

Paolo picked up Sydney's hand and kissed it.

"Just my hand?"

"Well, I don't want to..." Paolo paused. "You know, PDA," he said with a chuckle.

"Ah, yes, PDA. My daughter is something else. Please don't stop."

"I won't," he said, leaning forward and giving her an open-mouthed kiss.

Sydney sat back as she held his hand and stared into his eyes. "You realize I'm falling in love with you, Paolo."

"You realize I'm already in love with you."

"Yes," she said as a smile spread across her face.

Paolo gazed at her, immersed in the beauty of her eyes. His mind filled with the secrets he held close—secrets he now finally wanted to share.

"Paolo, what is it? What's on your mind?"

"I want to tell you something that I've never told you before." Paolo began to fumble with his hands.

"Yes?"

"I'm a little hesitant."

"You, hesitant? God, Paolo, we've known each other too long for you not to speak your mind."

Paolo stammered, "True."

"What are you going to tell me, you killed someone?"

Paolo paused.

"You killed someone?" Sydney repeated, a stunned excitement in her voice.

"No, I didn't kill anyone."

"Why did you pause?"

"Thought I'd be funny." He chuckled.

"You ass . . . not funny. So tell me, Paolo DeLaurentis, what's this big secret?"

"It's nothing bad," Paolo stammered. Sydney reached out and held his hand.

"It's okay, you can tell me. I won't run away."

"Someday you will." Paolo knew he could only discuss certain aspects of his gift. Because of Bill's assassination, he decided to omit many truths, because of his fear that his family and now Sydney would be harmed. His involvement with Rami and BOET—well, Sydney didn't have to know.

"Stop talking like an ass. I'm here to stay."

"Okay," Paolo inhaled deeply and began to tell the story. "When I was ten years old, I had an uncanny sense of knowing events before they occurred. I was clairvoyant."

The waiter approached the table with two cups of tea and the leather check holder. "Whenever you are ready, sir." Paolo pulled out his Platinum American Express card and gave it to the waiter. With a strange look on her face, Sydney removed her hand from his. She picked up her spoon and squeezed her tea bag.

He stared at her and said, "Maybe I should stop—you seem concerned."

"No, please don't. I want to hear. Don't be like Peter and keep secrets from me. I want to know."

"So, where was I?"

"Clairvoyant."

"As a child, I can remember the phone ringing. I'd tell my mother who was calling before she answered the phone."

"Can you tell me what the lotto numbers are?" she said with a smile on her face.

"Now you sound like my father. He wanted me to tell him who was going to win the football games."

Sydney moved closer and said to him in a whisper, "You were able to do that?"

Paolo came back with a curt reply. "Yes. I'm sorry, it's just . . ."

"What, Paolo?" With passionate sincerity, she said, "I believe you."

"I felt like I was in a freak show. My dad loved to bet football, so every weekend he'd ask me to pick the winning football teams. At first, it was fun. All I had to do was think about the two teams playing against each other. Out of nowhere I'd see the winning team and the final score."

"Holy shit, are you serious?"

"Oh, I'm serious. My father won seven consecutive weeks in a row. This went on for three years. He later told me the money he won paid for my college education and a family vacation to Hawaii. Dad won so much money, the bookies cut him off."

"Wow. What about you and me . . ." She stopped in midsentence, her head down as she spoke. "When I said I won't run away, and you said someday I will."

"I couldn't tell you. The thought popped into my head."

"Popped into your head?"

"Yep. Those thoughts that pop into my head helped me in my business. I can't explain it, I wish I could. I just know the outcomes of events and things that are going to happen. Sydney, I think a lot about you and me. Where will our future bring us? I have no idea. I have no precognition about us other than one recurring dream."

"A dream?"

"Yes." Paolo's face flushed in embarrassment. "Ever since I was a child, I'd dream about this woman who touched my heart, and we became one. A real dream—the type of dream you believe actually happened. I didn't realize it was about you until recently."

"How often have you had the dream?" Sydney asked, puzzled.

"A lot. I can't remember a month when I didn't dream of this woman."

"How do you know it's me?"

"I just do. Would you like me to describe the dream to you?" *I hope she says no.*

"Yes, please."

An awkward silence fell as Paolo recalled the dream before he spoke.

Paolo described the dream. *She floated toward him, her eyes focused on his. Mesmerized, he could not move. She began to speak, but he heard no words. Tranquility engulfed the two. Paolo knew he was dreaming; his heart began to race. She touched his face, her hand smooth; she looked in his eyes, her head tilted. Her hand dropped to his chest. He took her hand and placed it within him. She clutched his heart, withdrew her hand; she placed his heart onto hers. Their two hearts beating as one, she kissed him and disappeared.*

Sydney stared at Paolo in disbelief. "Wow, that's a hell of a dream."

"Sure is."

"So, tell me more about your clairvoyance?"

"Over the years, the gift came and went but I always knew the right choice—except for my marriage." He chuckled. "No, I'm very blessed. I have two wonderful children. And Victoria, she's a nice person—we were just wrong for each other."

"Gift?"

"That's what I call it." Paolo struggled to get the words out. "This is hard for me. Like I said, I used the gift to grow my business, specifically my investment in gold. And now the gift has led me in a different direction."

"A different direction?"

"Yes, I see . . ." Paolo was about to tell her about the vision he had and his involvement with BOET. Instead, he stopped and decided not to.

"You see what?"

"Never mind, I'll tell you another time."

"Okay, but you know I don't like secrets?"

"Yes, I know." Paolo laughed and rolled his eyes, trying to make light of it.

Sydney said nothing. She sat back in her chair and crossed her arms across her chest. An uncomfortable silence followed as each reflected on the other's words. Sydney leaned over and gave Paolo a kiss. She smiled, and changed the subject.

"Can you tell me when we're going to make love?"

Paolo smiled, "Soon, I hope, soon." Paolo was relieved when the conversation ended. He pulled the sleeve of his shirt back and looked at his watch. “It’s eleven-thirty. What do you say I take you home?”

“Yeah, good idea. Lisa and I have a busy day tomorrow. Mother-daughter bonding.”

“Nice. I’m supposed to spend the day with Rio, but I think she made plans.”

They left the restaurant hand in hand. When they reached Sydney’s driveway, she said, “I had a wonderful time, Mr. DeLaurentis.”

“So did I, Mrs. Hill, so did I.”

They kissed passionately for several minutes. Paolo walked her to the door and said goodnight.

He climbed the stairs to his au pair apartment at one in the morning and fell asleep, exhausted. Unexpectedly, he woke at sunrise, a vision in his mind. *A set of steel girders in a pile of rubble.* “This is the second time I’ve seen this vision, what do I do?” he asked aloud, to no one, as a ray of sunlight crept into his room.

The parts of the story Paolo didn’t tell Sydney were the tragic world events and incidents he witnessed in his mind. He had no control over his visions. In addition, he knew the gift was for the benefit of humanity and this secret would cause their relationship to take a roller coaster ride. Secrets bothered Sydney, but Paolo had no choice.

Chapter 37

I sit here with thoughts of you.
Your green eyes enrapture my soul.
I am lost in my heart, not knowing what to do
My mind preoccupied with when we will be together again

At times a few minutes seems like a lifetime
a lifetime with you seems too short
My dreams are filled with you and me

When you speak the words "I love you,"
My heart trembles with an unspeakable joy
How can it be I feel this way?

To love you is like a Hershey kiss
The excitement of a child anticipating the taste
The memory never leaves

The memory of you and me etched in our souls
Never to be forgotten
The love of you and me

LIFE MOVED FAST, too fast. Sydney's maternal devotion to her seventeen-year-old daughter's social schedule limited their evening dates. Sydney, like many mothers with teenagers, was the taxi driver. She was in the car so often it became her second home.

Paolo and Sydney changed their daytime schedules so they could be together. They would meet at nearby parks and stroll the grounds, holding hands in the spring afternoons. Paolo and Sydney talked, hugged, and kissed, their passions stopped by time. Their love blossomed. Paolo's dream was coming to fruition. Talk of the future always crept into their conversations—how they would grow old together, sitting on the porch in their rocking chairs, holding hands. Like a movie, everyone lived happily ever after. But in reality, life is not a movie, and sometimes the endings are not happy.

Nights were lonely for Paolo. He tried to occupy his time with dinners with his daughter, an occasional dinner with his mother, and once in a while, a men's night out with Steve, Tony, and Warren. Overall, he was lonely as hell. Paolo's release came from the words he wrote on paper, the thoughts from his heart and soul, and the love he had for Sydney. Deep in his heart, he understood their relationship would end. He didn't know how or why, he just knew. The idea of not having her in his life someday only increased the love he felt for her.

Paolo reminisced about their first passionate kiss. "A kiss to end all kisses," he would say. Sydney told him when their lips touched, a tingling sensation overcame her. She was unable to explain the sensation except that it was overwhelming. For Paolo, to be kissed by someone he truly loved and who loved him was a miracle.

Five weeks later, their passions ignited, the time for consummation finally came. Sydney and Paolo were to attend a meeting together at the Yale School of Business. Paolo was late due to an international phone call. He telephoned Sydney to let her know.

"Hello?"

"Hi. I'm running late."

"Okay."

"Would you like to make love with me after the meeting?"

He could visualize Sydney's face, red with embarrassment. "Sure."

The meeting couldn't end fast enough. Hearts raced and hormones raged as they ventured to the Brewster Estate. On the way, they laughed about their earlier conversation.

"I can't believe you asked me that question."

"I hoped you were surrounded by people," Paolo laughed.

She gave him one of those love punches to the shoulder, saying, "I thought you would never ask."

"I had to, I'm writing way too much about you," he chuckled.

"Writing about me? About what?"

"You. I told my therapist you are my Lara. Did you ever see *Dr. Zhivago*?"

"No."

"Someday we should watch the movie. To make a long story short, the doctor falls madly in love with a woman named Lara. He writes poetry about her to ease the pain of her absence in his life."

"You write poems about me?"

"Yep."

"When can I read them?" Sydney gave him another punch in the arm.

"In time."

"Where are we going?"

"To my new house."

"It's finished?"

"Almost, but don't worry—my bedroom is."

"Interesting."

* * *

Paolo drove the car through the open gate. He pressed a button on his visor and a gate to the left of the guardhouse swung open.

"Oh my god, Paolo, I can't believe all the work that's been accomplished in such a short time."

"Yeah, it's amazing." He drove around a bend, the stone wall to his left, and pressed a second button on his visor. A rear garage door opened.

"A garage with a back and front door. I'm impressed."

"Thank you."

Paolo opened the door. The alarm system buzzed. He entered his security code into the control pad. Together they walked into the twenty-five-foot-high foyer. Their footsteps echoed through the unfurnished house.

Paolo said, "Would you like the ninety-nine-cent tour?"

Instead, she wrapped her arms around his neck and kissed him. Paolo placed his hands on her face. They kissed deeply, their hands traveling down each other's bodies. Paolo whispered in her ear, "Let's go to the bedroom, or else this is going to end right here."

"Oh, we don't want that to happen, now do we?"

Paolo took her hand and climbed the unfinished hardwood stairs. At the top of the staircase to the right was the master bedroom suite. Paolo opened the doors. As if they were going through a time portal, everything changed. The room was fully furnished, like something out of *Architectural Digest.*

They shared the same worries as other first-time lovers—will it work? Not work? Is my breath okay? Will it be too fast? Clothes came off at a rapid pace and they fell onto the bed, intertwined. The room was dark, their bodies silhouetted by the hint of sunlight through the drapes. Her kisses, the smoothness of her body, her touch—Paolo was overcome. The memory of this moment would always bring him to her. Paolo had never experienced a love as intimate as when he was with Sydney. To his embarrassment, he wasn't able to make love with her. He made sure he satisfied her in every way possible.

They lay in bed. Paolo started to laugh. "I can't believe this. I'm a little embarrassed. I dreamt of this moment, and I had to get droopy. We should've stayed downstairs."

"Paolo, don't be embarrassed. I'm sure the next time everything will work just fine." Sydney cuddled up to him, her hand weaving through his chest hairs.

"I get a second chance?" They both laughed.

"Oh yeah, you get a second chance," she said as she kissed his lips. "I can't stay long. I need to pick up Lisa. We should get dressed and go."

As they dressed, Paolo said, "Remember, I leave for Los Angeles tomorrow. I'll be gone for about a week."

"Right, I almost forgot."

* * *

Paolo drove Sydney to her car. Before she got out, she leaned over and kissed him. "Thanks for the beautiful afternoon, you made me happy. Next time I'll make you happy."

"You already do."

"You know what I mean." She punched him in the arm. He laughed. As the door swung closed, Sydney said, "Don't forget me."

"That will never happen."

Chapter 38

PAOLO HAD PACKED his suitcase after saying goodnight to Sydney. American Airlines Flight 2 to Los Angeles departed at 9:35 a.m. He placed his first-class ticket inside his suit jacket. Paolo was scheduled to meet with a representative from the Chinese government to discuss a possible joint venture with several Italian and American corporations. His cell phone rang and the hair on the back of his neck stood up. He knew who it was.

"Hello, Colin."

"Paolo, how are you?" The sound of Dr. Payne's nasal voice turned Paolo's stomach.

"Fine, Colin, and you?"

"Fine. We haven't spoken in a while, how have you been?"

What a piece of shit. "Come on, Colin, my best friend was assassinated two months ago, how do you think I'm doing?"

"You're right, I do know. I saw you at the funeral . . ."

Paolo cut him off. "Yeah, I saw you. Why were you there?"

"I knew Bill, and I wanted to show my respect. I guess he pissed somebody off. It's a shame you had to witness his death. Like I told you when you were in my office, you have to be careful with whom you associate. It could've been you."

Paolo was stunned at the comment. *The balls on this guy.* The anger within him began to boil over. "What the hell do you mean by that, you little piece of shit?"

"Paolo, Paolo, calm down, there goes that Italian temper again. I didn't mean anything by it. I was just saying you have to be careful, that's all."

"Well, it sounds like you're saying something else."

"No, just be careful, that's all."

"I can take care of myself. Now, what do you want?"

"I've been meaning to ask you . . . do you still see the vision of the steel girders and the falling ash?"

Paolo was silent. I wish I'd never told him. "Yes."

"You still don't know where or when it will occur?"

"That's correct." Paolo's answers were blunt and to the point.

"The FBI was approached by a Cuban national with information about a potential terrorist attack against the country. I need you to talk with him. He happens to be in Los Angeles."

Paolo also wanted answers about the vision, so he acquiesced. "Sure, I'll meet with him."

"His name is Javier Castellanos. Contact Fred Birch of the LA branch of the FBI. He will arrange a meeting. And Paolo? Don't share the information with the FBI. Report directly back to me."

"Yeah, okay. By the way, Colin, how do you know I'm going to be in LA?" The phone call ended.

Paolo reached for the secure satellite phone and punched in the speed-dial number.

"Paolo, we believe he's sending you on a wild goose chase. Do what he asks, there is probably some validity. It's definitely a red herring. He just about told us that he had Bill shot. Be patient, my friend, and watch your anger. Our people will meet you in Los Angeles." The phone conversation ended.

* * *

Paolo walked out of the Los Angeles terminal into the cool June morning. His black Lincoln sedan with tinted windows waited at the curb. Paolo placed his bags in the empty gray trunk, then got in the rear passenger seat. He was surprised to see a beautiful woman sitting next to him.

"Hello, Mr. DeLaurentis."

"Hello, Christine Little."

"You know my name?"

"Yep. What does Rami have for me?"

She pulled a typewritten message from a manila envelope and handed it to Paolo.

Paolo, as you know, you are being watched. Our inside man discovered that you were the target in Venice, not Bill. Paolo read on. The Italians found the shooter dead in the Grande Canal. She was the same woman who was with Payne in Russia. "Shit, shit, shit." He crumpled the paper and put it in his coat jacket.

"Are you okay, Mr. DeLaurentis?"

"I've had better days and please call me Paolo. How long have you been with BOET?"

"Eight years, sir."

"Stop with the 'sir' crap. I understand you'll be following me during my trip?"

"Yes, and so will our driver, Tim."

Tim looked in the rearview mirror. His eyes communicated with Paolo, but he said nothing.

"Hello, Tim."

"Hello, Paolo, good to see you again." He placed the car in drive.

"It's good to see you again." Tim had been the waiter in Venice who took Paolo out of harm's way. "How many people are tailing me?"

"At least three men and one woman."

"Have we identified them yet?"

"No, General Ramirez is working on it."

"Okay, after you drop me off at the hotel, I'll find my own way to the FBI building. I know you two won't be too far behind."

"No, we won't," Christine said.

"I have to say, Christine, I've never had a beautiful woman protect me before."

"Thank you for the compliment."

"You're welcome."

* * *

Paolo arrived at FBI headquarters an hour later. After a five-minute wait, he was escorted to Special Agent Fred Birch's office, where he was to meet Castellanos.

"Hello, Mr. Castellanos."

"Hello, Mr. DeLaurentis. It's a pleasure to meet you." The two men shook hands. The short, slim, gray-haired Cuban wore white chinos and a teal blue shirt, untucked. He spoke with a slight accent. He sat across from Paolo in one of the FBI's private offices. A picture of the FBI director shaking hands with the president hung on the wall. An American flag stood in the corner.

"Please, call me Paolo."

Javier handed Paolo a small manila envelope. "Paolo, inside is a picture of three men. My brother in Cuba, who took the picture, said he overheard a conversation about a plot to attack an American city."

"Your brother is still in Cuba?"

"Yes," Javier lowered his head. "When Castro took over, my family fled the island. My brother and father were left behind."

"I'm sorry to hear that."

"It's okay; he works for the underground and is a bartender at a hotel, a local hangout for government officials. My brother provides us with a lot of information. This, however, was the first time he ever heard of a possible attack on our government." Javier pointed to the American flag in the corner of the room.

"I see. Well, thank you, Javier. I'll make sure Washington gets this information." The two men stood and shook hands, and Javier left the room.

Fred Birch entered the office. Paolo stood. "Thanks for the use of your office."

"No problem. What do you think?"

Paolo ignored Payne's warning not to discuss the conversation with the agent. "I think we have a problem. Would you like copies of the picture?" Paolo could see the surprise on the agent's face.

"That's a change—the NSC sharing information."

"It's your country, too." Paolo handed the picture of the three men to Birch.

"I'll go make copies and be right back."

"Sure." Paolo looked out the high-storied window. *I wonder what Sydney is doing?*

Paolo placed the photo of the three Cubans on the desk in his hotel suite, and closed his eyes.

His mind took him to a small kitchen. Three men in blue jeans and T-shirts sat at an old wooden table, eating rice and beans. Paolo recognized two of the men from Javier's picture—Carlos and Gustavo Batista, cousins. The cousins were tan, with tattooed portraits of Fidel Castro on their right arms, their brown eyes void of life. The third man seemed out of place. He had a smaller build and a thin face with a closely trimmed beard. His eyes were dark, almost black, and he had no tan. Paolo recognized him as Duman's associate, Abir.

A white two-burner stove stood next to a sink filled with dishes. The water faucet dripped in sync with the slow-moving ceiling fan. The blue lead-painted walls bubbled from the humidity. Carlos pulled a paint chip from his food and flicked it on the floor. The only furniture in the squalid three-room apartment was the kitchen table and chairs. Abir stood and walked over to a brown leather briefcase that lay on the floor. The Middle Eastern terrorist placed the briefcase on the table, entered a number code, and unlocked it.

He pulled out two envelopes and handed one to each cousin. "Gracias, Señor." Gustavo opened his envelope and inspected the five banded packs of hundred-dollar bills. "Must be at least fifty thousand dollars," he said.

The three men began to talk. Not able to understand Spanish, Paolo listened intently, trying to pick out a word he could recognize. He peered inside the briefcase. Inside were three airline tickets to Toronto, made out to the two cousins and Raul Gomez, for a flight two weeks from today.

Paolo was fluent in Italian and could recognize some of the Spanish words, but his understanding was hampered by the rapidity of the conversation. Frustrated, he opened his eyes. Paolo reached for his BlackBerry and emailed Rebecca for her to obtain a copy of Rosetta Stone Spanish.

* * *

"Hello, Rami. Listen, I viewed the Cubans. There was a surprise visitor, a Middle Eastern terrorist by the name of Abir. He was one of the men who tried to buy a nuclear weapon from Chambery."

"Are you sure?"

"Positive."

"Okay, in your report to Payne, leave Abir out."

"Why?"

"I have a hunch."

"Do you want to share?"

"Not right now."

"Okay, you're the boss. And Rami, thanks for the message. Any idea why Payne wants me dead?"

"Not a clue, and I don't know if we'll ever find out. Our inside man was almost caught, so we have to ease off for the time being.

"Great." Paolo said sarcastically.

"Listen, don't get yourself in an uproar. My people are the best, and they're not going to allow anything to happen to you."

"Okay, if you say so."

Paolo reread the message. *It should've been me. Pard died for me.* He crumpled the paper once again and threw it on the desk.

Chapter 39

I fall into your arms—
For a moment I am taken away to the depths of your love—
To the desires of my heart
I fall into your arms, like a dream floating among the heavens
In total bliss for a moment in time,
A moment bringing life to my soul, happiness to my being

My breath is taken away by your passion
As I lay next to you, I hold you, never to let you go
I have been awakened, the Italian singer pulling on my heartstrings
Tears trickle from my eyes—your skin so soft, your heart so kind

My mind wanders as you sleep, your breathing in rhythm with mine
Another place I go in time, a time of you and me

I fall into your arms so soft and gentle like a dream
Overcome with emotion, I embrace you
I stare deeply into your eyes, my mind goes blank, no words to explain
A love so deep as two souls meet

Love wanting, love desired—so much more
Moments shared, moments not forgotten
I fall into your arms, a day never to be forgotten

PAOLO SAT BACK and closed his eyes. He dragged his right thumb and forefinger across his eyelids until the fingers met at the bridge of his nose. *Maybe some fresh air will get rid of this headache.* From his balcony on the twenty-first floor, he gazed out over the city of Los Angeles. Hollywood nightlife churned as the lights glowed through the haze. Paolo imagined what it would be like to make love with Sydney again. This time no drooping body parts . . . he hoped. He sat in reverie as he remembered the afternoon they'd made love. Paolo started to get aroused. He said aloud, "Now you decide to work."

There was a knock on his hotel room door. Paolo walked through the two-room suite and gazed through the peephole. "Oh my God, what's she doing here?" He opened the door, and then realized he was in his underwear. He wedged his head in the doorway.

"Sydney?"

Sydney turned at his words. She'd already begun walking back toward the elevator.

"I'll be right back, give me a minute to get dressed."

He didn't realize that as the door shut, it also locked. Paolo was shocked that Sydney was in Los Angeles, let alone at his hotel room. He ran to the bedroom, put on an Oxford shirt and pants, and returned to the sitting room.

"Syd, Sydney." She was nowhere to be found. "Damn." Paolo went to the door and opened it. Sydney was leaning against the wall. She wore a black dress and her green eyes gleamed. The smile on her face caused his heart to ache with joy.

"May I come in?"

"Of course. I'm so sorry, Syd, I thought I left the door open."

"Sure you did. What are you hiding? Is somebody else with you?"

"What?"

"Kidding."

"Oh, duh," he stammered, in awe of her beauty. She entered the suite and gave Paolo a kiss on the lips. They embraced.

As she walked by him, she added, "I should have called you first."

She looked at the front of his pants and pointed to his zipper. "May I suggest you fix your pants," she smiled.

Paolo looked down and his face turned bright red. "Shit, I'll be right back." His shirttail was caught in his zipper.

"I'll be on the balcony, okay?"

"Sure. I have a bottle of wine on the bar, help yourself."

"Would you like a glass?"

"Please," he said as he rushed off to the bedroom.

After he fixed his pants and gained his composure, Paolo went back to the balcony. The closer he got to her, the more his heart began to race. *Sydney is here.* He was captivated by her beauty, her mind, and her soul—everything about her held his attention. Sydney stood as she looked out over the city, her bare back to him.

"You look absolutely beautiful."

Startled at the sound of his voice, she turned. "You scared me."

"I'm sorry. I was saying you look absolutely beautiful."

"Thank you. I poured a glass of wine for you." She reached over the table and handed it to him.

"Thanks. I'm so embarrassed that I locked you out of the room."

"Please don't be." She turned and faced the city once again.

Paolo's emotions ran high. He wrapped his arms around Sydney's waist as he held her from behind and kissed her bare shoulder. She moaned. Sydney held his arms across her stomach. Neither wanted the embrace to end. She pulled him in closer. A sense of comfort and security enveloped the two.

"I hope you don't mind me being here?"

"No, no, I still can't believe you're here. I'm so happy you are here." The joy in his voice was quite noticeable. They both watched the lights of Los Angeles. Paolo turned her toward him. Face to face, he kissed her deeply and passionately. The sighs and moans of a man and a woman echoed in the room. Finally alone together, they held each other as if a dream had come true.

Paolo took her by the hand and led her to the bedroom. They stood by the bed. Paolo wrapped his arms around her and kissed her. Sydney sighed. Her body tingled as he kissed and touched her. Paolo was in another world, his body going through an emotional outburst of joy and excitement. They slowly took off each other's clothes. Paolo touched her body; her skin was soft. Gently, he placed her naked body on the bed. The sensation overwhelming and indescribable, their bodies became one. Sydney wrapped her legs around him, the warmth of his body against hers. They moved rhythmically together. She let out a soft moan. She opened her eyes. Paolo smiled. Their bodies reached climax at the same time.

The passionate release over, the lovers held onto one another in a warm embrace. Paolo lay on his back, Sydney's head on his chest, as he stroked her blonde hair. Their voices were hushed whispers in the night as they talked, laughed, kissed, and hugged, at peace with one another. Of course, the topics of their laughter included his shirttail, and the first time they made love. With smiles on their faces, they fell asleep in each other's arms.

Paolo awoke, his arms wrapped around Sydney while she slept. *How beautiful she is, what a lover. I hope I was a good lover.* Never in his life had he experienced a love so deep, so physical, so passionate.

Sydney rustled and turned her body to face his. She placed her arm on his chest and opened her eyes. "Hi."

"Hi."

She kissed him, her lips warm. Her tongue probed. They made love again.

Dawn awakened Sydney and Paolo to a new life.

Paolo was already out of bed. Inspired to write in his journal, he wrote about music without knowing why.

From the earliest days of man, music has motivated, lit up the soul, and energized the masses—the harmonies, the melodies, the songwriter's words taking hold of the heart. The human senses are triggered by the sounds of music. The sweeping memories of joy, laughter, pain, and despair—all the emotions set off in a convoluted musical roller coaster ride of life. He then wrote about Sydney.

Sydney awoke, put on a bathrobe, and brushed her teeth. She

walked out of the bedroom. Paolo sat at the desk, quietly writing. Sydney stood behind him. She placed her hands on his shoulders and kissed him. Paolo jumped, surprised. "God, you scared me!" Paolo laughed. "Good morning, how did you sleep?"

"Excellent and you?"

"Excellent. How would you like to go to Santa Barbara today? We'll take a ride up the coast."

"Sounds great. What are you writing?"

"Just some words about you." Paolo folded the little piece of white paper.

"Can I read what you wrote?" With a little whine in her voice, she added, "Please?"

"How about I read it to you instead?"

"Okay."

Paolo stood and faced Sydney. He wrapped his arms around her waist and whispered in her ear:

You took my love; you made me whole
How I have longed for you, like a dream in the past
You have always been there, I knew you not—
Years of my life have gone, years of my life still to happen
Holding hands with you is like the cool ocean breeze
with the sun's warm rays on my face
The time I spend with you is like the smell of honeysuckle—it brings me to a time
When life was sweet and happy, the time today, tomorrow
A time to grow our love for one another, a time to hold hands
Life is sweet and happy with you

Sydney stepped back as tears ran down her face. She kissed him and took him to the bedroom.

Chapter 40

MUSIC FOR PAOLO was a lightning rod. The melodies and harmonies provided him a mnemonic trigger to remember facts and moments in his life. Paolo's personality was shaped as a teenager growing up in the late sixties, the era of protests, peace marches, and flower power. The cultural influence of music during that period helped to shape society. For a short period of time, the world changed and people became more tolerant.

Paolo rented an apple-red Mustang convertible for their drive up the California coast. They traveled Route 101, with the ocean to their left. Surfers rode the waves of the Pacific as Sydney's hair swept behind her. The sun shone on the two as they drove to Santa Barbara. A local suggested they dine at Aldo's, an Italian restaurant on State Street.

"This is quite the sight," Paolo said.

"What do you mean?"

"All the people, going about their business, enjoying the day, enjoying life."

"Enjoying life? How do you know that, Paolo?"

"Their eyes. They are alive. Some have hidden secrets, but for today, their escape is this street."

Paolo's voice was energetic and his words touched her heart. Leaving a hundred-dollar bill on the table, Paolo grabbed her hand. "Come on, let's go for a walk. I'll show you."

"Show me what?"

"Come on, walk with me?" They left the restaurant.

The waiter who had served them leaned over the black iron fence. "Sir, you forgot your change."

Paolo said, "Keep it, and have a good life."

"Thank you!"

"Look, Sydney," he said as his hands made a sweeping arc. "The people have smiles on their faces. They're enjoying the day and the warmth of the sun. Can you sense it?" She stared at him and smiled at the joy he exhibited. "Close your eyes," he said.

"Close my eyes? Paolo, what are you going to do?"

"Close your eyes." Paolo's voice was calm and reassuring.

"Okay."

"Take a deep breath. Can you smell the scent of the sea drifting up the street? The aroma of the food?" He paused. "The people are alive, their souls are shining." A broad smile crossed his face. "This is life." Paolo faced Sydney and gazed deeply into her green eyes. A deep warmth filled his being as he cupped her cheeks and kissed her. Sydney, overtaken by the charisma of his voice, acquiesced. Paolo took her hand and they crossed the street.

"Watch this."

"Oh, God. What are you going to do?" Sydney laughed, then giggled.

They walked past the Soho restaurant and stopped at the corner. Music emanated from the loudspeakers positioned on the street corner for all to hear. Paolo made an impromptu move as they began to cross the street. He grabbed Sydney's arm and pulled her to him.

"Dance with me?"

Sydney giggled, "Are you crazy! Not here."

Paolo once again gazed in her eyes. Sydney succumbed, overpowered by something within her. She wrapped her arms around the nape of his neck and together they danced in the street. Sydney laid her head on his shoulders. He held her tight. Car horns began to honk. People lined the street as the two danced. Paolo's eyes would meet theirs, as he mouthed, "How I love this woman, how I love her."

Traffic came to a standstill. Another couple got out of their car and eagerly joined them. Out of nowhere, more and more people started to dance in the street. Men and women held each other. The men said, "How I love this woman, oh how I love this woman."

A police officer saw the crowd and tried to stop the impromptu event, but by now thirty couples danced in the street. The officer's girlfriend approached and he threw up his hands and asked her to dance. When Sydney and Paolo stopped, people surrounded them in a circle. They clapped as he kissed her. Paolo whispered in her ear, "How I love you, Sydney Hill. You have no idea how much I love you."

"I love you, too, Paolo, my heart is yours. Let's walk to the beach and watch the sunset."

"Sounds like a great idea."

* * *

The sun had set, and a full moon rose in the sky as Paolo and Sydney sauntered hand in hand. The scent of the sea wafted on the twilight air. As Paolo stopped to look into her green eyes, a tear welled.

Sydney reached up and wiped his tear. "What's wrong?"

"Nothing. I just realized, Sydney, the idea of not having you in my life tugs at my heart."

"I'm in your life. What makes you think I'm going somewhere?"

Paolo said nothing. The notion of the secrets he withheld and the problem that would arise nagged at his consciousness. He leaned over and kissed her; their hearts beat a moment in time. The rays of the full moon highlighted the two as if under a stage spotlight. The beam's reflections danced on the ocean water. Their embrace was broken by a jogger and his barking dog.

The couple held their shoes in one hand as they walked ankle deep in the ocean. The tranquil summer night's breeze blew at their backs. The hills of Santa Barbara behind them, the light of the moon followed them. Sydney and Paolo walked to their car and drove back to Los Angeles.

* * *

They arrived at the hotel late that night. While Paolo packed his clothes in the bedroom, Sydney saw a crumpled piece of paper on the desk that looked like the poem Paolo wrote her. She opened the paper and read it, then fell back on the couch, put her head in her hands, and shook her head.

"Sydney, come look at this."

She gathered herself and walked into the bedroom. "Syd, are you okay? You look like you saw a ghost."

"No, I'm fine. What's up?"

"Look," Paolo pointed to the TV.

"A bizarre story out of Santa Barbara today: traffic came to a halt on State Street this afternoon, as people were dancing in the street."

The co-anchor responded, "Dancing in the street?" The pre-scripted banter between the two continued.

"Yes, apparently an unidentified couple decided to dance in the middle of the street and stopped all traffic. The man told passersby how much he loved the woman he was dancing with. You will never guess what happened next."

"Tell me, I can't wait," the blonde announcer said.

"Instead of beeping their horns and yelling, people joined in. People exited their cars and came out of the stores and started to dance. Everyone was saying the same thing, how they love this man or that woman. Witnesses stated even the local police officer was dancing with his girlfriend."

"Really? I don't think that would have worked in New York City."

"I don't think so, either. Only in California."

"Yes, Bob, only in California."

Chapter 41

THE LAST WEEK of June was backdropped by cherry blossoms, bright blue skies, and warm breezy winds. Three weeks had passed since the trip to Los Angeles. Paolo sat at his desk and looked at the aerial pictures of the Brewster Estate.

He pressed the intercom. “Rebecca?”

“Yes, boss?”

“I hate it when you call me that.”

“Sorry.”

“Remember I’m going to be out of the office for the remainder of the week.”

“Yes, moving day. Before I forget, the movers called. They’ll be at Victoria’s at nine tomorrow morning.”

“We’re using Augliera Moving, correct?”

“Yes. I spoke with Rob earlier today.”

“Excellent. I don’t need any screw-ups. The last movers were a nightmare. Thank you, Rebecca.”

“You’re welcome.”

* * *

“Paolo, Dr. Payne is on the line.”

“Thank you, Rebecca.” *Why is he calling on my office line?* Paolo reached under his desk and pushed a button; his phone conversation would now be monitored by Rami’s people. Rami’s words came to mind, "*Watch your Italian temper.*" He waited a moment before he picked up the phone.

"Good morning, Colin. How are you today?"

"I'm doing quite well. And you and Sydney?"

"Excellent. Thanks for asking." Paolo tried to remain calm. "You read my report on the Cuban exile."

"Yes. I guess you should take some Spanish lessons."

Paolo didn't respond.

"When you viewed, you only saw two men?"

"That's correct."

"And Paolo, next time when I ask you not to share information with the FBI . . ."

Paolo cut him off. "Get over yourself, Colin. They probably had the room bugged, and besides, we're all on the same team."

Payne grunted, "Have you experienced anything more about the vision?"

"No, I'm still seeing the steel girders in a debris pile with falling ash. A large building fell. What kept coming to me was we failed once, but we won't fail again."

"Any idea what country?"

"Yes, the United States."

"Any idea what city?"

"No."

"Call me if anything else occurs."

"Will do." With a hesitation in his voice, Paolo said, "Colin, this is still confidential, correct? They don't know about me?"

"No, they don't."

"Good. Talk with you soon."

Paolo hung up the phone and sat back in his chair. He closed his eyes.

He saw two men sitting. Dr. Payne placed the receiver on the phone. "Nothing yet," he said to the man in front of him. "I'll send you the transcript."

The president of the United States stood. "Thank you, Colin."

"No problem, Mr. President."

Paolo's eyes opened. "Someday, Payne, someday you'll pay. You son of a bitch."

* * *

Family and friends described Paolo as a passive, kind, and compassionate man . . . almost to a fault, other than his occasional Italian temper, triggered by dishonesty and deep hurt. They often said he allowed people to walk all over him; others said he had no balls. The reality was that it was all a ruse. Paolo waited for his time. He now knew Payne was behind the assassination of Bill. Still, there was the unanswered question: Why did he want Paolo dead?

It would be a cold day in hell before anyone got close enough to kill him. Rami and his elite team had his back. Paolo kept Sydney in the dark about the strength of his gift. His concern was that if the media ever found out—well, he could kiss his life with Sydney goodbye. In the end, right would triumph over wrong and once the truth was revealed, there was no way to stop the ensuing domino effect.

Paolo's release from the gift was his love for Sydney. As long as the emotional high of being in love was present, the gift remained clouded. Sydney put his mind in an oasis of peace and tranquility, muting the tragedies of the world. He gave her his heart in a way that he had never done before.

Paolo reached for the desk phone and lifted the receiver. "Rebecca, can you please come in here?"

"How was your conversation with Payne?"

"Okay. He's a scumbag, don't wanna talk about it. I need you to book Sydney and me on a flight to Colorado Springs for the end of October, around Halloween. Try to arrange reservations at the Broadmoor."

"How long do you want to stay?"

"What do you think? A long weekend . . . say, leave Thursday, come back Monday. How does that sound?"

"Sounds nice. Can I go?"

"You're the best, Rebecca. Have I ever told you how much I like working with you?"

She smiled, "Yes, you have, many times. How is Sydney?"

"Fine, she's away on business." Sydney was on a business trip to San Francisco. She was the guest speaker at a convention about women in business. Paolo had no idea why, but Sydney had become distant in their conversations. He had seen her once during the three weeks they'd been home. Her sudden absence confused him.

Rebecca recapped the itinerary and left Paolo's office.

Paolo reached for his phone and called Sydney.

"Hello."

"Hi. How is San Francisco?"

"Great. Can I call you back?"

"Sure, call me later." An uneasy feeling overcame Paolo; he pushed it aside.

* * *

That afternoon as Paolo packed some boxes in the au pair apartment, the vision of the steel girders covered in ash came to his mind. The vision was interrupted by the ringing of his cell phone. He shook his head and tried to erase the image.

"Hi, how is San Francisco?" Silence. "Sydney?"

"Yes, I'm here."

"How is San Francisco?"

"I'm not there."

"Where are you?"

"Home."

"What are you doing home? Is everything okay?"

"Yeah, fine."

"When did you get home?"

"Two days ago." Paolo's heart sank. "Two days ago? Why didn't you call me?"

"I didn't want to."

"Really. Well, maybe I don't want to talk to you right now." Paolo regretted the words.

"Okay."

An uncomfortable silence followed. Neither spoke. "Sydney, what's going on?"

"I don't know."

"What do you mean, you don't know?"

"I can't talk about it. I don't think we should be together."

Shocked, Paolo's voice rose an octave. "What?"

"I don't know if I love you."

"Wow," Paolo had no words. His heart began to ache.

"I'm sorry, Paolo."

"Yeah, thanks for the phone call." Paolo took his BlackBerry and threw it across the room. "What the hell."

The next morning, Paolo called the office. "Rebecca?"

"Yes, boss?"

"Stop calling me boss." Paolo was clearly angry.

"I'm sorry."

"Cancel the trip to Colorado Springs and order me a new BlackBerry." Paolo didn't allow Rebecca to respond. He slammed the phone down. He stood in the emptiness of the au pair apartment. Tears streamed down his cheeks. He picked up the house phone, called the local florist, and ordered a bouquet of flowers for Rebecca.

Chapter 42

TWO DAYS LATER, Paolo finally moved into his new home on the Brewster Estate. It was the second week of July. Almost a month since he had seen Sydney. The forty-eight-hundred square foot four-bedroom townhouse was surrounded by lush vegetation and tall evergreen trees. The location offered a quiet, peaceful, serene community; the majestic beauty of the complex had all the amenities of a five-star resort. Cobblestone walkways were lined with old-fashioned lampposts. One could envision the town crier waiting for twilight to light the oil lamps.

By the lake, a white pergola with a fireplace was used by the residents as a meeting place to discuss and analyze life, or to sit in front of a warm fire on cool nights. The body of water surrounded by park benches provided the small community a place to reflect upon nature's beauty. Although not yet completed, the complex had already been voted the best place to live in the United States. Property values increased fourfold with six months still left to complete the rest of the estate.

Rio and Giacomo helped Paolo unpack. He set up his new Dell computer in his study.

"Dad?" The young army major stood in the doorway, looking for his father.

"Under here, I'm attaching cables to the computer."

Giacomo walked into the study. The imposing, solidly built soldier said, "You need some help, old man?"

"Old man? I can probably still kick your ass."

"Sure you can."

"Do I detect sarcasm in your voice?"

"No sir, not from me." Giacomo chuckled.

Paolo came out from under the desk and stretched his legs. His son sat on one of the two couches and smiled at his father. "Nice house, Dad."

"Thanks, Giacomo." He looked at his square-jawed son, his heart filled with joy, "I'm happy you're here."

"Me too, Dad."

Paolo pointed to a white box. "See that white box over there?"

"Yes."

"Can you bring it to me?"

"Sure." Giacomo sprang to his feet and retrieved the box labeled Classified, Top Secret. "Classified, top secret . . . what are you up to, Dad?"

"Nothing special, I'm working on a government project." He patted his son's back.

Paolo opened the box and pulled out a series of electronic devices. Giacomo reached for one.

"Dad, what the hell do you need a phone scrambler for? Shit, is that a secure satellite phone?"

"Some tools I need."

Giacomo picked up the third device. He analyzed the thin black box. "What's this for?"

"I'm surprised you don't know. That, my son, is a silencer." Paolo held the device. "This box will emit a frequency that prevents people from eavesdropping on my conversations." Paolo sensed the bewilderment in his son. He placed his hand on Giacomo's shoulder. "Why don't you go get your sister? It's time the three of us talked."

Giacomo looked at his father. "Okay, be right back." He walked out of the study and yelled his sister's name.

Paolo held two plain white envelopes in his hand as he walked around his desk. He sat opposite his children and began to tell about his paranormal gifts—how his father used him for prognosticating football scores, the testing when he was a child, the time he saved Bill, Steve, and Tony at the sandpits. He withheld certain aspects—his apocalyptic visions, Dr. Colin Payne's involvement in Bill's death, and the fact that he was the target. Paolo decided to discuss with Giacomo his participation with Rami and BOET later that evening, if the matter presented itself.

The brother and sister listened in disbelief. Paolo could see shock on their faces.

"Why are you telling us now?" Rio chimed in.

"The time is right." Paolo handed them each an envelope, postmarked five years earlier. "Open them."

Rio opened hers and read the handwritten paper aloud. Giacomo read his silently.

"Thursday, July twelfth, two thousand and one. Giacomo and Rio are in my study, at a house I am unfamiliar with. Rio is dressed in blue jeans and a tan cashmere sweater. She has brown clogs and her hair is shoulder length. Giacomo sits to her left, reading his letter silently, wearing blue jeans, a white-and-blue rugby shirt, and Dockers with no socks.

"A great tragedy will soon occur in the United States. Terrorists will attack the country. I can see the burned, blackened steel structure of a building. Yet, I don't know where it is."

Rio folded the paper and placed it back in the envelope. "Holy shit, Dad."

Giacomo reached over and took Rio's envelope. He gave both envelopes back to his father. "I understand now."

"You understand what?"

Giacomo said nothing.

Rio spoke up. "Dad, can you give me the lotto numbers?"

"Come on, Rio," her brother rolled his eyes.

Paolo sat back. "No, my daughter, I can't help you with that."

Rio sat on the edge of the couch and pulled the tan cashmere sweater over her belt. "Who knows about this? Does Mom know?"

Giacomo leaned forward, as well. "Yeah, Dad, who knows?"

"Okay, both of you relax. There are very few people who know—

your grandmother, Rebecca, Jim, Danny and Jayne, and a doctor by the name of Colin Payne."

Giacomo interrupted. "The NSC member? Head of intelligence?"

"Yep, that's the one. He tested me when I was a young boy. Mom doesn't know. And of course, Pard knew." He left out Rami and a Frenchman named Arnaud. "Not everyone knows the extent and the depth of the gift."

Rio sat back. "Why do you call it a gift?"

"I don't know what else to call it. For some reason, I have an extraordinary power to know things. To be honest, I don't want to be a freak."

"Maybe you're a super-hero."

"A super-hero, my ass," Paolo said.

Rio walked over to her father and sat next to him. "You're my hero, Dad."

Paolo rolled his eyes. "Thank you, Rio. But I'm far from a hero. I sometimes feel like a loser—divorced, living alone, feeling guilty." His voice trailed off.

"Guilty about what?" asked Giacomo.

"I don't know . . . you, Rio, the divorce."

"Dad, Rio and I are fine with the divorce."

Paolo's head hung down, "Yep."

"Well, stop it. We totally understand, don't we, Rio?"

"Absolutely, even Mom understands. You've got to stop beating yourself up."

"Yeah, Dad, get over it. We are."

"Alright, alright, let's change the subject." Paolo looked at his watch. "Why don't we go get something to eat? It's already five-thirty."

"Sure Dad. How about Italian?"

Rio added, "Why don't you call your lady friend, Sydney? Maybe she can come with us. I thought we would've seen her today?"

"Italian sounds great, Giacomo."

Rio looked at her father. Paolo's eyes filled with tears. Nothing had to be said. Rio went up to her father and hugged him. "I'm sorry, Dad."

He tried to stave off the onslaught of tears. "Okay, you two, let's go." As he turned, he saw Giacomo mouth, "Lady friend?" Rio waved him off.

Paolo was surprised they didn't ask him about the vision. At this point, he was not going to bring up the subject. "If you two want, you can sleep here tonight."

"I can't, Dad, early class tomorrow."

"I'll stay over, Dad." The father and son looked into each other's eyes. "I'm sure we have a lot to talk about."

"Sounds great, Major."

* * *

The father, son, and daughter drove to Nataz's, a local restaurant that had no defined menu. The three were shown to their table and visited promptly by a waitress who spewed out a menu of delectables that left their mouths watering with delight. Paolo and Rio ordered zuppe de pesce while Giacomo ordered a double veal chop with a wine reduction sauce topped with a variety of mushrooms. Rio provided the laughter and the talk. Paolo sat in amusement and awe as he listened to his grown children. There was no mention or discussion about what Paolo had told them. After dinner, Rio got into her car and drove back to her mother's house. Giacomo and Paolo went to the estate.

Chapter 43

GIACOMO SAT NEXT to Paolo in the quietness of the study, waiting for the first word to be spoken. There was a silent, telepathic connection between father and son, but still the words had to be said. The subject had to be broached.

"What is it, Giacomo?" Paolo stood and walked to his desk.

"How strong are your ties with our government?"

"Why do you ask?"

The soldier looked around. Never short on words, he said. "Did you use your influence to help me?" His eyes diverted to the floor.

"Look at me." Giacomo's eyes focused on Paolo's. "Whatever you have accomplished and will accomplish in the future is all you. I've had no part in your career, other than supporting you one hundred percent."

"Really?"

"Yes, son, really. You don't need me. You have set your path, your course. Your life's journey is yours, not mine. It's hard enough for me to live my life, let alone yours."

The soldier smiled. "Thanks, Dad."

"So, my son, tell me . . . what's going on in the Army world?"

"Nothing much. I've been interviewed for a special operations unit."

"Sounds interesting."

"Yes, I'm looking forward to it. I can't really talk about it, if you know what I mean."

"Sure do."

"I ran into Rami the other day."

"You did?"

"He said to say hi."

Shit, he's applying to BOET? "What is General Ramirez up to?" Of course, Paolo knew, he'd spoken to him earlier in the day.

"He's the commander of the unit I hope to transfer to."

"Do you want me to give him a call?"

"No. Like you said, Dad, it's my journey."

"Alright then. See that cable over there? Can you bring it to your old man?"

"Sure. Isn't there a football game on tonight?"

"Yep, the New York Giants and the Dallas Cowboys, should be a good game. New York will win, thirty-one to twenty-eight in overtime."

"Sure, Dad," the major's voice was skeptical.

The two watched the game. Paolo fell asleep in the third quarter, only to be awakened by the screams of his son.

"Shit, Dad! How the hell did you know? New York just kicked a forty-yard field goal to win the game."

Paolo, groggy, stood looking at his son. "I just know." He patted his son on the back. "I'm going to bed, see you in the morning."

"See you in the morning, Dad."

Paolo turned. His son shook his head in disbelief. "Don't forget to turn off the lights."

"I won't. Goodnight, Dad."

"Goodnight, son."

* * *

The following morning after Giacomo left the house, Paolo called Rami.

"Hello."

"Rami, how the hell are you?"

"You know how I am. We talked yesterday. How's the new house?"

"Great. Thanks for sending the electronics. Everything has been installed."

"No problem. And the security of the compound?"

"I hate it when you use that word 'compound'."

"Paolo, the surveillance and the security system you have beats anything the government has, including the president."

"I hope your line is secure."

"You know damn well it is, or we wouldn't be talking like this."

"General, you take things too seriously."

The two men laughed. "Giacomo told me he saw you."

"That's why you're calling me?"

"Yep."

"I was gonna tell you, in fact, today he was accepted into the program."

"Not because of me?"

"No, the committee. I'll leave it up to you to tell your son about your involvement with BOET. Paolo, Giacomo scored the highest of any applicant ever to apply to the unit. One day he'll be my replacement—not because of you, because of who he is."

"Thanks, Rami. Listen, you're his commanding officer. If it's operationally necessary for him to know about me, I trust you to tell him. He'll understand."

"Okay. How are you holding up?"

"Okay, I guess. I feel paranoid with Payne watching me and knowing my every move."

"I understand. Hang in there, we almost have him. He'll eventually slip up—his greed for power and revenge will get the best of him."

"Revenge?"

"Yeah . . . we believe he has a vendetta against the United States, the Russian government, and you."

"I still can't figure it out, Rami. Why me?"

"Personally, I think he knew we were investigating him. And he feels you betrayed him."

"I guess that kinda makes sense . . . We have another problem, my remote-viewing capabilities have diminished."

"What do you mean?"

"Really simple, my ability to focus is disappearing. And the bigger problem is Payne won't believe me if I tell him."

"Hopefully we'll conclude this Payne business soon. Then you can go and live happily ever after with Sydney."

Paolo was silent. "Sydney ended our relationship."

"Oh, I'm sorry to hear that. Do you know why?"

"Yep. My secrets."

"You're a good man, Paolo, it will all work out. I'll let you know if anything crops up."

"I'm sure you will. Goodbye, Rami."

"Goodbye, Paolo."

* * *

That night, Paolo sat in his new library. Oak French doors opened to the dark blue-carpeted sanctuary adorned with built-in bookcases on three walls. The fourth wall contained a picture window that overlooked a rolling hill, a lake at its base. In the background, the Bose sound system played a CD by a Italian singer, Andrea Bocelli. The Italian lyrics punctuated the warmth and serenity of Paolo's inner sanctum. He took a small piece of paper with his written thoughts and placed it in his top desk drawer, where it joined other small pieces of paper and a journal.

Daydreaming about Sydney, Paolo took pen in hand and wrote:

My life is to be with you
I can see the glimpse of our life together
The memories of you and me in my mind
I just don't know the amount of time
For us
A nagging sense within me
My time is short, will we grow old together?
Will we be one?

I picture us asleep holding one another
Waking in the morning to kiss your cheek
To tell you I love you
The warmth of your body next to mine
Then I am gone
With just the memory of you and me

Chapter 44

Sorrow sweeps my heart
Another time maybe
In heaven maybe we shall meet
Life continues without you
Another day goes by
A night swallowed up by the dawning of the sun

PAOLO WAS IMMERSED in his own misery of not seeing Sydney. Three months had passed, time he spent revisiting memories of her. *What did I do wrong*? Paolo was baffled. *I guess I'll never know. I miss my friend.*

"Rebecca, I won't be in the office today."

"Okay, Paolo. Anything I can do for you?"

"Nope." He showed no signs of emotion. His statements were direct and to the point. The mornings were the toughest. He took long walks on the Brewster Estate. By noon, the reveries stopped. In the afternoons, he studied Spanish. By the middle of the second month, he had learned enough that he could understand and have an intelligible conversation.

Paolo closed his eyes. *His mind took him to a hotel room. He saw Gustavo, Raul, and Carlos around a table near a king-size bed. The television was on, showing a movie Paolo didn't recognize.*

"Raul, when will we get the explosive?" Carlos said.

"Within one week of the money being transferred. We will stay in Canada until then."

"How long will we be here?"

"I don't know."

"And what about the bomb for Russia?"

"Our Chechnyan counterparts are handling Russia."

Gustavo lit a cigarette. Inhaling, he blew smoke rings while Carlos and Raul continued their talk. "Is the plan still for us . . ."

Paolo's eyes opened at the sound of someone banging on his door.

"Rio, what are you doing here?"

"Hi, Dad. Can I come in?"

Paolo's mind was still in a flutter over the remote-viewing session. "Oh my God, of course."

Rio was dressed in blue jeans and a loose-fitting white shirt. She sported a summer tan, her dark brown hair tied in a ponytail. The father and daughter walked to the kitchen.

"Can I get you some lemonade?"

"Sure, Dad. What's going on? Are you okay?"

"I'm fine. The break-up with Sydney put me into a tailspin, but I'm okay now."

"Are you sure?"

Paolo noticed the concern in her eyes. He walked over to her and gave her a hug. "I'm fine, thank you for your concern." He kissed her forehead. "Sit down, tell me what's going on in your life?"

The two talked for a while. Sydney was never mentioned.

"Dad, are you going to the pig roast?"

"Wouldn't miss it. Are you bringing your new friend?"

"What do you mean?"

Paolo closed his eyes. "Eric."

"Shit, Dad, I'm not even going to ask how you know. Yes, I might."

"Good. I would like to meet him."

Rio picked up the glasses from the table and placed them in the sink. "Dad?"

"Yes, principessa?"

"If you need to talk, you can call me. If you want."

Paolo rose from the table and embraced his daughter. A tear trickled down his chin. "Thanks, Rio."

After Rio left, he placed the glasses in the dishwasher and walked to his study. He called Rami on the secure line and described what he'd seen and heard, particularly about a second bomb.

"Okay, let's keep this between us and see what develops. I'll call Sergei."

"Is that a good idea?"

"We have to, Paolo, we've got no choice."

"I guess you're right. Okay, talk later."

"Bye."

* * *

During the last week of August, Paolo was haunted continuously by the vision of blackened steel girders. He was unable to shake the vision from his mind. He remote viewed the Cubans but gleaned no new information. The vision would not go away.

Paolo continued to write about his love for Sydney, his written words helping to ease his grief. Each word he wrote removed a thorn from his heart.

Paolo sat at his kitchen table, reading the front page of the New Haven *Register*. "Hurricane Erin Creeps Up the East Coast." He sipped his black coffee. The phone rang.

"Hello, Warren."

"Paolo, how the hell are you?"

"I'm fine. It's great to hear your voice. How are Alicia, Dalton, and Bailey?"

"They're great, and your kids?"

"Everyone is fine. Pig roast next week?"

"Sure is, are you coming?"

"Absolutely."

"Great, I hope we don't get hit with Erin."

"We won't," Paolo said.

"Your words to God's ears. I'll see you then."

"Sure will."

* * *

Paolo sat back, a smile on his face. Warren was an old friend he'd met through Tony and Steve while in college.

Hurricane Erin churned up the east coast. The storm—Mother Nature's way of pummeling the earth—would cause havoc from the Carolinas to southern New Jersey before moving out to sea. She slammed into the Carolinas with the ferocity of a nuclear explosion. The Category 3 storm with winds of 150 mph had tentacles that reached Connecticut with strong winds two days prior to the Labor Day weekend pig roast.

* * *

The day was coming to an end and the pig roast went off without a hitch. Paolo and his friends sat around a blazing bonfire and discussed the day's events.

"Paolo?" Warren said, "I have to admit you were right about the hurricane. There was no damage here at all. Let me ask you a question, do you speak directly to God? Erin should have hit us big time."

Wayne chimed in, "We can all talk to God."

"Here we go again." Warren threw an empty plastic cup at his brother. Everyone laughed.

"I just knew." Not wanting to get into a philosophical conversation, Paolo said, "Listen, guys, I should get going. I need to take a shower, and get some rest. I'm getting too old for this."

"You'll be here next year," Alicia said. Warren's attractive, curvaceous wife stood, as did all the rest. One by one, Paolo said his goodbyes with hugs and kisses. He told each one, "I love you." As he walked away, Steve and Tony walked with him.

"Hey, guys, what's up? Steve, the sausage and peppers were outstanding. What a great time."

"Yeah, thanks." Steve lit up another Marlboro.

Tony said, "Go ahead, tell him."

"Paolo, we sold all the units."

"I know, congratulations."

"The problem is, we made a lot of money."

"That's a problem? You guys deserve it."

"Thanks, Paolo, but we can't keep it."

"Why?"

"Because it's fifteen million dollars and we don't need that much money."

Steve took a last draw on the cigarette, throwing it to the ground. "Yeah, Paolo, way too much."

Tony reached in his pocket, pulled out a check for ten million dollars, and gave it to Paolo. "We know, Paolo, this has to do with the day we were at the sandpits. Bill told us the story. We will always be friends, and we'll always be bound by that day. You don't have to feel guilty anymore. It was a long time ago and look, we're fine. Except for Steve's constant smoking."

The three laughed.

"Well, my friends, I appreciate the offer and the kind words, but I can't take it back. I'll tell you what you can do. Give some of the money to Warren and Wayne, so they can buy the farm and the field from their family so this tradition of love will never end, and the pig roast will continue free of charge. The rest donate to charity."

The two men took back the check. "That's a great idea."

"Hey, Paolo, who's the woman standing by your car?" Tony asked.

Paolo turned around. "Damn, Sydney is here."

"Who's Sydney?"

"The love of my life, Tony, the love of my life. I'll see you guys later."

Steve and Tony went back to the pit. Paolo walked along the field to his car. Sydney waited under the streetlight. With a broad smile on his face and an ache in his heart, Paolo approached the Jaguar.

"Hi," he said, his voice tentative.

"I hope you don't mind me standing next to your car?"

"Not at all. How are you?"

"I'm not too good." Her voice cracked as she tried to hold back the tears.

"I always thought you were pretty good," he said, trying to be humorous. In his mind, she was the best lover he had ever had.

"Stop joking, I'm being serious."

"Okay, I'll be serious. What's the problem?"

"You're going to make me suffer through this, aren't you?"

"Maybe," he smiled mischievously.

"When I was in your hotel room in LA, I read the note from Rami." She began to cry. Her green eyes melted his heart.

Shit. "You weren't supposed to see that." He took her in his arms. "Don't cry."

"I know, I thought it was one of your poems. I'm so sorry. Will you forgive me?"

"I'll always forgive you. I know you don't like secrets, and I couldn't tell you."

"But Paolo, someone is following you and . . ."

Paolo stopped her. "It's almost over. Soon I won't be working with Rami. I'm sorry I didn't tell you, but there is nothing for you to worry about. Everything will be fine."

"Are you sure?"

"Yep. Everything will be fine." *I hope.* "I'll be honest, Syd, you really broke my heart." He told her what had transpired over the last ten weeks—how he would write about her and how miserable he was without her in his life. Sydney asked to see the little white pieces of paper. They arrived at the townhouse together.

"I have to take a shower; my writings are in the top drawer of my desk in the library."

"You don't mind?"

Hesitantly, he said, "No, there are no crumpled pieces of paper."

"Not funny."

Paolo watched as she opened the drawer of his desk. Inside were at least one hundred, if not more, pieces of folded white paper. She chose one.

As I sit here looking at the rain
The color of your eyes comes shining forth
touching my soul with memories of you

The sun is not shining this day
The dreariness creeps in like the coldness of this day
Then the memories of you sidetrack my mind
And the sun shines again within me

Time passes slowly
The loneliness of the day
Surrounds me
Will the sun ever shine again?

Highlights of hope sparkle through
when I hear your voice
The love I have inside for you
So hard to contain
So much pain I feel

I await the day when it is you and me
For on that day I will dance in the street
With laughter in my heart
Tears of joy in my eyes
Love in my heart

When that day comes, you will be loved
Like no one has ever loved you before
I need your love in my life
As each day goes by
I need your love in my life
I need you in my life
I want to be a part of your life

In my dreams, in my heart
You will always be there
The future right now scares me

A day without you—the night cannot come fast enough
The mornings come too soon
It seems that all I have now is a dream
The memories, the memories of you and me

Like the songwriter's pen, the poet's soul is my only comfort
Love will conquer all—that is what I believe—the love of you
and me
No regrets do I have—for to have loved you one day
Made my life, filled my soul with happiness

Not able to read more, Sydney closed the desk drawer and silently wept. An hour had gone by. She walked in his bedroom, and found him sound asleep. She undressed and lay beside him. Tears streamed down her face as she whispered in his ear, "I love you, Paolo DeLaurentis. I love you." They slept through the night.

Chapter 45

NINE DAYS LATER, Paolo awoke in a cold sweat. His heart raced as if he were on amphetamines. The vision had been so clear—today was the day the vision of the blackened steel would come true. He reached over to the nightstand and called Dr. Colin Payne.

"Hello."

"Colin, today is the day something is going to happen. It's today."

"What do you mean?"

"The vision, Colin, the vision." Panic in his voice, Paolo said, "Oh my god, Colin, it's going to happen today, damn it."

"Relax, Paolo."

"Relax, my ass. Thousands of people are going to die today."

"Paolo, you've had this vision for over a year now. Go back to bed." The phone disconnected.

Paolo called Rami. There was no answer. He left a message. He talked to himself, "Shit." A deep dread engulfed him. "I'll call Sydney. No, I can't." Paolo sat down on his couch in the study and turned the television on. He waited.

"Terrorists strike at the financial heart of the United States," the news blared throughout the world. Headlines scrolled across the screen in fragments. Airplanes ram the World Trade Center. Thousands dead. Fire, smoke, people jumped to escape their burning fate, only to die when they hit the ground. Trade Towers collapse.

Gray ash falling from the sky. Blackened steel girders in a sea of rubble. The images tore at Paolo's heart.

He stared at the television in shock and disbelief, his paranormal vision now a reality. Paolo was angry and filled with profound grief and guilt. *Why couldn't I stop the attack?* Tears streamed down his face. His private phone rang

"Hello." He knew Colin Payne was on the other end.

"Paolo, I'm sure you've seen the pictures."

"You know I have," he said tersely.

"It's a shame you weren't able to give us any information on the Cubans."

"The Cubans had nothing to do with it and you damn well know it." *Watch your Italian temper*—Rami's words echoed in his head.

"They didn't?"

"No." *You know that, you piece of crap.* "I remote viewed them this morning. They were as shocked as we are. But—why are you calling me?"

"You screwed up, Paolo. If you came to work for me, we could've stopped this."

"You no good son of a bit . . ." The line went dead.

Paolo was furious. He called Rami.

"Paolo, he's pushing your buttons."

"But maybe I . . ."

"Maybe my ass. Paolo, this is over, you have to move forward now. Keep your mind focused on Payne—he's trying to throw you off guard. You're a good man, my friend, don't listen to that piece of crap. And you know what I think, Paolo?"

"What?"

"I think he kept you off track with the Cubans, so you couldn't discover what city."

"But why?"

"So when the time comes, he can discredit you."

"That makes sense, Rami. That son of a bitch."

"Be patient, my friend . . . like I said, he'll slip up."

Chapter 46

THE THIRD WEEKEND in September provided Paolo a respite from the agonizing thoughts of dealing with his apocalyptic visions. Something wasn't right. His subconscious gnawed at his mind. The memories of 9/11; his inability to prevent the attack; the destruction, the death and the grief of the families ripped at his heart. He needed quiet time—time with Sydney.

Lisa, Sydney's daughter, was away for the weekend. This provided the needed conjugal opportunity. Paolo spent the weekend at Sydney's house. They enjoyed a quiet Saturday evening together. Paolo cooked veal scallops with lobster topped with a drizzle of Béarnaise sauce. They watched a movie and went to bed.

Paolo usually woke with the sun, but on this particular day, he stayed in bed. The warmth of Sydney's naked body next to his gave him a sense of tranquility. A deep peace lay within his heart. He still couldn't get over the reality that he was in love with her and she with him. He could smell the scent of her hair. The color of her eyes brought memories of when they made love. He never said he made love *to* her, it was always *with* her. As the sun rose over the trees, its glimmering rays peeked through the blinds onto the couple. Aroused and not wanting to wake Sydney, Paolo got up and took a shower.

When he exited the bathroom, Sydney was no longer in bed. Paolo hoped he hadn't awakened her. He dressed and went downstairs. The sliding doors to the deck were open. Sydney's sweet voice broke the silence of the morning.

"Paolo, come to the deck." He walked through the open doorway into the waning cool morning air. Sydney sat on a padded lawn chair made for two. She wore a heavy blue cotton robe, slightly open. The skin of her breasts showed through the opening, ever so teasing. Her eyes lured him to her.

"Soaking up some sun, are you?"

"Absolutely," she replied with a coy smirk on her face. "Why don't you lean over and give me a kiss?"

Paolo leaned over and kissed her. She replied with an open-mouthed kiss and placed his hand on her breast.

Taken aback, he said, "Right here, outside?"

"Who's going to see?"

The sun crested over the trees. Their passions ignited, they made love in nature's paradise. The scent of honeysuckle filled the air. Two became one. A memory etched in their minds—after this, whenever the smell of honeysuckle was in the air, the memory came to life.

They lay holding each other, her leg on top of his. Sydney twirled his chest hair and they shared gentle kisses. Paolo gazed into her green eyes and was at peace. The rays of the warm sun touched their naked bodies.

"Can I make you breakfast?" he asked.

"That would be nice. I'm going to take a shower."

"Me too, can I join you?"

"No, you can use the other bathroom. Nice try, though."

They stood and embraced. "That was fun," Sydney said, kissing him on the cheek. "I might need a back rub later, the lawn chair was a little uncomfortable."

"No problem. With body oils?"

"You men are all the same. Give it a rest, will you?"

"Maybe," he smirked.

As she walked past him, her hand touched his. "I'll start to cook breakfast when I hear you start the hair dryer. Anything in particular you'd like?"

"Surprise me."

The warm water of the shower pelted Paolo's back. His mind

began to assimilate the morning's activities. *What is the stigma of a man? Why are we always the sexual aggressors in a woman's mind? Why can't it be the need to love? Yes, the needs are different; or do the needs of a man and woman change as they get older? Why is it when a woman wants to make love, the man had better not say no, but when a man wants to make love, he's simply acting like a man? The complexity of love. A man has no control when it comes to making love. Sure, he can pout and get angry, but the only thing he'll be holding is himself. Dad often said it's a man's world. I think you were wrong, Dad, there is no way this is a man's world.*

Chapter 47

PAOLO WALKED THE neighborhood outside the stone walls of the Brewster Estate. The colorful leaves of late October littered lawns and sidewalks, sparkling in the afternoon sun. Children jumped into the piles of red and yellow foliage. The serenity of the cool nights, the crisp, clean air, and the sounds of fall refreshed Paolo's troubled spirit.

Paolo was filled with excitement and apprehension as the holiday season approached. The cold and the beauty of winter would arrive in six weeks.

"What are you doing for the holidays?" Sydney said.

"Thanksgiving, Rio and I will be at my brother's house. Christmas, I don't know yet. Rio will be with her mother on Christmas Eve. And to tell you the truth, I don't know if I want to spend Christmas Eve with my family."

"But you love Christmas Eve!"

"I long for the family tradition, but everything has changed. The food, everything—it's just not the same anymore."

"How about you and I spend Christmas Eve together? You can cook for me."

Paolo was stunned. "Are you serious?"

"Absolutely. I would love to spend it with you, Paolo DeLaurentis. Maybe we can start our own tradition."

"What about Lisa and Andrew?"

"They'll be with their father."

"Excellent."

* * *

Paolo remembered the time-honored Italian family tradition of serving seven different types of fish on the festive night before Christmas, as holiday music played in the background and the padrones napped on the couch. Sometimes there was a light snowfall as the mothers and their children walked to midnight Mass, then home to open presents.

With Paolo's mother and aunt aging, the adult children took over the preparations and the cooking. Health concerns about how and what to eat became an issue. The fish was broiled instead of fried, in butter instead of margarine. The holiday changed and felt more like a chore than a celebration. Paolo knew that life changes, but why was the family tradition so difficult to continue? He came to realize that love was missing from the holiday—not necessarily from his family so much as from the world. People complained about commercialization; Paolo agreed. Everyone forgot God and His love for us. They believed Christmas was about children and presents. How wrong they were.

* * *

Paolo sat in his library as he wrapped Sydney's gift. The smell of simmering lobster sauce permeated the townhouse. Over the years of their friendship, Sydney had talked about wanting a diamond tennis bracelet. She clearly had the means to buy one, but she wanted the bracelet given to her as a present. Since her husband Peter never paid attention to her wants and needs, she never received what she wanted.

Paolo planned everything. He borrowed the Spode Christmas plates from his sister, the ones with a decorated pine tree painted on the front of each plate. The table was set with a red-and-green tablecloth with white snowflakes in the green squares, and a lit evergreen candle in the center. A fire crackled in the fireplace and its red and orange glow warmed the room. A sense of peace and comfort filled the air. Mistletoe hung in the doorway, waiting for the opportunity to share a kiss. In the background, Bing Crosby sang "White Christmas." Yellow roses, Sydney's favorite, adorned the coffee table. The setting resembled a picture taken out of *Good Housekeeping* magazine.

Paolo placed the silver foil-wrapped present under the tree. The Christ child absent from the manger sat atop the fireplace mantle, waiting for the midnight hour. Five stockings hung on the maple wood—for Sydney, Giacomo, Rio, Andrew, and Lisa. For Paolo, his present would be his desire for his children and her children to witness the true love of a man and a woman.

Paolo received a call from the guardhouse informing him that Sydney had turned the corner from Whitney Avenue to Cliff Street. Her license plate and face were scanned by a computerized optical system, which matched her face with the database. By the time the Audi 8 reached the gate, the computer had approved her credentials. Paolo gave the guard the final okay to let her into the estate.

Paolo watched the security monitor as Sydney drove along the evergreen-lined road with its cobblestone sidewalks to his house. A group of carolers sang by the pergola next to the frozen lake. Paolo opened the front door. He could hear them singing, "Noel, noel . . . ." The song drifted off into the chilly night air. The aromatic evergreen wreath, with its bright red bow, filled his senses with the holiday spirit. Sydney's car turned into the driveway. The sight of her on Christmas Eve enveloped his heart.

"Do you need any help?"

"No, I'm fine." She walked up the two steps where Paolo met her. Sydney was bundled up in a beautiful gray cashmere scarf. Her green eyes sparkled. Paolo was taken aback by her beauty. He stood, speechless.

"Are we going inside?" she quipped.

"Of course."

Sydney pointed to the mistletoe overhead. "Are you just going to stare at me or are you going to kiss me?"

Paolo surrounded her with his arms like wrapping paper around a Christmas present and kissed her. The passionate kissing of the two lovers warmed the chilly winter night. They broke apart when they realized the carolers were now singing behind them. Embarrassed, they thanked the singers and entered the house.

As Paolo warmed his hands in front of the fireplace, Sydney took her bag of presents, placed them under the eight-foot spruce, and stood next to him.

"The fire feels great. Nice and toasty." Sydney stood by his side.

"Toasty?"

"Yeah, toasty, like bread in a toaster."

"Oh, okay. That's a new one for me."

"Come on, Paolo, you never heard that before?"

"Nope."

Sydney wrapped her arms around his neck. "So, what have you cooked me for dinner? I'm starving."

"A vast assortment of fish, cooked with the love that I have for you," he said with a capricious grin.

"Sounds a little fishy to me."

"Ha ha, funny. I'm serving the traditional Italian Christmas Eve dinner—seven fish."

"I'm hungry but . . . you understand I can't eat all that."

"Yep, I know. I'm bringing the leftovers to my brother's house, tomorrow."

"Honey, I'm so impressed. The dinner table is absolutely beautiful. Do you need any help?"

"No, thank you." Paolo pulled a chair out. "Signora." He motioned for her to sit.

"Why, thank you."

"Prego—you're welcome. Would you like Chianti or Barolo?"

"Chianti, please."

Paolo left the dining room and returned with their plates filled with the ocean's delicacies.

* * *

"Paolo, I loved the lobster tails in the red sauce and the fried shrimp. God, they were good. I'm so stuffed."

"Me, too."

Paolo took his red cloth napkin and folded it lengthwise. He placed the cloth on the table underneath his arms. He leaned and stared at Sydney.

"Why are you staring at me?"

"Because I love your eyes, they're spectacular. Tonight when you walked into the house, your eyes were like sparkling emeralds."

"You love just my eyes?"

"No, other parts of your body as well."

"I'm glad to hear that," she said with a snicker.

"How would you like to go for a walk? Then we can come back and have some hot chocolate."

"Sounds like a good idea. Could I have whipped cream on mine?"

"Absolutely."

"What time is it?"

"Why, do you have someplace to go?"

"No, smart ass, I just wanted to know, so I can open up my presents."

"Eight-thirty. Another three-and-a-half hours till Christmas."

"Damn, can we open them now?"

"No. Christmas isn't here yet."

"Please," Sydney whined.

"Maybe when we come back. I'll go get our coats."

"Okay," she pouted.

The Southern New England winter night was not too cold, but cold enough for snow. The two lovers strolled along the brick walkway. The light of the lampposts glimmered in the darkness. The faint distant laughter of the neighbors traveled through the still, cool air. Hand in hand, they enjoyed the quietness.

A bright orange fire glowed in the fireplace by the pergola. The flames licked the cold night air, releasing red embers into the evening sky. The warmth of the burning wood radiated heat as the two walked to the railing overlooking the frozen lake. A spotlight aimed at one of the large evergreen trees showed fluffy white snow just beginning to fall. The stillness of the night was broken by the sound of a deer stepping on pine needles. Paolo's arm was around Sydney, her head nestled on his shoulder.

"You can almost hear the snowflakes hit the ground," Paolo said. "Tomorrow morning the estate will look absolutely gorgeous. We should probably get back before the snow starts to stick."

"But it's so peaceful here." Sydney snuggled closer.

"I know. Isn't it?"

Arm and arm, they walked back to the townhouse, saying little and enjoying the walk. By the time they arrived, the ground was already covered in pristine white snow, not yet victimized by the imprints of nature.

With joy in her voice, she whispered to him, "I guess I'm spending the night."

"I wouldn't have it any other way."

"Me, either."

"How about some hot chocolate with whipped cream on top?"

"That sounds wonderful. Do you need any help?"

"No, I think I can handle it. Go sit in front of the fireplace, I'll be right back."

Sydney sat with her knees pulled to her chest, soaking up the radiant heat of the fire.

"Here's your hot chocolate, my love."

"Why, thank you, kind sir. Care to join me?" Sydney patted the floor next to her.

"Absolutely."

They held the warm cups between their hands.

"So, what did you get me for Christmas?" The flickering flame painted her face in orange and red hues.

"Not until midnight, I told you."

"Oh please, just one." Sydney placed the mug on the coffee table. She began to kiss his neck.

"No, not until midnight, now stop."

"Please." Sydney began to rub the back of his neck as she whispered in his ear. "Please," she stretched out the word.

"Please stop."

Her hands traveled down his legs. She began to rub his thighs. Sydney flashed her green eyes. Paolo kissed her. The two undressed. The fire warmed the two naked lovers as they rhythmically moved in song with one another. The sexual tension of the evening released, they fell asleep in each other's arms as the glow of the red burning embers highlighted their bodies.

As the heat from the fire diminished, silently they awoke. "What time is it?" Sydney asked, her voice sleepy.

Paolo rolled over and searched for his watch amid the strewn clothes. "God, it's cold in here."

"I can tell," she replied. "Shrinkage." She stared at his groin.

"Not funny." He found his timepiece. "It's ten past midnight." Paolo leaned over and kissed her. "Merry Christmas, Sydney."

"Merry Christmas, Paolo. Let's get dressed before more shrinkage occurs."

"Ha ha."

They dressed and sat together on the couches. An assortment of colorfully wrapped presents lay neatly under the tree, stacked according to whom Paolo was going to visit on Christmas Day.

Sydney gathered the gifts. "You first." She put them on the coffee table.

He opened his gifts, in a slow, methodic way, teasing her with his slowness.

"Gee, you're like an old lady. Do you think you can open them a little faster? I'll be old and gray by the time you finish," Sydney quipped.

"Yes, dear." He continued to open one corner at a time, and then suddenly, in a fury, he ripped open the packages. Paolo threw the Christmas paper at Sydney.

"You are such an ass."

"Thank you," Paolo said with a smile. He sat back and folded his arms behind his neck. "That fast enough?"

"Yes," Sydney rolled her eyes. An assortment of cookbooks, a couple of shirts, a scarf and a picture calendar of Italy lay before him.

Sydney reached down and handed him Mario Batali's cookbook, *Simple Italian Food: Recipes from My Two Villages.* "Honey, read the inside cover."

"Okay." He read aloud. "'Paulo— to a great chef. I hope to meet you soon. Mario Batali.' Wow! Thank you. I love the way he cooks. What did he mean, 'I hope to see you soon'?"

"That's the best part. He's going to personally cook for you and me at his restaurant."

"Babbo?"

Sydney nodded her head.

"Excellent, when can we go?"

"I have his number. We just have to coordinate schedules."

With enthusiasm, Paolo said, "Thanks, what a present. I can't wait." He kissed her and then pointed to her presents, "Now it's your turn."

With excitement, she began to open her gifts. "Paolo, this is beautiful." She held the red cashmere sweater to her body. "Looks like the right size."

"Should be, your daughter helped me."

"And the Rolex watch . . . absolutely gorgeous."

"You forgot this one," he said, handing her the silver foil-wrapped package.

"Another present?"

"Nothing special. I thought you'd like this," Paolo said casually.

Painstakingly she unwrapped the present. Paolo's pulse began to quicken. She opened the black velvet Harry Winston case. Stunned, she stared at the ten-carat fifty-diamond tennis bracelet. Tears fell from her eyes.

"Are you okay?" Paolo said.

"Oh, I'm fine. This one caught me by surprise."

"Do you like the bracelet?"

Sydney nodded. "Thank you, thank you so much, this is beautiful."

"Well, try the damned thing on," Paolo said, a huge grin on his face.

Paolo took the bracelet and placed the diamonds around her

wrist. The brilliance of the precious stones sparkled in the glow of the fireplace, matched only by the brilliance of her green eyes. He wiped the tears from her face and kissed her.

Sydney wrapped her arms around him and whispered in his ear, "How I love you. I love you so much, thank you."

They sat on the couch while Sydney gazed at the bracelet. Paolo read Mario's book.

Sydney yawned, "I'm really tired."

"Me too, let's go to bed. It's already one-thirty." They walked to the bedroom, undressed, kissed each other and fell asleep.

* * *

As the sun rose, the evergreen trees were draped in fluffy white snow, carried away as wisps by the cold winter winds into the blueness of the December sky. In the distance, three deer roamed the grounds. Doves cooed in the crisp morning air. Paolo awoke, Sydney's head upon his chest. He gently moved her, kissed her cheek, and whispered, "I love you." He walked to the bathroom, showered, and went downstairs to cook her breakfast.

Paolo shook off the nagging headache. *I must've slept wrong.* The ache went away as he began to cook. Sydney entered the kitchen wearing one of Paolo's turtleneck shirts and a pair of his socks, her shapely legs bare. Paolo looked up to see her standing in the doorway. His heart skipped a beat.

"Good morning. Wow, you're sexy. Can I make love with you right now?"

"No. I'm starving. What are you cooking?"

"Darn, I was hoping for a little morning delight." He raised his eyebrows at her.

"Do I have to remind you, you're not twenty-five anymore?"

"No kidding, but the thought of making love with you . . . well." Paolo's voice trailed off.

"So, what are you cooking?"

"I've made your favorite, eggs Benedict."

"I can't wait."

After breakfast, they cleaned the kitchen, made their Christmas phone calls to their children, showered, and dressed. Then they sat by the French doors, holding one another and gazing out over the snow-covered park-like setting. Paolo seemed preoccupied.

"What's troubling you? You seem lost in thought."

"I was just thinking about you and me—the time we wasted when we weren't together."

"And that bothers you?"

"Yes. I don't understand why I'm just troubled today." He paused. "We're together now, so I'm happy today," he said, less than enthusiastically.

"I love you so much, Paolo. I'm in your arms now, and the past is the past. I can't wait for the day when I'll wake up next to you for the rest of my life."

"I can't wait, either," he said.

Together they went to ten o'clock Christmas Mass and then went their separate ways.

New Year's Eve came and went. They celebrated the holiday together with Rio and Lisa. They fell into a comfortable relationship; each understood the other's needs, wants, and desires—at least for the time being.

Chapter 48

The falling snow blankets the trees in the twilight of the evening
A fire blazing in the fireplace, two candles burning
Strangers no more
Wrapped in a blanket, alone at last
For a moment in time, a love satisfied
Evening turns to night
Night to morning
Embraced by the love of one another
You and I

APOCALYPTIC VISIONS CONTINUED to plague Paolo. His journal was now halfway full of the future tragedies that would befall humankind, both natural and man-made. He kept the secret of his journal to himself, only to be divulged when the time was right. As he thumbed through the pages, one vision began to haunt him.

People in the streets milled about. It was a normal day. The image was in black and white. A mother and her child walked hand in hand. A slight breeze blew a scrap of paper into the street. The morning air was crisp, a few white clouds moved to the east. A car horn honked as two men ran across the busy intersection. A young woman walked out of Starbucks, a grande cappuccino in her hand. An Asian man opened the door to his vegetable market, while another opened a kiosk that sold sunglasses and cigarettes. The dream turned to vivid color.

People walked in slow motion. A bright white flash erupted from a skyscraper. A rushing dark cloud immersed in a funnel of fire flew into the morning air. A massive wind tore down a bridge that connected the city, while the river below boiled. An immense heat swept through the streets. The scorching temperature incinerated those around him. A mushroom cloud hung over a city destroyed.

He gazed out his library to the snow-covered grounds. It was the second week of February and southern New England had just been pounded by a nor'easter. The roads still covered, Paolo stayed home. For whatever reason, his mind transported him to Dr. Colin Payne.

Payne sat at his kitchen table, talking on a satellite phone. "Good. Where is he? . . . You're sure he's the plant from BOET? . . . What do you mean, you don't know? . . . I don't care if you leave him on death's doorstep. I want some fucking answers, and I want them now!" Payne slammed the phone down. He picked up another phone and dialed. He spoke in Russian.

Paolo shook his head. Then the vision came to him again, but this time there was no mushroom cloud; the people of the city walked in peace.

"Rami."

"Paolo, how are you today? I hear you've got some snow up there."

Paolo sensed a note of hesitation in Rami's voice. "Sure do. We have a problem."

"What's going on?"

Paolo filled Rami in on the vision and his remote-view session of Payne. "Rami, email me a picture of our operative . . ." Paolo stopped in midsentence. "Shit, Rami, it's Giacomo."

"Yes. We know where he is, Paolo, our people are on the way. Paolo . . . ?"

Paolo ended the phone call as tears streaked down his face. "Hang in there, son."

His eyes glazed over; his mind transferred him to where his son was being held captive.

He easily recognized Giacomo, sitting next to a man he didn't know. Both men were stripped of their clothes, all but their underwear. Their mouths were duct-taped, their bodies strapped to floor-bolted chairs. Their heads swiveled on their shoulders like bobble-headed dolls as their interrogators pummeled them. They were in a darkened room. A ray of sunlight through *the closed drapes and a lamp on a table highlighted the tools of torture. The smell of human excrement hung in the air. Street noises could be heard in the distance. The walls behind the chairs were splattered with blood. The two Russians took turns battering the man Paolo didn't know.*

"Tell us what we need to know or you will end up like your friend," the man said in a heavy Russian accent to Giacomo. He reached up and pulled the duct tape from Giacomo's mouth. His eyes on fire, Giacomo tried to spit at him.

The bruised, battered face of the army major stared in disbelief at his captors. How he wished he could speak, but his vocal cords were bruised. If he could have, he'd have said, "When I get out of here, I'll kill you, you sons of bitches." But he couldn't utter the words. The pain from his broken cheekbones forced a soft moan. Paolo walked past the two Russians toward his broken son. Leaning over, he whispered, "It'll be okay, son. Dad is here." He placed his hand on his son's shoulder. Giacomo jumped at the touch, because he saw no one. Paolo turned around. The two men sat on a desk, smoking, as Giacomo twitched in agony. One threw his cigarette butt at him. "Let's get this over with," he said to no one in particular. Giacomo's eyes were swollen shut but he heard the prelude. Wind rushed past his ear as the baseball bat slammed into his shoulder, shattering bone and muscle. A searing pain traveled through his right arm and up his neck. *He gasped for air. The end was near. Paolo watched helplessly. Where the hell are they? Giacomo's head fell as he lost consciousness.*

A two-way communication device squawked a staticky warning to the two murderers. The words were simple and to the point: "Get out."

"Let's go," said the Russian the table.

The torturer, his mind on his soulless act, bent over and wiped Giacomo's splattered blood off his face, then said, "What?"

"They are coming! We have to get out! Shit, let's go!"

"Let me kill this bastard first."

"We don't have time."

"I'll clean up. You go."

"We don't have time."

"Go! I will be right behind you."

He ran up the stairs and escaped the building. Paolo followed, trying but failing to grab the bastard. Furious, he made his way back to the torture chamber.

The Russian had pulled Giacomo's head back and was about to spit in his face, when a loud, thunderous noise shook the room. It went dark with smoke. Stunned, the killer dropped to the floor and reached for his gun, but found he couldn't move his arm—it felt like someone was stepping on his hand, but nobody was there. Three BOET members burst into the basement. Infrared headgear in place, they swept their laser-sighted rifles as they searched for the two Russians. The savage torturer saw the sweep of the light of death and tried to lay still. Then, from nowhere, he felt a kick in his side and lifted his head in pain. A red beam of light centered on his forehead. The final sound he heard was the swish of a neatly placed fifty-caliber bullet entering his forehead and exploding through his occipital lobes in a mist of blood, brain, and skull.

The lead BOET member spoke, "Site secured. Extracting the major." The US Black Operations Elite Team rescued Giacomo and the body of the other man. They left the dead Russian extremist behind for the FBI to dispose of.

Paolo opened his eyes, reached for the trash bucket, and violently vomited. Stunned and trapped in his house, he sobbed. His satellite phone rang.

"Paolo, we have your son."

Paolo tried to stop crying. He sobbed, "Thank you, Rami. I saw it. Who was the other man?"

"That was our operative. We sent Giacomo over to get him when they were ambushed."

"Where are you taking Giacomo?"

"To Bethesda."

"No. I want him here at Yale."

"Can't do that, Paolo. We have to protect him. It will be best. I'll send a plane to pick you up."

"Don't need your plane! I've got my own. I'll be down there in a couple of hours. Make sure I get in to see him, General. I don't want any bullshit!"

Paolo slammed the phone down on the desk. His cell phone rang.

"Hello," his voice angry.

"Uh-oh, someone's in a bad mood. What's the problem?"

Silence. "Paolo, Paolo, are you there?"

"Hi, Sydney. I'm having a bad day." Then like a cascading waterfall, Paolo took the risk and spewed out the story of what had happened to Giacomo.

"Oh my God, Paolo. Is he alright?"

"I don't know. I'm heading down to Maryland in a couple of hours." His head pounding, he rubbed his temples.

"Who did it?"

Then, like a volcano, he erupted. "Who did it? I'll tell you who did it. Good old Dr. Payne. That miserable shit should drop dead." Paolo's face was red with seething anger. "Let me tell you something . . ." Suddenly he stopped yelling. An eerie silence replaced the words of disgust.

"Paolo, relax. This is not the Paolo I know. Am I speaking to someone else?"

"No."

"Paolo, I know that name. *Payne.* Doesn't he work for the government?"

"Yep. I can't get into it. Maybe another day."

"Another day? Paolo, your son will be fine. Why are you so angry? I've never heard you like this."

There was another long pause. "Paolo?"

"Sydney, my son was almost killed. And I saw it and I could do nothing about it."

"You were there?"

"No . . . not really."

"Paolo, you're not making any sense. Are you alright?"

"No, I have a monstrous headache." Paolo's words and anger were so uncharacteristic of his personality. "Do you understand, Sydney? I couldn't do anything about it. They have no concept of truth. The bastards look you in the eye and lie to your face. The sanctimonious sons of bitches! They should all rot in hell."

"Who are you talking about, Paolo? You're starting to scare me."

"I'm sorry, Sydney. I'm really sorry." Paolo tried to calm down. "Remember the story I told you about me when I was a child and the clairvoyance?"

"Yes."

"Well, Dr. Payne was the doctor who tested me."

"Oh, why didn't you tell me?"

"I didn't think it was important."

"Why?" Sydney's voice was puzzled.

"I have my reasons."

"They are?"

"I can't tell you. I'm sorry. I have to go."

"Oh." Paolo sensed the hurt in her voice. "Do you want me to go with you?"

"Thank you. But no, it's too dangerous."

"Dangerous?"

"I have to go, Sydney. I'll call you when I get home. And Sydney?" his voice hollow with resignation.

"Yes."

"I love you."

"Call me when you get home," she said coldly.

"Yeah, no problem," Paolo hung up the phone in disgust. "She can't even tell me she loves me."

Chapter 49

PAOLO CALLED TONY to see if the plane was available. By the time he arrived at the Key Air Hangar, the G-V was waiting with the engine running. Snowplows made a final sweep of the runway as Paolo drove his car onto the ramp. He stopped just short of the aircraft, jumped out of the Jaguar as if he were twenty years old, and two-stepped the stairs. Within five minutes, the aircraft roared into the Connecticut skies, leaving Oxford airport behind.

The plane arrived in Baltimore forty-five minutes later. The air traffic controller directed the plane to a taxiway. With the stairs lowered, Paolo raced out of the aircraft and jumped into the military helicopter that was waiting to take him directly to the hospital.

The Sikorsky Blackhawk landed on the roof of the fifteen-story building. Rami was there to meet him. Paolo exited the chopper and the two men headed into the hospital.

"How's my son?"

"Unbelievable—outside of the bruises and the damage to his shoulder, he'll be fine. The doctors expect a full recovery."

"What about his face?"

"Two small fractures in his cheekbones. He's definitely going to be sore when he wakes up. When they took him out of the building, he kept saying 'Where's my dad? My dad is in there.'"

"I was standing by his side—I guess he could feel my presence."

"Amazing," Rami said in disbelief. "I have a secure room where we can talk until he comes out of recovery."

"Good. I apologize for getting angry at you."

"Don't worry about it, I completely understand."

They walked down a hallway guarded by men holding M16 rifles. A sergeant stood at attention as they came to a door. The door opened. Inside was the president of the United States.

The president stood and walked over to Paolo. "It's so good to see you again, my old friend."

"Mr. President," Paolo said as he looked at Rami.

"I'm sorry to hear about your son. Rami told me he'll make a full recovery."

"That's my understanding, Mr. President. So, gentlemen, tell me what's going on?"

"Rami."

"Yes, Mr. President?"

"Fill him in."

"Yes, sir. Your son was able to signal us when he was ambushed. We had a pretty good idea of where he was. Within two hours, we found him and mobilized BOET. That's when you called, you know the rest. After we rescued Giacomo, I informed the president of our investigation, and the information you provided. He commanded the Secret Service to arrest Payne."

Paolo sat back, relieved. "Excellent. I can't wait to see that son of a bitch hang."

The president and Rami looked at each other.

"I'm sorry, Paolo . . . we believe Payne is no longer in the country, and we need your help to find him."

"Find him, Mr. President?"

"Yes, Rami filled me in about your paranormal abilities. What I didn't know was that it was you. Payne kept that from me. From what the general tells me, there is a strong possibility that he arranged the purchase of two nuclear weapons—one to be detonated here in the States, and the other in Russia. Go ahead, Rami."

"We were able to put some pieces together and they all revolve around you. We have no idea why, but they do. Okay, where do I begin? Let's start in France and your accidental viewing of Duman,

Abir, and Arnaud Chambery. Then the views of the Cubans. Now add the Chechnyans. What is the one common denominator?"

"Outside of me, the nuclear bombs."

"Right. We now believe that your paranormal ability will save millions of lives. When the general and I discussed your abilities—we both thought we were crazy. Paolo, neither of us is religious, but for some reason we believe you are the key to save mankind from killing itself."

"Whoa, gentlemen. You're starting to freak me out, as our friend Bill used to say. I'm not here to save anybody. I don't even know where the gift comes from. So please don't put me on a pedestal or any other place of honor. I'm just a simple man."

"Well, you might consider yourself a simple man. Frankly, Paolo, we need your help."

"Mr. President, I'll do what I can." Paolo didn't tell them of his vision of the city at peace and not destroyed—the outcome could be changed.

"That's all we can ask for. I'm sure you would like to see your son. Keep in contact with Rami. I've commanded the Secret Service to put a detail on you for your protection."

"That won't be necessary, Mr. President."

"Paolo, you won't notice them, they will work in conjunction with Rami and BOET. You'll still have your own autonomy."

"Yes, Mr. President."

The president walked over to Paolo and hugged him. "Godspeed, my friend."

* * *

Paolo walked into the stark hospital room. The battered face of his son made him nauseated and he turned away. The memory of Giacomo as a child came to mind, the dreams of the young boy wanting to be a warrior, the protector of the people. Sooner than later, his son's dreams would come to fruition. It seemed just a few years ago when he and Giacomo walked along Chapel Street while his son played the role of an Army soldier. He stood in front of his father, "Sir, requesting permission to scout ahead for enemy insurgents?"

"By all means, Sergeant. Carry on."

The young boy saluted his father. "Yes, sir."

Giacomo ran ahead of his father, stopping at street corners to peer around the block, hiding behind a stop sign. He'd yell at his father, "Sir, all clear."

"Thank you, Sergeant."

A tear fell from Paolo's eye. He knew in the years to come his son would witness horrific events. The days of innocence had been whisked away by time; the years disappeared in a heartbeat.

"Come on, I don't look that bad, old man." Giacomo's voice was strained.

Paolo couldn't speak. His throat tightened up, his eyes welled. He whispered, "No, you don't look that bad." He walked over to his son's bed.

"You wanna sign my cast?" Giacomo tried to sound lighthearted as he nodded toward the cast on his left shoulder and arm.

Paolo kissed him on his forehead. "Rest, my son, rest."

"Thanks for being there, Dad. The sound of your voice kept me alive." Giacomo fell asleep.

Chapter 50

"Hi."

"How is Giacomo?"

"He's doing great." Paolo paused, "Syd, I'm really sorry about the other day. I was so wrong in taking my anger out on you. Please forgive me."

"I'm trying to understand, Paolo, but you have so many secrets. I just don't know."

"I understand. I'll be home in two days. Why don't we get together and talk?"

"Give me a call when you get back. Tell Giacomo I said hi."

"Will do. I'll talk with you in a couple of days. Bye."

"Bye."

* * *

Paolo arrived in Connecticut the following Tuesday. Victoria and Rio were with Giacomo, who was up and walking around. The doctors said he would make a full recovery in nine months.

The casually dressed Paolo walked through the lobby to the elevators, briefcase in hand. He thought of Sydney and a smile crossed his face. The doors swung open with a swish. The wall bore the ancient crest of the village of Ottati and the words Ottati Consulting Ltd., in large gold letters. The video cameras recorded Paolo as he turned left toward the frosted-glass double doors. He slid his ID card in the reader and tapped his code in the security pad, and the doors automatically opened.

As Paolo walked into the reception area, he was greeted by his receptionist and his chief of security, who sat behind a twenty-foot half-moon console with a bank of monitors and telecom equipment. A camera strategically placed in the hallway snapped pictures of every person exiting the elevator; by the time they arrived at the glass doors, facial recognition software had confirmed their identity. The entrance was actually an x-ray portal that scanned everyone who entered the office. The body scan wasn't for weapons but for recording devices that could violate client confidentiality.

The high-tech system became operational a month after Bill's assassination and the revelation that Payne had tried to infiltrate Ottati Consulting. On the other side of the wall was another card reader and a security pad that controlled who was allowed out of the office.

Paolo's Chief of Security, Anthony Winters, stood and acknowledged his boss.

"Good afternoon, Paolo."

"How are you, Anthony? Have our friends arrived yet?"

"Yes, sir. Two Secret Service agents were here earlier. I provided them with live feeds to our monitors as you requested. How is your son?"

"He's doing great, thanks. Hello, Maryann. How are you today?"

"Great, Paolo. I'm sorry to hear about your son."

"Thank you, Maryann. You must be looking forward to your vacation. If I remember correctly, you are going to St. Maarten?"

"Yes. I can't wait."

"Well, have a great time. I hope you both have a good day."

"You too, Paolo," they said in unison.

Paolo walked down the carpeted hallway past the client center boardroom and took a right, passing through the next security door. He turned the doorknob and entered the realm of Ottati Consulting.

He stood before Rebecca. "Good morning, any messages?"

"Sydney Hill. She said she tried you on your cell phone, but it went right to voice mail. How's the major?"

"Unbelievable, Bec, he's doing great. Thanks."

"Don't forget Sydney called."

Paolo scanned his security card and opened the frosted glass door to his office. The cherry wood desk and matching bookcases sat on the plush green carpet. He looked out the fourteenth-story windows at the intersection of Church and Elm, busy with early afternoon traffic, then sat behind his desk.

How am I going to find Payne? What do I tell Sydney? Maybe I shouldn't play with the fates, let whatever happens happen. Why, God, are you taking a back seat?

Paolo took out his pen and wrote. *The earth's inhabitants are beginning the last act, the final eulogy of mankind. We can't live in peace—our ideologies so vast and so different, man killing man on behalf of a God who so loved his people. The incongruities between man and God grew pride and greed in the west and God's avengers in the east. Will it ever end or is it just the circle of life with no knowledge gained from history? Whether we believe it or not, there is a war, a war unseen to mankind . . . a war to be played out on the lands of the earth, a war so evil, bent on the destruction of humanity. And the kicker is we can't do shit about it.*

Paolo placed the pen down and massaged his face. He reached for the intercom.

"Rebecca, remember the trip to Colorado Springs I wanted to take?"

"Yes."

"Make reservations for Sydney and me for a month from today."

"Okay, will do. Don't forget to call her."

"I won't."

He dialed and spoke. "Hello, Sydney Hill. I hear you've been trying to reach me."

"Yes, where are you?"

"In my office. Apparently my cell phone isn't working. Sorry."

"Oh, okay. I thought about what you said, and maybe I'm a little paranoid about secrets.

I'm sorry and I'll try to understand. I know it must be difficult for you and maybe one day you'll feel comfortable enough to tell me. How about dinner tonight? Say, six o'clock, my house?"

"I'll be there. Thanks, Sydney."

Paolo hung up the phone, his heart filled with joy.

Chapter 51

THROUGHOUT THE NEXT month, whenever the opportunity presented itself, Sydney and Paolo made passionate love. Afterward, they would laugh, talk, and share dreams. When together, they were one. There was a wholeness about them.

"I can't believe, at our ages—you're almost forty-seven, and me . . . well, we don't have to go there—we can still have sex the way we do," Sydney said, her arm on his chest.

"Tell me about it. Two times in one day and no Viagra . . . whew, baby, you're hot."

"Viagra? Do you take those pills?"

"No, I was just saying, two times, damn . . . I'm not thirty years old."

"I know." Sydney rolled her eyes and grabbed the small, spare tire of a belly.

"Oh, aren't we funny." Paolo rolled on his side and propped his head on his left hand. He kissed her warm lips. "Should we try for the hat trick?"

"Hat trick? What's that?"

"Three times," Paolo raised his eyebrows.

Sydney made no response, just kissed him passionately.

Paolo and Sydney enjoyed making love. They had a mutual respect for one another. Their inhibitions gone, they became one.

Paolo took pleasure in telling Sydney he loved her, but for whatever reason, she couldn't say the words in return. This troubled Paolo deeply. He so desperately needed to hear those three little words from her.

* * *

Paolo tried numerous times to remote view the Cubans, Payne, and Abir, with no luck. His ability to view was stymied by his love for Sydney. A month later, Paolo and Sydney left for a long weekend in Colorado Springs. Both were excited about the prospect of being alone together.

Originally built in the early 1900s, the Broadmoor Hotel sat at the base of Pikes Peak. The facility had been updated over the years into a first-class resort. The hotel's nostalgic, romantic mood charmed all who stayed there.

Their suite overlooked the property with the mountains above and behind them and the city of Colorado Springs in the distance. The view was spectacular as the moon rose above the city. Exhausted from their travels, Sydney took a shower and got ready for bed. She gave Paolo a long kiss.

"Don't take too long—I might be asleep when you get to bed."

"I won't."

After his shower, towel wrapped around his body, Paolo walked into the bedroom. Sydney lay sound asleep. His body still warm from the shower, Paolo slid between the cotton sheets. He snuggled up to her and whispered in her ear, "I love you." He gently kissed her cheek. He saw her smile.

The smell of spring permeated the mountain air. The peaks were covered in snow, the vibrant green grass with its morning dew sparkled in the bright morning sun. The hotel courtyard had a brick walkway, which surrounded a man-made lake with park benches for the guests to sit and enjoy the fresh air. Mallard ducks waddled in the lake during the day. At night, the water glistened with the orange glow of the lighted lampposts.

Paolo tried to make their time together as romantic as possible. He quietly sneaked away, so he could plan little surprises for her. Sydney loved yellow roses, Paolo arranged for the florists at the hotel to deliver a dozen roses to her. To his disappointment, all they had were long- stemmed red roses—like the passion of his love for her.

The doorbell rang. "Sydney, can you answer that? I'm in the bathroom."

"Sure . . . who could it be? Did you order room service?"

"No."

Sydney opened the door. Before her stood the hotel bellman. He held a crystal vase with a dozen long-stemmed red roses and one yellow rose in the middle.

"Sydney Hill?" he said.

"Yes."

"These are for you," the bellman announced, extending his arms.

Sydney took the bouquet and smelled the roses. A tear came to her eye. Paolo had come out of the bedroom suite. He stood behind her and handed the man a ten-dollar bill.

"The roses are beautiful, Paolo, thank you." Sydney kissed him.

"They are beautiful, aren't they?" Paolo was surprised to see a yellow rose amid the red. *The florist said they had no yellow roses. I'll write him a thank-you note.* When the florist received the note several days later, he was surprised as well, for he didn't inventory yellow roses.

Sydney's eyes lit up when she saw the flowers, yet Paolo sensed a tentativeness to her joy. She placed the vase on the coffee table.

"Paolo, thank you so much! What a pleasant surprise. And look at this yellow rose! It is beautiful." She went over to Paolo and gave him a hug and a kiss. "They are so beautiful."

"I'm glad you like them. They are quite beautiful, I must say. For your second surprise, I arranged for us to have our own private massage at the spa."

"Together?"

"Not in the same room. If you want, you can also have a facial."

"Excellent, when do we need to be there?"

"In twenty minutes."

"Let's take a walk around the lake. That will bring us to the spa, and we can check out the restaurant. I heard someone in the lobby say the food was first-rate."

"Good idea, I can use the exercise," Paolo touched his stomach.

"Well, don't get too exhausted . . . you know you have to perform tonight."

"Oh really? Well, what if I want to go to sleep?" he quipped.

"I think I can change your mind."

* * *

Paolo and Sydney walked out into the main courtyard holding hands. Wherever they went, people openly stared at them. The two were a hard couple to miss. They strolled around the grounds of the resort, sat on a park bench, and kissed. Theirs was not the type of kiss teenagers do when their hormones rage wild. No, this was a kiss of love, a love between a man and a woman—a love envied by all who witnessed it.

They stood and continued their walk. They came to a group of evergreen trees. A deer and her fawn nipped at the ground. The fawn walked to Paolo; the mother lifted her head, looked at the two strangers, and continued eating. "Will you look at that? I wish I had some food to feed her." Paolo reached forward and petted the animal. He was awed at the sight. He reached for Sydney's hand. "Come on, or we'll be late for our massage."

"Paolo, I can't believe the deer didn't run away. And you touched it, wow."

"Yeah, bizarre."

As they left, another couple came over to see the deer, but the animals trotted away.

* * *

Relaxed after their massages, Paolo and Sydney sat in a large waiting area.

"Miss Hill?" A young woman stood in the doorway.

"Yes?"

"Whenever you're ready for your facial, I will be in room three, down the hall to your right."

"Thank you, I'll be there shortly."

Paolo stood, "Do you mind if I go back to the room?"

"No. I'll be fine. Are you alright?"

"Yeah, my mind is taking me someplace. I must be tired."

"Well, go take a nap. I'll see you later."

"Okay." Paolo leaned over and kissed her.

Paolo began to walk back to their suite. The late afternoon air was growing chilly. The sun set. As he passed the spot where the deer had stood, two young boys ran past him.

Paolo checked the call log on his new BlackBerry. He quietly walked to his room, haunted by a vision as he lay on the massage table: *a mushroom cloud devouring a small town.*

Exhausted, Paolo lay on the couch and fell asleep. When he awoke, Sydney was snuggled by his side. They enjoyed a romantic dinner with endless conversation and laughter.

* * *

The next morning the limo drove them to the airport. As they passed the airline terminal, Sydney asked, "Where are we going?"

"I have one more surprise for you." He pointed out her window. "That, my dear, is our personal aircraft for the day. It will take us directly back to Connecticut. My friend Tony lent it to me."

"Your old plane?"

"Yep."

"What airport are we going to?"

"Oxford. Two cars will be waiting to take us home."

"Nice. You're the best."

"Why, thank you. By the way, our flight attendant's name is Jayne. Her husband, Jim, is the captain and the second captain is Danny. They used to work for me when I owned the plane. Jayne used to be my therapist, before she became my flight attendant."

"Really?"

"Yep." Paolo changed the subject, not wanting to get into details. "You are going to love this."

The car drove up to the security gate. The driver pushed a button on the intercom system and spoke. "Two passengers for November Seven Papa Delta."

The gate swung open, and an orange Volkswagen Beetle with the words "Follow Me" written on the back escorted the limo to the aircraft.

By the stairway stood Jayne and her husband Jim, waiting to greet their passengers. A broad smile on his face, Paolo jumped out before the limo came to a stop, exasperating the driver. Arms outstretched, Paolo hugged first Jayne, then Jim. Paolo was more than a boss; he was a friend whom they loved.

Jayne was an attractive woman in her mid-forties. She had the most charming Australian accent. Paolo loved her like a sister. A retired psychologist, she often had long conversations with Paolo. Her husband Jim, an ex-Secret Service agent in his mid-fifties, was the glue to the husband-and-wife relationship and a pilot of unheralded accomplishment. Paolo trusted him with his life. The other pilot, Danny, was also a retired Secret Service agent; they served as Paolo's bodyguards when needed.

"Jim, Jayne—God, it's great to see you." Paolo's voice was excited.

"Paolo, you look great," Jayne said.

"Good to see you, Paolo," Jim remarked.

"And who is the young lady?" asked Jayne.

"That, Jayne, is Sydney Hill."

"The Sydney Hill from seven years ago?"

"Yes, the same Sydney Hill."

"Jim, didn't I tell you they'd end up together? I just knew you two would. Your eyes betrayed you, Paolo. Whenever you talked about her, your eyes brightened. I remember when we flew you to Italy after Sergio's dad died, you couldn't stop talking about her. You'd only known her for . . . what, a week?" Paolo nodded in affirmation.

"I do believe, Mr. DeLaurentis, you are blushing." Jim said with a broad smile.

Sydney approached the three. Paolo reached out and took her hand. "Syd, meet Jayne and Jim—two of the best employees I ever had."

After the introductions, Jim said, "Jayne, why don't you show Sydney around the plane? And don't forget to introduce her to Danny."

"I most certainly will, Captain," she said with a short salute.

As the two women walked up the stairs, Jim said, "She's beautiful, Paolo, actually kind of hot."

"Thanks, she is kind of hot, isn't she?" he said with a wide smile.

"Paolo, before we go on board..." Jim reached in his pocket, "I have a message from Rami. It came over the airborne fax."

"Secured?"

"Yes, it came through channel three encrypted."

Paolo read the note. "Thanks. I'll give him a call." After Bill was assassinated, Rami had reactivated Jim and Danny into the Secret Service. Paolo walked up the stairs and moved into the cockpit. Danny was seated in the captain's seat.

"So he's letting you fly today. God have mercy on us." Paolo said, laughing as he patted Danny on the shoulder. "How are you, Danny?"

"I'm fine, how about you, Paolo?"

"Fantastic, thanks for asking. How are Sharon and the girls?"

"Excellent, couldn't be better. My youngest is finally in college."

Jim stood behind Paolo and placed his hand on the shoulder of his benefactor.

"Okay, you two, you can talk later. We've got to get going."

"Aye, aye, Captain," Paolo said as he saluted Jim.

Paolo walked back into the cabin to find Sydney and Jayne talking as if they'd known each other for a lifetime. Sydney sat, her legs crossed. Her tight-fitting jeans accentuated the curves that had captured Paolo's eyes those seven years ago. The wide, deep-tan leather seats engulfed the two women. Jayne was telling Sydney about her home in Australia, a story Paolo had heard more than once. He stood between the galley and the cabin, a smile plastered on his face.

"Why are you smiling?" Sydney asked.

“Who better than me? I’m here with the two most gorgeous women in the world.”

“Please, I’m going to vomit,” Jayne said.

“I’m serious, Jayne, you two captivate my heart,” he chuckled.

“Please,” Jayne said with mock annoyance. She stood. “Can I get you a Pepsi?”

“Yep.”

“Sydney, would you like some tea?”

“Yes, thank you. Black, no sugar, please.”

“It will be my pleasure. Paolo, flight time today is just under four hours.”

“Thanks, Jayne.” Paolo sat across from Sydney. “Isn’t she wonderful?” Paolo said with a fondness in his voice.

“Yes, she is. You meant what you said, didn’t you?”

“And what was that?”

“The captivation of your heart.”

“Yes, I did, I’d die for her and Jim . . . .” His voice trailed as the engines spooled up.

“Here are your drinks.”

“Thanks, Jayne, are you going to sit with us?” Paolo asked.

“No, I think I’ll leave you two lovebirds alone. Besides, the taskmaster up front gave me all the paperwork to do.”

“Okay. Love you, Jayne.”

“Love you too, Paolo.”

The G-V departed Colorado Springs to make its way across the country. Sydney and Paolo reclined their seats and fell asleep. Paolo awoke startled¾the vision of the small town engulfed in a mushroom cloud entered his mind once again.

Chapter 52

PAOLO LOOKED OUT over downtown New Haven. It was early August and the hot humidity of the day caused condensation on his windows. Since their trip in March, Paolo and Sydney had grown apart, due to lack of face time and Paolo's secrets. He silently cursed the day Bill was assassinated; he had no desire to get so involved in the evilness of man.

His remote viewing of Payne, Duman, Abir, and the Cubans continued to be fruitless. Of course, it didn't stop the US and Russian governments from pursuing the traitors. Payne and his men were in deep hiding. One thing was certain; both governments knew Payne had two nuclear devices. And they were relying on Paolo to save the day.

Paolo knew that as the detonation time approached, his visions of the horrific event would increase in frequency. He waited. He had the vision at least once a week now, and was being pushed in a direction he didn't want to go. An external force propelled him into seeing the darkness and evilness of mankind—to what end, he wondered. Paolo was trapped by his gift, haunted by the consequences of man. His journal about the future events that would strike humanity was almost completed. His secrets piled up, and Sydney had no idea of his true paranormal abilities and his true relationship with BOET. He was caught in a lie—a lie to himself as to who and what he was.

"Hi."

"Hello, stranger."

Something in Sydney's voice troubled Paolo's spirit.

"How about dinner tonight?"

"I can't. I have to do something with Lisa."

"Oh," said Paolo. Sadness overcame him.

"Listen, I have to go. Call me later."

"Okay, bye."

Paolo sat at his desk, his silver Waterman pen in hand. An unsettled sensation traversed his body. Something was wrong with Sydney. A change had taken place. Paolo felt hopeless; his heart ached. He realized that keeping his secret from Sydney had created a rift between them, destroying the one true love he had in his life. *I'm in love with Sydney. This is not life. Where did we go wrong as a people?* He rubbed his right temple as he tried to rid his headache. He took out some paper and began writing an essay:

Our world has changed, our country has changed. We, the people of the land of the free, have lost the essence and the guidance of the forefathers of our great country. The American dream is soon to collapse, because we have lost sight of God and country.

The start of the counterculture revolution was fueled by a war in Vietnam. That war began the era of mass demonstrations, acts of true freedom. The first massive antiwar demonstrations were held in Washington, DC—more than 25,000 young people participated. In the future, that number will be a pittance as the people of our great country will take to the streets in mass protests against greed and selfishness.

It was a turbulent time and a misunderstanding of life. The sixties started the so-called counterculture revolution—a conscious and deliberate view of a world based on the ideology of peace and love. This philosophy, which has been proclaimed throughout the history of time, failed once again.

The young revolutionaries were pitted against the educated elders of the establishment. The caveat: youth of that era would influence all the generations to come, more than any other generation. This will lead to the last eulogy of mankind, a cry of regret and remorse for the missed opportunities of life. Mankind, unable to escape its own selfish desires, turned love into hate and greed. The selfishness of man, the agenda of future politicians, will evoke a world of chaos. The objectivity of man will be lost and overcome by incomplete truths, tiny white lies, and subtle evil.

Their ideology destroyed by the wanton greed of humanity, the societies of the future will be fueled by self-indulgence. Oblivious to the signs, mankind will fall to its knees, screaming for mercy. The foundations of the earth will shake with men's cries, unheard as they are whisked away by the swirling winds of deceit. The few that will try to save humanity will be mocked by society as the hippie culture of yesterday. The days of moral and social integrity are disappearing through the hourglass of time like a melting Popsicle on a hot summer day.

Don't be fooled, the subtlety of evil invades the consciousness of all humanity. The human race has begun to play footsie with the devil. And if we continue to ignore the cries of the poor and the innocent, our lives and our world will cease to exist as we know them today.

History will show we are no different from the societies of the past. The good will fade into the sunset. The bad will be swallowed up by the bowels of the earth in the darkness of the night. The winds of Mother Nature will sweep the truth under the clouds of the night sky, hidden from man's consciousness. Truth cannot be denied, it can only be hidden for a short period of time. The dawn of a new revolution awaits us. The time of truth is upon us this day.

Paolo placed the pen down, took an envelope, and addressed it to the editor of Time magazine. He folded the rough draft of his essay and placed the sealed envelope in his Out box. He went home.

Chapter 53

LABOR DAY WEEKEND arrived and for the first time, Paolo didn't attend the pig roast. At home with a pounding headache, he sat in his study and read the contractual agreement from *Time* magazine referencing his essay. The piece would appear in the Op-Ed section of the next issue of the popular magazine. His written work pleasantly edited, Paolo smiled and signed the contract.

Once again, the loneliness of the nights began to trouble Paolo. Sydney made excuses not to be with him and he understood she was slipping away. He missed her by his side. Paolo believed his angry outburst and his secrets frightened Sydney—they also frightened him. He felt he had no control over his life and who he was. The old saying is that love is patient, love is kind . . . but Paolo's patience began to run thin, and despair overtook his soul.

Paolo talked with Sydney two or three times a day. The calls were like a hot-cold water faucet—on some days, Sydney was warm and he couldn't get her off the phone; on other days, she was as cold as ice and the conversations were short. Paolo suggested they move in together; Sydney wouldn't hear of it. When he brought up the idea of marriage, she laughed.

* * *

Paolo arrived at his office on the anniversary of September 11. He still felt pangs of guilt that he could do nothing to stop the horrific attack.

Hopefully, he could prevent the next. He reviewed the morning's current gold spot reports, a cup of black coffee on his desk. Rebecca placed a series of manila folders next to it and exited his office.

His cell phone rang. "Hello, Sydney. How are you today?" Paolo's voice was upbeat.

"Paolo, we have to talk."

Paolo's stomach lurched as if he were on a roller coaster. Tentatively he said, "Okay, where do you want to meet?"

"I think it would be better if we talked over the phone." Sydney's voice was sullen.

"Alright . . . what's the problem?"

"Us."

"I'm listening," Paolo sat back and closed his eyes.

"I need some time alone."

"Oh. Exactly what does that mean?"

"I need time alone," she repeated, her voice adamant.

"So you need time alone. In other words, you're saying our relationship is over once again." There was a long silence. "Sydney, are you there?"

"Yes. Listen, Paolo, I can't do this. I have to go."

"But Sydney . . ."

"Paolo, I'm sorry."

The phone call ended. Devastated, Paolo took pen in hand and wrote about his sorrow and the love he had for Sydney.

I lie here without you by my side
The sounds of the night echo within my mind
An emptiness surrounds me
I toss and I turn
I toss and I turn
You are not here

Tears trickle down my face
The warmth of your body
Absent from my touch

The loneliness within my heart
When you are not here is like
The abyss of a great ocean

Will the loneliness ever end?
Will I ever have peace?
Will I ever be with you?

Chapter 54

PEOPLE IN THE streets milled about. It was a normal day. The image was in black and white. A mother and her child walked hand in hand. A slight breeze blew a scrap of paper into the street. The morning air was crisp, a few white clouds moved to the east. A car horn honked as two men ran across the busy intersection. A young woman walked out of Starbucks, a grande cappuccino in her hand. An Asian man opened the door to his vegetable market, while another opened a kiosk that sold sunglasses and cigarettes. The dream turned to vivid color. People walked in slow motion. A bright white flash erupted from a skyscraper. A rushing dark cloud immersed in a funnel of fire flew into the morning air. A massive wind tore down a bridge that connected the city, while the river below boiled. An immense heat swept through the streets. The scorching temperature incinerated those around him. A mushroom cloud hung over a city destroyed.

On Friday, September 30, Paolo awoke in a cold sweat. He looked at the clock; it was three in the morning. This time the vision was haunting and real. His body acted as if he had witnessed the actual event. Heart racing, frightened, he stood and tried to shake off the cobwebs.

His mind took him to the darkness of the city. *He stood between two parks and looked up. The street sign said Adams Street, another sign pointed left to Comerica Park. He was in the city of Detroit.* He put his head in his hands and cried.

He immediately went to his library and accessed a hidden wall safe behind the television. He removed a black transmitter that prevented any conversation within his house from being recorded by means of an ultrasound wave that distorted the frequency of human speech. He picked up the secure satellite phone and left a message for Rami:

"The city is Detroit, today is the day. Get there soon. May God have mercy on us all."

He tried to remote view Payne and the Cubans, with no luck. Twenty minutes later, the satellite phone warbled.

"Hello?"

"Sir," said a familiar voice.

It was Giacomo. Paolo was stunned. "Glad to hear you're back to work, Major."

"Thank you. Reference to your message, he's on his way. The general will be on site in Detroit with the team in one hour."

"You're in Washington?"

"Yes."

A wave of relief swept over Paolo. "Thank God. Major, have the general call me."

"Yes, sir. And Dad? I got a presidential promotion. I'm a colonel now."

"Congratulations, Colonel." The phone call ended. A tear welled in Paolo's already-red eyes. Five hours later, at eight o'clock in the morning, his satellite phone warbled again.

"Hello, Rami." Paolo described the vision again and what he remote viewed.

"We're here now. The Asian man opened his vegetable market, and we can see the ball park." The phone went dead.

"No, no. God, please no, don't let this happen." Paolo's face turned white. He wanted to vomit. He cried, "No, please no." He closed his eyes but nothing came to his mind. He ran over to the television.

"News alert. Pandemonium in the streets of Detroit as the Army National Guard is mobilized. We have been unable to get a news feed out of Detroit for the past five minutes. It's as if the city no longer exists." Wretched, Paolo cried, "No, no, no, damn it."

"We have just been notified the president will address the nation. Let's go to the White House."

The president stood before the cameras. "My fellow countrymen, I stand before you this day in sadness. Over the last two months, our American intelligence agencies, collaborating with our counterparts in Russia, have been tracking a terrorist group intent on detonating nuclear devices in our countries. I have been notified today by the Russian premier that a nuclear explosion has occurred in the outskirts of the Ural Mountains."

A Secret Service agent handed the president a piece of paper. He opened the paper and read the note. Tears ran down the president's face as he tried to recover. Someone handed him a tissue. "I have just been informed that a nuclear device in the city of Detroit has been neutralized. It's a joyous day here in our country today. Thank you, Paolo DeLaurentis." He regained his composure. "Let us pray for our lost Russian friends and their families who died today in the terrible attack on Russian soil." The screen switched back to the news program.

The newscaster, with disbelief on his face, said, "We pray for the lives lost in Russia today. We will be right back."

Paolo clicked the off button on the remote. "Thank you, God, thank you." The satellite phone warbled.

"Nice job, Rami."

"Not me, Paolo. If it wasn't for you, hundreds of thousands of people would have died—maybe more."

"Well, let's thank God."

"Paolo, the president would like to speak with you. We're patching him through."

"Paolo."

"Mr. President."

"Our country and our people thank you."

"Thank God, Mr. President, not me."

"I'll thank you both. I'm sorry I mentioned your name."

"No problem."

"Rami, do you want to tell him or should I?"

"You take the honor, Mr. President."

"Paolo, Colin Payne is dead."

"How do we know this?"

"The Russians had tracked him and Abir to the Urals. He was in the area of the detonation. We're confident that he evaporated in the explosion."

A wave of sadness overcame Paolo. The words of Sergio's father Vittorio came to mind. *In order to have true peace, you have to forgive.* "How many people were killed?"

"The Russians expect that casualties will be somewhere in the neighborhood of four thousand. They believe it was an accidental detonation. It could have been a lot worse."

"Yes, it could have, Mr. President."

"Rami, you can share your news with our college friend. I have a press conference that I have to attend. Again, Paolo, thank you."

"You're welcome, Mr. President." Paulo paused, then said, "Okay, Rami. When are you retiring?"

"Amazing how you know. Your gift."

"The problem is, Rami, it's inconsistent."

"Gonna retire next year. I've suggested to the president that Giacomo replace me. He has agreed."

"That's great. Does Giacomo know yet?"

"Yes, we've already started to transfer control. You should be very proud of him, Paolo. He's a good man . . . just like his father."

"Thank you, Rami, I am very proud of him. Stay in touch."

"I will, Paolo. Thank you for what you've done. Goodbye."

"Goodbye, General."

Chapter 55

NEW ENGLAND WAITED for the Indian summer of October while the world still reeled from the deadly terror attack on Russian soil. Although the United States celebrated the heroes who dismantled the weapon intended for them, a heavy black cloud settled over humanity.

Paolo faced the publicity that resulted from his name being mentioned with the honest acknowledgement he couldn't talk about it. Somewhat relieved that Payne was dead, he tried to move forward. The absence of Sydney in his life made his life seem meaningless. The love in his heart starved his being, an unquenchable thirst that could never be relieved without her being by his side. He spent his forty-seventh birthday with his daughter.

* * *

He arrived at Starbucks at four in the afternoon, journal in hand. Paolo ordered a cappuccino. The coffee shop was crowded but he found a table by a window and sat down with his thoughts.

In Starbucks without you
I've become a lost memory within you.
My heart, my life, shattered like a broken window
scattered on the ground.

"Do you mind if I sit down?"

Paolo was startled. "Not at all," he said, motioning with his hand.

Paolo offered the chair opposite him. "Please, sit." *Her face is so familiar.*

"I apologize, but . . . have we met before?" Paolo asked.

"I think so, but I can't place your face. I grew up in North Haven." Her blue eyes sparkled.

"So did I." Like a light bulb that turned on, Paolo recognized her. "You're Tina's sister, Cindy. I'm Paolo, Paolo DeLaurentis."

"Not the DeLaurentis from *Time* magazine?"

"Yep, that's me."

"Are you the same Paolo the president mentioned?"

Paolo grimaced, "Yep." He changed the subject. "How is Tina?"

"She passed away a couple of years ago of breast cancer." Cindy lowered her head.

"I'm so sorry to hear that . . ." Paolo paused reflectively. His eyes brightened. "I had this mad crush on her when we were in high school."

"She called you Paul."

"Yes, she was the only person ever to call me Paul."

Cindy sat back in her chair. Paolo felt her perfect blue eyes scan his face.

"I remember you now. You were always at the house. Amazing how life brings us back."

"So, do you still live in town?"

"No, I'm here settling my mother's estate. Mom passed away a year ago. She was eighty-six."

"I'm sorry. Was she sick long?"

"No, she never woke up, she died peacefully in her sleep."

"Your mother, God, what a wonderful lady. She always made me welcome, and she made excellent meatballs. Tina would call me when she was making them, so I could come over just as they were coming out of the frying pan. To be honest with you, they were better than my mother's. Don't tell my mother I said that," Paolo quipped. A smile on his face, he continued, "If I remember correctly, you went to Harvard, then married a lawyer. I actually remember the day you got married."

"You have an excellent memory."

"I have a talent for remembering things. So, Cindy, are you still married?"

"No, I got divorced about ten years ago. And you?"

"I'm divorced as well," Paolo paused. "Would you like to go out to dinner? There's a nice Italian restaurant down the street."

"Sure, I'd love to."

* * *

Dinner served, a bottle of red wine consumed, Paolo said, "I have to say, Cindy, time has had no effect on you. You're still a beautiful woman."

"Why, thank you. You look pretty good yourself."

Fascinated by Cindy's beauty and conversation, Paolo's thoughts were still of Sydney. He paid the bill and walked Cindy to her car. "I had a nice evening. Thank you."

"Me, too. If you're ever in Manhattan, please give me a call. I'd love to have dinner with you again." Cindy wrapped her arms around him and thanked him for dinner. They gazed in each other's eyes. Their faces moved closer, lips touched. Their embrace grew tighter and the kiss became more passionate. "My hotel isn't far from here. Would you like to come back for a nightcap?"

"Sure, I'll follow you." I have nothing to lose; somebody wants me, why not? Sydney doesn't care. She told me to date, so what the hell?

Paolo's reality for that one night was he was wanted. The need of two people to feel loved—to feel the warmth of one another even for one night—sometimes outweighs the risks involved. Cindy's hotel was several miles away, so Paolo followed her. When they got to the point of entering the hotel garage, he just kept on going. When Paolo arrived home, he wrote:

Why do I love you so much, Sydney Hill, that you destroy my heart? Why is my love for you so strong? Can anyone answer me? Why do I love this woman so much?

Paolo sat back in his chair and closed his eyes. In his subconscious, he heard: *Because you do, it is who you are—your essence—to love unconditionally, no matter what the pain and heartache, for it is better to have loved than not—for then your life would be truly empty. Your life is full because of the love you have for her.*

Paolo opened his eyes. It was clear he would never stop loving Sydney Hill. He couldn't. The love for her was imprinted on his heart, for all eternity.

Chapter 56

THE FIRST SNOW of the season fell in the second week in November. The thin white layer covered the sloped rooftops of the university buildings. Footprints tracked the pathways along the un-shoveled sidewalks. Paolo sat at his desk and stared at the New Haven Green from his office window. *I wonder what Sydney is doing? Maybe I should call her—after all, this is the holiday season. Thanksgiving is in two weeks.*

"Paolo?" Rebecca called through the intercom.

"Yes, Rebecca?"

"Sydney Hill is here to see you."

Paolo was bewildered. Sydney? What the hell is she doing here? He tried not to feel bitter, although bitter he was. She probably wants to return something. I poured my heart out to her, how could she do this to me? Paolo had totally ignored the warning signs—her need for independence, his keeping of secrets, her indecision about commitment, her fear of saying "I love you."

"Rebecca, tell her I'll be right there. Better yet, tell her to come right in."

"Yes, I will."

"Thank you. And Rebecca, I don't want to be disturbed."

"Yes, sir."

"Stop the 'sir' shit and let her in," he said tersely.

Sydney walked through the door. She wore a camel turtleneck sweater, a tan leather jacket, and blue jeans. She looked gorgeous.

Paolo noticed something in her eyes, a darkness of pain, hurt, and confusion.

"Hello, Sydney." His was not a pleasant hello. He stayed seated behind his desk.

"Hello, Paolo. Not too polite to Rebecca." It was a statement, not a question.

"I'll make sure I apologize. What can I do for you? I'm kind of busy."

"I came to apologize."

Darkness lifted off Paolo's shoulders. Still not giving her any slack, he said, "Okay, what does that mean?"

"You know I've not been myself."

"Tell me about it."

Angry, Sydney said, "Okay, I was wrong. I screwed up. But to be honest, your little tirade and little secrets scared me. For Pete's sake, Paolo, the president thanked you for saving the city of Detroit. Who are you?"

"Okay, okay," Paolo paused. "I apologized for my outburst, but still you didn't give me the time of day. You were like an ice cube. Now I'm a little angry. You really hurt me, Sydney . . . a lot. And the president thing, that's no longer a part of my life. Okay? I'm sorry." Paolo moved to the couch and sat opposite her.

"I'm sorry, Paolo, I'm not thinking right. My hormones are all screwed up."

"Your hormones? What do hormones have to do with anything?"

"Think back, Paolo. Every time I said something cold or dismissive, or wouldn't say I loved you? It always was about a week before my monthly cycle. When I get in those moods, I don't want to be around you, let alone kiss you. The thought of kissing you makes me want to vomit."

Paolo's eyes widened.

"I know my actions hurt you, so I thought it would be best if I broke up with you." She started to cry. "But it hurts too much not having my best friend around."

Paolo was shocked and tried to grasp the words she spoke. "Vomit?

Did you say vomit? The thought of kissing me would cause you to vomit? Well, that's not good."

"No, it's not. I saw a doctor a couple of days ago. The blood tests show I'm starting menopause."

Paolo moved closer to her on the couch. His empathic sense heightened, he felt her pain and sorrow. "It's okay, Syd, we can work this out."

She looked up at him. Tears streamed down her face. She kissed him. Her lips were warm and salty, and warmth filled Paolo's being. "Let's go out for dinner so we can talk. Where's Lisa?"

"She's having dinner at a friend's house."

"Okay, give her a call. Tell her we're going out to dinner and you won't be home late."

"Okay."

Neither of them ate much. They talked and decided they would try again. When Paolo arrived home, he looked up menopause on his computer. After an hour of reading, he went to bed, shaking his head.

God in his infinite wisdom created man and woman. He did this so man would have a partner in life. Man's stupidity—the temptation of Adam and Eve—screwed everything up. As punishment, man and woman were banished from the Garden of Eden and forced to set out into the wilderness to till the soil and live off the land. This biblical story has been handed down through the centuries. Theological scholars still debate whether it is symbolic or true. When man accepted the apple, everything changed—God's comic genius gave man and woman hormones.

Hormones, for the woman, guaranteed life would be a roller coaster ride. Granted, all humans have hormones. It's only in the female species that these hormones erupt on a monthly basis. Moreover, when the female reproductive cycle comes to an end, the ultimate eruption occurs—menopause, the final roller coaster ride.

For some women, menopause occurs early in life, sometimes by the age of forty. For the majority of women, menopause begins in the mid to late forties, usually ending in the early fifties, God willing. For man, God gave sports, outdoor activities, and hobbies—in other words, escapism. Then, once in a blue moon, a man comes along to try to figure it all out.

The upheavals, the emotional roller coaster of their relationship, troubled Paolo deeply. Why do people act the way they do? Why did he act the way he did? Paolo's deep and engrossing thought process nagged at him. Philosophers, psychologists, and scientists had pondered human behavior for eons. Still the academics didn't fully understand the inner workings of the human mind.

Paolo knew that childhood experiences influence who we are and how we act. Add hormones to the equation and all hell could break loose. The thoughts hung in the silence of his mind. Humankind's rationale of human behavior fell far short of the reality of man's existence in God's world.

Several days after their conversation, Paolo started to analyze their relationship from beginning to end—from when they first met to this latest incident. Sydney was right, a behavioral transformation in her personality occurred one to two weeks before her menstrual cycle. He reflected on the times their relationship had hit a roadblock, times when Sydney told him he should start dating other people, or said they were just friends. These all occurred within that time frame. He felt confident that there was no other man involved—this was something else, and if he could come to understand, then he could accept it.

Sydney started to have abrupt mood swings. Paolo became the punching bag, bearing the brunt of Sydney's anxiety, frustration and stress. She became depressed without understanding why she was depressed. She was no longer able to deal with everyday life—relationship, job, children. Paolo was put on the injured list, the designated hitter to be played again when life and hormones were balanced.

For Paolo, the love between them was real. He understood the outside influences that affected their love and damaged their relationship. Paolo had experienced a similar situation before, with his ex-wife and his mother. He decided to deal with the problem instead of accepting it.

* * *

Paolo went to Barnes and Noble, purchased several books on women's health, and then went home and spent the weekend reading them. He was amazed at what occurs to the female body and mind, all because of the pea-sized pituitary gland. He realized that Sydney exhibited all the symptoms—the migraine headache before her period, the mood swings, the fuzziness of mind and memory loss. It was as if the books were written about Sydney.

Then, in a comedic thought, he figured out why men his age date much younger women. Subconsciously men had figured it out—by the time their younger wives reached menopause, they would be dead.

Chapter 57

Winter approaches with its cold
The warmth of your heart, your love keeps the cold out
My fears undaunted by the knowledge you love me
And I love you
Loneliness envelops my heart when I am not near you
Emptiness surrounds me when I cannot hear your voice
Or feel your touch
Time seems so long without you
Hours with you are too short
Life without you I cannot fathom
Life with you seems like a dream
When you tell me you love me
You make my heart, my being, light up with joy
Oh, how I love you

The early November snowfall melted away. The fall leaves swirled along the roadside as Paolo drove his racing-green Jaguar to Sydney's house. The morning frost was not yet warmed by the sun when Paolo arrived for Sunday breakfast, just after nine.

Paolo drank his black coffee while Sydney sipped her morning tea. The *New York Times* was placed on a kitchen chair; warm gas-heated air blew through the vents.

"Paolo, do you want more coffee?"

"Sure, that sounds great." Sydney brought over the coffee pot. Paolo wrapped an arm around her backside and pulled her closer to him.

"Be careful, the coffee is hot."

"Yes, dear. I just love holding you near."

"Stop," she said, pulling away from him.

"What's the matter?"

"Nothing. Why does there always have to be something wrong? It's just my hormones." Sydney walked over to the counter, put the coffee pot down, and left the room.

"Well, I guess I said the wrong thing," Paolo said in a whisper as he shook his head. He reached over the chair, picked up the *New York Times*, and opened it to the sports page.

Twenty minutes passed before Sydney came back. She sat down next to Paolo and said nothing. Paolo placed his hand on hers. "This will all work out, it's just a moment in time."

"I don't have the patience I used to. You and me, everything . . . I don't even know if I love you." She sat with her arms folded against her chest.

The comment sent an aching pain right to his heart. Not letting on, he said, "Sydney, listen to me. I did some research. In my car I have a book you should read on menopause. The book might help you understand what's happening to you." Paolo continued, "Did you know the amount of sunlight, exercise, and how often and what you eat and drink can help alleviate your symptoms?"

Sydney placed her arms on the table and clasped her hands in a prayer-like manner. "No, I didn't."

"Menopause has a profound effect on all aspects of a woman's life—relationships, desires, body changes. Menopause is a life-changing moment. To be concise, your hormones go crazy. This craziness contributes to your mood swings, anxiety, and tears—and even the fuzzy thinking you've mentioned. And if you're already stressed out, then your stress becomes even more exasperated due to the fluctuating hormones."

Sydney listened.

"When I was at Barnes and Noble, I met two women—Mary and Rose. They were probably in their late sixties. Mary's story about the change of life was amazing."

Sydney stared at Paolo for a moment. "What did you do, go up and say 'Excuse me, have you gone through menopause yet?'" The sarcasm in her voice could have cut glass.

Paolo ignored the comment and went on to detail the conversation with Rose and Mary. "Let me go out and get the book." Paolo rose from the table and went out to his car.

When he got back, Sydney was shaking her head. "Paolo, I don't need this crap, I'm fine." He said nothing and placed the book on the table. She picked it up and skimmed through the first five pages.

Paolo left the house with a dull ache in his heart, an indescribable pain deep within him.

Paolo knew that in Sydney's mind, menopause was not the problem. What she failed to understand is what Paolo understood: he gave her the opportunity to change, but she decided not to. Sydney, being an independent woman, never relied on a man: she didn't have to change; Paolo needed to change, not her.

* * *

Over the next several weeks, the road got tougher. The Thanksgiving holiday was shared with family members, not with one another. Paolo figured by the middle of December, Sydney's hormones would be out of balance. Even though he realized this, he still asked her to share the Christmas holidays with him. Sydney held him off, and then on December 19, she said no. On December 21, she said yes. Paolo tried not to give her a hard time. He felt like a ping-pong ball and buried himself in his pain.

Paolo turned more and more to pen and paper, trying to alleviate the heartache with his written words. The pain, like a hook that speared his heart, never seemed to stop, and when he was not with her, it only increased. Paolo pondered day and night, asking himself why? What went wrong? There was no answer other than a change of life, a moment in time.

* * *

They spent part of Christmas Day together. "Merry Christmas, Lisa." She stood in the doorway. Paolo leaned down and gave her a hug.

Sydney stood behind her and said, "Merry Christmas, Paolo, come in." She gave him a kiss on the lips and took his overcoat while Lisa took the Macy's shopping bag filled with presents. The two walked into the living room. The crackling fire in the fireplace warmed Paolo's bones. The spruce tree was lit with red, green, and white lights. The song "I'll Be Home for Christmas" played in the background.

"Can I get you something to drink?"

"No, I'm fine, Sydney, thank you." The atmosphere was strained. "Lisa, in the shopping bag are presents for you and your brother. Where is Andrew, by the way?"

"Where else?" Sydney rolled her eyes.

"Ah yes, the girlfriend's house. Oh, to be in love," Paolo said with a sarcastic chuckle. Sydney didn't react to the sarcasm. "Lisa, can you make sure Andrew gets his present?"

"Sure will. Can I open mine now?"

"Lisa!" her mother said.

"Go right ahead, it's Christmas. We should all be happy."

Sydney sat down next to Paolo on the couch. The blazing fire lit up their faces. Sydney placed her hand on his leg. Paolo placed his hand on hers.

"Oh my God, Paolo, this is beautiful. Mom, look."

"What a beautiful present..."

"Rio helped me pick it out, thank her."

"Is it real?" Lisa asked.

"Lisa!" her mother exclaimed.

"Yes. It's so you'll never forget, a diamond lasts forever."

Sydney hit Paolo in the arm. "That's really corny."

"I can't help it," Paolo said as he rubbed his arm.

"What did you get, Mom?"

"Lisa!" Sydney exclaimed again. "Go and get the presents under the tree for Paolo. Paolo, open your presents first," Sydney said.

Paolo opened the present from Lisa and Andrew. He received old-style parchment paper for his writings. He unwrapped the present from Sydney. It was a 1920 gold-filled Mont Blanc fountain pen. "My God, this is beautiful. Where did you ever find it?"

"A friend of mine collects pens. She found it at an antiques dealer. I thought you would like it, since you like to write."

"Thank you, thank you, it's beautiful." Paolo gave her a kiss and said, "Now yours."

Some would say Paolo was a fool. He wanted to make Sydney happy, and he tried his best. Paolo gave her a wrapped shirt box. "This is a combined gift—you'll understand when you open it."

With a puzzled look on her face, Sydney opened the box. Inside was a card. Paolo snatched the card away and said, "You can read this later." Underneath the red tissue paper, she found a pair of plane tickets—one for her and one for him.

"What's this?" She took the tickets out of the boarding pass folder and started to cry. "This is the most wonderful present I've ever gotten." She threw her arms around Paolo and kissed him passionately.

"God! Why don't you two get a room?"

"Lisa!"

"Ah, Mom, get over it." They started to laugh. Lisa left the two and went to family room to watch *It's a Wonderful Life.*

One of Sydney's life wishes was to celebrate her birthday in Paris before she was fifty. The present was a fourteen-day vacation, with the first stop in Paris and the last in Sorrento, Italy. That night Sydney read the card.

I love you is all I can say
In the morning when I rise
You are on my mind
I love you is all I can say
Forevermore you are in my mind
I want to love you

When you are not near, I feel despair
How I long for you to be near

As the sun radiates the ground
Your love for me makes me sound
How I long for you always
And when the day ends
And my head hits the pillow
As the moonlight dances through the window
As I sleep through the night
I dream of you
I love you is all I can say
When the sun rises
And my day begins again
I think of you
I love you is all I can say

Chapter 58

THE WAR BETWEEN men was igniting, the evil tendrils of the devil reached for mankind. Paolo's journal was now three-quarters full.

Paolo learned to adapt during the times of the month when Sydney's hormones went haywire. He could do nothing, other than support her. Sydney's thought process was muddled. She avoided Paolo when the conflict between her heart and mind began. Paolo remarked to a friend that he was dating Dr. Jekyll and Mr. Hyde. He understood Sydney; the problem was the pain in his heart never left. The seven to ten days of upheaval tormented his mind. At one point, during one of her up mood swings, Sydney asked Paolo if he would move in with her and Lisa. For some reason, he replied, "Why don't we wait until we return from our trip in March?" Of course, he wanted to jump at the opportunity; instead, he restrained himself.

* * *

"Can you and Rio come over for dinner tonight?" Sydney asked.

"Of course, what time would you like us to be at your house?"

"How about six? You can come over earlier if you'd like."

"Six will be fine, depending on the traffic. Do you want me to bring anything?"

"No, just you . . . it's a shame the kids will be here. I'd love to be alone with you, if you know what I mean?"

"I most certainly do."

"Paolo?"

"Yes."

"I can't wait to be with you."

"Me, too."

Paolo picked up Rio at her mother's house. "Hi, Dad." She entered the car, leaned over, and kissed him on the cheek.

"How are you, my daughter? You look beautiful as always."

"Thanks, Dad." She flashed her perfect white teeth.

Rio was five feet seven, with flowing brown hair and beautiful green eyes. She could easily have become a model or an actor. Instead, she was in her second year of law school at Yale. The passion of Rio's soul to correct injustice, to fight for the little person and advocate for the downtrodden, made Paolo proud. He often told her she'd been born in the wrong era. He knew all too well the need for her services in the future. His legacy to her was the resolve and the financial strength to help when the time came.

It was a cold February day. As they approached the house, a light snow began to fall.

Sydney had made chicken cutlets Milanese topped with a lemon wine sauce, a favorite of Rio and Lisa, with spinach and roasted garlic mashed potatoes.

"This is delicious, Sydney," Rio remarked.

"Thank you, Rio."

"Yeah, Mom. This is superb," Lisa took a second cutlet. "Paolo, can you pass me the rolls, please?"

"Absolutely. Syd, this was an excellent meal." Paolo handed Lisa the basket of crescent rolls.

"Not as good as yours, I'm sure."

"Oh, I don't know. This is good, but this is my recipe, so maybe I can take a little credit." Paolo laughed.

"Dad!"

"Sorry, sorry."

"Paolo, are you excited about going to Paris?"

"Sure am, Lisa. Paris is a beautiful city, from what I hear."

"Dad, you've been to Paris before."

"You have?" Sydney quipped.

"Yes, for a short period of time."

"You never told me. Another one of your little secrets?"

Paolo picked up on the sarcasm. "National security business, I can't talk about it."

"National security? Come on, Dad, what are you, James Bond?"

"Funny, Rio. I did some consulting work there."

"Yeah, okay, consulting work." Rio rolled her eyes.

Lisa continued, "Well, James, are you going to Italy?"

"Yes, now Italy is truly beautiful. Not that I'm prejudiced, mind you, but Italy . . ." Paolo sat back, remembering the beauty and character of the place he wanted to retire to.

His mind took him to a room. *A person was face down on a desk, a jacket covered his head. A 9mm gun lay next to him.*

"Dad, Dad." Rio's hand shook his arm. "Are you there?"

Lisa's hand waved in front of his eyes.

"What, what?"

"Where did you go, Pops?"

Paolo tried to shrug off the vision. "Just thinking about Italy, sorry."

The three women looked at each other. Sydney said, "You're weird."

"Thanks, honey." The four laughed. Inside, Paolo wanted to vomit. Death was on somebody's doorstep.

"Can I go with you guys to Italy?" Lisa had just about gotten the words out of her mouth when Sydney replied, "I don't think so." She dragged out the word "so."

"I'll tell you what, Lisa. Giacomo will be home in the summer for a month. How about I take the six of us on a vacation to Italy and if you want, we can go to Paris as well."

Lisa's voice was filled with excitement, "Are you serious? Paolo, that would be totally awesome, all of us together. Wow."

"What do you say, Rio, do you think you can swing it?"

"A free trip? You can bet your ass I'll be there."

"Syd, what do you think?"

"Sure, but we have to check with Andrew to see if he can come, and the summer is still a ways off."

"Please, Mom, can we go?" Lisa begged.

"I think we'll be able to swing it, but first Paris for my forty-seventh."

Chapter 59

SYDNEY'S EAGERNESS TO visit the City of Lights with Paolo overshadowed the turmoil inside her. Her lifelong dream to celebrate her birthday in Paris now a reality, sharing the dream with Paolo or anyone else didn't matter.

For Paolo, the romantic city portrayed in movies provided the background for their escape. *In his mind's eye, he could picture the Eiffel Tower in the distance, Sydney and him in a quiet embrace as they stood on a bridge over the river Seine. Their bodies formed the silhouette of a heart. The two gazed into each other's eyes. Sydney's hair blew in the light breeze of the warm spring day. Their lips touched in a passionate kiss that made strollers envy the two lovers . . .*

Paolo's intercom snapped him out of his daydream. "Yes, Rebecca?"

"Your Federal Express package is here."

"Thank you."

Paolo, with a little help from Rebecca, arranged their itinerary. They would stay three days in Paris, then fly to Amalfi and tour Italy for eight days. Their plan was to drive along the Amalfi coast, spend two nights in Sorrento, three nights in Ottati, and end the trip in Rome with Sergio. A hopeless romantic, Paolo decided to throw caution to the winds.

"Rebecca?"

"Yes, Paolo?"

"What time is the limo picking me up?"

"At one o'clock."

"Good, good, good. Am I forgetting anything? Did Rio call?"

"If she had, I would have put her through." Rebecca stood in the doorway as Paolo sifted through his desk drawers. "Paolo, what are you looking for?"

"What, what?"

"What are you looking for?" She walked closer to him.

"My stupid passport," he said in exasperation. "I can't remember where I put the damn thing."

Rebecca shook her head and laughed, "Paolo, you gave it to me so you wouldn't lose it. Your passport is in the safe with your tickets and itinerary."

"I must be losing my mind, Rebecca. I don't want anything to go wrong. This trip is important to Sydney—it's a dream come true for her to be in Paris for her birthday."

"And of course you're going to make sure she celebrates her birthday in Paris."

"Yes." Paolo paused. "I sense a hidden meaning behind your words. Something on your mind?"

"Paolo, I realize you love her." Rebecca picked her words carefully. "But you're not the same person lately. She's hurting you."

Paolo looked at her with a slight irritation in his voice. "Rebecca, I care for you, and we've been together for a long time. And you probably understand me better than anyone else. Even my children don't know me as well as you do." He stopped and looked at her as he considered the right words. "You're partly right. But I need to figure this out myself." Paolo started to get flustered and curtly stopped the conversation, saying, "I don't want to talk about this right now. I'm going on vacation, and I'm going to have a fabulous time. Rebecca, I appreciate your concern, but I'm okay—there's nothing to worry about. Okay?"

Rebecca shook her head. "Okay, Paolo. Please be careful. You mean a lot to me, too."

"That's why we make a good team . . . now leave me alone," he said with a smile. "By the way, Rebecca, have I told you how much I like working with you?"

Rebecca laughed, "Yes, Paolo, many times."

As she walked out of his office, Paolo said, "Rebecca, Arnaud call yet?"

"No. Would you like me to track him down?"

"No, that's okay. He won't let me down. I told you, he got me the Belle Etoile suite at Le Meurice." Paolo used his best French accent although he sounded a bit like Inspector Jacques Clouseau.

"Yes, many times and yes, I know—for free."

"I guess it helps to have friends in high places," he retorted.

"Paolo?"

"Yes, my dear?"

Hesitantly, she said, "Don't do anything stupid, you'll just end up getting hurt."

With the movement of his hands, he swooshed her out of his office. "Go, go back to work." Paolo leaned back in his chair as she walked out of his office. *Is it that noticeable?*

"Paolo?" Rebecca said over the intercom.

"Yes?"

"Your booking agent is on the phone."

"Tell Dominique I'll call her when I get back from my trip."

"Okay."

Paolo's intercom buzzed again. "Yes, Rebecca?" His voice was strained.

"Sorry, Paolo. Dominique wanted to remind you that the contracts are ready to be signed for your speaking tour."

"Call her back and tell her to FedEx them to me at Le Meurice and I'll sign them."

"Will do. Luigi Luciani called as well, I told him you were on vacation."

"Thank you, Rebecca . . . and please, no more interruptions except for Sydney and Rio."

"Okay."

Luigi Luciani was the chairman of a national foundation trying to restore the morals and awareness of social injustice to future executives. He had approached Paolo after reading the article in *Time* magazine about his philanthropic efforts. A year later, after months of negotiations, Paolo finally agreed to do a speaking tour at area colleges. So far, Dominique had lined up Yale, Harvard, Columbia, Providence College, and Princeton. Paolo would speak about the declining economic morality of corporate America.

Rebecca appeared in the doorway with Paolo's jacket, passport, tickets, itinerary, and the Federal Express package. Paolo finished his phone call with Rio. "Okay, I will . . . I love you, Rio." He hung up the phone and looked at Rebecca. "The limo is here?"

"Yes, the driver took your luggage to the car. The car is in front of the building. The driver's name is Sam."

"Excellent. You know how to reach me if there are any problems." He stood and walked over to Rebecca, who handed him his jacket and papers. As he put on the jacket, he said, "Thanks for the concern, Rebecca." He leaned over and gave her a kiss on the cheek. "I'll see you in three weeks."

"Be careful and have a great time."

"I most certainly will." He left the office.

Chapter 60

Love has no boundaries, it is ever-consuming
It will always be the love
I have for you

SYDNEY AND PAOLO held hands as they boarded the Air France airbus. The flight attendant directed the couple to their first-class seats. The flight time to Paris was seven hours and twenty minutes; they would arrive at nine o'clock in the morning.

After the aircraft reached cruise altitude, they enjoyed a light dinner, and nestled into their wide-berth seats. They shared a kiss, whispered goodnight, and slept through the evening. Sydney awoke first as the sun rose over the Atlantic. The blue sky glistened and the overcast clouds below reflected the yellow and orange of the sun. She turned and buried her head on Paolo's shoulder and soon fell back asleep.

"Excuse me, Mr. and Mrs. DeLaurentis, we will be landing soon. Can you kindly put your seats in the upright position?"

"Of course," Paolo replied.

Sydney said, "Of course, but we're not married."

"Oh, I am so sorry! Please forgive me."

"It's okay," Sydney said.

Embarrassed, the flight attendant walked up the aisle as she checked the seat belts and seat positions of the other passengers.

"Mr. and Mrs. DeLaurentis sounds nice," Paolo said.

Sydney made no comment. She pointed out the window, "Look, Paolo! Paris! The Eiffel Tower."

Paolo leaned over and peered out the window. "It's a beautiful city," he said, matter-of-factly.

"Paolo, thank you so much for taking me to Paris." She kissed him and held his hand.

"Happy birthday, Sydney Hill."

As the aircraft taxied toward the gate, the flight attendant spoke. "Welcome to Paris. On behalf of your Air France flight crew, we would like to thank you for flying with us today. The weather is sunny, and the temperature on this first day of spring is currently fifteen degrees Celsius. We hope you enjoy your stay in Paris, the City of Lights. Again, thank you for flying Air France."

Paolo and Sydney stood in the aisle, stretched their legs, and exited the aircraft. Sydney walked ahead of Paolo. After they cleared customs, an older man approached them. Paolo recognized him and held out his hand. "Jean Paul." The two had met at a party at the Belle Etoile in celebration of the rescue of Arnaud's daughter, Emily.

"Mr. DeLaurentis, welcome back to Paris. Arnaud gives you his best. He regrets he will not be able to meet with you. You are not to worry, monsieur, Arnaud arranged everything for you. I am at your disposal. I shall take you to Le Meurice."

"Why, thank you, Jean Paul. It's good to see you again. This is Sydney Hill." Paolo placed the emphasis on Sydney's last name.

"Hello, Jean Paul. Please call me Sydney."

"Bonjour, Madame Hill . . . I mean Sydney . . . the car is right this way." They walked across the terminal, Paolo on one side of Jean Paul and Sydney on the other.

"It's been awhile, Mr. DeLaurentis; I didn't know if you'd still remember me."

"How could I forget you, Jean Paul?" Paolo placed a hand on his arm, "and it's Paolo."

"You are so kind, Paolo."

The three walked out into the beautiful Paris spring air. Paolo took a deep breath. "Fresh air, at last." Sydney and Paolo entered the black Mercedes sedan.

The French countryside whisked by as they drove to the City of Lights. Water from a recent rain lay in puddles on the brown ground. The farmers were ready to toil their fertile lands. It was early spring—the trees were beginning to bud and the flowers were starting to bloom. The forty-minute ride was quiet as Jean Paul segued to the city streets.

The sights of Paris began to come into view—the Opera Garnier on their left, the Eiffel Tower across the Seine. Paolo touched Sydney's thigh. "Look!"

Sydney had her eyes closed. "What? What?"

Paolo pointed, excited. "Sydney, Paris."

The car turned right on the Rue de Rivoli. Jean Paul said, "Monsieur Paolo, we will arrive shortly at the hotel."

"Thank you, Jean Paul."

"The Eiffel Tower," Paolo pointed. They were parallel to the Seine.

"What a beautiful sight!" Sydney moved closer to him. "I'm sorry about what happened on the airplane."

"What do you mean?"

"The last name thing."

"Oh, don't worry about it. Let's just have a good time, okay?" Deep within, Paolo hurt like hell.

"Excellent." Sydney leaned over, grabbed his hand, and kissed him on the cheek.

"Madame, the Louvre is ahead to your left." Sydney scooted across the seat to get a glimpse. Paolo kissed her neck as she leaned over him to get a better view.

"Stop." Sydney giggled as she shrugged her neck.

The Le Meurice Hotel, located opposite the Tuileries Gardens, was built in 1835 and renowned for its excellent service and accommodations. It was one of the most luxurious hotels on the Rue de Rivoli. The Seine and the Louvre were both within walking distance.

Sydney gasped at the sight. "Paolo, I feel like we're in a Monet painting."

"Yes, it's beautiful."

The sedan pulled up to the front of the hotel. Before Jean Paul could park the car, attendants on either side opened the passenger doors.

"Monsieur DeLaurentis and Madame Hill, welcome to the Meurice," the bell captain said in flawless English.

Jean Paul exited the car and opened the trunk.

"Please, allow us to take care of the bags," the bell captain said. "Right this way, Monsieur. We will take you to your suite, no need to check in. Mr. Arnaud arranged everything for you."

"Thank you so much." Paolo walked around the back of the car and approached Jean Paul, while Sydney walked into the lobby with the door attendant. "Jean Paul, thank you for picking us up at the airport." Paolo extended his hand. He placed a one hundred euro note in the palm of Jean Paul's hand.

"No, Paolo. I cannot accept this. Arnaud would be upset."

"I won't tell him if you don't," Paolo said with a smile. "Take your wife out to dinner."

Jean Paul took the money.

"Merci, Paolo, merci, and Madame Hill . . . yes . . . Paolo, she is beautiful and in the city of love—my Paris." He said this with a smile that spoke of the love Paolo had for her.

"I'll call you if we need you. As it stands, you will pick us up here in three days?"

"Yes."

"Very well, Jean Paul, have an excellent day."

"You as well, Monsieur. Merci." He held up his hand with the one hundred euros. "Merci, Paolo."

"Merci, Jean Paul."

Paolo entered the hotel. The lobby was decorated in Louis XVI furniture. Paolo walked across the gray-and-white marble floor. He saw Sydney in the distance, reading a plaque on the wall. Guests dotted the atrium. They stared at Paolo as he moved toward Sydney.

He overheard the quiet whispers, "Who is he? He looks so familiar."

"I have no idea, now stop staring."

"He's so familiar . . . I know him from somewhere," a woman said to her husband.

The husband ignored her; he looked more at the beauty of the woman reading the plaque.

Paolo wrapped his arms around Sydney's waist and embraced her tightly. "What are you reading?" he whispered in her ear.

"The history of the hotel," she said, continuing to gaze at the plaque. "Did you know it was originally founded in Calais in 1771, for rich British aristocrats on their way to Paris after crossing the Straits of Dover?"

"No, I can't say I knew." He kissed her ear.

"Stop it." She continued, "This man, Charles-Augustin Meurice, housed the travelers in his coaching inn in Calais, while he arranged for their transportation to Paris. He realized the travelers would be tired from their thirty-six-hour journey. In 1871, he decided to open another hotel, this time in Paris, naming it the Meurice. The hotel has been in this location since 1835."

"Wow, that's interesting," Paolo said, not caring, more interested in making love than in the history of the opulent hotel. She pulled free of his grip, turned, and kissed him lightly on the lips.

"What?" he said. "It is the City of Love."

"Men," she rolled her eyes.

Paolo laughed.

"Right this way," the bellman said.

They held hands as they walked to the elevator.

Chapter 61

The wind echoes in my mind
The thought of you, the love I have for you—will it ever end?
I stand here on the cliff of time, the cool salt-water breeze
striking my face
The reality of love, the despair of love, breaking my heart in two

THE COUPLE WALKED across the marbled lobby floor of Le Meurice past the main elevators.

"Where are we going?"

"Your surprise awaits, my lady. Follow the bellman," Paolo said in a mischievous voice.

The bellman escorted them to another elevator; he swiped the credit card key through the reader. The gold doors slid open to reveal a Charles X loveseat upholstered in a deep royal red. Sydney and Paolo leaned their hips against the sidewall rail, their images reflected in the mirrored doors opposite them.

Sydney wrapped her hands around the nape of Paolo's neck and kissed him gently and passionately. She whispered into his ear, "Thank you, Paolo, for this wonderful birthday present."

"You're quite welcome."

The bellman smiled as the doors opened to the seventh floor. Paolo and Sydney turned toward the front of the elevator and Sydney gasped in awe.

The Belle Etoile suite was considered one of the most spectacular hotel suites in the world. The 2,250-square-foot suite had two private entrances. Clearly the suite's most distinctive feature was its private 3,200-square-foot landscaped terrace. The terrace provided a 360-degree view of Paris.

"Monsieur DeLaurentis, if you follow me, I shall give you a tour of the Belle Etoile."

"That won't be necessary I'm familiar with the suite." Paolo handed the bellman a twenty-euro note. "Thank you. Is our luggage in the master bedroom?"

"Oui. Enjoy your stay. Merci, Monsieur."

"Merci." Paolo watched the elevator door close. He turned around to find Sydney was gone. Paolo walked through the gallery into the living room. The French doors opened wide to the terrace, a soft breeze drifted through the room. Paolo stood in the doorway and admired Sydney as she gazed at the city, her body outlined in the sun and the city of Paris in the background. He was captivated by her beauty.

Why do I love her so much? A smile crossed his face.

"So, what do you think? Did I do okay?"

Sydney turned and walked toward him. "I think you did better than okay, this is un-fucking believable."

Paolo was surprised at her vulgar description. "Wow, that was a hell of a comment. Un-fucking believable?"

"Oh my God, Paolo. Look!" Excited, Sydney began to point out the historic sights of Paris. "Over here, the Eiffel Tower. Over there, the Louvre. Notre Dame, the Musee d'Orsay, the Arc de Triomphe . . . did you do okay? Holy shit, you did better than okay." Sydney threw her arms around him and buried her head in his chest. "Thank you, thank you." She looked up into his eyes and kissed him. Their passions aroused, they walked to the master bedroom and made love, then silently fell asleep in each other's arms.

Paolo awoke. Sydney lay sleeping. He put on a pair of pants and a shirt and went out on the terrace. He absorbed the sight: the blue sky sprinkled with white puffy clouds, padded wooden lounge chairs interspersed with potted green plants. The sun cast its shadow on the late afternoon. The noises of the city below drifted on the warm spring air. Paolo sat quietly, immersed in the ambiance of the Parisian skyline.

Sydney found her way to the terrace. Barefoot, she wore one of Paolo's button-down shirts; her bare thighs glistened in the Paris sunlight. She stood before him as he sat on the lounge chair. He grabbed her waist and pulled her close to him. The palms of his hands lay on her silky thighs. Sydney pulled his head into her chest and hugged him. She lifted his head, clasped his face and looked into his eyes. "This is so unbelievable, Paolo. Thank you." She leaned down and kissed him.

Paolo grabbed her backside and looked up at her. "I hope this made you happy."

"I'm extremely happy, extremely happy."

"I'm glad. Now help me up."

Sydney reached for his arms. He stood and embraced her, then grabbed her backside. "I love your ass," he said as he squeezed her.

She grabbed him as well. "I love your ass, too."

"Thank you. How about a glass of wine? Then I'll tell you part of the story about how I first found out about this hotel and the infamous Arnaud."

"Sounds like a plan. I'll go get the glasses."

"Okay. I'll get the wine. White okay?"

"Yes, that's fine."

Paolo came back with a bottle of Château Lafitte Chardonnay. Sydney picked up two fine crystal goblets and asked, "Paolo, since you've been here before, can you give me a tour?"

"Sure, I'll give you the ninety-nine-cent tour." He opened the bottle and poured the delicate Chardonnay. He lifted the glass by its stem. "To you and me, may we always be together."

Sydney replied, "To Paris."

Not the answer Paolo wanted to hear. The glasses chimed as they lightly touched.

They walked through the suite and visited the living room first, with its early nineteenth-century Charles X style furniture. The inlaid mosaic with intricate wood patterns spoke of an era of extravagance and opulence. The kitchen, outfitted for a culinary chef, had all the utensils necessary to cook a gourmet meal fit for a king. After visiting the second bedroom, they went into the gallery.

"Do you think these paintings are real?" Sydney asked.

Hung on the walls were Monet's *Poppies Blooming*, Renoir's *Girl with a Hoop* and Van Gogh's *The Old Mill.* Strategically placed lights highlighted the vivid colors of the art.

"I don't think so."

"They appear to be authentic." Sydney ran her hand across the painting.

"I'll ask Arnaud."

"Why?"

"Because this is his suite, he lives here during the off-season, so he says. The reality, he visits once a month."

"Very interesting, it must be quite expensive."

"Extremely, and he can afford it," Paolo replied. "Come on, let's go to the master bedroom."

"Is that all you think about, sex?"

"No, you have to see the view, then we can think about sex," he laughed.

They entered through the double doors of the master suite. It featured a super-king-size bed off to the right, with a loveseat at its base. Full-length drapes covered the window.

"Sit here." Paolo pointed to the couch. "I'll open the drapes."

The only thing amiss was the music of a prelude. Paolo opened the curtains and the stage of Paris came into view. Multicolored roofs blanketed the city. In the distance was the Palais Garnier and Sacré-Coeur, the Catholic Basilica. Sydney walked toward the bank of windows, saying, "This is absolutely beautiful."

The two stood side by side in awe as they gazed out on the city of Paris.

"I'm sure you saw the marbled bathroom with the Jacuzzi," Paolo said.

"Yes, it is beautiful."

"The view from the Jacuzzi is breathtaking; can I interest you in a bath?"

"Why not? Will you tell me the story of Arnaud?"

"Oui, mon ami, but first, I shall go get the wine."

Paolo pointed to a thermostat on the wall outside of the bathroom. "If you turn the heat on, the floor will heat up. So your little baby feet won't be so cold," he said as if speaking to a little child.

"Oh, you won't warm me up?"

"I most certainly will," he said as he wrapped his arms around her and kissed her.

She pulled back. "Why don't you go get the wine, I'll fill the Jacuzzi. How hot do you want it?"

"I'll leave that up to you. I'll be back in a minute."

"I'll be waiting."

Paolo returned with wine bottle in hand. Sydney's clothes lay neatly on the bathroom floor. The lights dimmed, the room was illuminated by light from the windows filtering through the semi-opaque shades. Sydney was already in the Jacuzzi, the water up to her neck. Her naked body glistened in the bubbling tub.

"Hi, handsome. Care to join me?" Sydney said seductively.

"Absolutely." Without another word, clothes and all, Paolo entered the Jacuzzi with a splash.

"Oh my God, you have your clothes on. Are you crazy?" She laughed.

"Care for another glass of wine?"

"Only if you take your clothes off."

Paolo took off his shirt and fumbled with his pants.

"Do you need some help?"

"I can't unzip my pants."

Sydney moved toward him, "Let me try." Her wet, naked body tantalized him. She unzipped his pants.

"Boy, you're good," he said. He started to get aroused and kissed her neck.

"Not in the water."

"But you look so good," Paolo said with a boyish whine.

"No, not now. Later," she replied with a gleam in her eye.

"Fine." He pouted.

"Okay, so what's up with this guy Arnaud?"

"More wine?" He held up the bottle.

"Sure."

He poured the wine. "Arnaud . . . how do I put it . . ." Paolo paused. "Several years ago, before I knew you, I was doing some consulting work for the Italian government. The investigation brought me to Paris."

"Investigation?" Sydney asked.

"Yes . . . at first the situation appeared to be innocent . . ."

"Situation? What the hell were you doing?"

"We were working on a pretty touchy subject that turned ominous. I really shouldn't tell you."

"Oh, really?" She slid her body toward him. Their naked bodies touched side by side, legs outstretched. "I'm sure I can make you tell me." She placed her hand on his thigh.

"Now stop. That's not fair."

"Oh?" Her hand moved higher up his thigh.

Paolo removed her hand.

"I hate your little secrets." She folded her arms across her chest.

Paolo's voice changed. His eyes were less intense. He grabbed her hand, not wanting to start an argument. "I'm sorry, I know you do. Long story short, Arnaud's daughter, Emily, was kidnapped, and I happened to stumble upon the kidnappers."

"Why was she kidnapped?"

Paolo said nothing.

"Oh, I forgot—you can't tell me."

"No, I can. Arnaud was an arms dealer. By accident, I inadvertently stumbled upon his daughter's kidnappers." He lowered his head. "I used my gift to help rescue her."

"How? The clairvoyance?"

"Yep. Anyway, Arnaud and I have been friends ever since."

"Wow, so he feels obligated."

"Somewhat. I've helped him over the past couple of years, and he's made a lot of money with my influence. I'm really not sure he feels obligated. I know he's appreciative when it comes to Emily, but other than that, it's business."

"I'm sorry for prying. I know you don't like to talk about . . ."

Paolo changed the subject. "Shall we get dried off and get something to eat?"

"Sounds good. Can we eat in the hotel restaurant? I hear the food is excellent."

"It is."

Paolo stepped out of the Jacuzzi and grabbed one of the two white cotton velour bathrobes. He held the other robe open for Sydney. She stepped out of the Jacuzzi, her body gleaming from the rays of the setting sun that peered through the shaded window. Paolo wrapped the robe around her and began to rub her dry.

Exhausted, they had a quiet dinner and fell asleep in each other's arms.

Chapter 62

SYDNEY LAY ASLEEP. Paolo picked up his BlackBerry and looked at the time—seven o'clock, one in the morning in the States. He exited the hotel and made a left on the Rue de Rivoli. He passed an outdoor café filled with chatty Parisians and absorbed the aromas of the bakeries as they prepared the day's tasty treats. A hunger pang stirred at the pit of his stomach. *I could go for a croissant and a cup of coffee.* Paolo crossed the congested street to the seventeenth-century Tuilerics Garden, at one time the home of the Royal Palace. Two small children ran by, chased by their mother as she spoke in her native French dialect. Paolo could only imagine what she was saying: *"Come back here, you two; wait till your father hears about this."*

People are the same. It doesn't matter where you were born, everyone is the same. Differences in culture, yes; still, we humans remain the same. We want to love and want to be loved. Yes, not much difference between us.

He walked to the Grand Couvert, to one of the two cafes in the garden. He chose a table and ordered a cup of coffee and a croissant. When he finished, he stood and dusted the croissant crumbs off his shirt, and then started to stroll the gardens. Paolo's cell phone rang.

"Hello, Rami."

"Hello, Paolo, how are you?"

"I'm fine, in Paris enjoying this wonderful spring day. What can I do for you?"

"I'm sorry. I didn't know you were away. Call me when you get back. Have a great time."

"Thanks, Rami. I'll call you when I get back." A wave of uneasiness swept over him. Paolo looked at his watch. *A quarter past one in the morning on the East Coast. Why did he call me?*

Paolo inhaled the fresh, crisp morning air of the bustling city. The locals sauntered about the park. A police siren with its distinctive European sound awakened him from his daydream.

Paolo crossed Terrasse des Feuillants, a wide walkway with neatly trimmed trees on either side. He took a left down a similar but narrower pathway; the trees were almost at full blossom. The vivid green colors splashed across the blue sky. Paolo easily spotted the Louvre in the distance. He continued eastward. He stopped at one of the four fountains with its man-made ponds. Paolo watched the spew of water as it sprayed into the morning air.

"To your right is the Seine River," the heavily accented voice behind him said.

Paolo looked straight ahead. "Arnaud, my friend, funny meeting you here."

"Ah, Paolo, Paolo, my friend, you knew I would be here. That is why you are here," Arnaud said with a coy smile. "Remember, my friend, I am well aware of your gift. It was here that you reunited my Emily and me. I will never forget that, my friend." Arnaud was privy to Paolo's gift of clairvoyance. He reached in his back pocket and pulled out a wallet. With his elbow, he nudged Paolo's arm. The billfold opened. Inside was a picture of Emily.

"She's beautiful, Arnaud. Thank God she takes after her mother."

"Oui, my friend." He gingerly closed the billfold and placed it back in his pocket, as if it were a priceless gem.

Paolo began to walk toward the Seine. "Care to take a stroll?"

"After you, my friend," Arnaud said as he gestured with his cane to show Paolo the way.

They turned right on Terrasse du Bord de L'eau. Paolo said, "I'm glad to see you, Arnaud. It's been too long."

"Yes, my friend, it has. You know I'm with the DGSE?"

"Ah yes, the famous French secret police. Yes, I knew that. What's going on? When we last talked, you were supposed to be in Corsica at your estate."

"I was as of last night, until I received a phone call from the director inquiring why you were here. You've become a celebrity in the intelligence communities since your president mentioned your name on that terrible day. The director asked if I would speak to you."

"About what?"

"Why you are here."

"For one reason and one reason only. I'm on vacation with Sydney."

"Yes, that is what I told him. Still, he wanted me to come and speak with you. So since I have not seen you in quite a while, I thought I would come and say hi."

"Well, good to see you, Arnaud. The suite is beautiful, thank you."

"My pleasure. Your girlfriend is quite beautiful," Arnaud said with a leering smile.

"How do you know? That's a stupid question, of course you know. I'm being followed, aren't I?" Paolo was irritated. His relationship with Sydney was private, and he meant to keep it private. The fact that he was being followed annoyed him. "So let me ask you something, you little piece of French shit."

Arnaud was taken aback at Paolo's reaction. He stopped walking.

"Why am I being followed? I'm here on vacation. This is nobody's business but mine." Paolo's eyes flared. His penetrating gaze caused Arnaud to step back. A bead of sweat appeared on the Frenchman's brow.

"I am deeply sorry, my friend. I will disband the detail." His eyes to the ground, his voice remorseful, Arnaud touched Paolo's shoulder. "I am sorry. I will make sure from this moment on, you will not be followed. But you must understand, my friend, our world is different now . . ."

Paolo cut him off. "You don't know how different our world is. I came here to vacation with the woman I love. I want to be left alone. I'm not pissed off at you, Arnaud, and I appreciate you coming here to tell me, but . . ." Paolo rubbed the left side of his head; the pain caused his eyes to squint. They walked in silence.

"I'm sorry. I didn't mean to get angry with you. So tell me, how did you get involved with the DGSE?"

"After the arrest of the terrorists Abir and Duman, I had to inform the DGSE of my history—or, I should say, they already knew about my history. They recruited me, and I didn't have a choice—either join or go to jail. I chose to join."

"I understand."

"Then, after the nuclear explosion in the Urals, the director approached me about our relationship and how you helped your country find and neutralize the bomb in Detroit. I told him that our relationship was a business one."

"How did they know about us?"

"They had a picture of us sitting at the outdoor café, the day you gave Emily back to me."

"Do you think the director believed you?"

"No. If he did, I would not be here. He thinks you are in the intelligence community. He wants to make sure there will be no problems while you are here in Paris."

Paolo touched Arnaud. He looked into his eyes and said, with sincerity, "Don't worry, Arnaud, you can tell him there will be no problems."

"That, my friend, I know."

"Paolo, Paolo," the sound of a female voice came from behind them. A broad smile came across Paolo's face as he turned. Sydney was walking toward them.

"That must be Sydney?"

"Yes, it is."

"Well, I should be going."

Paolo held out his hand to stop Arnaud. "No, stay. I'd like you to meet her. Business is business—this is personal."

"Are you sure you are not in the Mafia?"

Paolo smiled at the joke. "No. Sydney was curious about you, I know she'd like to meet you."

"Ah, you know what they say about us French—we are irresistible to your American women."

"I'm not worried."

"Not worried about what?" Sydney kissed Paolo on the cheek.

"Oh, nothing. Syd, I'd like you to meet my friend Arnaud."

"Ah, the mysterious Arnaud." Sydney held out her hand.

Arnaud took her hand, looked into her eyes, and bent at the waist. Ever so gently, he kissed her hand. "Paolo surely understated your beauty. You are like a goddess."

"A goddess? I'm flattered. Paolo, I'm a goddess." She flashed a Hollywood smile at Arnaud.

Paolo rolled his eyes.

"I told you, my friend, they find us irresistible."

"Please. I'm going to get sick."

Sydney stared at the two with a puzzled face.

"Paolo, it is always good to be with you. I have an appointment that I have to attend. I hope you enjoy the Belle Etoile. If there is anything you need, please call me, my friend. My contacts in the City of Lights are many. Sydney, it was my pleasure to meet you. I envy my friend here. You are most spectacular."

"Thank you very much, Arnaud. Have a great day."

"I most surely will."

Paolo and Arnaud hugged. "Tell Emily I said hi."

"Most certainly, my friend." Arnaud turned around and walked toward the Louvre.

"What a line of B.S. What is he, a car salesman?"

"Pretty close," replied Paolo. "Pretty close."

"It seemed that the two of you were pretty animated—is everything alright?" Sydney asked.

"Everything is fine, just a little misunderstanding among friends."

"I see," Sydney responded tentatively.

"How about some breakfast? There is a café across from the Hotel Regina. Then we can go to Louvre. What do you say?" Paolo's voice was upbeat.

"Sounds like an excellent idea."

They sat next to each other at a small circular table. Their breakfast consisted of croissants and cheese omelets. Both were amazed at the amount of traffic that sped past them.

"Look at that, Paolo! A woman wearing high heels and a dress, riding to work on her bicycle."

"Yep." *Paris is a city unique unto itself—uncompromising in culture and yet beautiful and free-spirited, like New York. It's one of a kind.* Paolo and Sydney spent the remainder of the day at the Louvre and walked the streets of Paris while they shopped for their children.

They enjoyed an extravagant meal at the hotel. The restaurant was decorated in the style of Louis XVI; they sat in opulence, drinking wine and laughing. They ended the evening with a nightcap. Sydney and Paolo snuggled on one of the padded outdoor lounge chairs on the Belle Etoile terrace. The two watched the glow of the city lights and stared into the darkness. They fell asleep under the stars that twinkled above in the majestic night sky.

Chapter 63

So long, I must say to you today
I will miss you while you are away
My heart will ache because you are not near
Love has no boundaries, love is ever consuming
It will always be the love I have for you
So long, I must say to you today
And when you decide to come home
I will be here to love and to hold you

WHEN MORNING CAME, Sydney ordered room service while Paolo showered. She was dressed in a long, dark-blue, open-front cardigan, a tight body-fitting shirt, and jeans. Sydney looked as if she had stepped out of a fashion magazine. Paolo wore an Italian blue contrast shirt with French cuffs, brown khakis, and a blue blazer. He sat in the bright morning sun as he drank his black coffee and watched Sydney walk the terrace. The brilliance of the sun's rays laid shadow to her. Paolo stared as she gazed at the Parisian skyline. The Eiffel Tower loomed to her right, the Louvre to her left. His heart fluttered at the beauty that stood before him.

"I wish I had a camera. You look magnificent this morning."

Sydney turned and faced Paolo. She leaned against the railing between two potted plants. "Thank you. I don't feel magnificent."

"Well, you sure look magnificent." Paolo stood and walked toward her. "The city of Paris is a beautiful sight, isn't it?"

"Yes, Paris is beautiful." Her voice was melancholy.

"Are you okay?"

"I'm fine." She put on her best smile.

"You don't sound okay."

"I'm okay, probably jet lag." She placed her hand on his.

"Do you want some tea? A little caffeine might help. I'm going to get more coffee. I can heat up some water for you."

"No thanks, I'm fine. I'm going to walk around the terrace."

"Okay, enjoy."

Paolo poured himself another cup of black coffee and watched Sydney. *Why do I have such a hunger for this woman?* She was the woman in his dreams, the silent yet ethereal being that clutched his heart and nagged at his soul. He became a prisoner within his own heart. Even his children whom he loved dearly didn't have the impact this woman had on him. The questions loomed inside him. His eyes were clouded by the darkness of his love for her.

To truly love is to give up your life for others. It is to make yourself vulnerable—vulnerable to the hurt, the pain, the sorrow, the joy, and the happiness that love has to offer. It is to love unconditionally, not wanting anything in return, and to know you love another human being with a complete love that can never be questioned.

"Paolo, Paolo, are you there?" Sydney's voice broke the silence of the morning. She stood before him, waving her hands in front of his face.

"Of course I'm here, where else would I be?"

"You seemed to be zoning out, are you okay?"

"Yes, I'm fine. I was just thinking about how gorgeous you are. I love you, Sydney Hill. I love you with my whole heart." As he said this, peace settled over him, like a warm, gentle breeze. "Why, thank you. What are our plans today? Paolo, are you crying?"

"No, it's springtime allergies," Paolo wiped the tear from his eye and composed himself. "Today is Eiffel Tower day, so I thought we could . . ." His cell phone rang. "Hello? . . . Good morning, Jim . . . Excellent, thanks for letting me know . . . I don't think so . . . Tell Jayne and Danny I said hello. Thank you for calling."

“That was Jim. The plane is in London. They’ll arrive in Paris this afternoon. Tony wanted to know if we need the plane.”

“Do we?” Sydney said.

“I don’t think so. They’re not going to be here that long. Besides, we still have another two days in Paris, then off to Sorrento. I’ll check with Tony next week, and if the airplane is still in Europe, then we’ll take it home. How does that sound?”

“Sounds fantastic.”

“I need to make a couple of business calls, then we can get going.”

“Me too, I want to call Lisa before she goes on her hiking trip. Do you mind if I go do a little shopping?

“No, have a good time. Tell Lisa I said hi and when you come back, we’ll head over to Notre Dame.”

“Okay, I’ll be back in a couple of hours.” Sydney leaned over, placed her hand on his cheek, and kissed him. “Thank you, Paolo, you’re a wonderful man.”

“Thanks. Have a nice time.”

“I won’t be long.” Sydney walked back into the suite.

“I love you, Sydney Hill, I love you,” Paolo whispered. He went over to the balustrade and turned toward the east as he called his daughter. Then he called Arnaud to confirm the arrangements for dinner that night.

“Arnaud, Paolo. Are we all set for tonight? . . . Excellent, how much will it cost me? . . . Arnaud, you don’t have to . . . Forget about yesterday, that’s over with . . . How much? If you don’t tell me, I won’t show up . . . Euros or dollars? . . . Excellent, get me the bank info, and I’ll have Rebecca transfer the money . . . I’ll talk to you soon.”

Paolo hung up the phone and called Rebecca. He walked back to the lounge chairs and fell asleep in the cool spring air.

* * *

Paolo awoke to the blare of a car horn from the street below. He had a thunderous headache. He checked his BlackBerry for the time. Four o’clock. He had slept for five hours. In his search for some Advil, he came across a note Sydney left him. He read it and went to the bedroom.

Sydney lay on the bed sideways in a black baby-doll lace negligee. Paolo undressed and lay beside her. He touched her bare thigh, then gently kissed her cheek. Sydney smiled and snuggled close to him. He kissed her warm mouth. They embraced and made love.

"I have a surprise for you tonight."

"You do? I thought you just gave me a surprise."

"Besides that surprise."

"What is it?"

"I arranged—or I should say Arnaud arranged—dinner for us at the Eiffel Tower at Le Jules Verne." He said this in his best French accent.

"Oh my God, do you know how hard it is to get reservations?"

"Yes, Arnaud told me. Nonetheless, we're going to dine at Le Jules Verne. I don't know about you, but I'm starving."

"Me, too. I'm going to take a shower and get ready."

"Okay, I'll use the other bathroom." Paolo leaned over and gave Sydney a kiss. "You are absolutely beautiful."

Sydney pushed him gently. "Thank you. Now get going before we spend our entire vacation in bed."

"Oui, Madame."

* * *

Paolo walked into the dressing area of the bedroom. Sydney sat before the mirror putting on her makeup.

"Are you almost ready to go? The concierge called, our car is here."

"Yeah, I'm just about done." She put on lip gloss that made her lips shine.

"I still don't understand why you use makeup. You're already beautiful."

"You men will never understand." She stood up and straightened her outfit. "I'm ready."

Paolo smiled. "You look stunning tonight."

"Thank you." She kissed his cheek.

They walked to the private elevator, and traveled the seven stories to the lobby in silence. When the door opened, Jean Paul was there to meet them.

"Jean Paul, what a pleasant surprise," Sydney said.

"Oui, Madame. It is such a pleasure to see you again."

"Good evening, Jean Paul."

"Good evening, Paolo. Arnaud said I am to be your driver for the evening. Wherever you would like to go, I shall take you."

"Excellent, Jean Paul. First stop, the Eiffel Tower. We're having dinner at Le Jules Verne."

"Very nice, monsieur, you have a beautiful night for it, the sky is clear."

Paolo turned to Sydney. "The restaurant is four hundred feet in the air. We'll have a fabulous view of Paris tonight."

"I hear the food is superb."

"I hope so. If not, we'll have exceptional food when we get to Sorrento."

They walked through the hotel lobby, past a young couple talking to the concierge about dinner reservations. Paolo overheard their disappointment; they couldn't get a reservation at Le Jules Verne. "Sydney and Jean Paul, I'll be right back—I want to talk to these people."

"Okay, we'll meet you in the car."

"Okay, I won't be long."

Paolo approached the couple. "Excuse me, you need a reservation at Le Jules Verne?"

The young man, in his late twenties, said, "Yes, they're booked. Tonight is our last night in Paris, then we head back to the States. We're here on our honeymoon and when I made the plans, I forgot to make reservations."

"It's okay, honey, it's not the end of the world," his young wife said.

"Hi, my name is Paolo. I might be able to help."

The newly hired concierge raised an eyebrow in fascination. His expression said, *These Americans, what do they know? If I can't get them a reservation, nobody can.*

"Let me make a phone call. What are your names?"

"I'm Mike, and this is my wife Kathy." Mike offered his hand; Paolo reached out and shook it.

"Glad to meet you, Mike and Kathy, my name is Paolo DeLaurentis. Give me a minute and let me see what I can do?" He turned away and walked a short distance, then called Arnaud.

Kathy whispered to her new husband, "Do you know who that is? That's the guy who was on the cover of *Time* magazine."

The concierge interrupted their conversation. Unaware of who Paolo was, he said, "I do not think this Paolo whatever his name is will be able to help. I can get you a reservation here at the hotel restaurant if you let me . . ."

Paolo returned to the newlyweds. He heard the concierge and interrupted, "If you don't mind waiting an hour and a half . . ."

"Not at all," the husband chimed in, "Not at all." The couple's faces lit up as they said in unison, "Thank you so much. Thank you, thank you."

"It's no problem."

"Should we give you our last name?"

"All you have to do is just show up in an hour and a half." Paolo turned to the concierge. "Would you like me to get you a reservation as well?" he said sarcastically. Mike and Kathy giggled to themselves as they walked away.

Paolo walked out into the evening air. Darkness had descended upon the City of Lights. Jean Paul stood by the car and opened the door for Paolo.

"Jean Paul, I've made reservations for the young couple I was talking with at Le Jules Verne. If you don't mind, could you come back and pick them up in an hour and a half?"

"It would be my pleasure. I will come back here in an hour. That way I will not miss them. What are their names?"

"Mike and Kathy."

"I will pick them up as you requested."

Paolo leaned over and entered the car. Sydney said, "You're too good. How did you ever get them a reservation? The restaurant is usually booked months in advance."

"I made them an offer they couldn't refuse."

"Ooh, that type of talk turns me on. Now really, how did you do it?"

"Like I said, I made them an offer they couldn't refuse."

"You Italians," she said, leaning over to kiss him.

* * *

They held hands for the fifteen-minute drive. The Eiffel Tower glistened in gold light. Its majestic beauty impaled the evening sky. Comprised of seven thousand tons of iron and paint, the tower was built in 1889 as a centennial tribute to the French Revolution. Almost torn down in 1909, the structure had become the iconic symbol of Paris. If you cared to walk to the top, plan to climb over sixteen hundred steps.

The car came to a stop at the corner of Quai Branly and Pont d'lena. "That is absolutely beautiful," Paolo said. He looked through the archways at the lights of the Ecole-Militaire on the horizon. Jean Paul opened the door and offered his hand to Sydney. Tourists and Parisians roamed the base of the tower. The night sky with its brilliant stars, the clean spring air, and a slight chill captivated the romantic side of Paolo.

"Paolo, this is beautiful." Sydney's eyes sparkled in the evening light. She squeezed his hand.

"Yes, it is. I believe the elevator is over there," he said, pointing to his right.

"You mean the one that says Jules Verne on the awning?"

A door attendant approached them. "Mr. DeLaurentis?"

"Yes."

"Your table awaits you, sir, right this way."

As the ground below them grew smaller, they watched the cable carry the elevator to the second platform.

"This is beautiful. We should bring the girls here. They would love it."

"What they'd love is the shopping. It would cost us a fortune if we brought them here," Paolo chuckled.

The doors opened. Music played in the background. Claude, the general manager of the restaurant, met them. "Good evening, Madame Hill and Monsieur DeLaurentis. We have been expecting you. Please follow me, I will show you to your table."

The diminutive man led the way. Sydney pulled on Paolo's arm. "Paolo, we're the only ones here?" Her voice cracked.

"Yes, just you and me, for at least an hour and fifteen minutes. Claude, when Mike and Kathy arrive, please let me know—I'd like to speak with them. I'm sure you will seat them away from us, so they may have their privacy as well."

"Oui, monsieur."

"Please call me Paolo, and this is Sydney. I'll pay for Mike and Kathy's meal. Whatever they want, please give it to them."

"Oui, Paolo. Please feel free to walk around and enjoy the view."

"We most certainly will, thank you, Claude." He turned to Sydney. "Hello, are you there?" Paolo waved his hand in front of her face.

"I, I . . ." Sydney stuttered, "I'm speechless. I can't believe you did this all for me?"

"Yes, I did, because I love you and I want to make you happy."

"Wow, thank you so much. What a view," she exclaimed. "Look, the Ferris wheel at the end of the Jardin des Tuileries."

"Look over here." Paolo pointed to the north, "The Arc de Triomphe."

"Absolutely breathtaking."

The Champs-Élysées glowed as they peered through the glass. The tower's steel girder legs swept past them. Down below and over the horizon was the most spectacular view of Paris. The city's lights dotted the horizon. Paolo and Sydney wandered the restaurant. A waiter offered them glasses of white wine. The air was filled with romantic French music as three musicians serenaded them.

"Would you care to dance?" Paolo asked.

"I'd love to."

They held each other tightly, swaying to the rhythm of the music. They went back to their table hand in hand, past the kitchen located at the center of the restaurant. Paolo pulled Sydney's chair out for her.

"What a gentleman."

"Thank you."

Sydney sat down. Paolo leaned over and pulled back her hair. He kissed her neck.

"The chairs are comfortable and the tableware . . ." She paused and picked up a fork. "Look at this, Paolo."

"Yes, quite interesting."

The tableware was made specifically for the restaurant. It had a unique, contemporary flair and mimicked the inside of a Jules Verne airship.

"I hope you don't mind, but I took the privilege of ordering for us."

"Not at all. What did you order?"

"I ordered you beef tournedos with foie gras and vegetables. For me, roasted veal. And for dessert, a chocolate soufflé and dark chocolate, praline, and hazelnut ice cream."

"That sounds better than sex," Sydney quipped.

"Well, I don't know about that."

* * *

"This was excellent. I can't wait for dessert."

"Yep, it was great. The veal was very tender."

The waiter cleared the table and the musicians played "La vie en rose."

"I love that song; I wish I understood French," Sydney said.

Paolo took hold of her hand and said, "Hold me close and hold me fast, the magic spell you cast, this is la vie en rose. When you kiss me, heaven sighs, and though I close my eyes, I see la vie en rose. When you press me to your heart, I am in a world apart, a world where roses bloom and when you speak, angels sing from above. Everyday words seem to turn into love songs. Give your heart and soul to me and life will always be la vie en rose."

"Are those actually the words?" Sydney asked, incredulous.

"Yes, they are," he continued. "Everyday words seem to turn into love songs. Give your heart and soul to me, and life will always be la vie en rose." Paolo reached into his blazer and pulled out a Harry Winston box. He opened it and said, "Sydney, will you marry me?"

Sydney stared at the two-carat pear-shaped diamond ring. Stunned, she picked it up and held it to her chest. A tear trickled down her face. "I can't." She reached for Paolo's hand, "I don't know if I love you." She placed the ring on the table, stood, and left. Paolo sat stunned, his heart broken in two, ravaged by the words she'd spoken.

Claude approached. "Monsieur, Mike and Kathy have arrived."

"Thank you, Claude. When Sydney returns, tell her I'll be right back."

Claude said apprehensively, "Paolo, Sydney got on the elevator when your friends arrived."

Paolo looked past his reflection in the window and gazed out into the darkness. Unable to look at Claude, he bowed his head into his right hand. "Oh, okay," he said. Claude walked silently away.

Paolo stared out the window. The cold, stark iron pillars lay placid in the blackness of the night. His soul was drenched in sorrow. Tears flowed down his face into his hand. He grabbed a white linen napkin and wiped his face. He composed himself in his hurt and heart-wrenching agony and stood to meet the newlyweds. A nearby waiter saw the ring on the table.

"Monsieur, you left this." He held the two-carat diamond ring in his hand.

"It's okay, I don't need it anymore. You can keep it." Paolo was visibly upset.

"Monsieur, I cannot accept this. Maybe you should sit down. I will get you a drink."

"No, no, I'm fine, thank you." Far from fine, his face ashen, Paolo said with a stern voice, "I'll be insulted if you refuse my gift."

"Oui, Monsieur, thank you."

Chapter 64

The memory of your voice, the memory of your touch
Will put me at ease, so lonely I will be.
My longing for you will seem like an eternity
So long, I must say to you today
Goodbye, I cannot say
How I would love it if you would stay

PAOLO SPOKE WITH Mike and Kathy. Their exuberant faces acknowledged the gratitude they had for this man they didn't know.

"Thank you so much," Kathy said.

"Yes, this is unbelievable. I can't believe we're the only ones here. Would you care to join us?" Mike offered to get a chair.

"No, thank you, I must get going."

"My wife thinks you were on the cover of *Time* magazine."

"Mike," Kathy said, stretching out his name.

"Yes, I was."

"Mr. DeLaurentis, please excuse my husband." Kathy gazed into Paolo's eyes. "You are a very kind and generous man, thank you."

"No problem. I hope you enjoy the evening." Paolo started to walk away. He turned back and said, "If we should never meet again, have a wonderful life filled with love for one another."

The couple didn't know what to say, other than "Thank you."

Paolo was met at the elevator door. "Monsieur Paolo, Jean Paul is waiting for you downstairs."

"Thank you, Claude. Your staff is outstanding." Paolo was silent for a moment and then said, "If we should never meet again, Claude, may your life be filled with joy and love." The elevator door opened and Paolo stepped inside. Paolo saw the sadness in Claude's eyes; he knew the man would revisit the story of how two lovers' hearts were broken in the Jules Verne. The waiter would donate the ring to an orphanage.

Jean Paul met Paolo by the elevator. "Did you take Sydney to the hotel?" Paolo's voice was sullen.

"Oui."

"Was she alright?"

"She was crying. She said nothing except thank you when we got to the hotel."

"Oh."

Jean Paul held the car door open. "Back to the hotel, Paolo?"

"Not yet. Take me for a drive . . . toward the Arc de Triomphe and down the Champs-Élysées." Paolo hoped the drive would be long enough that when he got back to the hotel, Sydney would be asleep.

Jean Paul drove toward the Arc. "Paolo, do you wish to stop someplace?"

"No, I'll be fine, Jean Paul." After a pause, he went on, "I don't understand women, I guess . . . the mixed signals, the hormones . . . the sad part, Jean Paul, is . . . she loves me."

Jean Paul listened.

"I had everything planned. I'd ask Sydney to marry me, the lights of Paris below us. She would say yes, a long embrace, a passionate kiss in the city of love. I would whisk her off to Sorrento to the hotel with the balcony overlooking the bay. Two lovers standing on the terrace, we would watch the sunset. A warm evening breeze would blow the curtains into our suite. I'd hold her in my arms, kissing her in the way that made her body tingle. We would make love. Our lives together would be as one." Paolo sighed deeply. Tears trickled down his cheeks. “I guess that plan didn’t work,” he said with a whispered chuckle.

As the car sped past the Grand Palais, Paolo’s cell phone rang. He answered with the hope it was Sydney.

“Hello.”

“My friend, are you alright?” Arnaud said.

“I will be in time, I suppose.” Not wanting to talk, Paolo added, “We’ll probably check out tomorrow. Thank you for the suite, Arnaud, I appreciate what you did.”

“Paolo, you can stay as long as you want. I will stay at my villa in the country.”

“Thank you, but no, life goes on.”

“Goodbye, my friend.”

“Goodbye, Arnaud.”

* * *

Sydney Hill walked out of Le Meurice, still crying, with her suitcase in hand. Black mascara ran down her face. The attendant opened the car door for her. “The car will take you to the airport, Madame.” She bent over to enter the Mercedes limo, then looked up and stopped.

“Excuse me, I thought this car was for me?”

“It is, Miss Hill. Would you care to join me? My name is Dr. Colin Payne.”

At that same time, the doorman pushed her into the back seat. He ran to the driver’s side, jumped in, and sped off down the Rue di Rivoli.

“Duman, to the chateau.”

“Yes, Dr. Payne.”

Chapter 65

JEAN PAUL PULLED in front of the hotel just as a Mercedes limo sped off down the street. Paolo leaned forward in the car and put his hand on Jean Paul's shoulder.

"Thank you, Jean Paul. Please stay in the car, I can manage myself."

"I am sorry, Paolo."

"Thank you."

Paolo went into the hotel, his head down and his hands tucked into his pockets. Oblivious to the sights and sounds of the lobby, he felt overcome by a sense of the surreal. Paolo's heart ached. He dreaded the confrontation that would take place—not one of anger but of sorrow and disappointment.

What will I say? What will she say? Thoughts rambled in his brain. *Perhaps she will change her mind and realize the true love she has for me.* This thought was fleeting. Paolo understood Sydney wouldn't change. He did know she loved him—no one could convince him differently. Paolo sensed the love she had for him. He battled the demons within himself. He questioned himself and now he had to confront the fact that Sydney had said she didn't love him. *Instead of letting her go, I continued to pursue her. I love her so much, I couldn't let her out of my life. I should have waited. No, I had to find out. Why couldn't I leave well enough alone? So what if she couldn't say she loved me. Her actions showed me she did.* Stuck in a quagmire of thoughts and denial, he didn't recognize where he was when the elevator doors opened to the suite.

Distraught, his heart racing, Paolo walked through the gallery to the living room. A note was taped to the lampshade. He sat on the plush couch and held the folded piece of paper in his hand. Tears streamed down his face as he read the already tearstained note.

"My dearest Paolo, I am so sorry. Words can't explain how I feel about you. To know you are hurting because of me rips at my heart. I am deeply fond of you, and I care so much for you. I am sorry I can't marry you. My own demons confront me every day—your secrets, my emotions—you know better than I do. I should have listened to you and gotten help. I sometimes want to spend the rest of my life with you and then other times I don't care—that is the conflict within me. How I hurt, knowing I have hurt you. Our friendship over the years has been a special gift we share. Your love for me is so powerful I can't grasp its meaning. Maybe that is what scares me. I can't love you the way you love me.

"This beautiful birthday present—what can I say, it is a gift I will never forget.

"By the time you read this, I will be on an airplane heading back home. I thought it would be best that I leave. I couldn't bear to see the pain on your face. Paolo, you are the nicest, kindest, gentlest man I have ever met and I am probably making a big mistake. I am so sorry that I hurt you. Please forgive me.

"Sydney."

The words *I can't love you the way you love me* struck Paolo deeply. The realization that the love he had for her was divine and unconditional gave him no repose. Paolo tore up the note and whispered, "So long, Sydney Hill, have a great freak'n life." He reached for his cell phone and called Tony, and then Jim.

"Hi, Jim, hope I didn't disturb you and Jayne."

"Not at all, Paolo, we're still on eastern time. What can I do for you?"

"What's going on with the airplane over the next couple of days?"

"Nothing—we're actually waiting to hear from you."

"You guys up to going home tomorrow?"

"Absolutely."

"How soon can we leave?"

"You tell me."

"How does tomorrow morning at nine sound?"

"Fine, I look forward to seeing you and Sydney tomorrow."

"Jim, Sydney won't be with us," Paolo said with sadness in his voice.

Jim paused, then said, "Okay. We'll be waiting for you."

Paolo hooked the phone to its charger. He went into the bedroom and packed. He could smell Sydney's lingering perfume. He sat on the bed and cried himself to sleep.

Chapter 66

I sit here in the solitude of my mind thinking of you
The sun glistens over the water
The waves break against the sea wall
As my heart beats to your memory
All entwined as one, my being not without you
For you are in my heart
How I long to be with you
I sit here with the sun splashing on my face
With you on my mind

JEAN PAUL PICKED Paolo up at the hotel at eight o'clock the next morning and brought him to the airport.

"Thank you, Jean Paul, for these last several days. I hope to see you soon." Paolo handed Jean Paul two hundred euros.

Jean Paul accepted the offering. "I wish you all the luck, Paolo. You will see—she will come back."

"From your mouth to God's ears, Jean Paul."

Paolo walked into the private air terminal, where he cleared customs. Danny, the other pilot, met him at the gate.

"Hello, Danny," Paolo said in a subdued voice.

"Hello, Paolo."

"How long to Oxford?"

"Almost eight hours."

"Excellent. Jayne on board?" Paolo's statements were short and to the point.

"Yes sir, she is."

"Is El Capitan flying today?"

"Yes, he is." They continued their walk to the fifty-million-dollar jet in silence.

Paolo climbed the ten steps. Jayne stood in the doorway and waited for her friend. "Good morning, Paolo."

"Good morning, Jayne." Paolo made a quick left turn to the cockpit and patted Jim on the shoulder.

"Hi, Jim."

"How are you, Paolo?" The question hinted that the crew was aware of his breakup with Sydney.

"Shitty." Paolo moved to the cabin and sat in the rearmost forward seat. Jayne followed.

"Hi again, Jayne."

"Hi, Paolo. Are you okay?"

Paolo immediately sensed the sincerity in her voice and the sympathy in her eyes. "Word travels fast."

"Tony called and gave us a heads-up."

"Certainly is nice to know people care about you," Paolo's voice cracked.

"Yes, we do. Can I get you some coffee?"

"How about a shot of tequila?" he suggested with a grin.

"So you think tequila is a good idea?"

"Probably not. Coffee would be fine. Thanks, Jayne."

Jayne brought Paolo a cup of coffee. She walked forward to the crew quarters. Paolo reclined the leather seat as the plane hurled down the runway and pulled away from the French airstrip. The sound of the synchronized engines gave rhythm to Paolo's mind as he began to analyze what had happened with Sydney.

Paolo closed his eyes and recalled the times Sydney had ended their relationship and brought the emotional roller coaster to a stop. Sydney's explanation was that she loved him so much, it was easier for her to say goodbye than endure the pain of him leaving her.

"This is bullshit. I'd give you anything and everything; I would sacrifice everything for you; I'd die for you, Sydney Hill," he whispered.

As he sat, some forty-eight thousand feet above Europe, Paolo realized his behavior was destructive. His continued acceptance during her emotional breakdowns took an unforeseen toll on his mind and body. Paolo became a prisoner to her love and the love he had for her. His desire not to allow their love to fade away only imprisoned him more.

Paolo remembered the happy times. How he loved the sweet sound of her voice when she greeted him. The concern in her tone when she asked how he was doing filled him with happiness and hope. Then, when the relationship fell apart, the absence of her love almost drove him to despair. Paolo waited and hoped for Sydney to call, just to say hi, to say anything. Every morning for a month, he went to a local Starbucks, making excuses to Rebecca for his absence from the office. His stomach would be in knots as he waited for Sydney to call. Stranded with his cappuccino, Paolo wrote down his thoughts and feelings. Pen in hand, words flowed from his soul onto little pieces of white paper. Entrenched in deep sorrow, Paolo would walk the Brewster Estate in solitude into the late hours of the evening. He lay awake at night, unable to fall asleep, deep in thought. His only outlet was the endless harmony of words churned out onto white paper bought at the corner drugstore. The story would become his life. His soul was laid bare to all who would read about the eternal love he had for a woman. He took the blame for the demise of their relationship upon himself. He often wondered what he had done wrong. Now, he had to relive it again. He dreaded being alone.

* * *

"Paolo, can I get you some more coffee?"

Paolo snapped out of his reverie. "What?" he barked.

"Can I get you some more coffee?"

"Sure, Jayne . . . I didn't mean to jump down your throat. Are you interested in talking to an old fool?"

"Of course. It's what are friends for," Jayne said, sitting opposite him.

"I need to let Sydney go. I can't convince her to love me. The best

I can do is be her friend." With resignation, he sighed, "I need to finally let her go. My problem is, Jayne, how do I handle the pain of her absence? The pain of losing her and not having her to love." Tears welled in Paolo's eyes and his voice cracked. "The pain won't leave, nor will the love I have for her." Paolo's mind rambled on in random thoughts. His eyes closed for a brief moment. He took a deep breath, sighed, and opened them. He stared out the oval window, his head propped up in his right hand.

"I believe God put her in my life, so I'd understand what true love is. The question I ask myself is, would he also take her away from me?" He stopped and wiped a tear from his eye, then looked at Jayne. "I guess so."

"I'm sorry, Paolo, this must be extremely difficult for you." Jayne went on, "There are many people who say love is a choice, and feelings are circumstantial. You chose to love her, you accepted the love God put in your heart for her. Now you need to use the love in your heart for others. We can never understand the ways of God. We can only trust that where we are in our life is where God wants us to be, even if it hurts like hell." Jayne paused, "Paolo, I think this love is different, this love will touch the fabric of many people."

Paolo absorbed her words. "It's funny, I know the love in my heart for her always existed within me. I believe if we had met in a different period of time the love I have for her would still be here in my heart." Paolo placed his hand on his chest. "You've heard the saying that actions speak louder than words?"

"Yes."

"Well, her actions were contradictory to her words. Sydney couldn't tell me she loved me, yet she loved me with her actions. The meaning of life is based upon both words and actions, not one or the other. Actions and words are of equal importance to me, to all of us. Words can kill the heart as easily as being stabbed with a knife. And now my heart is slowly dying."

Jayne sat and listened. Paolo continued, his words coming from his soul, a soul touched by the hand of God.

"What I couldn't comprehend was the underlying issue to

her psyche, what made Sydney tick. What I found out—" Paolo paused, "was that part of the problem was she was going through menopause. The other part—my secrets—only compounded her stress. Her hormones were in such disarray that her rational thinking was turned off. Now, couple that with a lousy marriage and painful divorce . . . it's no wonder she couldn't commit. I asked myself why she didn't understand I loved her for who she was as a person, an individual. Why couldn't she accept the fact I fell in love with her because she warmed my heart? All I wanted to do . . . was make her happy with the love I had for her. Maybe we as a people can't accept love anymore, we've grown too callous."

Jayne leaned forward and placed her hand on his knee. "In life, our fears often dictate our choices, thus destroying our happiness. We often forget our earthly existence is short-lived. Do you think she held back her love for you because of her own fears of rejection?"

"Possibly. Will I ever find out? Probably not."

Paolo stopped his diatribe, stared out the window for a moment, then turned and faced Jayne, his face stained by tears. "I still can't understand what happened. My life is now in the hands of God. Sydney has touched something deep within me. The bond I have with her is too strong to break, at least up till today." He turned his head and looked out the window again into the cloudless sky.

"I have some shrimp cocktail, if you want?"

"Sure, that would be fine. And please get me some Advil. I have a terrible headache."

Chapter 67

PAOLO FINISHED HIS shrimp cocktail. His face looked more at peace, even though his inner self was still in turmoil.

"Were the shrimp okay?" Jayne asked.

"Not bad. The cocktail sauce was not as good as my friend Warren's."

"Warren?"

"Yeah, you'll meet him soon enough, great guy. Tony will invite you to the pig roast in September. When you go, you'll see the true love of family and friends." Paolo paused, looked reflective, and smiled. "Sydney and I reconciled our relationship there." He stared out the window. "Jayne, I'm going to take a nap."

"Okay. I've got paperwork to do. Sleep well."

"Thanks for listening. I find talking helps. It relieves some of the pain, and makes me realize not all is bad. For me, a good talk gets the thoughts out of my head. It keeps me from dwelling. Talking frees my mind."

"Anytime."

* * *

Four hours later, Paolo awoke to the sound of Jim's voice. "Ladies and gentlemen, this is your captain speaking. We will be landing in Oxford soon. Kindly fasten your seatbelts."

The Gulfstream's wheels screeched as they touched the runway. As Paolo prepared to get off the airplane, Jayne gave him a hug. Paolo said, "You should have kept your psychology practice. Thanks for listening."

"Anytime."

"I have something for you to read. I wrote this last night. I have to move forward now." Paolo handed the white piece of paper to Jayne. "I'll see you soon."

The sorrow never leaves, the hurt always present
Hiding in the shadows of these words
A new reality has dawned
That sometimes life never changes
Don't wait too long
Because I might not be here
For I have to stop my pain
Looking back in time
Through the windows of my mind
The memories of you rain down on me

As Paolo entered his car, he looked back and saw Jayne reading the note with tears in her eyes.

Chapter 68

THE DRIVE FROM Oxford airport to his townhouse took thirty minutes. When he got home, he called his daughter and got a quick update on the family.

"Dad, why are you home so early? I thought you were going to Sorrento."

"I thought so, too, but I had to get back early." He gave no explanation.

"I'm sorry—you must be disappointed. How is Sydney? Did she enjoy Paris?"

"Yes, she was quite surprised, to say the least."

"Is everything alright, Dad?"

"Yes, I'm just a little tired, and I have a headache."

"Do you want me to come over? I'll cook you dinner."

"No, I'm okay, honey. I'll be fine, a little rest will do me good."

"Okay, but if you need anything, call me, okay?"

"Thank you, principessa. I will be fine. Besides, I need to prepare for my speaking tour. I'll be able to get a head start on it."

"Okay, Dad. I love you."

"Love you too, Rio. Bye."

"Bye."

A tear fell from Paolo's eye.

Life's often-bitter road with its many winding curves and one-way streets seemed to beckon in Paolo's direction. His spirit unsettled, his empathic ability was thwarted, and he was free from the haunting nightmares of man's incredible stupidity. His love for Sydney grew ever stronger and deeper as the days went by. His knowledge of time counting down to some type of cataclysmic event nagged at his consciousness. He felt helpless—the love of his life gone, human death on the doorstep. The only message he had left was the message of love.

Exhausted from his trip and his long conversation with Jayne, Paolo sat at his desk. He opened the drawer with the little white pieces of paper. He neatly piled them in bundles of ten and placed elastic bands around them. He kept only one, a poem titled "Yellow Rose." Paolo walked to the fireplace and gently placed the secrets of his heart in the cold open hearth. The next time the fireplace was lit, his words would be whisked away in clouds of smoke.

"Goodbye, Sydney Hill," he said. Tears rolled down his face.

His soul was touched to the very core of his existence with the love he had for Sydney. Influenced by this overwhelming sense, he reached deep within himself and realized it was a gift from God. Nevertheless, why did he feel this way? For what purpose should a man or woman feel such pain, such despair? Whether it was divine intervention or the rationalization of man, Paolo decided the love in his heart was the love God has for his people, who blinded by their own selfish existence, fail to realize and accept the love God has for them.

Chapter 69

PAOLO AWOKE THE following Monday morning to a new dawn. He accepted the love he had for Sydney, even though the void in his heart hurt like hell. Paolo left his protected estate for the first time since his return from Paris, and began his four-mile, twenty-minute drive to his office. On his car CD player, Andrea Bocelli sang "Sogno." The words of the song touched Paolo's heart. *Va ti aspettero—qui ti aspettero w rubero i baci al tempo. Go, I will wait for you—here, I will wait for you and steal kisses from time.* Paolo thought of Sydney's kisses, the softness of her lips. He shook his head and turned the love song off. Instantly he came out of his reverie. He turned the radio on and listened to "Imus in the Morning."

The comfortable ride of his racing green S-type Jaguar calmed him. Paolo's mind wandered as he recalled Jayne's advice to bring his love for Sydney into his talks on the lecture circuit. The car stopped at the corner of Humphrey and Whitney. Yale's Nuclear Structure Laboratory, on the right, housed the largest Van de Graaff nuclear accelerator in the world. The conversation with Jayne once again popped into his mind. The car crossed Trumbull Street, the back of Saint Mary's Church on his right. "God placed the love in your heart for her."

Yes, he did. Out of nowhere, like a blowing wind that you can't see, a renewed enthusiasm overcame him. The passion he expressed, written on those white sheets of paper; the feelings in his heart, and the love deep within him, exploded. *Yes, I will use the love within my heart. Will it be enough to heal my memory of Sydney or will it only cause me more pain?*

He parked his car in the garage of the office building. Head high, Paolo walked to his office. Matt, the attendant, opened the door for him. "Good morning, Mr. DeLaurentis. How was your vacation?"

"Good morning to you, Matt. Let's just say my vacation was enlightening."

"Have an excellent day."

"You too, Matt."

"Good morning, Rebecca. Did you miss me?"

"Why, of course I did. How was your vacation?"

"Do I really need to answer that?" Rebecca shook her head no, not knowing what to say. "I know Jim spoke to you."

"I'm sorry, Paolo."

"It's okay. Any messages?"

"Yes, Arnaud has called you several times."

"Really? He called my cell phone several times too but didn't leave a message. I'm sure he's pissed off at me. I left the hotel maid a substantial tip. To be honest with you, Beck, I really don't want to talk with anyone."

"Yes, sir," she replied. "My old boss is back," she whispered.

"I heard that."

Inside his office, Paolo gazed out the window. He noticed two men standing on the street corner. They seemed out of place. "Paolo, your son is on the phone." Rebecca's voice chirped on the intercom.

"Hi, Giacomo, how are you feeling?"

"I'm doing great, Dad. Shoulder is a little sore but other than that, doing great. How are you, Dad? Are you okay?"

"Yeah. Good days and bad days, but overall I'm fine. When are you coming home? Your sister and I haven't seen you in a while."

"By the end of the summer."

"Be careful, my son. I love you."

"Love you too, Dad."

Paolo hung up the phone. A tear crept down the side of his face.

"Be careful, my son," he whispered. Paolo pressed the intercom and summoned Rebecca.

She walked into his office. "Yes, Paolo?"

"What is my schedule over the next two months?"

Rebecca, always prepared, had a copy of his lecture schedule. "Next week, April 15, in Providence; April 22, here at Yale; Columbia, April 24; Boston College, May 11; and your last one, NYU on May 17."

"I guess I'll be a little busy."

"Paolo?"

"Yes, Rebecca?"

"Did I ever tell you how much I like working with you?"

A broad smile crossed Paolo's face. "No, you didn't, and isn't that my line?"

"Yes, I thought I'd beat you to the punch."

"Funny."

"Anything else?" Rebecca asked.

"Yes, one other thing," Paolo paused.

"Yes?"

"Rebecca, have I ever—"

Rebecca shook her head and walked out of his office before he could finish the question.

Chapter 70

THE UNIVERSITY SPEAKER circuit paid Paolo a considerable amount of money; his fee ranged from seventy-five to one hundred and fifty thousand dollars per lecture. He kept up with his philanthropic efforts, and donated fifty percent of the money to various civic causes. The remainder of his fee was given back to that university's general scholarship fund.

The topic of his speeches was "The declining economic morality of corporate America." The lectures were an enormous success among the university population. Contrary to popular opinion, the youth of the day wanted answers to the meaning of life. Paolo discussed with the student body the need to give back to society. Paolo stipulated there was nothing wrong with being wealthy, but openly flaunting your financial status only builds upon the greed of society. He told the students: "Your responsibility to society is not to hoard and loathe the poor, the needy, and the sick. Your responsibility is the opposite—to give back to society openly with a true, charitable heart."

* * *

Paolo arrived at his office. Rebecca followed him to his desk. "How did it go today in Providence?"

"It went well. Dean Richards asked me to give the commencement speech next year. I wrote the date down here." Paolo handed Rebecca a piece of paper with the date and time of the Providence College graduation.

"You must be pleased."

"I am."

"Then why do you look so worried?"

"Just something I saw—or I should say, someone I saw."

"Who did you see?"

"Secret Service agents."

"Why?"

"I don't know. My best guess is they're protecting me from being hounded by the media. After the president mentioned my name, he felt bad about the slip."

"That could be. We've been called by just about every news organization out there. Even though it's been six months, we still get calls."

"Strange . . . I guess it kinda makes sense. Can you get me some Advil?"

"Sure, no problem."

Rebecca came back in the office with a glass of water and the Advil. Paolo looked straight ahead.

"Paolo, Paolo."

"Oh, thanks, Rebecca." He took the medicine from her hands and with a swig of water, downed the pills.

"You know you were zoning out?"

"Yep. Has Arnaud called back?"

"No."

"Okay."

"What was your talk about?"

"For the first time I talked about love and the need to give back to society and how we are a misguided people. I ended the speech by saying you can change the deplorable moral attitude of society with a simple act of unconditional love."

"That sounds great. What was their reaction?"

"Are you ready for this? A standing ovation."

"Impressive."

Paolo swiveled his chair and stared out the window at the New Haven Green. He thought of Sydney. A moment later, his cell phone rang, then stopped. It was Sydney. He didn't answer the phone.

Chapter 71

THAT NIGHT PAOLO sat in his study. The doorbell rang. To his pleasant surprise, his son and daughter had come to visit.

"Giacomo, Rio, what a great surprise." There was something wrong; Paolo could see it in their faces. Rio had a tear in her eye. Paolo tried to ignore the foreboding sense within him. His son and daughter walked into the foyer.

"Dad, we need to talk."

"Sure, Giacomo. Come on in—but first, let me take a good look at you." He hugged his son tightly, then released him, tears in his eyes. "Come, let's go to the study." He walked ahead of them, as if he were going to his execution.

"Okay guys, what's up?"

"Sit down, Dad."

Paolo sat on the couch. Rio sat next to him. "Is my mother dead?"

"No, Dad . . . it's Sydney."

"What do you mean, Sydney?"

"She never came home from Paris."

"What! What do you mean?" He jumped off the couch and reached for his cell phone, his hand shaking.

Giacomo reached over and took the phone out of his hands. "Dad, Sydney has been kidnapped."

"What? By whom? That can't be—she called me. Look at my phone log—she called me today. Look, Giacomo, look—she called me." His eyes filled with tears. "She called me." His voice was somber, almost a whisper. "She called me."

Rio wrapped her arms around her father. She held back a deep sob. Her lower lip quivered as she said the words. "She's dead, Dad."

Paolo slumped to the floor. "No, no, she can't be. Not my Sydney. No." He sobbed. His children sat with him on the floor and cried with their father.

An hour went by. Paolo stood and looked out the window. His children sat on the couches. "Tell me, Giacomo, what happened?"

"Rio got a phone call from Lisa last week asking when you and Sydney were coming home. She had forgotten the date."

Rio explained, "I knew you were already home and originally not expected to be back until tomorrow. I didn't know what to say, so I told her tomorrow. Then I called Giacomo and told him."

"When I put a trace on her name, the customs computer showed she never reentered the country. At the same time, Rami received a phone call from Arnaud Chambery saying that the security cameras at the Meurice had captured Sydney being pushed into a black car."

"Now I understand why Arnaud was trying to reach me."

"Yes, he mentioned that. He was extremely upset. Rami told him we would contact you."

"Were you able to get facial recognition on the kidnappers?"

Giacomo hesitated, "Yes . . . the man who pushed her was a Middle Eastern by the name of Duman. The man inside the vehicle was Colin Payne."

"What? Payne? He's dead."

"We thought so too, Dad."

"That son of a bitch." Paolo's face was red with anger. "That son of a bitch. Do we know where he is?"

"No."

Paolo's voice choked, "Where's Sydney's body?"

"We don't know."

"What do you mean, you don't know?"

"We don't know. Arnaud and his people are looking for the body."

A hint of hope was in Paolo's voice. "How do you know she's dead, then?"

"We received a picture of her dead body several hours ago."

"Oh," his voice trailed off. "She's not dead."

"What, Dad?"

"She's not dead, Rio, she's not." He sobbed. "I want to see the picture, Giacomo."

"Dad, that's not a good idea."

"Giacomo."

"I'll see what I can do."

"Any contact with Payne?'

"Yes—a simple untraceable email."

"What did it say?"

"Nothing, Dad."

"Tell me. I want to know." Paolo's gaze was uncompromising.

"It said, 'I told you, you have to be careful with whom you associate. You picked the wrong side. You thought you could use your gift against me. Think again.'"

"That son of a bitch. Do we have any idea where he is?"

"No. The DGSE and Arnaud are searching."

"That's why the Secret Service agents are watching me?"

"Yes, Dad, as well as Rio. We have deployed BOET personnel around Brewster just in case."

"Alright. I'm going to get changed, then I'm going to tell Lisa and Andrew."

"I'll go with you, Dad."

"Thanks, Rio."

"I have to get back to Washington. I'll be back in a couple of days."

"Okay." He hugged his son, "Be careful."

"Don't worry about me, Dad."

Paolo went upstairs and showered.

To Paolo's dismay, Giacomo shredded the gruesome photo of his father's true love without showing it to him, for no one should have to bear that much pain. Paolo forgave his son but denied Sydney was dead. In his heart, she was alive.

Chapter 72

A MONTH HAD GONE by since Sydney's memorial service in late April. The body was never found. Paolo still lived in denial. His love for Sydney was real and his heart still ached. The long nights, the absence of her in his life, overpowered him. He continued to write about her; the thoughts and feelings became his lectures. Paolo folded the little white pieces of paper etched with his words. At night, he'd gather them and place them in the fireplace. The bundled papers gathered dust, waiting for the first cold winter night.

Paolo honored his lecture circuit dates and his speeches were a success. The news traveled and his office and agent were inundated with offers for him to speak at universities throughout the country. He longed to spend a portion of the fall season in Ottati, in the mountains of Italy, where the air was fresh and clean and life was simple.

The speaking engagements were Paolo's way of escaping the heartache. He found himself once again a sought-after commodity—not for his business acumen this time, but for the moral betterment of those who attended his talks. Paolo's spoken words were published in school newspapers. Word traveled fast. By chance, the secretary-general of the United Nations attended one of Paolo's lectures. Impressed with the message, he arranged to meet with Paolo. After their three-hour meeting, he invited Paolo to speak before the General Assembly.

"Good morning, Mr. President."

"Good morning, Paolo, how are you?"

"I'm well, sir. You and your family?"

"Everyone is fine. I want you to know that I support your talk before the General Assembly. Go light some fires, my friend."

"Thank you, Mr. President, I will."

* * *

Paolo looked out from the podium. It was his last talk before he left for Italy. The members and guests of the United Nations sat before him. The translation rooms filled with translators and assembly members donned their headsets. The room was packed; there was standing room only. Rio sat next to Sergio and the Italian representative. Paolo reached for the glass of water to his right, took a sip, and began.

"I stand before you and I see the people of the world—a world that has gone to hell, a world that we have made, we have manufactured. Each and every one of us has contributed to the pain and suffering of people. We, the inhabitants of this planet—a place where we are only visitors—have succumbed to the subtleties of evil."

Paolo paused. Unsettled, the audience moved in their seats. "Strong words, yes. They are meant to be. It is time that we as a people, brothers and sisters of this planet, unite and defeat the hatred, selfishness, and greed of humanity. The time has come to stop the evil of the world.

"We must realize that evil exists and that our minds have been influenced over time by tiny lies that have been carried through the generations. Our minds are so confused that we don't even recognize what evil is. Simply put, evil is the opposite of love. When we destroy, when we disregard the poor, the lowly, and the destitute, when we trample on one another to attain our own agenda, an agenda that hurts and destroys—that is evil.

"If we believe in God, a higher being, whatever you want to call it—for me, God—then this nonsense has got to stop. For what purpose do we exist? To fight God's battles? No, God is greater than us. He doesn't need us—we need him.

"We exist to love one another, to forgive, to live in peace, to live a simple life and to love God. I warn you, if we don't start today to bring peace, share love, and forgive one another, we will destroy our world, our people. A time will come when devastating events will take place that will forever change us. My fear is that the last eulogy of mankind has begun." Paolo's voice began to crack and a tear welled in his eye. "The evilness of man is a one-way ticket to our destruction. We must begin to love today, to throw away our history of indifference and begin anew—before God does it for us. Time is short, eternity is forever. There is a hell, and there is a heaven. Where do you want to spend your eternity?" Paolo paused to wipe a tear from his eye. "I love you and ask that the love you have inside of you be released from the prison of evil and given to your fellow man. Thank you."

A tumultuous standing ovation erupted. For one moment in time, the representatives of the countries of the world experienced love for one another. Paolo's words touched the members of the one hundred and ninety-two states in a way that forever changed the world organization.

The message Paolo presented was published in the world's newspapers and drew critical acclaim. His words did not go unheeded by corporate magnates. Increasingly, CEOs began to donate vast amounts of money to help fund society's needs. Though the liberal media knocked his philosophical talks of love and forgiveness as bunk, one couldn't dispute that Paolo spoke the truth. Paolo's lectures were contrary to the syllabus taught in the hallowed halls of the universities. Paolo's insight about liberalism took hold with the youth of the day. He continually attacked society's idealism with his message of love. Paolo shared with his audiences in unbridled terms that their era was coming to a rapid conclusion. A period of devastating consequences to humankind would begin. He spoke of the tribulations about to occur. He made sure everyone understood humankind was at fault. Man's failure to recognize the subtleness of evil, the rejection of God, would be its cause. Paolo was careful not to divulge the tragic consequences that would transpire. He continued to proclaim, not preach. It was too late for a sermon. The priests, ministers, rabbis, and imams of the world had already spoken homilies from the pulpit to the deaf ears of their congregations.

Paolo spoke not of bitterness; instead, he talked of hope, love, and perseverance. The events documented in his journal, though painful, would establish a better earth. Humanity would experience a cleansing, an awakening realization that God exists. Over seventy-five percent of the population believed a new way of life beckoned humankind, if only humankind would open its eyes wide enough to see the meaning of life.

Chapter 73

THE LAST WEEK in August was particularly cool. Paolo kept to himself, still driven by the denial of Sydney's death. He often had lunch with Tony and Steve, and had dinner with Rio on most nights. Sundays he saw his mother, brothers, nieces and nephews. Outside of that, he had become estranged from the world. For the second year in a row, he wasn't going to attend the pig roast. He gave his apologies. His friends understood. Ottati Consulting would soon become Rio's business; her desire was to continue in her father's footsteps and help society. On the first of October, Paolo would venture to Ottati, where he planned to spend some time relaxing.

Paolo's intercom rang.

"Do you want a cup of coffee?"

"Sure, I'll have a tall cappuccino with two raw sugars. Sprinkle a little bit of cocoa on top."

"Okay. Be back in fifteen minutes."

"Bye."

Paolo gazed out the windows of his office. Dark rain clouds appeared from the west. Paolo called Rio and left a message on her voice mail. A tear trickled down his chin.

"Paolo? Paolo?"

Paolo swiveled his chair around. Rebecca stood before him. She placed the coffee on his desk. "No luck?"

"Nope. I've lost the gift; I can't remote view for shit. I've tried for the last four months— nothing but headaches. We'll never find the bastard." Paolo rubbed his head.

"I'm sorry, Paolo. Want some Advil?"

"Yep, please. I don't understand why I can't remote view anymore, Rebecca. I just can't do it."

"Maybe it's not meant to be, Paolo."

"What do you mean?"

Rebecca said nothing and walked out of his office.

Not meant to be. The words touched Paolo. His mind began to flash back over his life—Vittorio, his father, Antonio, Sister Mary, Pard, Sergio, Jayne, the birth of his children, his time with Sydney. He cried. Elbows on his knees, he wept into his hands. He reached deep within himself and cried out in his mind: *I forgive you, Colin Payne. I forgive you.*

A beam of sunlight broke through the clouds and shined on Paolo. He stood and walked out his office door.

"Rebecca, I'm going home, Thank you." Paolo leaned over and kissed her cheek. "Thank you."

"You're welcome."

"Goodbye, Rebecca. Say, have I ever told you . . ."

She smiled. "Goodbye, Paolo."

Chapter 74

Sad for now—my friend you will always be
The writer said true love is to let go
And should you come back, my arms will be open
My heart at peace
And while you are away I will try to understand
For I know you love me and I love you
Every love song I hear is about you and me
Like the blood that flows through my veins, that sustains my life
Is the love I have for you

PAOLO CLOSED HIS now-full journal and made a note to himself to get another writing tablet. He walked to the fireplace, gathered the little white pieces of paper, and placed them in a shoebox on the dining room table. He still held onto the piece titled "Yellow Rose" and slipped it into his pocket.

He put on his navy blue jacket and went outside. He strolled through the Brewster Estate in the twilight of the evening. Photoelectric sensors turned on the 1850s-style streetlights and they began to glow. Paolo's path illuminated by the light of the lamps, he walked by the pergola. A slight chill was in the air. Hands clasped behind his back, Paolo let his thoughts ramble. He talked to himself quietly. "We as a people failed to see life's warning signs. The choice was made long ago, in ancient generations—we took the love of one another and tossed it into the wind, to be blown into the four corners of the world in a mist of confusion and chaos. All man's choices were made with total disregard for love. All the people that will suffer because of our own stupidity . . . " He shook his head, rubbed his right temple, and tried to rid his thoughts of the past. The world was in chaos and he was at the forefront, but his mind couldn't let go of Sydney. *What was this thing called love?* The question lingered in his mind like the smell of cigarette smoke on clothes. *What went wrong? What didn't I do? What was right? What was wrong? What has happened to humanity?* His thoughts became disjointed. *Why, why am I here? What is my purpose? I speak to thousands about the importance of love, but here I stand, walking alone in this cocoon of silence.* A headache erupted as he walked and tears streamed down his face. His brain became numb to the outside world. A deer entered his peripheral vision and nuzzled in one of the many gardens, looking for food. The distant voices of his neighbors faded and the chilly night suddenly filled with silence.

Overwhelmed, Paolo sat on a park bench under a lantern. He gazed at the wispy clouds that raced before the full moon as it rose over East Rock Mountain. His body was highlighted by the blue-silver glimmer of the moonlight and the Big Dipper hanging in the western sky. His headache grew stronger and a searing pain traveled through his skull. Paolo tried to focus on the beauty of the night. He closed his eyes for a moment.

* * *

Paolo was awakened by the sound of the security golf cart. The flashing yellow strobe light penetrated his closed eyelids. He struggled to wake up.

"Paolo, Paolo, Mr. DeLaurentis, are you okay?"

"Yes," he said groggily. Paolo realized he was slurring his words. *Did I have a stroke?* He struggled to sit up. The security guard rushed over to him.

"What time is it?" Paolo managed to say.

"Almost two a.m." replied Bryan, the guard. He was a fifth-year architecture student who had worked for BOET before going back to college. Paolo's face was ashen under the glow of the streetlight. Bryan reached for his cell phone and dialed 911.

Paolo tried to focus on Bryan's face. He clutched his head and said, "I don't..." Paolo tried to stand, but collapsed and hit his head on the cold iron rail of the park bench. Within fifteen minutes, an ambulance arrived and loaded the unconscious Paolo. Sirens wailed as Paolo was taken to Yale New Haven Hospital.

The ambulance took a circuitous route—Whitney to Chapel to Park to Howard and finally to the emergency entrance at Davenport. Paolo's face was easily recognizable, and the EMT notified the emergency room a VIP was inbound. At the same time, Bryan notified his BOET counterpart.

A protective order was issued from the White House. Strict orders were given to the New Haven police department to protect Paolo DeLaurentis until the Secret Service arrived. The phone calls were made: Jim Collon left his house in Seymour, Colonel DeLaurentis was transported to New Haven via F16 fighter jet, Rio was on her way.

A recent issue of *Time* magazine lay atop the nurse's station. On the cover was Paolo's picture. The caption read, "The Messenger from God?"

Chapter 75

PAOLO AWOKE TWO days later, his children at his bedside. He heard the audible beeping of the heart monitor, and a hissing sound accompanied a squeezing pressure on his left arm. To his relief, his head no longer hurt. He opened his eyes and focused on the cork bulletin board that hung on the blue wall in front of him. His eyes vacant, he tried to understand where he was.

"Rio, I think Dad is awake."

Rio leaned over. "Dad? Dad, are you okay? Giacomo, go get a nurse." Giacomo leaned over and pushed the call button.

Paolo replied sleepily, "I think so, did I have a stroke?"

Giacomo answered, "No, Dad, you didn't have a stroke. We can talk about it later." He touched Paolo's arm.

"My mouth is dry. Can I get something to drink?"

"Sure, Dad," Rio reached for the blue plastic pitcher of water and poured him a glass.

Paolo tried to sit up. Giacomo gently placed his hand on Paolo's shoulder. "Don't try to get up, Dad."

"Yeah Dad, wait till the nurse comes." Rio gently lifted the back of her father's head. She placed the cup on his lips. Paolo sipped some water.

"How long have I been here?" Paolo asked.

"Almost two days," Rio replied with sadness in her eyes.

Paolo understood by the look in their eyes that his prognosis was not a good one.

"How bad, Colonel?"

"Not good, Dad. It looks like you have cancer."

"Brain?" Paolo asked sullenly.

"Yes," Rio said. She turned and tried to hold back the deep sigh within her.

Both his children had tears in their eyes. Paolo said, "Everything will be alright, we can fight this. Come closer." Paolo took each of his grown children's hands and kissed them. He said, "I guess I should've kept on sleeping. This brain cancer thing can ruin your whole day," he laughed, putting on his best face. Rio broke down and sobbed. Giacomo enfolded her in his arms and cried, too.

"Excuse me, you two, but I'm the one dying here," Paolo said sardonically.

They turned and looked at their father. He smiled at them. "A long time ago, a man told me that tomorrow waits for no man—even in death, there is always a tomorrow. You will always have a tomorrow. I'll be a memory in your hearts, life will continue, and it's up to you to seize the day, to grasp life, and most of all, to love. It's so important to love." An inner strength overcame Paolo. He continued, "Physical death is every person's outcome. Apparently my physical death will arrive early. For me, my life will continue within the minds and hearts of those I loved and those who have loved me. Colonel?"

"Yes, Dad?" Giacomo took his forefingers and wiped the tears from his eyes.

"Help me sit up?"

"You shouldn't sit up, Dad," Rio said.

"What could happen? I'm already going to die." He laughed. "Come on, help your old man sit up."

"Okay." Rio leaned over and kissed her father on the cheek.

"How long do I have?"

The brother and sister looked at each other.

"Well?"

"Maybe six months with treatment," Giacomo said. Rio turned her head and wept.

"Rio?"

"Yeah."

"Turn around, my principessa." She turned, tissue in hand, and wiped her eyes.

"Listen, this is not the end of the world. I will always be with you and your brother. I'll never leave your hearts."

"I know, Dad, but it hurts."

"It's okay, Rio." Paolo pushed himself up. Propped on a pillow, he slid over. "Come here, sit down next to your father." Rio placed her head on his chest and silently cried. Paolo stroked her long brown hair. "It will be okay, Rio." After a few minutes, Paolo said, "Okay, you two, a few things. First, I don't want to die here. Second, I still want to go to Ottati. Third, and most important, I love you guys so much—never ever forget that, okay?" They nodded their heads. "One final comment, I understand this is sad for both of you and to be honest I'm not too happy about it either, but this is life. I want my last days, no matter how few they are, to be filled with life and happiness. Can we agree on that?"

"I'll try, Dad."

"Thanks, Rio. And you, Giacomo?"

"I'll try my best, Pops."

"Pops—that's what I used to call my dad." A broad smile crossed Paolo's face.

The door to his hospital room opened. "Mr. DeLaurentis?"

"Yep, that's me."

"Hi, I'm Dr. Carr."

"Hello, Dr. Carr, nice to meet you." The two shook hands. "Tell me, Doc, is it as bad as my children say?"

"I'm afraid so. The tumor is embedded deep in your temporal lobe. Because of the depth, we were not able to perform a biopsy. Our experience has been that this type of tumor is always fatal. Outside of your headaches and the seizure two nights ago, have you had any other problems?"

"Such as what?"

"Memory issues, emotional problems?"

"My memory, hmm . . . for the last several months, my mind has been like a movie, replaying my life over and over. Emotionally? Well . . ." his voice trailed off.

"Your children told me about your loss, I'm very sorry. Have you had any problems distinguishing sounds? Have you experienced slurred speech?"

"No."

"I take it your children told you the tumor is inoperable."

"Yes."

"We feel confident that radiation and chemotherapy will shrink the tumor, but that will not completely eradicate the cancer cells."

"So, what you're telling me is I'm going to die soon."

"More than likely. I'm sorry."

"How long do I have without the treatment?"

"Hard to say . . . maybe a month or two."

"With the treatment?"

"Six to nine months."

"Well, as my daughter would say, that sucks." The doctor made no response. "Okay, this is what we're going to do." Dr. Carr's eyebrows rose. "First and foremost, I have to be in Italy in six weeks. This is not negotiable. How long is the treatment?"

"With radiation and chemo, four weeks. But I have to tell you, Mr. DeLaurentis, this treatment will take a toll on your body."

"I'm sure it will. So technically I can still go to Italy?"

"Technically, yes."

"Very well. When do we start?"

"Tomorrow."

Paolo looked at his children. "Guys, do you have any questions?" They shook their heads no. "Okay, thank you, doctor. I appreciate your honesty and candidness. Now, smile, enjoy your life. You're a good man. And the next time you see me, call me Paolo."

"Yes, Paolo." The doctor left the room.

"Dad, why do you have to go to Italy?"

"I want to see Ottati one last time. I want to sit in the Piazza Umberto overlooking the Valle del Calore, the lush greens below, and feel the fresh mountain breeze of fall. I want to see the bright orange-colored roofs, the ancient stairways. Maybe have a warm chestnut or a fig and listen to the voices of the children playing. And celebrate my birthday. That's all I desire—to see the beautiful vistas of my grandfather's home, my home, one last time."

Rio and Giacomo both replied. "Okay, Dad. We're coming with you."

"Absolutely, Rio."

* * *

The stress and heartache of losing Sydney took its toll on Paolo's body. Diagnosed with brain cancer, Paolo resigned himself to the fact he was dying. Memories of the past faded in the face of life with all the daunting tasks that beseeched him. One would think you could easily escape into the fantasy of the mind, ignoring all reality. In this earthly existence, the reality of life can come crashing down, slapping you in the face with a wrecking ball.

While undergoing radiation treatments, encased in the desolate room behind the closed, vault-like door, under the cold machine aiming its lethal rays at the alien mass within his brain, Paolo's one desire was Sydney. What was in his being that made him love this woman to the point of self-sacrifice? The thought was always the memory of her. The remembrance of her and him kept Paolo alive until the time was right.

Paolo's gurney was nestled in a corner of a hallway. Like a stray dog held in captivity at a kennel, Paolo waited patiently for the orderly to take him back to his room. The queasiness in his stomach started to brew. He closed his eyes in hope the sickness would go away, and Sydney was by his side, then just as quickly, she was gone. Paolo hallucinated almost daily—his mind played tricks on him, caused by the desire within him for her. The hallucinations gave him no repose, no peace.

They say hell is the total, complete absence of God. Hell is the absence of love, the desire to be with God and not being able to quench the desire. Hell was the never-ending epiphany that God does truly exist. Was he in hell? Did the epiphany of love escape him?

During the third week of his treatment, when Paolo was lucid enough, Marge, his nurse, would write down his words of love and forgiveness. He made an agreement with her that she would write everything that he blabbered from his mouth.

"As I lay here at what appears to be death's door, I can only think of you. My life seems so insignificant when I see all the suffering around me. How blessed I am with the knowledge that I have loved you, and you have loved me. You were with me yesterday as I lay in the hallway on my gurney. Soon I shall probably be lying on the same gurney with a sheet over my head and I hope I will be with you once again in heaven. I pray I'll be in the hands of God resting in peace with you by my side. I find that as the days go on, my hallucinations increase, and for whatever reason, you are always present before me. They do bring me comfort, even though I know you're not really here, for how could you be? I love you and will love you for all eternity.

"Time passes slowly. All I have now are my memories. I have some visitors; they usually come after Marge leaves for the day. Family, mostly. Steve, Tony, and Warren come by almost every night. I managed to keep my illness quiet, for I want no fanfare. It hurts me when my mother and brothers and sisters come to visit, which is on a daily basis. My mother's suffering with the knowledge that her child will die breaks my heart. It's a terrible, terrible tragedy for a parent to watch their child die, no matter how old the child. Giacomo and Rio are here constantly. I tell the kids that even though my life is ending, I'll live for eternity in heaven and will always be with them in their hearts and minds.

"At times, I'm afraid, yet an inner peace envelops me in the knowledge that love exists. Strangely, I sometimes look forward to my passing. The pain will finally end and I will be with you. Thank you for the kiss you just gave me, your lips, the softness of your lips. How the mind can play tricks. I guess you're not here. Marge always ruins these hallucinations. Sorry, Marge, I don't want to hurt your feelings. How I wish you were here, Syd. I love you," he said as he drifted off to sleep.

Paolo became quite the personality at the hospital. The staff was well aware of who he was. Paolo was a major benefactor and his stay was kept quiet. The fourth and final week of treatment came. His face was gaunt and gray, he had lost over thirty pounds, and he appeared to be on death's doorstep. Paolo no longer resembled the photo in *Time* magazine.

The nurses would tell their co-workers about the patient in Room 542. Paolo's words touched the hearts of those who heard him. Afterwards, they became richer. Many took the love within them and gave it to their loved ones. Some went so far as to share their love with strangers. How they wished to be loved the way Paolo loved Sydney.

Paolo would often go into discourses about love. One time, during one of his discussions with Marge, a group of twenty people gathered in his room. Nurses, doctors, aides—even the orderly who took Paolo to his radiation treatments—lined the doorway. Some would say the hallucinations got the better of him, but others felt as if God talked through Paolo to them. At times—more often than not—the listeners left his room emotionally touched.

"Love is more than a choice. God put people together—whether stranger, foe, or friend—to share with one another all aspects of life. Love is not transient. It's up to you to keep it alive. Accept each other, as you are, the complete package of human nature. Your life is a life of love only strengthened by your desire to open your heart. You'll find love everywhere, from the tiniest blade of grass to the largest predator who tries to feed its young.

"The human thought of pride and ego stops love. The choice a person makes can inhibit it. The unwillingness to be vulnerable to love will leave a hole in your heart and soul. Live your life with no regrets. Accept what has occurred in your life, seek forgiveness, and open your heart to love. Love one another and you will be at peace." Paolo ended his talks by falling asleep or with the simple words "I love you." The love he had for Sydney was more than passion and desire. It was the love God has for all his people. That love was in his heart for her.

Moments of his life were played back by the cameras of his mind. His life created an illusion within his consciousness. Those memories triggered the senses and the senses triggered the memories. For him, the recollections of Sydney Hill would be with him until the day he died.

Marge was constantly with him. The two became close friends. A bond of love and respect united them. Before that came to be, however, a catharsis had to take place.

Marge was a middle-aged African American woman with the grace, kindness, and love so common to her race—a race stigmatized by society's opinion.

During their time together, Paolo often apologized to her for the way people treated one another because of their prejudices. The bigotry within humanity hurt him deeply. The pain, the sorrow, the narrow-mindedness of the human race bewildered him. The ache of this evilness overwhelmed his empathic senses. Paolo viewed all people the same, no matter what their race, skin color, nationality, or religion. All of humankind wanted one thing: love. It was a simple equation with a difficult solution, for in order to receive love, you had to give love. "Love exists in all people, inhibited by the social inadequacies of mankind," he often said.

At first, Marge was appalled and angry. "How dare he apologize to me?" Paolo overheard her say to a colleague. "The white man killed my two brothers, one at the bottom of an elevator shaft and the other bleeding in the street. This honky white man is apologizing to me!"

She kept her anger hidden, buried deep within her, for thirty years. Then one day, Paolo's room empty except for the two of them, he closed his eyes and touched her arm.

"Marge?"

"Yes, Paolo?"

"I love you." In a whisper, he continued, "The image of your love surrounds me."

"It does?"

"Absolutely, you are a child of God. His love surrounds you. Now is the time to forgive."

"Forgive who, Paolo?"

"You know."

Marge sat and gazed at the man who sat at God's doorstep, puzzled. "Who, Paolo?"

"Captain Bobby Sullivan, the police officer who killed your innocent brothers."

Marge pulled her hand from his as the anger within her began to explode. "How dare you? How do you know?"

"God just told me."

Then a profound peace came, a sense of guilt swept over her like a thunderstorm that opened the floodgates. She wept, and as she wept, she sensed a hand on her shoulder, and peace once again filled her heart. When she opened her eyes, Paolo was sound asleep. This man who lay before her, Paolo DeLaurentis, was God's modern-day prophet.

Marge grew up in the south in the era of Rosa Parks. She knew firsthand about prejudice and faith. Because of her faith, she tried to put prejudice behind her. That day she came to realize her own prejudices. She sat by Paolo's bedside and wept, not in sorrow but in joy, in the knowledge that this man who labored through his pain loved her, not because of the color of her skin but because of who she was inside. Paolo had the gift to love unconditionally. Up until that day, Marge Wentworth Robinson had never kissed a white man, let alone a patient. She knew she would miss Paolo terribly. In the years to come, Marge would fight the prejudice within her own race and all people, not by force but by the example of a man's love for a woman, Paolo's love for Sydney.

Paolo slept. As she prepared to leave for the day, she leaned over and kissed him on the forehead.

Chapter 76

BY THE END of the fourth week, the tumor had shrunk in size. The frequency of Paolo's hallucinations decreased. The pain was still present but dulled by narcotics. His passion for Sydney never left him. Paolo continued to dwell upon the true love of his life. There were so many memories of the love they shared. Images and scenes flowed through his brain as though through a movie projector onto a big screen.

Paolo was discharged from the hospital on a Tuesday morning. The day was bright and sunny with a cool breeze. Rio and Giacomo would take him home. He struggled to walk, but he looked forward to his trip to Ottati. Dr. Carr was still reluctant to let him fly.

"Listen, Doc, you know and I know, I'm going to die. You can't stop it and I sure as hell can't. So what's the big deal?" Paolo still had his characteristic gaze, he held the doctor's eyes.

"You're right, Paolo. May I make a suggestion?"

"Sure."

"Take Marge with you."

"She's already coming."

"You're a smart man, Mr. DeLaurentis."

"Thank you, Doctor. I hope you have a great life. I have a funny feeling we won't be seeing each other again."

"Goodbye, Paolo." The doctor took a tissue and wiped his eyes.

"Fall allergies, Doctor?"

"Yes, fall allergies."

* * *

The father, son, daughter, and nurse arrived at Oxford airport. Tony stood by the G-V as the car pulled up to the aircraft. Tony had visited Paolo in the hospital, so it wasn't a shock when his childhood friend stepped out of the car.

"Tony, how are you?" The two friends embraced.

"I'm fine."

"Wish I could say the same. Lost thirty pounds and look," Paolo rubbed his almost-bald head. "I look like Mr. Clean."

"You look great to me."

'You're full of crap. At least I don't feel too bad, other than an occasional headache. I'm getting my strength back."

"That's good. Hi, Rio. Hi, Giacomo."

"Hi, Tony." Rio hugged Tony and Giacomo shook his hand.

"This is my friend Marge, who is actually my nurse."

"Hello, Marge, I'm Tony D."

"A pleasure to meet you, I've read your books."

"I hope you liked them?"

"Yes, I did."

"Okay, you two, maybe you can have this conversation later?"

"Hey, a fan . . . I don't have many."

"Sure, after how many books, ten? I think you have fans. Danny and Jim on board?"

"Sorry, Paolo, only Danny and Jayne. Jim had some government business to do."

"Oh," Paolo's voice was sullen. "I'd hoped to see him."

"He'll pick you up, I guarantee it."

"Okay."

Rio and Giacomo climbed the aircraft stairs. Paolo hugged his friend goodbye. He grabbed the railing and walked up the stairs. Marge was right behind him, her hand on his back keeping him straight and steady. He was met at the top of the stairs by Danny and Jayne.

"I look that bad?"

"No, you look great."

"Nice try, Jayne." She hugged him, her eyes wet.

"How are you, Paolo?" Danny offered his hand.

"I've been better. Good to see you, Dan. How's your family?"

"They're great, thanks for asking. Flight time to Salerno is seven and a half hours, we've got great tailwinds."

"Who is in the right seat?"

"Tim—you've met him before."

"Yes, a couple of times. I remember him . . . a good guy. I'll come forward once we get airborne and say hi."

"Sounds good."

Marge gave Paolo his medication. He fell asleep and awoke just before the plane arrived in Salerno. He looked out the window as they flew between the islands of Corsica and Sardinia. The morning sun glinted on the bay. The aircraft passed over the Amalfi coast on its approach to the airport and taxied to the area reserved for private aircraft.

Still a little groggy, Paolo leaned on Giacomo as he made his way to the door. He held on to the stair railing with his left hand while Giacomo held his right arm. His longtime friend Sergio waited for him.

"Sergio, my God, what a pleasure to see you." The two friends hugged and gave each other kisses on both cheeks.

"Paolo, it is so good to see you, my friend. How are you feeling?"

"I could be better, but I'm getting stronger every day, which is a good thing. How is the family?"

"They are all fine. When you get settled, we will come over, have dinner."

"That sounds great. I'd love to see them again."

Sergio walked over to hug Rio and Giacomo. There were tears in their eyes.

The four stood as the black Mercedes SUV pulled up to the aircraft. A police car followed. The officer opened the door and walked to Sergio to hand him a piece of paper.

"Giacomo, this is for you."

"What is it, son?" asked Paolo.

"I have to get back to Washington."

Paolo felt his son's despair. "It's okay. I'm not going to die anytime soon. Do what you have to do."

"I'll be back as soon as I can, Dad."

"I know you will, son." They hugged. A third car arrived and whisked Giacomo away to a waiting military aircraft.

Paolo hugged Jayne and Danny. "Till we meet again, my friends. May your lives be filled with happiness, I love you both." A tear welled in Paolo's eyes as he entered the front seat of the SUV. Sergio arranged for a police escort to Ottati.

The car followed the shoreline through Pontecagnano, then past the hotel owned by Sergio's family. The sea was to the right; the day was crystal clear with the summer haze long gone. The car took a left on 161 and began the hour-long drive to the mountain village of Ottati. As they passed the village of Castel San Lorenzo, Paolo asked the driver to stop at a scenic outlook. The driver radioed ahead to the police escort.

Able to get out of the car on his own, Paolo beckoned Rio and Marge to come with him. They stood on either side in the warm sun. A slight breeze cooled their faces. Paolo pointed across the valley below to the mountains.

"Can you see it, to your left? Castelcivita, Ottati in the center, and Sant'Angelo a Fasanella over there to the right?"

"Yes, I see it, Dad."

"Paolo, it's absolutely beautiful! The farms below, the rolling hills . . . and the mountains. Wow, the mountains."

"Wait, Marge, till we get to the other side—the view is spectacular. I know of a nice restaurant in Fasanella, we'll go there for lunch."

Chapter 77

THE SUV ENTERED the commune of Ottati and pulled into the Piazza Umberto. A sense of peace came over Paolo. A man sitting at one of the tables along the fence got up and walked toward the car.

"Paolo DeLaurentis, my old friend, so nice to see you again."

Paolo stood and took a deep breath. "Sabatino, so nice to see you. You look just like your father did thirty years ago."

"I hope that is good?"

"Yes it is, my friend. This is my daughter Rio and my nurse Marge."

"It is a pleasure to meet you." Sabatino gave the customary two-cheek kiss. He embraced Rio a little longer than Paolo would have liked.

"Sabatino, is the house ready?"

"Yes, just the way you left it."

"Thanks so much."

"Paolo! Paolo!" A middle-aged, attractive woman walked from the restaurant in the piazza, wiping her hands on a kitchen towel.

Paolo turned. "Maria, Maria!" Paolo walked in front of the SUV and hugged the woman.

"How are you feeling? I heard you were sick. I will make you better with my food."

"I'm sure you will. Maria, this is my daughter Rio and my nurse Marge."

"So nice to meet you. Come, sit down. I will make you lunch."

"No thank you, Maria, I have to lie down. I'm tired."

"I understand, mi amore." She placed her hand on his face.

"Sabatino, we'll talk later. I'll stop by your office."

"Sure, Paolo. Ciao."

"Ciao, ciao Maria."

Paolo pointed to an alley. "My house is right over here. I know you have a lot of questions, Rio. I'll explain when we get inside."

"Yes, mi amore," said Rio, raising her eyebrows.

Her father wrapped his arm around her shoulder. "You will always be mi amore." The two laughed.

Paolo turned left, walked down three steps, and turned left again.

"Holy crap, Dad, this is beautiful."

"Wow, Paolo, is this yours?"

"It is for now." The trio walked to the three-story stone building. The short walkway was lined with potted plants. To the right, another three brown-tiled steps led to a terrace that overlooked the valley and the mountains to the west. Black wrought-iron railings surrounded the three small balconies, their windows shuttered. The interior was simple: a main living room with two couches, a television, and an empty bookcase; large floor-to-ceiling windows provided a panorama of Ottati's orange-roofed houses and the valley below. A study and master bedroom completed the first floor. The second floor had a large kitchen and dining room with an entrance to the patio. The third floor had three bedrooms. Marge went up to the third floor to unpack.

"So Dad, what's up? How do these people know you? And this house? I'm kinda puzzled."

"I'm sure you are. Well, my dear, you're looking at my hideaway. I haven't been here in almost four years. I was only able to get here twice. In that short time, I became friends with Maria and Sabatino. I had met their parents when I first came here. I don't know why but we had a connection. I found peace here, peace from the world. When I bought this house, I believed it would be a great place to retire to. And now, I guess . . ."

"Please don't say it, Dad."

"Okay . . . a place to live life."

"Much better. Dad, can I ask you a question?"

"Of course, Rio."

"With your gift, how come you didn't know you were sick?"

"I really don't know, honey. The gift has been absent for months."

"Okay, but why didn't you know like a year ago?"

Paolo paused. "Life is a journey with a beginning and an end. In the middle of life, we travel a road filled with curves and ups and downs. What would life be if we knew when it was going to end? Life is a mystery. We must travel the road in faith and expectation that God will take us home. If we knew when death would occur, it would take the fun out of life."

"I guess that makes sense."

"Good. I don't know about you, but I'm tired, so I'm going to take a nap. Go walk about. Take Marge with you and talk to the people—you'll find that you have a lot in common."

"Okay, Dad, sleep well." Rio kissed her father's cheek.

"Principessa?"

"Yeah, Dad?"

"Dinner at Maria's place tonight."

"Ooh, mi amore." She chuckled and climbed to the third floor.

Chapter 78

THE SECOND WEEK of October, on Paolo's birthday, he had a mild seizure as he sat outside of Maria's restaurant drinking his morning cup of espresso.

"Dad, do you think we should go home?"

"Why, because I had a seizure?"

"Yes."

The father and daughter sat out on the patio. Purple vine flowers cascaded up the stone wall next to the entrance of the house. The blue sky was dotted with clouds.

"Do you know the name of those flowers?"

"No, and you're avoiding the subject."

"I know. Not yet, I want to stay here a little bit longer."

Marge walked out of the house. "Paolo, it's time to take your meds."

"Okay. It's a beautiful night, isn't it?"

"No, Dad, it's morning."

"Oh yeah, I was just testing you. I need to take a nap. Don't forget, we're having a dinner party in a couple of days. Have we heard from . . ." He bowed his head as the words slurred.

"Giacomo?"

"Yep."

"Not yet. Go take a nap, Dad."

"Yep."

Marge helped him walk back to the house.

* * *

Two days later, Paolo was back to his normal self, making his morning walk to Maria's for his espresso, having a game of chess with Sabatino in the piazza. He was excited and upbeat. Sergio and his wife were coming for dinner, along with Sabatino, his wife, the mayor, Maria and her husband, and a couple of Paolo's neighbors. With the help of Rio and Marge, Paolo was going to serve veal Milanese, homemade pasta with tomatoes, fresh mozzarella and basil, and figs drizzled with an aged balsamic vinegar.

The table was set for twelve and colored lights were strung around the terrace. The guests were to arrive at seven. The forecast was clear with a full moon and temperatures in the mid-sixties.

Paolo stood by the railing in the late afternoon, gazing out over the valley below. *You would have loved this, Sydney.* A tear came to his eye. He reached inside his pocket and pulled out a piece of wrinkled, white paper. He unfolded the paper and read the title: "Yellow Rose."

"Hello, Dad, quite a place you have here."

Paolo turned. Giacomo stood at the tiled steps. As he crossed the patio to his father, Paolo folded the paper and placed it back in his pants pocket.

"Giacomo, thank God you're back." The father and son hugged each other. "How did everything go in Washington?"

"Actually, I ended up in Paris, and everything went amazingly well."

"I wish I'd known you were going there—I have a friend who lives there."

"I didn't have much time, Dad, I was really busy."

"Well, I'm glad you're here. Your sister and Marge took a walk to Saint Biagio's church. I think they're praying for me."

"That's good. Nothing wrong with a little prayer."

"You're right about that. I'm so glad you're here, Giacomo."

"How are you feeling? Rio told me about the seizure. Sorry I missed your birthday."

"No problem—my birthday present is having you and Rio here

with me. I feel great today, but I have a funny feeling I won't be this way much longer. Maybe we should go back to the States next week. So, how do you like your house?"

"My house?"

"Well, yours and Rio's."

"It is beautiful, Dad."

"Help me sit down, will you, son?"

"Sure, Pop." The two walked over to a lounge chair.

"Did you see my hair is growing back?" Paolo rubbed his head.

"Yeah, it looks nice—reminds me of a drill sergeant I had in boot camp."

"Thanks." Paolo chuckled. "Why don't you go inside and change, your bedroom is on the third floor. I'm going to take a little nap. And Giacomo?"

"Yeah, Dad."

"I'm glad you're here."

"Me, too."

Paolo lay back and fell asleep in the warmness of the sun's light.

Chapter 79

THE GUESTS MILLED about the patio as the sun began to set. Tall outdoor heaters were lit to warm the patio area as the night air cooled. Wine glasses in hand, the guests enjoyed a light appetizer of cured meats and cheeses. Italian music played quietly in the background.

Paolo tapped his water glass with a spoon. "Ladies and gentlemen, I'm so glad you're here. Please, sit down." A police siren echoed through the streets, fading. The voices of the party quieted. Maria said, "Sounds like the polizia are in the piazza." She told her husband, "Roberto, go get some more wine and make sure the restaurant is alright."

"I'll go help you with the wine," Giacomo said. The two men left.

"Wow, you can see the blue flashing lights in the valley."

"It's probably nothing, Marge. Come on, Rio, let's go check on the food."

"Okay, Dad."

"I will come with you, mi amore."

Paolo and Rio looked at each other and smiled.

Five minutes later, Paolo, Rio and Maria walked back out to the patio. A fresh, familiar scent wafted across Paolo's nose in the cool night air. By the tile stairs stood several familiar faces—one wore a beret and had a cane in his hand, the other two were Jim and Rami.

A broad smile crossed Paolo's face. "Oh, my God, what are you three doing here?" In the same breath, he added, "Where the hell are all my guests?" Like the great sea parting, the three men stepped aside.

Paolo stumbled forward and grabbed a chair. Rio was behind him. "It's okay, Dad, it's not a hallucination."

There in the sparkling light of the moon stood Sydney Hill. Paolo began to weep. "I'm not hallucinating?"

"No, Dad, you're not."

"Oh my God, oh my God. How?"

Sydney walked to Paolo. He met her halfway. Under the bright light of the moon, the two embraced. Out in the alley, people began to clap and cheer.

Arnaud walked to them. "Bonjour, my friend. I hope you are as happy as I was that day when you returned Emily to my arms."

Paolo could say nothing. Speechless, he looked into Sydney's face. The dazzling green eyes captivated his soul once again. "I don't understand. I don't understand. Are you okay?"

"I'm fine, my love, I'm fine." She tenderly rubbed his face and kissed him.

"But you're dead."

She pulled back from him, took his hands, and placed them on her face. "No, I'm not. See? I'm real."

"Dad, why don't you sit down?"

"Yeah, I think that's a good idea. Rio, can you get me a glass of wine?"

"Sure, Dad."

Everyone piled onto the patio. As if it were Christmas Day, joy and laughter filled the air. The village of Ottati came to life. Maria sent her staff over to the restaurant to get more food. Wine flowed as people chatted away in Italian and English. The celebration ended by ten, the doors to the patio closed.

Paolo, Sydney, Arnaud, Jim, Rami, Giacomo, and Rio sat on the couches in the main living area downstairs. Marge had gone upstairs to sleep. When the shock was just about gone, Paolo asked, "Okay, tell me what the hell happened?"

"Dad, it's a long story."

"I have all night, I'm listening."

"After we realized Sydney had been kidnapped, Arnaud and the DGSE sent out search teams. Now, mind you, the Russian government was also looking for Payne. Between the three countries, we were able to pinpoint his whereabouts—at least, that's what we believed. Every time we thought we had him, he eluded us—to this day, we still don't know how. In early September, we captured Duman. Through various interrogation techniques, we were able to ascertain where Payne was. This time, only Arnaud, Rami, Jim and I knew the location.

"That's why you had to leave when we got to the airport?"

"Exactly. I led the raid. The funny thing was, it was almost a non-event. He was holed up in an estate outside Paris. There were two armed men, a maid, and Payne. The two guards gave up immediately. We found Payne in the library, reading. He looked up and said, "Finally." Then he pulled a gun from his drawer and killed himself. For some odd reason, I covered him with my jacket. We found Sydney in a secluded part of the house. We immediately took her to an army hospital and debriefed her."

Sydney explained, "When I was first captured, I thought he was going to kill me, but that wasn't what he wanted. We moved a lot for the first month or so. One day I awoke with what I thought was blood all over my neck and chest. Payne's people had drugged me and mocked my death. When I finally recovered from the drug, I realized we had moved to the château. I questioned Payne, why? He never gave me an answer. I had my own living quarters with a kitchen, bathroom, and living room, but I was not allowed to leave. I even had a television. I saw your speech before the UN, Paolo. It was magnificent. I tried numerous times to escape, but the doors were barricaded. The last couple of weeks, he would come and have dinner with me— always civil, and with a bodyguard. He looked sick and troubled. He said he had radiation poisoning and soon I would be free. Then one morning I heard a gunshot, and Giacomo came walking through the door."

"Amazing. And he never harmed you?"

"No."

"Do we know why he did it?"

"Sorry, Dad, we have no idea. We've looked through all his records, computers—nothing."

"Sad, that's very sad. May God have mercy on him."

Arnaud shook his head. "I will never understand you, my friend."

"What about Andrew and Lisa?"

"We had a video conference call, they're fine and looking forward to seeing me."

"I'll ask Tony to send over the G-V, and we'll get back to the States tomorrow."

"The plane is already at the Salerno airport, waiting," Jim said.

"Excellent."

"Dad, I think you need to get some sleep. Arnaud can have my room. I'll sleep in Marge's room in the spare bed. Maria has two open rooms at her place for Rami and Jim."

"Thanks, Rio."

They all stood. Paolo embraced Rami and Jim. He wrapped his arms around Arnaud, and the two men cried. "Good night, my friend. I'll see you in the morning."

Paolo hugged Giacomo, "Thank you, son, thank you."

"No problem, Dad."

He kissed Rio, whispering, "I love you, mi amore." He stepped back and looked in her eyes, and the two laughed.

Rami and Jim left to go to Maria's. Rio, Giacomo and Arnaud walked upstairs. Paolo turned to Sydney. Looking in her eyes, he asked, "Would you care to sleep with me, Ms. Hill?"

"I thought you'd never ask, Mr. DeLaurentis."

"Just so you know . . . I might not be able to perform."

"You don't have to. Your warm body is enough."

Paolo reached in his pocket for the wrinkled, white piece of paper and gave it to Sydney. She opened it and glanced at the words. "Will you read it to me?"

Paolo wrapped his arms around her and whispered in her ear as a tear fell from his eye.

A yellow rose I give to you
To say how much I love you
Though we are apart and I am often blue
I think of the days that I gave a yellow rose to you

The smile on your face
The twinkle in your eye
The sound of joy in your voice
For the yellow rose I gave to you

I sit here in my dark hour
Because you are not here
Nothing else seems to matter
Until I can give you a yellow rose

A yellow rose can come and go
But the yellow rose of my heart
Will always be you.

"I love you, Sydney."
"I love you, Paolo."

Epilogue

MEDIA ACROSS THE world broadcast news of Paolo's death. His funeral was attended by both the elite and the downtrodden of society. They offered their respects to a man who so loved a woman, his words changed the lives of many.

Colonel DeLaurentis, Rio, and Sydney went to dismantle the townhouse. Under strict orders from Paolo, no one was permitted to enter until after his death. The property was willed to Rio.

The three entered the house. As directed by his father, Giacomo went to Paolo's study. Once there, he was to open his father's safe. Inside was a safety deposit box to be opened on October 28 the following year.

Sydney and Rio entered the kitchen. On the table was a shoebox with Sydney's name on it. Over two hundred pieces of folded white paper lay inside—the story of the love Paolo had for Sydney.

* * *

The following spring, the scent of nature's new birth filled the morning air. Sydney DeLaurentis walked around her house, looking at her gardens and the work she had to do. The loneliness in her heart, the absence of Paolo in her life, filled her with sorrow. Whatever had gone wrong seemed inconsequential—the loss overwhelmed her heart.

She came to her red rose bushes. As she knelt down to clear

some leaves, she began to sob. Then a tranquil peace filled her being. The pain gone, the memory of Paolo was present to her. Hidden in the barren bushes was a fully blossomed yellow rose. The fragrance overwhelmed her senses. She thought of Paolo and said, "How you will always be the yellow rose of my heart." In the years to come, wherever she lived, there appeared a yellow rose. She never forgot the true love a man had for her and the love she had for him.

* * *

A beam of sunlight streamed through the big window. It was October 28, the following year Giacomo and Rio sat on a couch in the corner of what had been their father's study. Not much had changed. There was a new Oriental rug, and law journals had replaced the various business books. Paolo's old desk was still cluttered with papers. Pictures of the twins and their parents were scattered throughout the room.

"How are you feeling, my older brother?"

"Better, now that I'm finally out of the hospital."

"Tell me about it. Mom and I were worried sick. I can't believe your fever was so high."

"Yeah, the doctors were definitely puzzled."

"Sounds like the story Dad told us about when he was a boy. Did a white light surround you?"

"No, no white lights." Giacomo changed the subject. "Do you have the key?"

"Yeah. Came yesterday by FedEx. I found the box hidden under the floorboards over there by the window. I'm surprised we received the package, considering how much damage Hurricane Adam caused."

"Did you see the news footage of Florida? Totally devastated. How are they going to recover? Not to mention, how is the government going to pay for it?"

Rio wiped a tear from her eye. "Those poor people. This is unbelievable; our world is going to hell. The coastline flooded to

Lake Okeechobee, and hundreds of thousands are homeless. I don't understand how a flood could be that bad."

"The president told me this morning the satellite pictures show a tsunami hitting the

coast. They estimated the first wave at over one hundred fifty feet. Thank God most people were evacuated—Adam was a category 5 when it slammed into the shoreline."

"Unbelievable." She shook her head and handed the key to Giacomo. He opened the box. Inside was a note attached to a journal. They read the pages together.

My dear children, if you are reading this I am dead. I always wanted to say that.

Giacomo and Rio laughed.

> I hope you are both well. I am sure you are. Attached is my journal containing all the visions I had. I give this to both of you. Giacomo, with your contacts, and Rio, with your legal mind, and with all your financial resources, maybe the two of you can do better than I did. I love you both. What you hold in your hands is a burden, I know—I lived with it for many years. Giacomo, if you and your sister feel the burden is too great, you have my permission to give the journal to the president. Whatever you do will be the right thing—there is no wrong decision.
>
> I love you,
> Dad

Brother and sister leaned back on the leather couch, tears in their eyes. Rio reached over to the coffee table and picked up the journal. She sat close to her twin and opened the prophetic book. Together they read the first page.

> When Adam, the giant hurricane, hits the coast of Florida and Lake Okeechobee becomes part of the Atlantic Ocean,

humankind will enter an era when the earth will shudder and quake. The meteorological events will tax the economies of the world, igniting a maelstrom of want and greed. The nations will rise against each other as foretold, until a new era of peace, a new dawn awakens humankind . . .

CPSIA information can be obtained
at www.ICGtesting.com
Printed in the USA
BVHW040711240219
541009BV00020B/709/P